"A tender, precise book filled with strangeness and beauty, *Lovelier, Lonelier* casts a beguiling spell. The novel asks the big questions: what does it mean to love? How much of our lives are written in the stars? How can one be free? These are questions that can only be answered in its ambitious scope. Yam builds entire worlds spanning decades and continents that echo, overlap, intersect, linked by a delicate thread of serendipity, and it is a pleasure to inhabit them."

—Rachel Heng, author of *The Great Reclamation*

"Melancholic, peripatetic, flexuous."

—Amanda Lee Koe, author of *Delayed Rays of a Star*

"Yam's prose is fresh and contemplative—one that I'm excited to read again in the future."

—Lee Jing-Jing, author of *How We Disappeared*

"A sensitive, assured piece of work with a strong sense of feeling at its centre."

—Sharlene Teo, author of *Ponti*

"A beautiful and hallucinatory mediation on life, love (or what passes for it) and the elusive nature of reality. The intertwined lives of four friends intersect with historical events and inexplicable, fantastical incidents in a genre-bending novel reminiscent of Haruki Murakami."

—Victor Fernando R. Ocampo, author of *The Infinite Library and Other Stories*

"In this novel lies the journey across museums and galleries in Kyoto, New York, Madrid and Singapore that you have been dying to crash. If you love meandering paths and performance art, this massive existential road trip will leave you drenched in heartbreak. Enter and lose yourself."

—Heman Chong, artist

First United States edition published 2024 by Gaudy Boy

Original title: Lovelier, Lonelier
© 2021 by Daryl Qilin Yam.
First published by Epigram Books, 2021.
Published by arrangement with Agence littéraire Astier-Pécher.
All Rights Reserved.

Published by Gaudy Boy, LLC,
an imprint of Singapore Unbound
www.singaporeunbound.org/gaudyboy
New York

For more information on ordering books, contact jkoh@singaporeunbound.org.

ISBN 978-1-958652-04-6 / eISBN 978-1-958652-05-3
Library of Congress Control Number: 2023943311

Cover design by Flora Chan
Interior design by Jennifer Houle

LOVELIER, LONELIER

DARYL QILIN YAM

PART I

RANDEN

Kyoto, 1996

Happiness lies beyond the clouds;
Happiness lies above the sky.

—Kyu Sakamoto, "Sukiyaki"

1

It wasn't love, really. They were just trying to make something out of their lives.

When Jing met Isaac, in 1996, she was in the midst of losing her mother, a loss that, looking back now, she might have supplanted with a man she'd come to love, or what she had assumed was love. She would find herself thinking about this years later, at one of Isaac's work parties, one of the few she had attended out of an unspoken solidarity. They were at the clubhouse of a condominium, located at one of the offshoots of Orchard Road; the host was a theatre-maker who wanted Isaac to star in one of her plays, regardless of whether his renewed contract with Mediacorp would allow it. Jing remembered the look on Isaac's face then, a very well-known face at that point in time, but a face she liked to think she knew most intimately as he stared out of a window: she saw the way he gazed past the treetops, and the way his features were lit, dappled even, by the shimmering surface of the pool several metres below. She saw the way his eyes were trained towards the hazy skyline of the boulevard's glittering buildings, not so much with yearning or despair, but with some other emotion she had yet to pin down, even after all the time they'd spent together.

The year was 1999; the new century would be upon them in a few minutes' time. Standing in a corner of the room, watching various couples find one another, reach for one another, all of it in an atmosphere of palpable anticipation, Jing was struck by the idea that there were perhaps some things she would never know about him, had never known about him, probably since the day they'd first met. With this came the conclusion that it wasn't solidarity that Isaac needed from Jing that night: it was solitude. He wanted to be alone, or perhaps, he needed to be alone; it might even be a fundamental part of his nature, this loneliness. She became increasingly convinced of this, even as a countdown eventually began, causing her husband to finally tear his gaze away from the window.

She'd seen that same look before as well: on Mateo, her best friend, in that restaurant in Shinmachi-dori.

It was the night of the 22nd of March, 1996. They showed up to the restaurant at 7pm sharp, standing underneath an umbrella large enough to accommodate them all: her, Mateo and their other friend, Tori, who worked and lived at the ryokan they were staying at just two streets away. Jing and Mateo had met Tori in their final year in London, in the spring term of 1994, at a house party in Stoke Newington: even though Jing had exchanged a few kisses with Tori that night, it was never serious, because the real intimacy, Jing knew, lay strictly between Tori and Mateo instead. To her they shared an innate connection, an understanding that bordered on the telepathic, resulting in an intense, triangular friendship over the remainder of that term, one that undoubtedly made Jing jealous of the other two at times. Jing watched Tori then, in that restaurant in Shinmachi-dori, wondering if she could see what must have been plain to her too: that Mateo was in trouble, had been in trouble over the past few days in Kyoto, and that he might possibly be at the breaking point that evening. He had already taken to staring out the window just minutes after the three of them had been seated, in a place that should have appealed to all of Mateo's sensibilities: the dining area replete with hinoki floorboards and furnishings, with servers dressed in linen from head to toe, and that overly large juniper bonsai standing in the middle of the dining area, casting grotesque shadows on the ceiling.

Instead Mateo partook in the drizzly weather outside, the droplets still clinging to the wires between the telephone poles, the only landmark of note in an otherwise featureless part of town. Jing wondered if Tori knew what was going on with their friend, as she caught her giving Mateo a quick glance. She wondered if any of them knew what was really going on with each other's lives.

Tori began to scan the menu. Jing made the effort to do so too, even though everything was in Japanese. Tori then told her it was okay, that she would do the ordering, although her finger did hover over the few options they had, the cheapest one priced at 3,500 yen.

Jing made a face. Ugh, she said. That's going to hurt.

I agree, said Tori. She flipped the menu, trying to see if there was another page—there wasn't. Oh no, said Tori, smiling at Jing, and Jing couldn't help it: she smiled back at her too. Tori asked if Jing was still returning to Singapore on Sunday, the twenty-fourth, and Jing said yes, I suppose so, though with a little hesitancy. Tori asked her what the matter was, and Jing didn't reply immediately: instead she quickly shot Mateo another look, before saying that there were still things she needed to settle. Things she needed to do.

In Kyoto? said Tori. Kyoto, specifically?

Jing nodded. She allowed herself to look at Mateo more firmly then, just as Tori stared at her with her question. But Mateo's gaze was still fixed towards the window: it made him appear more impenetrable than ever, what with the watery light from the streetlamp shining into the restaurant, casting a grey, nearly opaque finish over his face, his glasses, the collar of his shirt. Tori then asked them both, her and Mateo, what it was that Jing needed to do in the city, and Jing felt like she had no choice but to say that she was sorry, and that now was not the right time.

To what? asked Tori.

To tell you, said Jing.

Jing and Tori kept quiet then, for a few seconds. I see, said Tori. I understand. She smiled again. We have not spoken in the past two years, so I should not . . . I should not pry, she said, causing Jing to feel an onset of shame.

Don't misunderstand; it's got nothing to do with that, said Jing. It's just—there's a story I can't tell, not now. I'm still in the middle of it. You get that, don't you? she asked, and at this Tori nodded, saying yes, I do. I do, actually. Do not worry. Tori then turned to Mateo, and asked if he knew what was going on with Jing.

I've been helping her, actually.

Oh. Over the past three days?

He nodded.

And are you also leaving on Sunday?

Mateo looked down at the table, and shrugged. I don't know, he said, making a pointless flip of the menu before him. He still hadn't made a decision on his open return; he didn't know when he would be flying back to Spain. To Madrid? asked Tori, and Mateo shrugged again. Maybe, he said, most likely Madrid, after which hung a long pause, a pause that Jing used to watch him again, her friend from long ago, wondering why there was so much the three of them had chosen to hide from one another. She wondered how they had got so comfortable with this, this arrangement of not knowing. But in her mind she knew that different friends had different agreements with one another.

Hey Mateo, said Tori.

Hmm?

Is it sad?

Mateo cocked his head to the side, with a half-grin on his face: for just a few seconds, Jing thought, he looked like his usual self again, like she'd always remembered him. What is? he asked, to which Tori said, Jing's story, causing Jing to laugh, mortified at what they were saying. So is it not? asked Tori, smiling once again, and Jing shook her head, saying no, no, I don't know. Forget it. She laughed a little more before she took a sip of water. It's fine, she said. I'll tell you one day, Tori, the whole thing. The whole story.

Mateo's face lit up just then. He reached a hand out, tenderly, to touch the window.

Oh, he said: Fireworks.

Jing remembered turning, almost immediately, with the eagerness of a child—but there was nothing, nothing, even though that was the moment when everything had begun to change. Where? she asked Mateo, and he quickly tapped his fingers on the windowpane, before the light could fade away.

Right there, he said—there, look. You see it, no?

Tori stood up behind Jing, and took a step towards the window. Jing remembered feeling Tori's hand on her shoulder, a light grip that left her tense.

I don't see anything, she said.

What?

Tori appeared to remain unconvinced. I don't see anything, Mateo, she said again. Some might—some might say it is too early.

He didn't understand. Too early?

For fireworks, she said. Tori then explained it to him, to the two of them: how hanabi, as they were known here, typically take place during the summertime. It is the custom, she insisted. Tori then asked if he was sure about what he'd just seen, and he said that he was, he was certain about it. And that was when Mateo revealed that he had been seeing fireworks every night, actually: grand ones, large ones, fired over the city. Over the main river, in fact, the Kamo River, that threaded through the city centre. He would hear the fireworks first before he'd see them, many of them, burst all over the sky above.

Every night? asked Tori.

Mateo nodded. Every night, he said. And that was when Jing finally made eye contact with Mateo that evening, as he added: I can show you.

The friends didn't stay long at the restaurant after that. They settled the bill, and proceeded to walk back to the ryokan, under a much lighter rain this time. There is a bar, said Mateo, a bar that he could take the girls to, to show them that what he'd seen was real. Jing remembered failing to understand why the fireworks had mattered to him so much, but she also remembered the way that Tori looked at Mateo too, with a sudden seriousness that surprised her. This is important to you? said Tori, and Mateo said yes, it was important, very much so. Then okay, said Tori, I will go with you. And when she turned to Jing to ask if she would join them too, Jing found Tori holding her hand, with the same firmness she'd felt on her shoulder just moments ago. Come on, said Mateo, join us. Just like old times. Jing then looked at him, and then at Tori, with the distinct feeling that they were caught in an undertow, somehow, the three of them too weak to resist it. Sure, she said to Mateo. Let's go out.

The three entered the ryokan and took their shoes off; they were about to settle on a time to regroup when Tori appeared distracted by a pair of trainers, shelved away in a corner of the genkan. She began to head down the corridor of the first floor, towards the common kitchen, in a manner that compelled Jing and Mateo to follow.

There was a guy inside, a tall one, with hair that'd grown past his eyes. He turned out to be a recent friend of Tori's, a guest at the ryokan a few weeks ago, before he went travelling around the region. He called her every other day, from whichever payphone he could find, just to tell her where he was; Tori hadn't known, however, that he would be coming back to Kyoto that evening. I also didn't know, the guy said, smiling. Tori asked if that was why he called her a second time today, and he said yeah, I guess. In fact, he just got to the ryokan half an hour ago, just in time before the front desk closed for the night.

Tori glanced at the tinfoil packet, heating up inside a pot of boiling water. Instant curry? she asked.

To go with rice, he said. Plus a banana, the guy added, pointing at the plastic bag beside the rice cooker.

He then finally turned to her, to Jing and Mateo, asking if they'd eaten already. Jing remembered being struck by Isaac's handsomeness then, an almost unfair attractiveness that pushed past the unkempt hair, the uneven shave, the hollowness in his cheeks. It was also hard to tell if he was older or younger than she was: he had a natural complexion that betrayed his youth, but also a demeanour, an air about him, that told her he'd been through something difficult, profound—something only he could understand. In years to come, this aura of his would compel strangers to be kind to him, unfailingly so, and even propel him to stardom; that same aura would protect him too, from the lingering presence of most people, as though afraid of overstaying their welcome. It left only a rare few in his innermost circle, a circle Jing couldn't even be sure she was a part of at times. But she wouldn't have an inkling of this, wouldn't have the ability to foresee such a thing in the ryokan that evening, not on that Friday night in March, 1996; as they shared their names with one another, she wouldn't be able to tell if her attraction to him was due to some gravitational effect that he had, or because she wanted to be pulled towards him instead, to be close to someone, to have the presence of something decent in her life. When Isaac revealed that he was from Singapore, Jing remembered feeling heartened by the coincidence. It felt uncanny to her. Oh, she said, me too, which left an awkward, almost embarrassing silence in its wake.

Mateo spoke up. He asked Isaac if he would like to join them later, to a bar he knew in the city. Isaac said it was okay: he wanted to rest tonight, take his time at the bathhouse after his dinner. He felt like he had come a long way, even though the journey hadn't actually been that far.

Where were you? asked Mateo. Jing then watched Isaac turn back to Tori, tentatively, just as he gave his reply: Nishinomiya.

A frown and a smile both quivered over Mateo's face. Isn't—isn't that where—?

Tori nodded. Yes, she said. Where I grew up. And for a moment the four of them fell quiet once again, filled with questions they didn't know how to ask one another. They were all so young.

2

On the day he left home, Isaac made sure to take a couple of things with him, on top of the other items Sherry had written down on a list. First, he took a lighter and a pack of candles from his field pack, as well as his tin can, for eating on the go. He then went into his parents' bedroom and pocketed his father's Oakley sunglasses, hanging from a hook behind the door, and took the Walkman too, standing by his father's side of the bed, which also doubled as a radio.

He popped out the cassette tape. It was an old favourite of his father's, *Bad Girl*, the 1985 album by Anita Mui. As Isaac put the tape down, wound halfway along its A-side, he recalled not the music, but the cover art, the singer in bright jewels and a purple dress, staring through the hollow of a man's fading silhouette.

Isaac went over to the other side of the room. He swiped a half-empty jar of sour plum candy from the top of his mother's bedside cabinet, a leftover treat from Chinese New Year. He then found more sweets, which he took as well, as he worked his way down the cabinet's drawers. From the fourth and final drawer, Isaac managed to find a disposable camera, with eleven shots left in the roll, as well as his birth certificate, laminated and slotted into a fraying, A4-sized manila envelope. ISAAC XAVIER NEO JIALIANG, it said. 01/03/1973. Isaac placed the certificate back into its envelope and filched that too.

He returned to his bedroom, his and his sister's. The only thing that Isaac took from her was a photograph, stuck on the wall above her mattress. As he peeled it away from the Blu-Tack, he could sense his sister stirring, looking up at him, drool already pooling over the side of her mouth.

Isaac knelt beside her. He used her bib to wipe her saliva. He then got her to look at the photograph, for what would be the last time between the two of them.

The year in the corner said 1982: Isaac was nine, his sister seven, his parents still in their early thirties. They were at the zoo, all four members of the family, seated on a giant, artificial log. There was a monkey too, squatting in the middle—golden-haired and red-faced, unbothered by the way his sister had wrapped her arms around its body. As Isaac held the photo closer to their faces, Isaac could see the monkey's trainer standing by the side, smiling proudly, it seemed, at both the way the primate was behaving, and the unbridled enthusiasm his sister had for the creature.

Isaac considered the other faces too. It was easy for him now, to see how they might have borne traces of a future they would each come to inhabit. His father looked content for one, but wary, clearly anxious about the animal; you could see the sweat coming down his sideburns, dripping down the length of his forearms. His mother, eyes half-open, sported a lazy smirk as she placed her hands around her daughter's shoulder, oblivious to her husband's worries. And there was him, of course, his mouth wide open in a perfect smile, holding up a peace sign next to his face: the only one ready for his shot.

Isaac and Sherry got the idea to run away on the 17th of January, 1995, about a year before they managed to carry out their plan. It was a day off in National Service for Isaac, a Tuesday: Sherry met him at Khatib Camp, first thing in the morning, and followed him back to Chinatown, to his flat in Jalan Minyak, where his family lived on the twelfth floor. They had arrived with food, a steaming packet of chwee kueh and two cans of F&N Grape, and heard a thump, from his and his sister's bedroom; when they opened the door they were immediately assaulted by a horrible stench, followed by the sight of Isaac's sister on the floor, squirming and struggling towards him like a worm. Just beside the mattress was his mother, who kept on sleeping, snoring like a cow, even with the smell of her daughter's shit wafting from a day-old diaper.

Zach, said Sherry, you wanna wake your mother first? Isaac quickly spotted the bottle of zolpidem pills in a corner, and shook his head.

Help me carry my sister, he said instead.

They hoisted her to the back of the flat, their feet nimble enough to avoid the flecks of waste that dripped onto the floor. Sherry then brought the radio from the living room, her father's Walkman, with a Faye Wong cassette tape inside it this time, and placed it next to the door of the toilet.

Isaac laid out a few sheets of newspaper on the floor before he undid his sister's diapers. He and Sherry grimaced, and held their breath, as he skipped over to the rubbish chute and tossed it out of sight. Sherry waited till Isaac had settled back down and started the water before she extended the Walkman's antenna, adjusted the dial for the radio, and turned up the volume.

93.3FM was Sherry's favourite station. Isaac had always known, ever since the two had started dating in their second year of poly, that it had been her dream to go into radio one day, even though he had also seen how that dream would shrink, or take a different shape from time to time, to accommodate other roles in the media that she could do. Now her aspirations went largely unspoken, a year after they had graduated; Sherry still worked at her mother's printing shop, failing to put anything they had learnt in their media and communications course to use. Whenever Sherry played the radio next to him, Isaac could only think of the way their lives were already adjusting even further, and hardening, some might say, within the fast-shrinking confines of a foreclosed reality.

There was a news segment then, on the radio: the first item was about a major earthquake that had struck Japan several hours ago, at 5.46 in the morning. The tremors had lasted for twenty seconds, and measured at a magnitude of 7.2 on the Richter scale. Isaac and Sherry exchanged a quick look, certain that the same question had arisen in both their minds: what in the world did a 7.2 entail? What was a 7.2 relative to a 5.2, a 6.2, an 8.2? The answer soon came: an estimated 3,000 lives lost in the city of Kobe alone, a number the newscaster said was sure to rise over the rest of the day. And as the news segment concluded, the two looked at one another, dazed as though in an aftershock of their own, broken then by the most horrific sound, a sound Isaac found hard to believe he was hearing: it was laughter. The radio deejays of the morning show were laughing, over a joke one of the co-hosts just made. It didn't matter what the joke was even about.

That's horrible, said Isaac.

Yah, said Sherry.

He found it hard to speak. I can't believe—

Believe what?

Isaac shook his head, to stop himself from commenting further. And yet he felt surprised when he heard Sherry's voice, as though she were completing his sentence: We are so lucky to be here. Right?

His first instinct, believe it or not, was to laugh in response. Right, he thought. They were so very lucky to be where they were. And while the two of them smiled at one another, Isaac knew that Sherry was imagining the same thing he was: of Singapore shaking, uncontrollably, 7.2 on the Richter scale, just to see what it felt like, for once—just to see what it meant to crumble, for once. It was not a frightening thought for him to entertain. And even though Isaac was playing with the bidet now, causing his sister to clap and snigger under the fresh spurts of water, he could still feel Sherry's gaze upon him, along with all of the anger and shame and self-loathing that they shouldered between them. Remnants of his sister's shit floated towards the drain of the toilet as he said:

Do you want to leave?

The dazed look came back into Sherry's eyes. Oh yah?

Yah, said Isaac. Let's leave.

They saved money over the following year. The weekend before his National Service ended, Isaac and Sherry got together and counted everything they had in the bank. They counted and then recounted, and then counted again. At the end of it all they asked one another, did they really know how much it would cost to take a bus, a train, a ferry, a flight? What about hostels, other places to stay? What about food? Isaac and Sherry frowned, unsure of what to say.

Isaac still remembered that day, spent at the void deck, tallying up coins and bank notes, and sums on their passbooks over a mosaic-tiled chess table. The void deck was in one of the estates in Bishan, where Sherry and her mother lived in her maternal uncle's flat; she had just come back from the hospice, where her father was warded, paralysed after an accident in the army. Isaac saw that Sherry had worn lipstick that day, and a bit of blush. She had eyeliner on too, and her eyebrows were plucked into thinner lines.

Make-up, he said to her.

Yah, she said, keeping her eyes down on her passbook. Nice, right?

He nodded. It's new, he said. It's nice.

She smiled.

Thanks, Zach, said Sherry.

That was a thing Isaac never figured out: how she had arrived at this nickname of his, the shortening of his name to Zach. It was what she called him ever since they became a couple. To her, he would always be Zach, while to him, Sherry would always be Sherry.

The following Saturday, Sherry asked Isaac if he wanted to try something new. It was a small request from a friend, with some money tied to the end of it. It's nothing complicated, she said, and it could be done in one morning. Nice, said Isaac, that's super cool, even though he had no idea, really, what it was she was getting him to do. Isaac then asked if he knew this friend of hers, and Sherry said no, don't think so. He's someone new, she added.

Sherry then told Isaac to meet her at her mother's printing shop at 10am on Monday, and he told her he'd see her then.

Isaac liked going to the printing shop. Sherry's mother was a tall woman with even taller hair, and she had a great, great laugh. She was the kind of woman who'd get invited to host auctions or sing karaoke on stage every time getai season rolled by. He'd see Sherry's eyes, her nose and her teeth every time he looked at the woman, and it amazed him, the resemblance. And whenever he visited he'd bring food from the kopitiam next door, and Mrs Wong would laugh and say aiyoh, leng zai, so sweet. She'd take the food with her glove-covered hands and pass it around the shop, causing the heavy musk of hot paper and fresh ink to be imbued with the scent of whatever food he got them that day. But as he stood outside the printing shop on Monday morning, he found himself horrified by the realisation that he would not miss this. He would not miss these smells, these recollections. It shocked him to think that he would not even miss the sounds of Sherry's mother greeting him, laughing at him, calling him handsome. What was the point? he thought. It made him wonder what he was truly capable of achieving; it made him wonder how far he'd go to excavate himself, if it meant that he could run away. He would miss nothing, he thought, as Sherry opened the door.

Hey Zach, she said.

He stepped inside. The shop was closed on Mondays, so there was no one in besides the two of them. Sherry locked the entrance and led him to a photocopier, the one standing at the rightmost corner of the place. Isaac pointed at the tall stack of A5 paper beside it.

Flyers?

Dui, said Sherry, nodding. She must have already started before he showed up, thought Isaac. Sherry picked up a separate stack of A4s and passed it to him.

Cut them in half, she said. Can?

He nodded. He then looked at the A4s and the A5s—at the same face that was smiling on all of them.

Is this Zoe Tay?

Sherry cast him a quick glance. Dui, she said again.

He peered closer. There was text in English and in Chinese, printed at the bottom of the flyer: *ZOE TAY. MOST POPULAR FEMALE ARTISTE. STAR AWARDS 1996*. He must have looked rather puzzled, for when he raised his head again he saw Sherry staring at him.

You dunno, right, she said.

Yah, he said. No clue.

Sherry handed him one of the flyers. She told him that the Star Awards was a TCS awards ceremony that started two years ago. It rewarded the best in Chinese Singaporean television, super glam and everything. So you dunno about *The Golden Pillow*? Sherry asked, and Isaac said in response: What pillow? It was a drama starring Zoe Tay, and it had just ended the previous month, said Sherry. In the first episode, set in Thailand, Zoe Tay's character, Xiao Dan, gets caught in a love triangle between two men: there's the one who wants to marry her, a you qian got money kind of guy, and there's the one she wants to marry, her childhood friend, who she'd been in love with for the longest time. But the you qian ren then gave 1,500 baht to Xiao Dan, signalling his intent to marry her, while Xiao Dan moves along with her life, carrying around the 1,500 baht, with no idea that the money could mean this kind of nonsense thing. Only at the end of the episode does her childhood friend finally tell her: Someone wants to marry you. You sure you dunno, Xiao Dan?

Wait, wait, said Isaac. But she wants to marry her childhood friend, right?

That's right, said Sherry. Ren Niang.

And is Ren Niang also a you qian ren?

She shook her head. Xiao Dan's life would be simpler, said Sherry, if she could just forget about Ren Niang. Just marry the you qian ren. But what to do?

Isaac looked at her then, unable to tell what was going through her mind. Yah, he said. What to do.

Sherry didn't respond. Instead she turned back to the flyers, to all of Zoe Tay's photocopied faces.

That's how I know.

Know what?

That I really love Xiao Dan, said Sherry. That I was going to love the show. Xiao Dan is so strong, so brave, all because she's in love with Ren Niang, who's also strong and brave as well, said Sherry. No matter where he goes, there she will be, because she loves him no matter what.

Isaac looked at the flyers again. It was the first time he ever heard Sherry say she loved anything in her life; it was also the first time he felt like he was learning something new about Sherry again, even though it made sense, of course, that she would fall into this kind of thing. Okay, he said. I get it.

At 12.45pm they were done cutting all the flyers. Isaac went out and bought them both lunch, fishball noodles from the kopitiam. At 1.30pm a man came by the shop, a skinny dude with running visors; Sherry handed him the entire stack of flyers, all 1,500 pieces of Zoe Tay. The man opened his backpack and handed Sherry an envelope filled with $2, $5 and $10 notes.

Sherry returned to Isaac's side. Together they counted the money, both of them performing mental sums under their breaths. When Sherry was done counting she said: Okay. Take it.

He felt like he had to ask. Everything?

She nodded. Yah, she said. You keep.

And then the day to leave came, on the final week of February. Isaac placed the lighter, the candles and the Oakley sunglasses into the tin can, before putting it at the bottom of his backpack. He then gathered all his mother's sweets into a ziplock bag and placed it inside as well, followed by the camera and his father's Walkman. In also went the manila envelope, containing both his birth certificate and the photograph of his family at the zoo. All of it sat alongside his essentials, the things that Sherry had listed for him, which included an extra set of clothes, some toiletries and station-ery for making notes with. His passport, his way out of town, was kept in a separate ziplock bag, while his wallet was fastened to the waist of his jeans with a metal chain. He was good to go.

He heard a moan, then, from the corner of the room. He wondered if it was cruel of him, packing his bag in front of his sister. Isaac looked at her one last time, and found her staring back at him, her hand opening and closing, as though grasping at some invisible thing.

I'll always remember you, was all he managed to say, before he left for good.

The sun was quickly setting. Isaac made his way down the hill, towards Chin Swee Road, before cutting across the park at Pearl's Hill towards Chinatown. Even then he thought that he might have lost all memory of his neighbourhood already, overcome by the realisation that all roads had a way of looking the same, all paths too, all under the common denominator that was the night. When he got on the bus that would take him directly to Golden Mile, Isaac placed himself on one of the seats beside the windows. As soon as the bus reached its next stop, he thought he was on the verge of retching, of heaving, only to realise that he was crying, sobbing, so painfully that he had to bite into his fist to muffle the anguish. When he could finally reopen his eyes, he found that the seats closest to him were clear of people; only the few who had remained along the perimeter managed a glance at him, before fearfully looking away.

Sherry was already at Golden Mile, waiting for him on the steps of the main driveway. She had a fanny pack around her waist, while her backpack, a bright purple Eastpak, sat beside her feet.

Hey, Sherry, he said.

She must have noticed how puffy his face was. Hey, Zach, she said anyway.

Isaac rubbed his nose, and looked around. There were other people too, people with suitcases and rucksacks, staring at the road. You ready? he said.

Sherry nodded. You leh?

He nodded back. I think so, he said to her. He then felt another sharp pain, squarely in the middle of his ribs this time. And then he had to bend over, his chest tightening.

Zach. Zach.

Yah?

You can do this, Zach.

Okay.

You are going to take this bus and leave everything behind, Zach.

Okay.

It will take you to a new life, Zach.

I know.

Do you?

Yah.

You sure?

Hmm.

Okay, good.

Their bus came at the appointed time, at 7.50pm. Sherry reached into her fanny pack and took out their tickets. Isaac trailed behind her as they queued for their seats. It took everything in him to be grateful that here, even now, he still had Sherry Wong, the one who understood him the most. The one who knew what it meant to have this rage of his, an incandescent rage, one that would clear a path forward for his and Sherry's new lives. The driver asked if they had any luggage, and it was clear to Isaac, so clear: these bags on their backs, it was all that they had with them. These bags were the sum total of their new lives, with spaces they might or might not fill. He would do anything in his power to protect what he had left with him.

Sherry chose a pair of seats in the midsection of the bus. As Isaac settled in beside her, she held tightly onto his hand, placing it firmly on her knee.

Hey, Zach?

Hmm?

Say it to me.

Say what? he said. And then he stopped himself, shook his head; he knew what she was talking about.

You can do this, Sherry.

Hmm.

You are going to take this bus and leave everything behind, Sherry.

Hmm.

This bus is going to take you to a new life, Sherry.

And Sherry looked at Isaac, her eyes boring into his. What could Isaac say about this moment, seated in this bus to Malaysia? That her eyes were hardening and then softening, and then hardening again; that they wouldn't loosen their grip on the other's hand; that he wouldn't know how long they would stay that way in the bus, after the doors closed and led them north, out of Singapore and over the Causeway, away from everything he had known before. They went into the strange and the wondrous, towards the only things he knew for sure now, which so happened to encompass the passing view, the blurring signs—the too-wide and half-dreaded unknown.

3

Fear, Mateo thought. Love is everywhere.

He thought Daniel had called, on his fourth night in Tokyo. It was a leap day, the 29th of February, 1996: Mateo stood by the sink of his toilet, in the serviced apartment that the gallery had rented for him, smoking a cigarette whose taste he was beginning to enjoy. He turned to the box, flipped it on the counter, reread the label on the front: Golden Bat Cigarettes. Sweet & Mild.

He left the door to the toilet ajar, by just a sliver. It was enough for him to watch his companion for the evening, a man whose name he had long forgotten or probably misheard. They had met in Ni-chome, at one of those hole-in-the-walls that were friendly, welcoming even, to the patronage of foreigners: a guapo approached him and danced with him, the Cher song they were shimmying to nearly over at that point. Mateo could still recall the sensation of the guapo's mouth at his ear, asking if they ought to sleep with one another, and Mateo had said yes, yes. Let's leave, right away.

Mateo tapped his ashes into the sink. Here, in the ambient lighting of his room on the eighth floor, he inhaled the last of his cigarette and exhaled over the scene, over the sight of his companion, compressed within the gap between the door and its frame.

Anyone could look like anybody, given enough smoke.

He stubbed out his Golden Bat, flicked it into the toilet bowl. He then reached for a second, a third, a fourth; he knew that life would continue to be like this, this endless reaching for things, so why should he stop now? It also explained why, at 1.15 in the morning, he found himself dashing out of the toilet in his bathrobe, towards the phone that just began to ring. He picked it up and went, Hola—Daniel? only to cringe, and swear under his breath, when he heard a woman's voice instead. It was Jing, a former room-mate from his time in London, asking who this Daniel was.

Ha ha, he said. My bad. Hey, Miss Singapore.

Hey, your foot. Come on, Jing said to him. Who's Daniel?

Mateo eyed the man on his bed, deep into REM. The corner of his mouth twitched, as well as his brows, before he turned his body to the side. An ex, said Mateo, his heart palpitating. Huh, said Jing. You never told me. Do you want to talk about it? she asked, and he had to lick his lips.

He had a vision, then: he saw Daniel in the toilet, through the gap in the door, standing by the sink. Standing where he used to be. Not really, said Mateo, sorry. He changed the topic, even though what he really wanted was to hang up right now, smoke another cigarette. So you got my postcard? he said, and Jing said yes, she did. She asked how long he was going to be in Tokyo, and what kind of work he was going to be doing there. Three-week secondment, baby, Mateo replied: admin, logistics, sales, networking. Everything, basically. Jing then asked if he was planning to return to Madrid, and he found himself locking eyes with Daniel again, the vision of Daniel, watching him chat on the phone. He told Jing about his plans to travel around Japan instead, to at least see their old friend Tori, now that he had finally got a hold of where she was based. She works at an inn now, like, at a guesthouse in Kyoto, he said. I even have the address.

Mateo then heard a sigh over the phone, a rush of static over the speaker. Jing asked if he ever felt that life had a way of working out sometimes, to which his answer was a prompt no. Miss Singapore, he said. Not at all, love. But he got her to explain while he watched, and waited, for the vision of his former lover to pass. He couldn't keep his eyes away.

———

They decided to walk to the bar, now that the rain had stopped. Mateo didn't have the exact address of the place, but he knew it was near the west end of the bridge that overlooked a delta in the Kamo River. Tori then told them about a route, a shortcut across the city—one that involved walking through the Kyoto Gyoen, the national park that surrounded the Imperial Palace.

There was a moment, just before they left, when Jing caught Isaac leaving the kitchen, making his way down the corridor towards them. Jing quickly returned to tying her shoelaces, pretending she hadn't noticed. Eventually she felt his presence, or more accurately his long shadow, cast over them all in the genkan. Take care, you guys, he said.

You sure you don't wanna join us? asked Mateo. Isaac said it was okay; Tori wished him a good rest.

I will see you tomorrow? she asked.

Can, he replied. I'm not going anywhere.

He didn't move then; he seemed intent on watching them go, before returning to his dinner. It gave Jing the courage to crane her head up towards him, to ask if he knew when he was going back. Back where? said Isaac, a response that left her dumbfounded, surprised. I meant Singapore, she said.

Oh, said Isaac. She found it hard to read his face, a face half-shrouded in shadow. I'll let you know, he said to her, tomorrow.

The three then walked northwards, for about a kilometre or so, towards Marutamachi Station. It marked the southern corner of the Kyoto Gyoen, according to Tori. While they walked, Jing observed how the rain seemed to stop, after several days of intermittent downpour, dwindling at last into something like a fine mist, unfolding over them and the city: she heard nothing but the sound of their briskly moving feet, and their steady breaths; she could hear the rainwater too, falling from the eaves of nearby rooftops, as cars and motorcycles dashed over puddles on the road.

At some point, Tori finally asked Mateo if he could tell her more about the fireworks, and he asked if she was sure. Yes, said Tori, I want to know.

Jing then caught Mateo looking at her too, and she nodded, even though she was mostly following Tori's lead. Just tell us, she said.

He told them that he'd seen his first firework on the 19th of March, his first night in Kyoto. He said he wasn't altogether sure of where he was, though it was midnight, last he'd checked. He had lain on top of his futon with his eyes open, unable to sleep, unable to reconcile his back with the tatami floor. He remembered looking at Jing, lightly snoring on the other side of the room, soft but operatic. He heard his G-shock beep the time, 2400 hours, which was when he had got up, changed and grabbed his wallet. Mateo stepped out of the room and went downstairs, where he found Tori, in the kitchen, with her colleagues round a large table. He saw the drink in her hand, and the way everyone was still laughing, still eating. He crept into the vestibule and slipped on his shoes, sliding through the main entrance, confident he hadn't been seen. Had you though? asked Mateo then. Had you seen me leaving? And Tori smiled, and said she hadn't, though she later noticed, while retreating back to her quarters on the second floor, that his shoes were missing from the genkan.

It was his favourite season, spring. April was his favourite month in Madrid, what with all the frequent showers: rain was the gayest weather, said Mateo, it had nothing but style, nothing but drama. Here, in Kyoto, it was as though the rain were speaking to him with hushed whispers, gracing him with little touches like a familiar friend in another city. When Mateo had slipped out that night, he only knew of the bathhouse, round the corner of the ryokan; he then walked down another road, aimless and happy to wander, until he eventually came across a Lawson. He bought a box of Golden Bats there, as well as a six-pack of Asahi. Everything else after that was a good blur, he said, the kind that he welcomed, he wanted. He savoured it, the cool moisture on his skin and in his hair; he could imagine the rain hissing against the burnt cinders that he nursed in his lungs.

At one point he didn't know where he was any longer; it didn't matter to him, really. He said this just as the three friends stopped at the crossing of Nishiyoko-cho, waiting for the light to change. At some point he had caught his first firework, watched it flash over the street, he said: it prompted him to turn, to look over his shoulder, just in time to catch it flare into brightness, into fast-fading gold—and while it did so the whole city seemed to shine. And while it shone he found himself bursting into a smile too—he was drunk, yes, but he was alone, more importantly, and the quiet horror of knowing this had filled him with a pleasure he couldn't quite explain. Mateo smiled for the length of time the light had stayed with him in the air.

They walked past Marutamachi Station, towards a FamilyMart, where Tori used the toilet while Mateo bought himself a new lighter. When Tori rejoined the group, Mateo was already smoking, while Jing stood closer to the bicycles parked outside the store, staring at the large intersection just ahead. She was looking at the large compound across the road, walled by stone and a perimeter of trees. The Gyoen.

Jing watched Mateo stub out his cigarette. He began to tell them about his second night, about how he had waited for Jing to fall asleep again, before slipping out of their room. While making his way down, he got caught by Tori this time, seated in the lounge beside the main staircase. He'd seen the variety of small dishes that Tori had set in front of her, as well as the magazine laid open to the side. He asked if her shift had just ended, and in turn Tori asked if he was heading somewhere. Mateo grinned, bit his lower lip. He was going to get a drink, he said, causing Tori to remark, Without Jing? Sí, said Mateo. Is that naughty of me? And Tori had wiggled her nose, asking if she could join; Mateo clapped his hands together and told her yes, Miss Japan, of course. Not sure where, though, he admitted. Tori then quickly heaped her remaining food onto a single plate.

Let me take you somewhere, she said.

They had walked as well, that night, to the izakaya that Tori frequented in Pontocho, an alleyway of teahouses and restaurants situated next to the Kamo River. But first they had to wade through Shijo-dori, inundated with people; Tori said that she went to the izakaya whenever she wanted to be alone but not alone, if he knew what she meant by that. Mateo asked if that happened to her often, the need to be alone, and Tori said matter-of-factly: Loneliness is normal for me. It is a completely normal part of my life. And you? she asked. Mateo remembered fixing his gaze on his friend, who was still waiting for him to reply; as they wove their way through the night-time crowd, he wondered if something had necessitated this level of frankness between them, caused by all that time they hadn't spoken to one another, or if she had always had this ability, to see him for who he really was. You are still the same, said Tori to him, as they neared the alley of Pontocho. You only feel valued when you are desired. I understand that very much.

The alleyway had been just as crowded that evening, swarmed with tourists. Mateo and Tori each ordered a highball the moment they were seated at the counter of the izakaya, wedged into a narrow gap between two teahouses. Sābisu, said the bartender, placing a small plate of fried tofu in front of them. Tori asked if Mateo needed anything else to eat, and he shook his head. The food was more than enough, he said.

The izakaya got talking, at some point. It began when one of the German diners asked about the gramophone crackling in a corner. What's that song? he said. From *Porgy and Bess?* The woman seated beside him spoke up next: Traurig, she said, that sounds depressing, for the bartender had pulled out the sleeve of the vinyl and pointed at the title of the current track. Act 1, Scene 2, recited another person: "My Man's Gone Now".

There were about a dozen of them in the conversation, all from different parts of the world: there was the pair from Munich, executives of an automobile company; there was another pair too, from São Paulo, in Kyoto for their twentieth wedding anniversary. One man who came alone was a musician from Iceland, a double bassist close to retirement, if there was ever such a thing. The topic so happened to be about everyone's first loves, and they did so by going down the counter, taking turns to tell their stories, and it had pained him, Mateo, to realise that his turn was only a matter of time. At one point the izakaya burst into protest, over something that the double bassist from Iceland just said: he declared that he had never been in love before, which caused the bartender, a long-time friend of his apparently, to wag his finger at him, saying no, no. Muri. You are lying, he insisted. But the German woman leapt to the musician's defence, saying no, I believe him, I do. I know people, perfectly content people, who have never experienced the feeling in their lives before. But then it was the Brazilian couple's turn to speak, and they told their story, a heart-warming one, which lightened the atmosphere once again; once they were done, the couple looked at Mateo, who was next. Mateo found himself smiling at everyone, Bartender-san included, not knowing what to say. When he turned to Tori, he found her smiling back at him too, saying: Go on.

Mateo looked down at his drink; he watched an ice cube break into two, bobbing on the surface of his whisky. He took a swig, then cast his eyes down again as he said: I fell in love many times. When I was young, especially. But I was only ever loved back once.

He looked up. Everyone at the izakaya was silent, waiting for him to continue. Even the opera playing had seemed to soften.

I met him last summer. In New York City, said Mateo. One of the Japanese diners asked where, where exactly in the city, and Mateo said: At the Museum of Modern Art.

And then he didn't speak anymore. He kept quiet, and the izakaya stared at him, realising that that was all he was going to share that evening. He felt Tori tap him on the shoulder, asking if he was okay. He turned to her.

I'm going to head out, he said. A quick smoke.

Are you sure? she had said. You can smoke in here.

Jing finally looked at Mateo, at this point in the story. The three of them were in the middle of the Gyoen now, where it was dark and bright at the same time. Everything about the park felt extremely vast, with gravel paths that must have been twenty metres wide, making it hard to even see the trees that stood by the side; it had the effect of making everyone inside it feel awfully small.

I'll see you in a bit, Mateo had said to Tori in the izakaya, and he stepped outside, where he could take a deep breath, even though every intake of air felt shallow. Nothing felt enough. He made his way out, back onto the main alley: there were still so many people, so many passers-by in Pontocho that he had to find his way out of that too, and he finally stumbled upon a small park, one that overlooked a section of the Kamo River. It was here where the feeling finally relinquished its hold over him, loosening its grip over his chest, dissipating into something lighter, freer.

There were people about, down at the riverbank. (Jing looked about her: it was almost bleak, really, to feel like they were the only ones in the park.) Lovers, loners: everything amber-lit, on either side of the stream. Even in the dark he had known he could fall in love with this place, this river, so adept at catching the many lights of the city, and so adept, too, in making them dance in its grasp. (A wind picked up then: nothing stirred, not even the trees to the side, bearing their leaves in the dark.)

Mateo had heard it then: heard it whistle, and pop. He remembered looking upwards, northwards—upriver. And then more fireworks, again and again, lighting the water and its many patrons, the river alive, as though aflame. Every time another went off, he imagined a pair of hands striking a piano, a chord in minor key: he imagined Daniel beside him, witnessing the spectacle with him, until he was really there, loving him back, both of them happy and content to remain in the shadows of this soft-lit city. That night he thought back to that summer day, in New York, in search of West 53rd Street like all the other fucking tourists, trying to intuit which way was uptown and which way was down. He was short-sighted, it turned out, he needed glasses; he couldn't read any of the road signs, right on the verge of realising that what he had was a problem, that this was not how other people perceived the world, in a blur. Watching the fireworks, he remembered why he was there in the first place, why he had thought of heading to MoMA that day. It was *RANDEN*, he recalled; it was on display. It was one of the nine installations at the Barbara London show, *Video Spaces*, in the René d'Harnoncourt Galleries. In the brochure was a picture of the artist, Han Aw, heavily pregnant, standing amidst a clearing within a bamboo grove.

Jing's mother.

More claps resounded across the sky. (A wind continued to blow through the park; Jing had to pull her jacket tighter around her, while her friends had to stop, close their eyes, hold their hair back.) Mateo had watched each firework go up in a soar, not just golden ones this time, but silver ones too, even a few in emerald green. Each one appeared to dissipate in a sigh, each one reminding him of what he really had: the grandeur, the uncanniness. The illusion.

It ruined him.

They sat by a road. They were in the middle of a small neighbourhood, at the northwestern exit of the Gyoen: nothing but low-lying buildings, packed tightly together into a grid. The three decided to rest outside a minimart, one with an impossibly bright sign in white and lime green. Tori went inside and quickly came back out, handing the two of them a bottle of beer each.

I didn't know, said Jing, the first time she'd spoken all evening. She knew that Mateo had taken a look at *Video Spaces* that summer, had even managed to catch her mother's artist talk. He had written to her, telling her how cool it was to see *RANDEN* in a space like that, the only pre-1990 work in the show, placed between the Stan Douglas and Chris Marker installations. But Jing didn't know that that was how Mateo had met Daniel; she hadn't even heard of his name till a few weeks ago, over the phone, when the relationship had already run its course. In that moment, Jing could have asked for any number of details, like what was Daniel's surname, for instance, or what the guy did for a living. She knew nothing about this man. Instead Jing asked Mateo if he had hated it, being with her, when she had asked for his help in Kyoto. No, said Mateo, he didn't hate it. It just reminded him of things, is all.

Tori was glancing at the two of them. What is going on? she asked. You have to tell me, she said, looking pointedly at Jing, and although Jing bristled at her friend's insistence, she knew that there was no avoiding it now, the story. She asked if Tori still remembered who Jing's mother was, and she said that she did, of course. Mateo had just mentioned it earlier, the performance artist. Tori asked what the matter was with her mother, and Jing said that she was dying. From throat cancer, she said: Stage 4. She had a laryngectomy last month, though I don't think it bought her that much time.

Tori was aghast; she looked pale in the illumination of the minimart's sign. I have to ask, she said, but what is a, a—a laryngectomy? Jing demonstrated by placing a hand over her neck. They take out your entire larynx, she said, and create a hole on your neck, to help you breathe.

Tori blinked. A hole? she said. An actual—

Yes, said Jing. The hole. The doctors put a plastic case over it too, to protect it.

Tori nodded, before looking down at her feet, at her own bottle of beer, held in both hands. Jing knew that she was trying to imagine it, having a hole in her own neck. But how to tell her that nothing could compare to the sight of the actual thing? How to tell her friend the sheer number of steps involved, just to take care of it at home, on a twice-daily basis? How to tell her about the way her hands had shook, as she swabbed the skin around the opening, the stoma—or the way she had winced, and shuddered, as she watched her grandmother remove and reinsert the inner cannula, that plastic tube, through her mother's neck? Some stories were truly impossible to tell, thought Jing—especially the one about her relief, really, to be here in Kyoto. She felt relieved, grateful even, to be sent here instead of being stuck at home in Singapore, with her mother dying in her makeshift bed on the living room couch.

Tori took a drink from her bottle. So what is the connection? she asked again. Between Han Aw and Kyoto?

Mateo cleared his throat. He readjusted his glasses. Jing's mother wants her to recreate an artwork, he said.

Jing sighed. Yes.

What artwork? Tori asked, and Mateo explained: in 1970, Han Aw travelled around Malaysia and Indonesia, conducting research on an ethnomusicology project. She discovered she was pregnant with Jing, on the same day that Paul McCartney announced he was leaving the Beatles. It prompted the artist to make a series of works that would define the rest of her career: she gave lectures and stage performances about the nature of having a child, about the responsibility of bringing a child into the world, the politics of being pregnant, giving birth, making life. That same year she performed at the first Pride parade in New York, said Mateo. Han Aw made a bunch of friends there, gathered a small crew of cameramen, and flew all of them here, to this city, where she would film a work known as *RANDEN*. Have you seen it?

Tori shook her head.

It's a great film, said Mateo. You need to imagine, Tori, this woman with very long hair, wearing a white dress, facing away from the camera. She's in the middle of Kyoto, standing completely still for like, what, forty seconds? And then she *screams*.

Tori gasps. She what?

Sí, said Mateo. The bitch screams, for fifteen seconds. And then she goes quiet for five seconds, before the scene changes, and it's her again, except she's standing somewhere else, another place in the same city. And again, forty seconds of silence, until—

She screams?

Uhuh, said Mateo, for another fifteen seconds. The scene then changes again, and the artist screams again, and then it's another scene, another place—

How many times?

Jing held up the number with her fingers. Seven, she said. I even have the places memorised: the rock garden at Ryoan-ji; the Sanmon Gate at Nanzen-ji; the landscape garden at Taizo-in Temple; the Shariden Garden at Rokuo-in Temple; the dry waterfall, Ryumonbaku, at Tenryu-ji Temple; the Shishi Rock, in the grounds of the Hogon-in Temple. The seventh one is tricky, but—

It's Arashiyama, said Mateo, the bamboo grove. It's the one place we haven't filmed yet.

Yet? said Tori. So the two of you have been—

Filming, yes. I am the cameraman, said Mateo.

Tori looked at Jing, a look that now held wonder alongside the fear. So you've been—

Screaming my head off? Yah, said Jing, I have. And before they knew it she and Tori were laughing, clutching one another's hands, leaning against the other by the roadside. Mateo watched the girls with a smirk on his face, and took another swig from his bottle. Jing and Tori soon righted themselves, finishing the rest of their beers.

Do you remember where we started filming? said Mateo.

Yah, said Jing. At Rokuo-in.

Mateo nodded. You had the stills from *RANDEN* printed out, just to check we were at the exact same spot.

That's right, said Jing. I also passed you my mother's Handycam.

Mateo nodded again. You did, he said. And I did my best, you know, to make sure I captured the same spot at the same angle, the same stone-paved path that extended from the main gate. You stood a few metres ahead, asking how was your position, and I gave you an *okay* sign, telling you to stay where you are, surrounded by maple trees. And then you took off your jacket, and pulled out this white blouse from your bag. Mateo smiled. It was a reference, right, to your mother's original white dress? he said. And you know, Jing, I found it really funny, the concept, funny to the point of absurd: continuity, it's not just a thing of films, I realised, but of memory too, of the images we hold onto. He paused. I didn't know, for instance, how long the image of Daniel was standing next to me, there at the Shariden Garden, he said. But there he was anyway, fully formed, like the real thing, dressed in cargo pants that nearly touched the ground. And he had his, his prescription sunglasses too, with that *horrible* leather cord slung around his neck. And there was a way I *swear* that Daniel was gazing at you, Jing, standing right beside me: the same gaze on his face the first time we met last summer, fixed instead on your mother's back that time.

And I don't know, said Mateo. I don't know if you noticed this moment, Jing, but I—I put the camcorder down. I had to. I had to look at this Daniel, here with me in Kyoto, staring straight ahead, paying me no mind. Like *I* was the one who wasn't there. Like *I* wasn't the one staring at *him*, at this, this man, this man with the cargo pants. But he knew, didn't he? He knew I didn't care about art anymore; all I cared about was this guy I found at the museum. I wanted to ask if he knew that I was already memorising every part of him, every ridiculous detail.

Did he know how easy it was? said Mateo that night. To, to bring him back, to bring him—bring him here? How the real difficulty lay elsewhere, within myself? I wanted to show him, you know, the, the dark corner where I put all kinds of stuff, a whole assortment of things, where they would suffer from more than the usual neglect. I wanted him to see it, said Mateo, show that place to him. I wanted him to know that I still love him, I do. Needless to say.

4

Lately Tori had allowed herself to feel comfortable again, at ease. On the 1st of March, 1996, she began her shift as usual, by taking a spray to the front desk and wiping the counter down with a cloth. She then flipped opened the room register and checked the day's log, to see which guests were checking in and which ones were leaving. She brewed a pot of tea for herself too, to last her throughout the day. She then reached behind the counter and switched the heater off, for what might have been the first time that year.

The telephone rang. She picked it up and sent her first morning greetings over the phone, to the concierge of a serviced apartment in Tokyo. He would like to book a room for two, on behalf of a guest, he said: six nights in total, from the nineteenth to the twenty-fourth. The dates were still two weeks shy from the cherry blossom forecast, which should mean good news for the concierge. Tori checked the register, and said they had a few private rooms on the fourth floor available.

Excellent, said the concierge, I'll have one of those rooms. He then asked if he could confirm one other thing, and Tori told him to go ahead, as she marked the dates out with a pencil. The concierge cleared his throat, and asked if there was a person named Tori Yamamoto working at the ryokan.

Tori paused: her hand froze, the tip of the pencil hovering just above the page. Why do you ask?

The concierge seemed to have picked up on Tori's trepidation. He replied, rather apprehensively: My guest says that he is a friend of hers.

Tori told herself to take a breath. She asked if she could have his guest's name. The concierge told her that he had the names of both guests actually: Mateo Calvo Morales and Jing Aw. He asked if he needed to spell their names out for her, he could go letter by letter if necessary, and she said no, that was not needed. I'm Tori Yamamoto, by the way, she said to the concierge. I'm the one they're looking for.

The phone rang again, twenty minutes later: it was Mateo, naturally, calling her from Tokyo. He asked if she remembered him, and she told him that she did, of course. She kept her voice as level as possible, and asked Mateo how he had found her. He said: I sent a postcard to you, to the mailing address you left me and Jing. And guess who left a message for me at my apartment?

Tori didn't have to work hard to remember: there could only be one address she'd given him. Regardless, she asked: Who?

Ay dios padrastro, said Mateo. Your stepfather, Tori.

Both hands tightened around the handset. It was harder to keep her voice level now, as she asked Mateo what the message was, and he had to pause, just like the concierge, sensing that something was not quite right with the conversation. He gave me the number to your workplace, said Mateo. Told me to check on you, see if you're well. Standard daddy things, you know?

Tori closed her eyes. So they know, she thought. They must have tracked her down, somehow, before deciding to let her be. Right, she said in reply. Standard daddy things.

There was another pause over the line. In any case, said Mateo finally: I can't wait to see you. There's no one quite like you, Miss Japan.

Tori smiled. He did say that a lot, Miss Japan, Miss Singapore; Mateo was Miss Universe, of course, Miss Universe 1994. She was relieved to find that the nostalgia she was filled with was a simple one, uncomplicated; it was something she might be able to live with, even enjoy. It has been a while, said Tori. I hope you're well. She told him that she couldn't wait to see Jing too, before putting the phone down on its cradle.

The rest of her shift proceeded relatively normally that day. In the evening she walked to the nearby sento and put her clothes away. She then made sure to take a long shower, letting the hot water run over her body. There was a mother on the other side, shampooing her two young daughters. Tori turned her tap off and walked over to the mosaic-tiled tub, where she found herself not just sitting, but reclining, letting the water lap over her shoulders, her neck, and then up to her ears, so that the only thing she could hear was the muffled churning of the water in the bath, the sounds of other people reduced to mere murmurings, while her voice continued to repeat itself in her mind, saying: They know, they know. They've always known. They've known, all this while.

Hello? someone said, as though from above. You okay?

Tori blinked: she had no idea where she was. She tried to breathe, but she couldn't—she then winced, and found her hands and knees bruised, from being on all fours on the pavement. She tried to breathe again, and coughed; she blinked once more, only to shed tears this time, plenty of them, dripping over the concrete like rain.

Hey, said the voice again. You know English?

The voice belonged to the pair of trainers, standing right in front of her. She nodded.

Oh, said the voice, oh good. Are you okay?

Tori nodded again. The stranger was kneeling in front of her now, sliding a packet of tissues towards her on the ground.

You want?

Her hands and knees continued to hurt. Tori took a tissue from the packet and quickly wiped her face.

We don't need to talk, he said. But let me take you home, okay?

All right, said Tori. Thank you. He looked kind, she told herself—she figured him to be a backpacker, someone who must have just arrived in the city. He never touched her, only hovered about her, protectively, when she rose to her feet. He asked her what happened, and she shuddered, looked around.

Bad dream, was all she said, though it was the truth. It was. She was still in her nightclothes, barefooted and without any trousers on. She allowed herself one hard look at Kyoto Station before turning her back on the place; there was no screaming, no ruin, no pain. It had been more than a year, she reminded herself.

Tori asked for the time. The stranger checked his watch: 5.51am.

She nodded; she'd only been like this for a few minutes, then. And do you—do you have a spare pair of jeans? she asked.

The backpacker put a hand to his head, thinking quickly. Um, uh—I got shorts, he said. Can?

Tori nodded another time. He quickly opened his backpack and managed to dig them out, a pair of denim shorts. She put them on.

You need slippers also?

Tori could have cried again, at the kindness this stranger was showing her. She kept her voice steady as she said yes, yes please.

She slid her feet into flip-flops two sizes too big. But they felt spongy, well worn. You sure nothing happened to you? asked the stranger, and Tori shook her head.

No, she said. Lucky me.

She knew the way back was just straight ahead, northwards, with a quick left at Takoyakushi-dori. She asked the stranger if he was looking for a place to stay that day, and he said that he was, but only somewhere cheap, like at a hostel or something. Tori understood, and nodded at him, telling him to follow her, to Shinmachi, where the ryokan was located. She switched the light on over the front desk and flipped through the register, noting the spare bed she still had in the men's communal room on the third floor. Only then did Tori finally think to ask him for his name, and instead of telling her he reached into his backpack and handed her his passport, kept safe in a wrinkled ziplock bag. Singapore, said the front cover; that's how she recognised his accent, she thought.

Tori took his details down. As she did, it surprised her to see that today, technically, would be the man's twenty-third birthday. Tori handed his passport back to him, wincing, still, from the slight bruise she had on her palms.

Thank you, Isaac. Welcome to Kyoto.

———

The first thing Isaac and Sherry did at the hotel was fuck, which was to say that they did so urgently, clumsily, desperately. Sherry hooked her arms around Isaac's neck and remained silent, hoisting his sex into hers, her body this nimble, frightening, but also wondrous thing to him. Every time she came she threw her head back and let out this low, guttural sound and grit her teeth together, not in a way that suggested restraint, but the need to compress it, contain it, the violence and the pleasure and the feeling. After they were done, Isaac lay on their bed, tired and utterly spent. Sherry hopped off his body, tossed his condom into the trash and cleaned herself in the shower. When she came back out she picked up the phone and ordered room service.

What's the cheapest thing you have? she said into the phone. Okay. Yah. Terima kasih.

Sherry hung up, then turned to Isaac and patted his arm.

Hope you're okay with instant noodles, she said. After that we have to go out and buy stuff.

Isaac was still sweaty, panting. Can, he said.

Sherry rolled her eyes, and looked through her Eastpak for her spare bra. You got see a supermarket around here? Anything nearby?

He shook his head.

Right, she said. Tonight.

That evening Isaac and Sherry found themselves before a Giant outlet a few blocks away, with more aisles of produce either of them had ever seen in their lives. Sherry took Isaac to the bread section and chose a loaf with nuts and raisins; at the fruit section she picked out bananas, apples and pears. She would say things like: This is good, this won't need to be in a refrigerator, you can just eat it whenever you feel it's time. That or: This is healthy, Zach, it will make you full, you don't need to eat anything else. She would then ask Isaac if he understood, and he would nod and say yah, he did. Sometimes she would ask him a second time, and he'd have to go yah, yah, he got it.

Try to drink only bottled water if you can.

Okay.

Sometimes tap water might be okay, but most of the time it's not.

Okay.

Also always keep your plastic bags, you don't know when you might need them.

Okay.

Do you know how to fold? Into small tight squares?

I think so.

Sherry narrowed her eyes at him, even as she gave him a smile. I show you later, she said.

Isaac would later count the things that Sherry made him get: ponchos, insecticide, bandages, powder, packets of sweetener, a comb. After they paid for everything Sherry handed them all to him, just for him, to keep. This is how it starts, he thought at the time; this is how their lives would begin to fill, starting with these little things. He only hoped that his backpack would be big enough.

Back at the hotel they entertained themselves by taking pictures, with the disposable camera Isaac had taken from his mother. They took pictures of the bed, the toilet, the view out the window. They took pictures of one another, alone and together, striking various poses before they decided to fuck another time. It started when Sherry placed one hand on Isaac's arm and placed the other on his pants; he looked at her, saw the intent in her eyes once again, and got instantly aroused. It was then he thought: it doesn't take much to love someone like Sherry. Sherry was beautiful, and available, and strong. Sherry was a leader, a guide. Sherry knew what to do and knew what she wanted. And now she wanted him, and she was wanting him all the time, it seemed. But Isaac made sure he was in charge this time. He held her wrists down as he pumped into her, again and again and again, asking her if she liked it, if she liked how it felt, was she sure that she did? Did she want him to come, and was she close to coming? Did any of it feel good? he asked, as Sherry's lips curled into a smile. After they were done they cleaned up and settled back into bed, unclear if it was still day or night. Who knew where the sun was any longer? And then another thought occurred to Isaac as he lay on the bed.

Can I ask you something? he said. Can I ask you about that show?

What show? said Sherry, looking at him. *The Golden Pillow*?

Isaac nodded. He asked about the show's name: Is there, like, an actual golden pillow? Sherry nodded back and said yah, there is. It's a gold-coloured stone that Ren Niang's father gave his mother a long time ago. Ren Niang? asked Isaac—Xiao Dan's childhood friend? He then asked what was so important about this stone, and Sherry said: Love lor. It's love, Zach. When Ren Niang's father left for Singapore, he gave his mother this stone to remember him by, and she held on to it, slept with it, used it as pillow. She did this for more than twenty years, loving Ren Niang's father but hating him also, counting every day he doesn't come back for them. But does he? asked Isaac, and Sherry said yah, he does. Ren Niang's father is still in love with his mother, even though he has this whole other family in Singapore, all in this crazy big house. So he runs to Thailand? said Isaac, and Sherry said no, more like the other way round. He gets them to come to Singapore.

There was a siren, then, wailing past the hotel. Isaac stared at the ceiling of their room, waiting for the sound to fade away before he asked: Is he a good guy?

Who? Ren Niang's father?

Sure.

Yah, said Sherry. He's a good guy.

And Ren Niang? asked Isaac. Is he a good guy?

Yah, said Sherry again. He's a good guy also, Zach.

Isaac turned his head, to smile at Sherry. He found that she'd been staring at the ceiling too. Do they get together? he asked. Xiao Dan and Ren Niang? And Sherry looked at him again, shaking her head. I dunno actually, she said, with tired eyes. Isaac told her he didn't understand. I also dunno, she said. No one knows who is with who by the end of the final episode. It's too heartbreaking for anyone to decide.

Isaac turned away—he felt a sudden pain in his head. Okay, he said, I get it, even though he wasn't actually sure if he did. He closed his eyes, and Sherry switched on the television, flicking past the Malaysian channels until she finally hit Channel 8, at the tail end of the day's *Singapore Today*, broadcast through a haze of static. *People around the world can expect brilliant views in the night sky from the 1st to the 3rd of March*, the newscaster said, *as Comet Hyakutake, also known as the Great Comet of 1996, becomes the closest-flying comet to Earth in more than two hundred years*. While Sherry strained to listen to the newscaster's voice, steadily increasing the volume on the TV, all he could hear was the static, the haze, the noise. Isaac reached for a pillow and placed it over his head.

A while passed; he didn't know how long. Isaac was hoping he could touch her, at least, perhaps feel her lying next to him, though it was clear that she was no longer on the bed. But Isaac could still hear the TV, hear people speaking to one another, not with words but with interference, electrical interference, which caused his head to buzz with the noise too. He figured that Sherry was still in the room, just seated somewhere else, like perhaps the window, the toilet, or even the floor, until he finally heard that other noise, of the door opening and closing, and then not opening again, no matter how long and how much he willed it to.

She'll be back, he thought. She will be. He balled his hand into a fist and put it in his mouth, until the TV began to clear up again, with *News 8 at 10*.

He would never forget her either.

Sherry took care to leave a few items behind: a set of timetables from the railway station; a pocket atlas, containing maps of every country in the Asian continent; a folder of cash in several currencies, like rupiah, pesos, yuan and yen. No baht, he noted ruefully, the number 1,500 coming to mind.

He found the flyer a few hours later, for the talent show *Star Search*, inviting interested applicants to register and audition. He discovered it as he was flipping through the pages of the pocket atlas, absentminded and then suddenly alert: it'd been wedged in the final pages of the small book, the ink on the paper long worn out along its edges.

She had told him about the show before, the difference between *Star Search* and the Star Awards. *Star Search* is an acting competition, which Zoe Tay had won, of course. She was the show's first ever champion in 1988. The competition has since taken place once every two years, he remembered, which led Isaac to look at the flyer once again, at the year that was printed beneath the title.

1996.

Isaac checked out of the hotel on Friday morning. He asked the receptionist for directions to the rail station, where he bought a one-way ticket to the airport in Selangor. He studied the large dashboard in Terminal One, confused but not daunted by the constantly changing information, at the numbers and letters rattling and turning, always turning. The time was half past nine, and he walked over to the customer service counter, where a lady gave him a smile.

How can I help you?

Hi, said Isaac. What's your name?

I'm Huda, sir.

Hi, Huda, I'm Isaac.

Isaac reached over the counter to shake her hand. Huda took his hand and smiled at him, with a slight hint of irritation crossing her eyes as Isaac placed his backpack on the counter. I'm sure you got see guys like me all the time, he said to her.

Huda didn't nod, though she did continue to smile. You want to know what is the first flight out of here?

Yah, he said.

International or domestic?

I-international.

Budget?

Uh, he said. As cheap as possible.

All right, sir. Please wait.

A few minutes passed as she made a phone call in Bahasa Melayu. Huda then showed him a list of the various flights and destinations she managed to obtain: flights to Jakarta, to Hanoi, to New Delhi—it was surprising, Isaac realised, how long this list could be. Huda, Huda, he said. Listen to me: you need to help me decide.

Ah, is it?

Yah.

Huda let out a sigh. Isaac.

Yes?

I'm not very impressed, she said. Did your girlfriend just leave you? Or something like that?

Y-yah. Yes. That just happened to me, yes.

And how was that relationship like?

Meaning?

Well, said Huda. Who took care of who? Who looked after who, in this relationship?

He didn't have to think about it. Sherry, he said. She looked after me.

Okay, said Huda. She drummed her fingers on the arm of her chair. Who was the prettier one? she asked.

Isaac had to think harder this time, and said: We're about the same.

I see, said Huda. She stopped drumming her fingers. You need to be stronger, Isaac.

Yes, Huda.

There are some things only you can do on your own, Isaac. Only you. You and no one else. Sherry doesn't want to play a part in your life anymore, you understand?

He nodded. He then cast a quick glance behind him, to see if there was a queue forming. There was no one.

Huda, he said. Huda, ma'am. I know exactly what you are saying.

Good.

I know I'm weak, I'm stupid, I really need to grow up.

All right, sir, I never—

I need to do better. I know. I swear I will, the moment I get out of here.

Huda looked at him, sadly. You still want me to decide.

Isaac nodded; it scared him to think how close he was to the verge of tears. Yes, ma'am, he said. I just need a push.

All right, said Huda. She turned to her phone, before adding: You know this won't end, right? If you don't think this is a problem?

What problem? he asked.

This reliance on other people, she said.

Isaac stared at Huda, not knowing what to say.

All right then, she said again. Huda picked up her phone one final time. She kept her gaze fixed on Isaac as she ran a pencil down her list, eventually circling a line entirely at random. That's the one, he thought. That's the one. The moment her call connected, Huda took a quick look at what she just circled before speaking more Bahasa Melayu into the phone. Isaac took his wallet out from his jeans as a machine on Huda's desk started to print his itinerary.

This happens too often, said Huda, in a lower voice. Sometimes I think the world is full of lonely men and women, roaming about the earth with no idea how they got there. It comes with working at an airport.

He nodded, solemnly. We're all a bit lost, Huda.

She shook her head. People are only lost if they want to be found, she said, handing him his ticket. Don't wander for too long, Mr Neo.

His boarding pass said he was headed for Kansai International, in Osaka. Isaac didn't know if he ought to be excited or afraid: once he was past security he reached into his backpack and took out Sherry's pocket atlas, flipping open to the Japan section, where there was thankfully a map of Osaka itself. He noticed that Sherry had drawn a few asterisks, indicating to him multiple neighbourhoods of interest in the city. There were asterisks over Tokyo as well, and Hokkaido. Kagoshima, Okinawa, Hiroshima; there was an asterisk over Kobe, too, wedged between Osaka and Kyoto, in spite of what had happened there. All places where he could be, if he so chose.

Isaac got on his flight. He vowed he would spend only a day in each city, maybe two. He wouldn't be sentimental about it, he told himself. In the city of Osaka he walked the lengths of its beautiful canals, where the setting sun had dyed their waters orange. And when it got dark, too dark, he found his way into a police station and asked what was the best way to get around the country. The one policeman who knew English recommended taking an overnight coach. To where? asked Isaac. To Kyoto, the policeman said. It was a generalisation, the policeman said, but he believed there were more English speakers to the east, although Isaac could try his luck with Mandarin speakers to the west. No, no, said Isaac—he would go eastwards. He then thanked him, thanking all of the policemen on duty, who seemed sad to see the young and handsome traveller go. At the bus terminal Isaac washed his face and brushed his teeth in the toilet, rinsing his mouth with a can of coke he bought from a vending machine.

He then got a seat on the 11pm coach. Isaac took his place beside the window, finally falling asleep as he drowsily thought, the roads: all of them look the same, the same. All under the night.

And that's how you came to Kyoto? Tori asked.

Isaac nodded. When I woke up, I was at the station.

And while you were walking down the street—

Yah, said Isaac. I found you.

————

Tori treated him to dinner that evening. She took him to the one place she knew she could rely on, a diner near Nishiki Market that served okonomi-yaki. And because Isaac had never heard of the dish before, Tori took it upon herself to ask what his favourite ingredients were, and whether he liked a drink. She then made the pancake for him on the griddle, mixing and shaping and then letting the batter fry on its own. She flipped it, expertly, and got him to flip hers too, just to give it a go. While their okonom-iyaki was cooking she told him how much she loved this diner: how it was walkable from the ryokan, so good and yet so affordable, and how it was open all the time, 24/7. She already had a habit, she said, of finding the best possible okonomiyaki place to eat at, every time she found herself in a new city. It sounded like she'd been to a lot of places, said Isaac, and Tori said yes, that is true. He then asked if she liked travelling, and she said yes, she did. She did, once. Can you recommend some places in Japan then, he said next, and Tori said sure, she can. First we shall eat.

Tori, rather than drizzle the mayo in stripes, used the bottle to squeeze the numbers "2" and "3" over Isaac's okonomiyaki instead. How is it? she asked, as she watched him take his first bite.

Isaac nodded, still chewing. Shiok, he said.

What?

He laughed. Sorry, he said, and gave her a thumbs-up. Super good.

Tori set her chopsticks down, and took a swig from her highball. I know someone from Singapore, she said. She will be coming to Kyoto quite soon, actually.

Wah, he said. And?

Tori shrugged. I never heard her use that word.

"Shiok"?

Yes, she said, that one.

Isaac made a face. Weird.

Tori wrinkled her nose; she liked girls, yes, and so was glad to be immune, somewhat, to the man's obvious attractiveness. Jing might have code-switched, actually, to blend in, said Tori. We met in London.

Wah, said Isaac again, dragging the word out this time. London. Why?

Is it, uh—nice?

You mean, shiok? said Tori, amused. It can be. Very rainy, though.

Like Singapore lah, said Isaac.

I guess, said Tori. She took another swig from her highball. She then asked him why he was in Japan, and Isaac paused, setting his chopsticks down too. He looked down at his plate for a curiously long time, before glancing up at her again, asking how much she wanted to know. And Tori sat up, straightening her back, with an ever more curious look on her face. Everything, she said to him; everything is what I always want to know. And so he told her his story, for which she felt immensely grateful.

Can I ask you something? he later said to Tori. She nodded. Why did you come back?

She frowned. Come back?

To Japan, he said. You were in London? And you, uh—you said you liked to travel?

Ah, said Tori; she loved hearing other people talk, which meant that she wasn't used to talking about herself very much. She told him that she was just an exchange student in London, and that she had to return to Japan once her visa had expired. Isaac then asked if she'd return to London if she had a choice, and Tori said no, she would not. Why not? asked Isaac, and Tori said, surprising even herself: It is too far. From what? asked Isaac, and Tori managed to catch herself, nearly saying this time: *From my family*. But even though she hadn't uttered the words, Isaac seemed to know; he smirked, though not unkindly, at the truth she had stopped herself from admitting.

You love them? he asked. Your family?

Tori nodded, blinking rapidly.

But you ran away, as well?

She nodded again, staying mute for a while longer. I did, she finally said; I still am. And you? she asked. Do you love your family?

Isaac looked at his plate, picked up his chopsticks again. He took one in each hand and tore a slice from his pancake, shredding it methodically. I'm not sure, he said.

Not sure?

He looked up at her, for just a few seconds. There was something holding him back too, she thought, something that felt akin to shame. When Isaac said no, however, and returned to his food, Tori realised that it wasn't shame after all. It was resentment.

Tori met him by the front desk the next morning. She had gone through the pocket atlas his ex-girlfriend left him, and handed it back, with all of the places he should check out dog-eared and marked with Post-its and stickers. Sherry did a good job, said Tori. It felt like she wanted the best for you. Isaac gave her a sad smile. He told her he'd travel as much as he could, as much as his money would allow. He'd call her too, from time to time.

Just to chat?

He shrugged. Yah, he said. Can?

She nodded. Sure.

And then I'll come back, he said.

Here?

He nodded. I want to see my friend one last time, he said, before I go anywhere else.

5

July, 1995. New York City.

Mateo excused himself early from work. It was his fifth day in town on an eight-day work trip, but he was already certain that he knew the way to MoMA. It didn't matter that he could barely read the road signs, or that it was sweltering hot in the city—or that the people seemed to be talking to themselves, talking while always seeming on the verge of breaking out into a run. He adored the trash, the stink, the shoptalk, the shouting, all of it pressing upon him the moment he emerged out of Bryant Park, and headed uptown on Sixth Avenue. Mateo adored all of it in the way only a transient figure like himself, a passing traveller, could afford to adore it. Take this morning, for instance, as he was exiting the subway, walking down a pedestrian tunnel: a man from the same train, same carriage—seated right across from him, reading the morning's paper, in fact—had burst out suddenly into song. It was stunning. In an instant the tunnel lit up with his voice, and it was a marvel only to him, and no one else. Mateo found himself back in that tunnel again, in the spirit of that tunnel, as he walked up Sixth Avenue, buoyed all day by the sense of feeling complete, of being totally filled with sound, with the songs of strange, impulsive men. This was his first time in New York City, and he was primed, he was ready; he was about to fall in love.

*　　*　　*

Mateo purchased a ticket to the Barbara London show. After a quick walk through, he headed back to the ground floor, to the Edward John Noble Education Center, where the artist talk with Han Aw was about to begin.

The artist had a kind face, with round eyes and a slender nose, and especially thin lips; she had her hair tied back too, in a single, large braid that reached beyond her waist, and with mostly white and grey strands. Mateo had always thought that Jing didn't look entirely like her mother, and would at times wonder which features were hers and which belonged to her father, though the greater struggle was reconciling the public persona of the artist—passionate in her younger years, mellower in her later years—with what Jing had told about him about her parenting style, which was really a matter of delegation, apparently. Her mother made no pretence of being interested in single parenthood: looking at the number of times she'd performed and exhibited around the world in the seventies and eighties, it was little wonder to Mateo when he heard that Jing was mostly raised by her grandparents, in the house where Han Aw had grown up and still lived. She told him too that amongst the plants in the garden that her grandfather tended to, there was one that stood for her, his youngest child, which somehow ended up being the tallest, dwarfing the chillis, the bougainvilleas and the mango tree that represented the other members of the Aw family. She was the tabebuia tree, which bore a shimmering crown of white flowers twice or thrice a year. Its life began as a large branch that her grandfather had snipped from the main road and replanted in the corner of his garden; in a childhood devoid of Han Aw's presence, all Jing had was the tree, which, by the time she'd left for London, had already grown as tall as the house. It became the only thing she could see from her bedroom window.

The artist picked up her microphone, and placed it in her lap. She remained quiet while Barbara London, the moderator for the evening, began her introduction of the artist. Han Aw has done a great many things: she practises mainly in the fields of performance, using a combination of voice, physical work and multimedia, the curator said. Han Aw has also taught seminars at the Nanyang Academy of Fine Arts in Singapore, loyal to the institution and the faculty that gave her and many artists of her generation their one and only diploma. The artist also gave lectures and masterclasses abroad, and is often cited amongst other names such as Meredith Monk, Kimsooja, Joan Jonas, Yoko Ono. She received both the Young Artist Award and the Cultural Medallion within a span of fifteen years, a feat matched by no other artist in the Republic of Singapore. As an artist, she could be defined by two highly recognisable aspects: the first being her voice, which sang, and lectured, and protested, and more iconically screamed, before adapting a wordless lexicon in her more recent work. The second involved her use of inscriptions, instructions to herself, which she'd write by hand on a piece of paper or textile. A year ago the artist debuted a new performance work at The Substation, inscribing a biography-slash-manifesto on the floor of the gallery, with lines that spanned from wall to wall. The work ended the moment the artist had reached the gallery's doors, said Barbara London, prompting Han Aw to get up and leave, and I mean literally leave, never to return inside the institution for the rest of the day. The work has since been performed in Hong Kong, in Gwacheon, in Stockholm, in Argentina and just last week, in Chicago. For those still around this weekend, said the curator, the artist will be performing the work at the Galerie Lelong & Co in Chelsea. Ladies and gentleman: Han Aw.

The audience clapped. The artist flashed everyone a demure smile before bringing the microphone up to her lips. I know this is called an artist talk, but I'll try to use as little words as I can today, said Han Aw. The audience began to murmur: the artist's voice sounded especially hoarse that evening, as though she was in desperate need of a cup of water, prompting Barbara to nudge a bottle of Evian closer to the artist. Everyone laughed again. Oh, I'm just old! said Han Aw. Let's begin. And although the rest of the artist talk did proceed as planned, Mateo found himself still concerned about the condition of the artist's voice, wondering too about how Jing would react, hearing her mother speak about the year 1970, the year she was conceived.

It was a unique year, said Han Aw. I certainly didn't plan to be pregnant. In another world I wouldn't be, wouldn't have allowed it to factor into any of my work. But it was my life, you see, it was . . . it was changing. Once so keenly individual, but now, now not. The artist then paused, and looked to the audience. Do you understand what I mean by this, everyone? To know that you could never be free again? To feel your own existence split apart, while also knowing that, that you would be forever tied, *yoked*, not just to this other life that you now carry within yourself, but also to that great system of life, the sequence, that unending chain . . . The artist paused another time, and held up the end of her hair. To be, well—braided? she added, to more laughter from the audience. And as the laughter died down, Mateo turned to the man seated a few seats away, still chuckling to himself. He watched as he ran a hand over his face, and shook his head. The man then flashed Mateo a knowing look, a quick one, a look that did its job. That was Daniel, of course, though he had yet to know his name at the time.

Mateo watched him remove his glasses, letting them hang via a cord around his neck; he watched him rise from his chair and leave the room. And Mateo followed him, noticing that he walked with a slight limp. He followed him through the corridors of the museum, which had already begun to empty of people. He followed him till he found himself back at the show, at the René d'Harnoncourt Galleries, where *Video Spaces* was being exhibited. He didn't question the lack of guards stopping them from wandering around the building at this hour; in fact he noticed it, the conspicuous, glaring absence of them, all the while wondering: was this embarrassing? Cruising, like this, on a work trip? At the freaking Museum of Modern Art? Mateo kept some distance behind Daniel as he stopped to admire the various installations, putting his glasses back on his face. The man then disappeared, through a gap between the walls, inside one of the more remote installations, where the space felt cavernous, seemingly boundless, its walls painted in a dense, illusory black. A tower of gadgets stood in the middle, beaming onto the walls moving images of ghost-like performers in the nude, oftentimes wandering, if not running, if not dancing across the perimeter of the room. It was otherworldly, watching the performers themselves enter a trance-like state, possessed by repetitive, robotic motions. Whenever the images of the bodies overlapped, there was no recognition of the other's presence, no intimacy. No love.

Daniel was standing in the centre of this room. Mateo approached, one careful step at a time, with his hands in his pockets, maintaining a careful, casual nonchalance. Even in the darkness, he realised, the sight of Daniel shimmered in concordance with the soundscape of the room, an intermittent, metallic ping; several golden lines, dramatically intersecting, forming the shape of a crosshair, and then a crucifix, and other potent configurations, as Mateo stepped closer to the man. And there were words too, flashing across the projected bodies; he was near him, near the man he had his eye on, while the words,

> *fear*
>
> *love is everywhere*

flashed across the image of two fleeing figures.

Eventually he managed to stand beside the stranger. He feigned distraction, while his heart pounded against his ribs: they were hardly more than a metre apart as they watched, transfixed, at the arrival of a final image, that of the artist himself: Teiji Furuhashi, in the nude, just like his fellow performers. And he was beautiful too, Mateo thought, in an ascetic sort of way, as the artist spread his arms open. Mateo could almost feel the artist's hands reach into his chest and curl around his heart, as the projection curled its arms back into a self-embrace. A patron saint of sick and lonely men.

Mateo turned his head to the left. And his companion was looking at him, finally, knowing that they have found one another at last: two figures, in the flesh, mercifully ordained to meet under the bright auspices of Teiji Furuhashi.

Mi llamo Daniel, he said to Mateo. Hola.

———

We gotta go, Mateo kept saying. We gotta get *moving*, ladies. But where the hell were they going? Jing wanted to know. Where are we going! she said, when neither of her friends seemed capable of answering her. Tori burst out laughing, saying she knows, she knows (*Know what?* Jing mouthed to Mateo); she got up and began to walk, forcing Jing and Mateo to follow. And in the drunken magnitude of the moment, their accomplishment, their collective, magical thinking (*What the fuck was in their beer?* Mateo mouthed back), there the three were, paralysed before another immense intersection, except this time Mateo could spy with his eye the tail end of the bridge that crossed over the river. The delta.

There was a small crowd across the street, gathered at the foot of a tall office building, standing in the middle of an otherwise large and empty allotment. The crowd gathered on a gravel driveway, waiting to enter the bar via a flight of stairs at the back of the building that led into the basement. As Mateo crossed the street Jing asked how he knew of this bar, and he said that he had been alone again, the night before, walking down the riverbank. At some point the river lit up, right on cue, sounds popping from the sky and then echoing all about, like it was fucking Las Fallas. And as he squinted at the fireworks, and the thick strands of silver, whooshing (Whooshing! said Tori) into oblivion, he knew he would remember it, this sight, the sparks blossoming and then fluttering into so many brilliant points, sparkling over the surface of the Kamo River. You were drinking again? Jing asked, and Mateo said no, no actually, he had been completely sober last night. He just wanted to be with himself, he said, but he had also wanted to find the source of the fireworks, you know—he wanted to know where they were coming from. And that was when he saw a bicycle ramp ahead, connecting the riverbank to the bridge above. He took a few steps up the ramp and caught a shadow, a familiar-looking one, staring at him from the top. He could just about feel his own heart fill with light when he saw the way it stood—the way it seemed to stand on one leg more than the other. He ran up the ramp, only to slip over the slick surfaces; when he got up again, and went up the length of the ramp, he managed to see the shadow flicker round a corner of the road. And that was how he found himself here, in this driveway. Mateo pointed to a poster pasted on the wooden fence that bordered the allotment, and Jing went towards it. All she could read were the words PRISMATIC and DUMB TYPE, which didn't make any sense to her. But the main graphic was that of a firework, pale gold against a muted, green sky.

Tori read the poster, as more people began to stream towards the allotment. She told them that Prismatic wasn't just a bar—it was a club. And Dumb Type? Jing asked. Tori said she didn't know, though it seemed like they were the night's act. Mateo then asked Jing if she was sure that the name of the group didn't sound familiar to her, and she said nope, no idea. Who are they! she asked, over the increasing din of the excited crowd, and he said they were the name of a collective, based in Kyoto, founded by Teiji Furuhashi. He was part of the group show, said Mateo, at *Video Spaces*. Do you remember now? And Jing looked at her friend, struck by how happy he seemed in that moment. Imagine, he said to her, the coincidence! The serendipity, really! He wanted to know if he could actually meet him tonight, the artist, the one who had brought him and Daniel together, and Jing said, We'll see! We'll see. Let's get another drink, she said, and just then the crowd began to move. People started cheering as music began to blast from the bottom of the stairwell. And while Mateo cheered along, Tori put her hands on Jing's and Mateo's shoulders, telling them to go ahead, go downstairs, she needed to find the toilet first, especially if they were going to dance. And as Jing saw Tori walk towards the office building, she felt Mateo grab her hand, leading her to the end of the driveway; he skipped down the stairs, into the basement of the building, where the two soon waded into a sea of people, gathered under the blessings of two, no, three, no, *four* disco balls, spinning and glittering, refracting and then blinding, breaking a hundred colours into a thousand, no, ten thousand colours. A new one seemed to appear in every second, every moment, which must have given the club its name, Jing thought. And as they pushed through the heat of the crowd, Mateo still holding on to her hand, she felt like she could scream, and scream properly this time, scream until her voice cracked wide open.

Is Tori back? Mateo had to yell in Jing's ear, and Jing found herself shouting back that she didn't know, it was impossible to tell. Mateo then said, Fuck it, it doesn't matter; he ordered them a glass of cherry vodka each from the bar, and the two did a quick cheers—Salud! Kanpai!—a full glass that they downed like a shot, without even meaning to, both of them alarmed and then egging the other on. And then Mateo spoke into her ear again. Wanna hunt someone down? he said, and she said what, Tori? And Mateo said, Teiji! Teiji Furuhashi, you dumb bitch, the artist! And then he told her to come, to follow him into a corner as they pressed through the sea of people, there were so many of them, dancing and lip-syncing to songs they had never heard of, songs that every person at the bar seemed to know by heart—but there was a constant beeping sound too, crystalline and bell-like, incessant pings of sound, and it made her somewhat anxious, claustrophobic. Jing now wanted to know where Tori was, and with a wild hope, wished that she could conjure up her friend's face, summon her to her side, only to discover that she had lost Mateo too, her only friend in the world. Mateo! said Jing. Where did you—? And as she looked around, desperate to find a familiar face, she found herself spinning, she was being spun around, literally, by a group of people she didn't know; they screamed at her, laughed at her, all with their hands and their drinks in the air, and she too spun, she too screamed. She found herself dancing while holding her still-empty glass, which she threw onto the floor, causing everyone to scatter, to flail, to dramatically point at the site of the incident— and Jing, she felt herself being pulled away again, so grateful but also so terrified, only to see it was Mateo, her friend, who looked so truly happy now—he appeared joyous, so joyous, it made her feel the same too, and he started to shout into her ear, saying Jing, Jing, I found him, this is Tei. And there he was, the artist, Teiji Furuhashi, standing behind Mateo, his slender jaw nestled in the crook of her friend's shoulder. But before Jing could even say hi to the artist, Mateo was yelling again, at the two of them, saying that they ought to head outside, where it was cooler and they could talk—and Jing found herself linking hands again, with the artist this time, his right hand holding on to her left, which she had to squeeze, several times, as though to confirm it was really him. But it was him, for sure—she hadn't seen him before, hadn't even known who he was before—but surely it was him, no? She was startled by the purity of his plain tee, throwing off a radiance, it seemed, with the intense heat of starlight. And Jing felt not the joy that Mateo felt, but the breaking, finally, as her eyes began to widen, and tear up—she felt the artist squeeze her hand back, just as they were nearing the exit. He turned his magnanimous head towards her, not to speak but only to smile, as though to say it would not be long now, my dear, we shall be out of here soon; we're nearly there now, all of us, just trust me.

Jing had to fan herself, back outside; earlier, as she dashed up the stairs, she had to squeeze past a couple of incomers, the whole group carrying with them the heavy smell of beer and cigarettes. But the air was sharp out on the driveway—Jing found a wall and leant against it, just to steady herself, as she gulped on this newer, fresher air.

You okay? she heard Mateo ask, and Jing had to say yah, thanks. I'm good. She just needed the spinning to stop, haha. Jing then felt the artist's hand on her arm, patting and then smoothing the fabric on her jacket. It will take some time, said the artist, in a clipped and charming manner, and she believed him.

The artist asked her friend if she mixed her drinks. No, said Mateo, before he made a face. Yes. They had beer and then they had vodka, quite a lot of it, he said, and the artist laughed in response, a light laugh, sharp yet gentle. When the spinning finally slowed to a manageable pace, Jing righted herself and looked around, at the empty driveway and its wooden border. She expected the artist to have some kind of set-up, there on the driveway, for Mateo's fireworks, but there was nothing, just them, no one apart from them and the small stones beneath their feet. Jing then heard a crunching sound: she saw Mateo dash away, back down the stairs into the club.

Where's he going? she asked the artist, and Teiji Furuhashi said, Water. O-mizu. I told him to get some for you, honey.

Oh, said Jing, thank you, touched by his use of the endearment. Jing took another look at the artist's face, and saw that he was silver. They were both silver, all over, because they were seated underneath a spotlight attached to the side of the office building. The artist got up, and got her to relocate with him, the two moving down to the middle of the driveway, where they could be away from the glare. And yet the artist remained shining somehow: he glowed as he got her to lie with him, down on the gravel, the stones crunching under their backs as they held one another's hands. They breathed in unison as they stared up above.

The sky is clearing, said the artist. The clouds are parting. Do you see?

Jing did. She watched as the heavens seemed to heed his command, the clouds rolling over the earth, the land, the city of Kyoto. She then turned her head back to him.

You know Han Aw, right?

The artist was still staring up at the sky. Who?

Han Aw, she said, another artist. My mother.

Tei blinked; he turned towards her. Hmm, was all he said. Jing asked if they had ever met one another, and he didn't nod. He merely stared at her, with his still-shining eyes.

Yes, he said.

Yah?

Yes, he said again: Yes. I see her form, her dark shape. I see her life over yours, all over you, sweet honey. But you have to look, he said. Look, he said again, pointing up to the sky: I'm trying to show you something.

And Jing looked. There, in the sky, in a parting of the clouds, was something she'd never seen before in her life: a comet, iridescent green, with an azure, powdery tail.

Look, said the artist: it's the most wondrous event in human history. But you have no idea, don't you, dear Jing. No idea about its significance, its importance. Its impact. Jing then felt the artist tap her head, in the space between her brows, once, twice, thrice. This is why, he said. This is all why. You only see what's in front of you. Your pain, your suffering, your story: all of it has made you blind, just blind, all of you, blind as fools. The artist then sat up, abruptly. Someone was running towards them, Mateo, then handing her a plastic cup filled with water. Teiji Furuhashi watched Jing take her first sip and broke out into a smile.

I want to take you somewhere, he said to Mateo.

Jing watched her friend's face freeze in delight. Where?

The artist kept on smiling. Let me take you, he said. He then stood up, and held out his hand; Mateo took it, and Tei said, Let's run—and they did. Mateo looked behind him, over his shoulder at Jing, taken by surprise and all the more delighted. And as Jing watched them go, down the remaining length of the driveway towards the street, she rose to her feet, and attempted to run as well, to chase after them, trying to follow where the artist was taking her friend. Wait, she said, to the two of them—wait! But the pair rounded a corner, and vanished. They disappeared, Mateo and Teiji: wherever they had gone, it was a place she couldn't see.

She told herself to breathe. She then squeezed it, unthinkingly, the plastic cup she still held in her hand. The water spilled all over her jeans, her shoes; she stood by the roadside, facing the large and empty intersection before her, finally giving in to the breaking she'd felt earlier, the swell, the surge. And then she heard her, Tori—she heard Tori call out her name. She turned and saw Tori walk towards her, asking if that was Mateo she just saw. And that other man? Tori asked. Who was that? And Jing shook her head this time, still on the verge of tears. You just missed him, she said, turning to where she'd last seen them—the artist, she said, he's wonderful. But I don't know where they went; I, I don't know where they are. And Tori's voice was soft when she told her to stand still, to keep steady, that she could lean against her if she wanted. And then she told her that they had to go back, back to the ryokan. There is something very wrong, she said, something very strange that is happening in the city. And Jing looked at her, confused. Why? she asked. What's going on? And so Tori told her: the artist, Teiji Furuhashi, died last year. He passed away from AIDS.

Jing flinched. She could still feel the spot between her brows, the tap of his strong fingers against her skull. What—what artist again? she asked, and Tori answered, emphatically: Teiji Furuhashi, the performance artist. The one Mateo wanted to meet tonight. He passed away in October, five months ago. Jing then felt Tori's hand on her arm as she said, You have to believe me, Jing. It is the truth. And Jing felt the spinning come back to her, faster, wilder, harder: she keeled over, and squatted, and sat on the ground beside her friend's feet. She needed to think but she couldn't, she was so damn drunk. She pressed her forehead against the pavement, thinking, death. Oh, death. Oh, Tori, she said, just stop, stop—stop talking.

6

Isaac opened the door to the phone booth and stepped inside. He counted the number of coins he had in his wallet, and put the requisite amount into the slot. He then took out the card that Tori had given him and dialled the number to the ryokan, a number he was close to memorising by now, after three weeks of calling his friend. Hey, he said, once Tori picked up. Guess who.

Tori sounded amused over the phone. Are you trying to tell a joke?

He paused. I—I dunno, he said. I don't have any jokes.

I know one, said Tori. Shall I tell it?

Sure.

Okay, said Tori. Knock knock.

Who's there?

No one.

No one who?

No one but you, said Tori.

Another me?

Yes, she said, another you: walking away, never to return.

Isaac sighed. It was an awful joke, he thought. He allowed himself a glance out of the phone booth, at the nearby bench, on which sat an animal, a monkey—a macaque, to be precise. He watched it examine the contents of a discarded plastic container, fished out of a nearby trash can.

Where's the other me going? asked Isaac over the phone, and Tori said she didn't know. It wasn't up to her to decide. She asked where he was calling her from this time, and he said he wasn't sure. He could barely even remember what the date was anymore, and had to check his watch: the 19th of March, 1996.

The macaque then spoke. Miyazu, it said, still staring at the plastic container. We're at Miyazu, it said again, and Isaac quickly relayed the information back to Tori. Amanohashidate Station, the macaque said next, and Isaac found himself unable to repeat what it said this time. Ama—Amano—

The sandbar?

Yes, said Isaac, that one. Amanohashidate was a sandbar three kilometres long, stretching across the mouth of the Miyazu Bay: "bridge to heaven" was what the name of the sandbar meant. Tori told Isaac that she had never been there before, and Isaac said, Never? Never, she said, though it was a place she had always wanted to go. It is very popular with tourists. Right now are there many tourists? she asked, and Isaac eyed the macaque once more, still seated on the bench.

It's not bad, he said. I have company.

You do?

Isaac nodded. I got a friend, he said, before ending the call.

Isaac stepped out of the phone booth, and walked towards the bench. The macaque had thrown the container down onto the ground, and was now staring at it in disappointment. I can buy you food if you want, said Isaac to the animal, and the macaque looked up at him, tentative but hopeful.

Your treat? it asked.

He nodded. My treat. What do you want?

The macaque blinked once, and looked around. It then leapt off the bench, and stopped by the side of the road, waiting for a car to pass by. There was a 7-Eleven nearby, the macaque said, and together the two of them crossed the road. Isaac followed it as it led the way, scampering on all fours past a row of shophouses. He recognised the novelty of the situation, aware that people didn't seem too concerned by the presence of the animal. Just a week ago he was at another station, one whose name he'd forgotten as well: he had been staring at the large map before him, unable to decipher where he was or decide where he ought to go to next, when the animal appeared beside him, squatting on its haunches, staring up at the map with one hand on its chin. It soon proceeded to relay to him a series of instructions, which Isaac obeyed without question. You need a ticket also? he asked the macaque, and the macaque shook its head.

You don't remember me, do you, it said instead.

Isaac looked down at the animal. It peered back at him with its beady, amber-coloured eyes. Isaac quickly set his backpack down and found the manila envelope, where he'd kept the photo of his family at the zoo. Is this you? he asked, showing the photo to the animal, with a finger placed over the monkey. The macaque took a quick glance.

This photo was taken in 1982?

Isaac nodded.

Then no, it said. Yes, in a way—but no. Nice try.

Isaac looked at the photo. To him, the two creatures were nearly identical, though it was hard to be sure. Fine, said Isaac.

He placed the photo and the manila envelope back into his backpack, thinking: I'm not freaking out. I should be freaking out. The macaque then shuddered, and turned away from him, scampering towards the ticket gates. It led him to the correct platform, and then brought him to one of the quieter carriages of the train, where the macaque could sit by the window. It was happy to tear open a bag of salted peanuts as it relayed to Isaac several basic facts about its species. It taught him how to spell the word "macaque", for one, as well as its various other names: snow monkey, nihonzaru, *Macaca fuscata*. It taught him the matrilineal customs of the Japanese macaque, and their particular fondness for cold weather, natural hot springs and potatoes dipped in seawater. It spoke to him about the pride the macaques had for their glossy coats of blonde-to-silver fur, and the bright and vibrant redness of their faces and posteriors. And yes, it said to him;

that monkey you just showed me, squatting in the middle of that photo—that's a snow monkey too. The macaque then took to staring out of the window, its face nearly pressed against the glass, as it gripped the bottom of the windowsill with its small grey hands.

You still don't remember me, it said to Isaac, soft and yet clear all the same.

Isaac kept quiet. The animal was right: they had met before, somehow, he and this monkey. They must have, in circumstances that involved their speaking to one another. He just forgot about it, the what and the when. But Isaac also had the feeling that the memory would come back to him, the memory of whatever previous encounter he and this talking monkey had in the past. All he had to do was wait, and to be careful about the waiting, certain that the answers would come in time. Isaac watched the macaque, still staring at the view, and asked if it had a name.

I have no name.

Why not?

I am not an individual. I do not lead an individual life, it said. The macaque then looked over its shoulder, meeting its gaze with Isaac's.

You have a name, it said. But your life is not yours alone. The macaque then turned back to the window, saying not another word.

Isaac stepped out of the 7-Eleven. The banana he bought was wrapped in plastic, and the macaque grunted and hooted in excitement as it watched him tear the wrapper away. In turn, Isaac watched the macaque reach for the fruit with outstretched hands and peel the skin off with a single dextrous motion.

The macaque quickly swallowed its first bite. We eat more than bananas, you know. We eat all kinds of things, it said.

Isaac nodded. I know.

The macaque took another bite. Just thought to remind you, it said, staring at Isaac's empty hands. It asked him what he was eating, and he shrugged. I'm not hungry yet, replied Isaac, though that was a little bit of a lie.

They made their way to the sandbar. The southern entrance was a small bridge over a narrow passage of seawater; on the other end lay Amanohashidate, which mainly consisted of a well-worn route, flanked by pine trees on both sides until the sand touched the grey waters of Miyazu Bay. Isaac and the macaque walked for about twenty minutes or so, until they reached what seemed to be the midway mark. They went towards the shoreline and sat facing the open water.

There was a family of four not far away from them, eating sandwiches from a Tupperware container. You have family? asked Isaac.

The macaque grunted. I do.

They don't need you?

No, it said. Not right now.

Isaac asked him why. Before it chose to reply, the macaque simply stared at the sea, unblinking, the light gold of its fur gently brushed by the salty breeze. They have the pack, it said to Isaac, before lapsing once again into silence. The macaque was still gazing into the distance when it added:

You were eating a very sweet apple when we first met.

Isaac had to swallow. I was?

The macaque nodded. You had two apples, actually; you passed one of them to me. It then turned and looked at Isaac, its eyes boring into his. You still don't remember, it said. Would it help if I told you that you stole those apples?

No, he thought. The fact didn't surprise him. There were more things he'd stolen in the past, and they were all packed into his bag right now. Really, said Isaac, and the macaque grunted. It wasn't really stealing though, it said, confusing Isaac this time. He said he didn't understand. The macaque grunted again.

Never mind, it said. You will get what I mean, once the memory comes back to you. The macaque then turned back to the sea. Does that happen to you often?

What, stealing?

No, it said. Forgetting.

Isaac grew quiet. He knew the answer. He could already see the flashes of his previous life, counting money at the void deck, washing the shit off his sister's legs, Sherry passing a stack of Zoe Tay flyers to her friend. He could see her mother's mouth widen with laughter as she called him leng zai, could just about picture the colour on her painted nails as she passed around the lo mai gai he'd bought for the other aunties to eat. And then Sherry came back again, the memory of her, her body on top of his as they fucked in that hotel room in Kuala Lumpur. He forgot nothing, Isaac; his problem was that he still remembered everything, everything from his other life, the one he'd meant to leave behind: the sound the sleeping pills made whenever his mother had to pop a few into her mouth, or the sound of his father's slippers shuffling away down the corridor, heading towards the lift. It took next to nothing to hear it, the little moan her sister made when she wanted to say hi.

Isaac covered his eyes. He forced himself to breathe, to breathe through the burning that pricked his nose, his eyes, his mouth. He did this until the feeling passed. And when he looked to his side he found that the macaque wasn't there any longer, which was about time, he supposed. It happened like this, randomly, the macaque appearing and then not appearing. Still he checked anyway, looking up at the pine trees and the remaining stretch of beach. He stopped checking once he reached the other end of the sandbar, and took a bus that brought him around Miyazu Bay.

The animal would return. It would return, so long as its mission remained incomplete. He knew this.

Isaac found a hostel, and paid for two nights in a six-bed room. He took a quick shower and put his things away in his designated locker; he headed back to the main entrance, hoping to ask where he might have dinner that night, only to find the macaque again, squatting by the side of the road. It was checking its coat for fleas, its nose half buried into the fur beneath its armpit. It only looked up when Isaac stood in front of it, smiling and saying, Guess who?

The macaque flashed him a look of irritation. Why are you so happy? it asked.

Isaac blinked. Oh, he said—I just, uh—

The animal put its arm down. Do you think this is normal?

What?

Do you think this is okay? Natural? My being here, talking to you?

Look, uh—I never said—

You are acting like you have all the time in the world, it said. But you don't! You do not. It then got on all fours, skipped away a couple of paces down the sidewalk; the macaque turned its red face back towards him, telling him to hurry up. Come on, it said. I want curry tonight.

Guess who, said Isaac.

Not again, said Tori.

What, said Isaac. You already tired of me, is it?

No. You just need a different greeting, said Tori. She asked Isaac if he had found a joke for her yet, and he said that he hadn't.

Isaac, said Tori. I gave you two days. Your lack of jokes is making me very concerned.

He looked out of the phone booth: the macaque was back on the bench, the same bench outside Amanohashidate Station, picking grains of corn out of a styrofoam cup this time. Just wait, okay? I'll think of a joke for you, he said. He then asked her how the birthday was, and Tori said she didn't know what he was referring to. Oh, she then said, the staff party—that was two nights ago, yes. It was okay, she told him; I try to drink as little as possible when I am drinking with colleagues. Did you have fun? he asked her next, and Tori said: It was educational.

Isaac didn't get it. Hah?

Hmm, said Tori. Let us just say . . . I learnt a lot?

Like what?

Hmm, said Tori again. There are rumours.

Rumours?

Yes, she said: the rumours were many. They came from all over the city, so many that it was hard to discern what was and was not real; for weeks she'd been hearing things from guests, and now she'd been hearing things from colleagues too. Tori also said it was hard for her to sift through the rumours and see which ones needed paying attention to, and which did not. Hey Isaac, she said to him then—have you heard of tengu?

What? he said. No. He asked her what they were, and she said that they were creatures of myth, beings with long noses and the wings of a bird. Do they do anything? asked Isaac, and Tori said, Some are protectors. Some are troublemakers. Some take people away, kidnap them, bring them back to wherever they live. Some are said to be signs of worse things to come. Tori then paused, sensing she'd gone overboard somehow; she asked Isaac how the sandbar was, and he described it to her, the bridge and the sand and the pine trees, the families he spotted spending time on the beach. It surprised her, the families. Did they *swim*? she asked, and he told her no, it was too cold, of course. They kept to the sand. Tori then fell into another silence.

Hey, Isaac, she said: I am going to ask you a question.

Sure, he said.

Have you seen anything—anything weird, maybe, on your travels so far? asked Tori. Isaac looked immediately at the macaque, still at the bench, now licking its fingers. Weird? said Isaac, and Tori said yes, anything weird, anything out of the ordinary. The macaque then paused: Isaac watched it stiffen, sit upright and leer at him.

No, he said in a low voice. Nothing's weird.

Tori sounded unconvinced. Nothing?

No, said Isaac, still staring back at the macaque. Why?

Hmm, said Tori. Nothing, she said once more. Oh, she then added—my friend from Singapore is here.

Hmm, said Isaac. Until when?

Until Sunday, said Tori. Will you be back in Kyoto by then?

He paused. He looked down at his watch; it was Thursday, the 21st. He told Tori he wasn't sure, and Tori said she understood. I am the same, she said. I would not want to see anybody from where I am from.

Isaac looked at the macaque again. It had its hands in its lap now, its eyes a pair of bronze-coloured marbles, still fixed upon him, unblinking. Somewhere in the backdrop a group of elderly people poured out of the main exit of Amanohashidate Station, outfitted in parkas and track pants, all of their visors winking under the bright morning sun. Hey, Tori, he said. Where *are* you from?

Pardon?

He repeated himself: Where in Japan are you from?

Tori paused. She almost seemed to be holding her breath. Why do you want to know?

Isaac's gaze shifted back to the macaque. It continued to leer at him, insistent. He watched the tourists again, relieved that no one seemed to be headed their way.

Tori then told him the name of her hometown. Isaac slung his backpack to the front and unzipped it, reaching for his pocket atlas. Uh, he started to say, where—

It is on the page with the star, said Tori.

Oh, said Isaac, still flipping the book. You mean a sticker, right?

Yes, said Tori, a sticker.

He soon found it, the page, with the sticker in the shape of a golden star pasted right above the name, Nishinomiya. The city was just east of Kobe.

Be careful when you are there, she said. Whatever you do.

Isaac paused. He asked her why. Tori sounded almost surprised by the question. The earthquake, she managed to say, before the call between them got cut off.

*   *   *

Nishinomiya was literally on the other side of the country. It lay directly south of Miyazu on the pocket atlas, as south as any city could possibly be.

The fastest way to Nishinomiya was a three-hour bus ride from the front of Amanohashidate Station, according to the macaque. It would lead them to the Umeda district in Osaka, where they could then take a short train westward on the Tokaido-Sanyo Line. Isaac bought his bus ticket and waited twenty minutes for the vehicle to be ready; once onboard, he counted the remaining bills in his wallet while the macaque, seated by the window, told him not to worry. He could always check his bag.

Isaac looked questioningly at the macaque. The plastic folder, it said to him: I believe there is money in other currencies that you have yet to use.

Right, said Isaac. It didn't surprise him anymore, the way the animal knew more about him than he could ever recall: it made him afraid of the creature at first, before inspiring a quiet awe within him. The macaque had a mission, and fulfilling it entailed leading him, guiding him, accompanying him on his travels; it entailed pointing the way forward and watching him take it, without question, no matter how aimless or opaque the whole process might seem. Isaac opened his backpack and took out the plastic folder, holding it open for his companion to see. The macaque peered inside and nodded, telling him that there ought to be plenty of money changers in Umeda. You're not planning to go anywhere else, are you, it said.

Isaac nodded, and gave it a weak smile. He had suddenly thought of Huda, the lady from the airport who sold him his flight ticket to Japan, and the recollection filled him with sadness; it was a problem, she'd said to him, his reliance on other people. But now, more than ever, he thought—I don't want to be alone. I don't know how to be alone. He looked at the macaque and found it gazing back at him, saying, You are sad, which caused Isaac to nod again. That's good, it said next; it's important to keep feeling, even when you are heading towards the inevitable. Isaac had to ask what the last word meant, "inevitable", and the animal scratched an ear, thinking. It told him: That which you cannot avoid; that which you cannot change, run away from; that which always catches up to you in the end. Isaac asked the macaque what that thing was, the thing he couldn't run away from, and the macaque seemed to smile back at him this time, almost out of sympathy.

Isaac, it said to him, my friend: that, as always, is for you alone to find out.

It was roughly five in the afternoon when the pair arrived at Nishinomiya Station. Though the ride on the Tokaido-Sanyo Line was short, it offered enough evidence, even to Isaac, that the region was still healing from the earthquake that struck fourteen months ago. The railway cut across a dense urban landscape west of Osaka, marked crosswise by three paved rivers; whenever Isaac looked out at the view, there was always a vacant lot, or a building with missing windows or a wall caved in, sometimes even a pile of rubble. Violence was everywhere, he thought; it was a violence that barely sought to conceal itself, rupturing reminders of a pain buried away. If this was Nishinomiya, he thought, he couldn't imagine what Kobe must be like. And the macaque remained beside him, never once fading out of sight, choosing instead to keep quiet, letting out none of its usual hoots and grunts. It remained silent even when the doors to their carriage opened at Nishinomiya Station, and Isaac sought to make a move: the macaque took hold of his leg, and didn't let it go, stopping him from disembarking. It then raised a single finger with its other hand.

One more stop.

The next stop was Kōroen Station. The macaque leapt out of the carriage, and Isaac followed it, all the way out of the station: he followed it down a short road towards an underpass, leading out onto a broad riverside avenue, lined by cherry trees, the tips of their boughs dotted pink and white with still-budding flowers. There were pedestrians around them, and cyclists too, and parents pushing their babies about in prams. Buildings stood just beyond the distraction of the trees, but he kept his attention ever ahead, where the river, he could tell, was beginning to widen. He could detect a faint saltiness on the evening breeze, and could just about hear the crashing of distant waves; they were soon approaching the point where the mouth of the river would meet the sea.

A large and imposing sea wall greeted them at the end of their route. Isaac watched the macaque scamper up a flight of steps carved into the side of the wall; he climbed after it and encountered what looked like a man-made beach, with patches here and there of weeds and grass. Isaac was about to step foot on the sand when he noticed that the macaque was seated now, on the sea wall, no longer leading the way but merely watching, observing. The two stared at one another, wordless, the macaque's eyes and face betraying nothing, just patience.

Isaac turned back to the beach. It looked empty, he thought; it might be getting a little late. He began to wander in an almost automatic fashion, ready for whatever was about to happen.

It took him mere minutes. There was a coin purse, made out of woven leather, lying hidden amidst a growth of weeds, concealed even further by the twilight that was taking hold over the sand, the sea, the horizon. He picked up the purse, small but heavy; he unfastened the clasp and found money, a half-used packet of pills, and what looked like a shopping list, meticulously handwritten, with squares drawn before every item. Isaac turned back to the macaque, to confirm if this was it, the thing that it said was inevitable, only to find the monkey back on all fours, leaping down the steps along the sea wall, flashing only a glimpse of its bright rear end. By the time Isaac thought he had caught up with it, it had disappeared completely. The macaque was nowhere to be seen.

A streetlight flickered to life behind him. Isaac went through the remaining contents of the purse, and found what must be an identity card bearing the image of a middle-aged woman—she was staring at him through thinly-rimmed glasses, though her name, printed in Japanese, was impossible to figure out. The next item was a photograph, folded up into fourths: it was the picture of a family, of a mum and a dad, an older sister and a younger brother, all smiling with abandon. They were in a sandpit, in a playground, awash in a golden hue; he looked at the face of the mum and knew he was travelling back in time, re-encountering another version of the coin purse's owner: younger and happier, not alone, donning thicker and larger glasses. The year, printed in the corner of the photograph, said 1982.

Isaac took a deep breath. He placed the photo back into the purse, before keeping the purse inside his backpack. He felt the finality of this day, this moment; he felt like he was being hollowed out, as though it wasn't just the day and time he was losing sense of, but also his sense of place, of distance. And yet he remained mindful of what he needed to do, for now. He returned to the train station, going back the way he came. He knew he'd have to find another hostel for tonight, for however long this part of the journey will take. He knew he was all on his own, for sure, this time.

Still, he called Tori the next morning, using the payphone in the lobby. She asked him if he was there already, at Nishinomiya, and he told her that he was. Oh, said Tori, allowing herself a pause. You actually did it.

Isaac held the speaker to his ear, wondering how much longer the silence could last between them. He asked if she wanted to know where he was exactly, and she told him it was okay, she didn't want to know. How long will you be there? she asked, and he said, Not sure. Why not? she asked. He said, unhelpfully, I dunno. He told her he had a feeling that he might be spending more than one night here, and Tori asked him why. What's making you stay? she asked, and again he said he didn't know. And then he added:

Sometimes I think I'm just—I'm acting.

Acting?

Yah, he said. Or maybe, more like—like I'm just this person, you know? This very small, not important person. And the world is really huge.

Yes.

It's so huge, that maybe I think—I'm not in control.

Yes.

I'm not in charge of my own life.

Yes.

And though I dunno why I'm here, he said, I'm just—I'm just playing along. Like I know what I'm doing, like that, except I don't.

So by acting, said Tori, you mean you might be following a script?

Yah, said Isaac, his voice soft, unsteady. But I can't read the words. They're right in front of me, I feel, but I just—I can't read them. I can't make sense of them.

The two fell quiet again. Maybe you should come back to Kyoto, said Tori. When? Isaac asked, and Tori said, I do not know, but soon. Isaac asked why, this time, and Tori said: Because I do not like that place. I do not like Nishinomiya. I do not like what it does to you.

Why? Isaac asked again. It makes you crazy, is it?

No, said Tori. Because it makes you stop. It makes you not want to move, Isaac. It traps you, it—it holds you in its place, and does not let you go. She paused, and he could hear the sudden rush of her breath over the speaker. Do you ever wonder why we became friends? she asked.

Sometimes, said Isaac.

What did you conclude?

I dunno. I'm not very funny.

Yes. You are not.

I dunno any jokes, he said.

None! said Tori. You are too serious.

Yah, too—too loser, you know?

Yes, I do know. I am a loser too.

No lah, Tori.

I am, she said. I have—I have lost so much, Isaac. He then heard her breath again, before saying: But you were there.

Yah, said Isaac, with a gentler voice. I remember. Why were *you* there? Me?

Yah, said Isaac, you.

I told you, said Tori. I had a bad dream.

7

Every star is a sun has an Earth has a person. That's just something Tori's father told her once.

He took her hiking on her fourteenth birthday, to the Kabutoyama Forest Park. They met first at 10am, at Kōyōen Station, which lay at the end of the Hankyū Kōyō Line. After cutting through a network of hillside houses, her father passed her his water bottle, asking if she wanted a drink. She told him she was okay.

Are you sure, Tori?

Tori looked at all the houses around them. Yes, she said, before adding: I wonder where we're going. She'd been to the park countless times actually, in elementary school—just not this way, and not with her father. It wasn't till they had walked past their final house that they finally found a sign that looked promising.

Down the road were nothing but trees at first, before houses reappeared, built along the side of the narrow road. There were small fields too, fields for farming, which surprised her. The two kept walking till they arrived at their pit stop, at Kannō-ji, the temple, where they would eat their packed lunches with a panoramic view of Nishinomiya city.

Tori's lunch was made by her mother. In her box were baby tomatoes, mini-sausages and pieces of tamagoyaki. Her father's lunch was three balls of onigiri, wrapped in cling film, clearly home-made. Each onigiri was stuffed with a large pickled plum. She asked if they were his favourite, pickled plums, and he said that they were indeed.

He pointed at her lunch box. Do you like tamagoyaki?

She nodded.

That's great. Did your mother make them?

She nodded again. She looked at his half-bitten rice ball, and at the diced pieces of pickled plum, buried in the rice like the hard pit of a peach.

Who made your onigiri? asked Tori.

Her father smiled. My wife, he said. You've met her, yes?

Oh, she thought; of course. Tori nodded a third time.

Another hour passed. Tori found herself before a giant statue almost nine metres tall. It stood over a mound of rocks, arranged almost to resemble a pool; the statue itself was a human-like figure, with arms like wings, cast in white marble from head to toe.

The character for "love" was carved into its pedestal. Tori had no idea why that was necessary in the first place. To her the statue looked too much like a bird trapped in stone.

Tori, she heard her father say. Come here.

She went over, as directed. He sat on the edge of a picnic mat, with a woman and a boy seated next to him. They'd been waiting for her apparently, the whole time she and her father went hiking. And although she'd seen the woman before, she had never met the kid.

Would you like some hot tea? the woman asked Tori, who didn't say yes, but held her hand out anyway. The woman smiled at her father before handing her the thermos. Happy birthday, Tori, she said. You're so grown up now.

The woman had a pretty smile, thought Tori. She had a pretty shawl too, wrapped around her neck. She then turned to the boy, who also wished her a happy birthday. Tori asked him what his name was, and he said it was Kaito. She then asked Kaito how old he was, and he said he was eleven.

Kaito was a gifted boy, according to his mother. He's way ahead of all his peers. He's being made to read all kinds of books now, isn't he, books meant for older students? Kaito nodded, and said he was going through the short stories of Akutagawa at the moment. He was stuck on this story called "The Spider's Thread", which has got Buddha in it, said Kaito, Buddha and hell, before asking Tori if she'd read the story too. And then her father stepped in, and told him to stop. Today was about her, he said, not him. Remember that, please.

Tori studied Kaito a while longer, before turning to Kaito's mother. She then glanced down at the lunch laid out before them, and the other varieties of onigiri she had also prepared—braised pork, egg salad, tuna mayonnaise—all the while thinking: there were so many people in her life. There were the people she lived with, her mother, her stepfather and Hideo; then there were the people she didn't live with, who were these people, with whom she somehow shared the same surname. It was confusing, she thought, like being split into two all the time: if she thought too hard about it she felt like her skin would tear.

Tori lay down on the picnic mat. She looked up at the sky. She squinted her eyes against the sun, and felt its heat spread all over her. Being warm on a cold day was the best, she thought. But Kaito was soon yelling at her to stop. Sit up! he said. Sit up right now! The sun will cause you to go blind! Tori couldn't help but smile when Kaito's mother told him to pay her no mind.

I'm so sorry, Tori, said Kaito's mother. The boy can't help but lecture every time, can he . . .

But Kaito didn't seem to take instructions very well; he would not stop paying attention to her. He wanted to know everything about her, he declared. In the car home Kaito wanted to know why Tori hadn't gone blind yet, after staring at the sun; he wanted to know how she could look at the sun and still be able to see. Kaito's mother turned to her from the passenger seat and smiled.

That's because she's lucky, she said. Aren't you, Tori?

Tori looked at her. I am, she said. Super lucky.

Kaito had a question: What does it mean to be lucky? he asked. Kaito's mother thought about it.

It means . . . nothing bad will ever happen to you, she said.

The boy made a big O with his mouth. The revelation held him for precisely fifteen seconds, before something new came to his mind. Hey, Tori, did you know, he said, that we are made of the same stuff as the sun?

Tori turned to him. She held up a hand, and looked at it. You learnt this in your special class?

Yep.

What stuff? asked Tori.

Carbon, he said. You, me, Mummy, Daddy. Every single one of us, every single human on Earth. Everyone is made out of the same stuff as the stars.

Tori looked down at her hands. I didn't know that, she said. So what?

So what?

She nodded. So what if we're made of carbon? she asked. But Kaito merely lit up at the challenge, and said:

When we die, we go back to the sun.

The sun?

Yes, said Kaito. The sun. And then it'll take us and reshape us and spit us back out. And then we'll be made new!

Kaito's mother burst out laughing: it was a pretty laugh, thought Tori, prettier than the way she smiled even. Oh my, oh my, she said, slapping her father's arm. Shin'ichi, she said, this is *your* doing, isn't it? What in the world have you been saying to him?

It was her father's turn to laugh now. Tori's ears perked when he did so, snapped immediately to attention: she had never heard him laugh before.

Every star is a sun has an Earth has a person, he said. Everyone is connected, one way or another. Tori then caught him looking at her, via her reflection in the rear-view mirror. That is what it means to be a part of the universe, he said.

———

The rumours were many, said Tori to Jing by the roadside. Some said it was the work of a variety show, as part of a series of scripted gags; others said that they were the schemes of the local government, machinations of an over-the-top tourism campaign; several of the more superstitious folks blamed the incoming century, even though it was still four years away. And Chisato, one of the cleaners at the ryokan, thought it might be King Sojobo instead—ruler of a thousand tengu, prankster lord of Mount Kurama—up to no good once more. Too long had he remained in his cave! said Chisato at the staff dinner last Tuesday. And that old creature, she'd added, he's probably baffled by us at this point. By what we've become.

But even then, said Tori, the rumours:

One guest at the ryokan brought tales of a smell at Kyoto Tower, a smell that morphed from sweet to sour to smoke, for the few who attempted to trace its source. Another mentioned the appearance of an island, in the middle of the Kyōyōchi Pond in Ryoan-ji. Another spoke about a restaurant, situated between two buildings that used to stand side by side: it had a Spanish name, this restaurant, or it might have been Italian; it served nabe, in any case, and was identifiable by a plain white T-shirt hung on a pole in place of the standard noren.

Another guest described being the only one seated at a matinee show, at the Minamiza Kabuki Theatre last weekend. It was a strange show, Jing heard Tori say: the only thing that happened on stage was a flurry of snow, coating a resplendent plum tree in full bloom, with long and claw-like branches. It was a tree that trembled at first before it began to groan, shivering and moaning under the cold, begging for someone, anyone, to chop it down on the spot. When the guest had finally re-emerged from the theatre, she looked around the busy intersection at Gion-Shijo Station, and at the masses that crossed the Kamo River and thronged the sidewalk around Takashimaya, wondering: How could it already be nightfall? It was still morning, the guest had said to Tori, when she had wandered into the theatre.

Jing then heard Tori tell her about one especially vivid rumour, taking place at a random intersection within Nishiki Market. This was a rumour supplied by Tori's boss himself, something he'd experienced about a week ago. It was about an okonomiyaki stand, fully furnished, with buckets and trays of the standard toppings, and a row of stools at the front for passers-by to stop and sit down. But how did they first hear it? The sound? Neither of them actually knew, but one of them swore (swore!) that he had heard the sizzling and the crackling of a well-oiled teppanyaki, and the scraping and the slicing of spatulas working across the hot griddle. And that was how they had come across the stand, said her boss—it had appeared to him and his friend, quite out of nowhere one night, after they had got drunk on beer and sake at a previous joint.

Jing looked at Tori. There was still music, coming from Prismatic, though the two could still hear one another perfectly fine. And did they sit down? Jing asked. To eat?

They did, yes, said Tori. The thing was, there was nobody standing behind the stand. They waited and waited, but nobody came. Nobody came, in spite of what they'd heard earlier.

So nothing happened?

Tori nodded. She then told Jing about how, at that point of the staff dinner, Chisato had reached across the table and taken the final steamed yam. Tori and the rest of the table watched as the elderly woman peeled the aluminium foil away, with all of the delicateness her roughened fingers could lend her. Tori then took another swig of her whisky highball and asked: What do you think? You reckon King Sojobo is behind this?

Chisato chuckled, blowing on the steam that wafted from her yam. She then barked directly at the boss, asking: You didn't hear wings as well, did you?

The boss looked stumped, just as he was about to reach for something else with his chopsticks. Wings? he said. N-no.

So no wings, said Chisato, no flapping noise . . . ?

He shook his head. Chisato took a bite from her yam. Too bad, she said, as she began to chew on the yam. Not even the tengu want anything to do with you.

Jing's head began to throb—she'd become much more of a lightweight ever since she started working as a journalist two years ago—which meant that her hangover must already be settling in. She asked if the rumours were why Tori had been so keen to hear Mateo's story earlier, and why they were here now, wasted by the side of the road. It's because of whatever—Jing began to wave her arms around—*whatever* you think is going on, right? And Tori said yes, that is why. The rumours. Jing then asked if it was possible to separate what was real and what was make-believe, from all the rumours she'd heard so far, and Tori said that she tried, she did. But it was impossible. Why? asked Jing. Because, said Tori, because—everyone believes what they say to be real.

Jing looked at Tori. They were insane, the rumours, but even what Tori just said to her still had a kernel of truth. She asked Tori how she had known about the artist, and Tori said that she had been coming back from the toilet earlier when she saw a group of people outside the building, smoking and drinking together. One of them said hey to her, and she said hey back. And he said, in Japanese, You don't look familiar, and Tori said, Oh? You know everyone who comes here? The guy then asked if Tori was from Kyoto, and she said no, she just worked here. He asked about the club next, and how she had come to know about the place, and she told him about Mateo. I then asked if they knew the artist, Teiji Furuhashi, said Tori, and the group, well, the group fell really quiet. Jing asked what she meant, and Tori said it was like everyone not only stopped talking, they stopped looking at her too. And then around me rose the group, she said, one by one. They walked away, back towards the club.

One member stayed behind, the one who said hi to me earlier, said Tori. Tei was our friend, he said. Was he yours? No, Tori quickly said, no, two hours ago was when she'd first heard his name. Ah, that makes sense, said the guy. He said that Teiji Furuhashi had AIDS, and that he had been living with it for a while, sick but still making art. They had partied a lot too, before Tei passed away. They partied, right till the very end: 29th of October, 1995.

That's the date? Jing asked.

Tori nodded. I hope Mateo is safe, she said, and Jing nodded back. I hope so too, she said, just as something occurred to her: she looked up, at the sky, and found that it was overcast again.

What? said Tori, looking up as well. Is it—?

Jing placed a hand on her friend's shoulder. The artist, he—he told me something.

Tori turned back to Jing. Yes?

Is there a comet, she asked, passing in the sky right now? And Tori frowned, saying there is. There might be. Jing asked if they could check the news, see if any papers at the ryokan might say something. And Tori wrinkled her nose this time, saying: Shall we—shall we go back and check?

Jing nodded. She nearly let out a sigh of relief, wanting nothing more than to rest right now.

Tori got up on her feet. She looked up and down the road. Mateo can find his way back without us, right?

Two points of light surged into view, though it was just a taxi, driving on the other side of the road. Tori waved at it, frantically, hailing it down; the taxi braked, just as it drove past them, and made a sharp U-turn.

Tori opened the door to let Jing clamber in, urging her to be careful. The driver spoke up, shortly after Jing secured her seat belt.

Where to, miss?

Shinmachi, please, said Tori, and gave him the address to the ryokan. Do you know the way?

Roughly, said the driver. You might have to guide me later, hope you don't mind. A few seconds passed before he asked Tori if they were tourists. Whereabouts are you from, miss?

Tori looked at Jing: her friend was already easing herself into the corner between the door and the seat, eyes closed and ready to sleep. My friend here is Singaporean, she said.

Ah, said the driver. And you? Which part of Japan are you from?

Tori didn't immediately reply. I'm from Nishinomiya, she said, eliciting a short pause from him.

Beside Kobe?

Yes.

Oh, miss, said the driver, with a slight strain in his voice. It was terrible, I heard.

Tori tried to catch the driver's eye in his rear-view mirror. She could barely make his face out beneath the brim of his cap. Are you from Kobe? she asked, and he said, Oh, I'm not, miss. He said he was born in Kawasaki, and was raised there for a few years, before his mother took him and his siblings to Kasama, a much smaller city in Ibaraki Prefecture. And then back to Kawasaki, the driver added, which is the city I so happen to remember, anyway. Those five years in Kasama were all a blur to me.

Another pause fell between her and the driver, just as the taxi slowed to a stop. The red light bled into the vehicle, staining the leather on the seats with a rouge-like patina.

I have to be honest, miss. I was probably asleep.

Tori didn't understand. Asleep?

During the earthquake, he said. Happened so early in the morning, miss, I slept through the whole thing. And you know what's the best part?

He waited for her to respond. What? said Tori.

I might have dreamt it, said the driver. I can't remember what I was doing in the dream, but I remember being shaken, shaking, right till the moment I woke up. By then it was all over the news.

Tori looked out the window; the taxi had resumed its course, driving down an empty thoroughfare. This city is nice, she said, in an attempt to fill the conversation, to which the driver said that it was a beautiful city indeed. I like that the tallest building is Kyoto Tower, and nothing else, he said. He then asked if she worked here, in Kyoto, and she said that she did, the second time she'd been asked that evening. She worked at the ryokan they were headed to, in fact. The driver asked if she'd always been in this line of work, and she said no.

I was an interpreter, in my previous job.

The driver sounded surprised. Oh? What languages?

Tori smiled. Japanese and English, she said. It was a good job, actually. I got to travel all over the country, attend all kinds of meetings. It was quite fun.

Interesting, said the driver. So why the switch?

Tori looked at Jing: her friend was now fast asleep, with her mouth half-open. I was in Kyoto when it happened, said Tori: the earthquake. I was still an interpreter then. I had only meant to be in the city for two days.

And then?

Tori glanced back to the rear-view mirror this time. She caught the driver looking at her, and saw the smile in his beady, childlike eyes. They looked like a pair of crescent moons, she thought, as she said to the driver:

And then I stayed.

Tori had been on the phone with Hideo, the day before the earthquake struck. It was a simple funeral, he said, dignified—that's what our father thought anyway. And he liked what they'd done with the flower arrangement too.

Tori couldn't help but ask, How were the flowers arranged?

Like a fish.

A fish?

Yes, said Hideo, like one giant, white tuna.

She grinned. A tuna.

Something to that extent, he said. Maybe Shin'ichi liked fishing?

Tori didn't know how to respond; she had no idea what the man liked or didn't like, though the image of the onigiri did come to her, like it always did: a ball of rice with a purple heart, held in his large hand.

How was our mother?

She cried.

Ah.

Don't sound so surprised, said Hideo quickly. She was in love with him once, remember?

Tori winced. This was their relationship now, one in which her younger brother had the moral authority to scold her. Still, Hideo always knew when to change the topic, and asked if she had ever gone fishing before. She said no, not ever, and asked him why the question. Hideo had an interest in fishing, it turned out: he and his classmates were thinking of going to Kanagawa soon, where they could go fly fishing in the mountains. If all went well they might plan a second trip, to Hokkaido.

Have you ever been?

Where?

Hokkaido, he said.

It's a big place, said Tori. Which part of Hokkaido?

Huh, he said, not sure. And Kanagawa?

Several times, said Tori. I'll tell you about it tomorrow. Hideo took that as his cue to go over their plans for the following day: Tori would board the 6am train at Kyoto Station and disembark at Nishinomiya Station an hour later. He'd pick her up with the family car and drive her home.

Oh, one more thing, he said: the dog's coming along. I'll take him on my jog around the shrine before you arrive.

So you'll be early? said Tori.

I guess so, said Hideo. The dog's got to poop somewhere, and he won't do it if I ain't next to him. Plus I'm not brave enough to drive on my own yet! he added, his voice going a pitch higher over the phone. The dog relaxes me.

Tori smiled. Doing things on your own can be tough, she said, and she could still remember the way Hideo had paused, and softened his voice, as he scolded her the second time over the phone.

You make it look so easy, though, he said.

It was Tori's turn to pause now. She looked out of the small window of her hotel room, at the sight of Kyoto Tower standing in the distance. She hadn't seen anyone from her family, let alone the new Labrador they had adopted, ever since she graduated from high school. She moved to Tokyo, and then to London, and then to Yokohoma, where the HQ of her agency was based. Tomorrow would be the first time she had set foot in Nishinomiya in years.

How are they, by the way?

Who?

Shin'ichi's family, said Tori, as the afternoon came back to her once more. She could even recall the pattern of the picnic mat they sat on, positioned in front of that strange statue. They seemed fine, according to Hideo, although Kaito did ask where she was that day, and the day before that too. I used the excuse you gave me, said Hideo: I told him you had a last-minute assignment in Kyoto. I told him tomorrow was the only day you could come by.

Tori thanked him. It's true, you know.

What's true?

The assignment, she said. I was just done with it an hour ago. Now I'm back at the hotel.

Hah, said Hideo. Whatever you say. As long as you're home tomorrow, he added, before hanging up.

In her mind Tori had it all perfectly timed. Everything was perfectly placed.

She kept a wide berth around Nishinomiya city. Her agent had first sent her to jobs all over Tokyo, before sending her to far-flung places like Nagoya, Fukushima, Fukuoka. The economy was booming all over Japan, and she didn't mind travelling at all, to wherever that needed her services. She'd fly to Yonago one week and then to Sapporo the next, and then to Niigata the one after that. She got to meet gangsters, entertainers, fashion designers, anthropologists. She rented a pre-furbished apartment in Yokohama, just to have a place to keep her things, and to have a billing address for her bank account. When she found out that the lease was close to expiring, she was tempted, for a week, to do away with having a place altogether. She'd gladly live out of her worn leather suitcase, she thought.

Hideo was the one who had told her about Shin'ichi's stroke; at that time, Hideo was the only one she was willing to speak to within her family. He'd had a bad fall, down the steps that led to Inokashira Park, said Hideo. Kaito and his mother later learnt that it was a stroke that had caused him to fall, a stroke fatal enough to have incapacitated Shin'ichi either way. Tori didn't hear more about her father until Hideo called her again, this time with a final update.

It happened again, said Hideo, another stroke. He passed away peacefully in his sleep this time. And even though the man was based in Tokyo, with Kaito and Kaito's mother, it was in Shin'ichi's will that he be cremated in Nishinomiya, where his family had always been cremated. The funeral proceedings would most likely start in a day or two, said Hideo.

Tori called her agent then. She asked if he had any jobs for her, anything near Nishinomiya—anything that needed help right now. Her agent told her about an emergency assignment in Kyoto, in one of the hanamachi, a job that would cover her hotel and train fare, even a free kaiseki dinner. After confirming the exact date and time of the job, Tori told him that she would take it. She knew the job would keep her adequately preoccupied, but reasonably close by; it would be the excuse she'd use to miss the first day of proceedings, as well as the inevitable family gatherings that would occur the day prior. But once this job was over she'd concede, she told herself, and do the right thing. She would head home, finally, to the place that made her feel the most wretched.

The thing was, Tori had nothing against her hometown. Nishinomiya was a perfectly nice city. It had access to lovely mountains, as well as a share of that coast along the Seto Inland Sea. It just so happened to be the place where all her pain was located too, the place she knew she had to leave, and stay away from, or she would die. Every star is a sun has an Earth has a person—that's what her father told her once. And while the cosmos was mappable, no matter how vast it actually was, the same could not be said of the heart. And the same, surely, could not be said of the soul. How far could the soul go, she thought, before it was finally out of reach? Before it could be free from the hurt, the suffering, and the knowledge that love, even love, was finite? No one, not even Tori, could say.

Tori had a quick dinner that evening, and made sure all of her things were packed. She then popped out, having done a bit of research on the city, and found the izakaya tucked in the middle of Pontocho. She noticed the old gramophone, playing opera in a corner, and knew she got the place right.

Yonosu was the name of the small establishment. It was empty that evening, save for another woman, seated at the other end of the counter. Whenever Tori thought back to how they'd met, she'd recall a few key details, such as the martini the woman held in one hand, its olives still in their pick; a smear of lipstick, staining the rim of her glass; even the way she grabbed food with her chopsticks, and the way she puckered her lips to eat them. Her name, she said, was Emi.

Emi, repeated Tori. She felt something stir within her. Have I met you before?

The woman tossed her hair over her shoulder. Why, she asked—do you think it's destiny? It's a popular name, she said, and Tori had to close her eyes, to savour the tenor of her companion's voice.

They went back to her hotel. Tori had to close her eyes every time Emi spoke into her ear. So this is your kink, she said, your fetish? And Tori had no choice but to arch her back, and say yes, yes, it was. She could feel her mind irradiate with desire (yes), feel it course down the side of her neck and then down (yes) her spine, ending in a wild and warm dampness (yes). They were never quite done making love to one another that night, even when it had persisted into the morning. Emi suggested that they take a break, have supper, have some proper food—but the only place Tori could think of was an okonomiyaki diner, near Nishiki Market, open 24/7. Wouldn't it be better, Tori suggested, if they tried to sleep instead? The suggestion caused Emi to laugh, and purr even more into her ear.

Ah, she said . . . You want to *sleep*?

Tori took her things a few hours later, and slipped out. She wanted to kiss her companion on the cheek, say goodbye. But it was nearly half past five, according to the clock on the nightstand: she'd barely have enough time to check out, head to Kyoto Station, maybe grab a coffee on the platform. She'd have to hurry, either way—Hideo might even be out by then, letting the Labrador into the car; he might even be driving down to the station already, ready to go on his jog with the dog.

Tori checked out of her hotel, and left quickly for the station; she was buzzing, flustered, still high with endorphins. She would no longer be afraid, she decided. Everything she ever owned at that point, all that she ever needed, was stuffed into the leather suitcase in her hand; she'd take all of it, all of her, and finally go home.

The driver abruptly turned, at one point, to ask Tori a question: Do you know how or why planes crash?

Tori sat back in surprise: it was her first and closest glimpse of the driver's full face. He had a wide smile, with near-perfect teeth. And his eyes, she discovered, curved upwards like the edge of a clipped fingernail.

I'm asking, he said, because I have a flight to catch.

Where?

Osaka! he said. From Haneda.

Tori frowned. Haneda was all the way in Tokyo, she thought. Taking a train from Kyoto would only take you half an hour, she said.

The driver turned back to the road. I'd rather fly, miss. I don't want to be on a train when another earthquake strikes. I've had one too many bad dreams about it already. He looked at her again, via the rear-view mirror this time. I take it you were not hurt, when it happened, miss?

No, said Tori. I wasn't. I suppose I should have been squashed by a falling pillar, or even a toppling fridge. I could have fallen through a hole in the floor, a hole in the ground.

Hmm, that is right. You are very right, miss.

But I'm still here, she said.

Indeed you are, replied the driver. You are the Luckiest, Most Fortunate, Number One Girl in the World.

Tori turned back to the rear-view mirror, just as the driver stopped before the glare of another red light. What did you say? she asked.

Hmm?

What you said earlier, she said—what was that?

I do not know, he said. I cannot seem to remember. He then raised a hand to his dashboard. Shall I turn the radio on, miss?

Tori failed to give him a response; the driver turned the dial nonetheless. Sound and static filled the interior: music began to play, an old pop song from the sixties, and she had to look at Jing again, to see if she was still asleep. And before she knew it, she found herself strangely compelled to tell him, the driver, about a bad dream that she had too, one that she had a few weeks ago, at the end of a long day at work. She was on her way to Kyoto Station, in that dream, when she felt the ground move beneath her feet. She fell to her hands and her knees, rendered deaf not by the tremors that shook the sidewalk, the lampposts, the overhanging cables, but by her fear. She heard a window shatter, several cars braking to a stop; she was crouched over her suitcase in the dream, even though, in reality, she remembered holding on to it instead, the knuckles on her right hand ground into the pavement. Tori then witnessed a peculiar sequence of images later in that dream: she must have been a bird, or better yet, a mere speck in the cosmos, watching a fissure crack the earth open, a subduction of the Philippine Sea Plate creating incredible movement across the Nojima Fault, a jagged line over the planet where day had yet to break. And then Tori was back on the pavement, curled up with her eyes shut, thinking, yes, of course: this is as good as it will ever get, Tori Yamamoto. This is as close as you'll ever come to Nishinomiya in your life. And in the dream the tremors stopped shaking, even though her body continued to sway; she dared herself to look towards the station, where there were people scrambling to their feet and rushing outdoors. Here her dream had come to an end, even though in reality Tori had got up, and tightened her hold on her suitcase, her things. They were still in her hand. In reality she told herself to turn around, and find shelter somehow; she would have to stay put in this city till she had a better grasp of what had just taken place. And her brother, Hideo, yes, Hideo— even Hideo, her family, the dead man who brought her into this life: all of them would have to wait.

And then the taxi began to move again. The driver stepped on the pedal, and the music cut off, the radio filling the interior of the vehicle with breaking news: of three religious statues that had gone missing, at Kurama-dera, a temple far north of the city on Mount Kurama. Each statue was an object of worship, a National Treasure of Japan, kept safely in the temple for centuries. Tori asked the driver if he could turn up the volume on the radio, not because she was enraptured by the story, but because it was the voice, the voice that was broadcasting the news: it reminded her of someone she'd met fourteen months ago, at an izakaya in the middle of Pontocho.

Emi.

I'm dreaming again, said Tori out loud. This can't be real.

The driver watched Tori once more from his rear-view mirror. Miss, he said, permit me to ask: of all the horrible and tragic and senseless things that have happened to you—how much of it is made up, you think? How much of your trauma is a product of your own imagination—and how much of it dares you, simply, to believe? But before Tori could answer she felt the taxi come to a sudden stop. We are here, the driver announced, and he was right. She looked out the window: they were indeed outside the ryokan.

You'll have to wake your friend, he said.

Tori felt dazed. She still couldn't believe that Emi had just spoken on the radio, and she blinked and shook her head as she stepped out of the taxi.

Tori crossed over to Jing's side and released her friend's seat belt, stirring her awake. We're here, said Tori.

Jing peeled open an eye. Where?

The ryokan, she replied. Come on. Tori slung Jing's arm around her shoulder, and hoisted her out of the car. You need to try walking, please, she said to Jing, just as the driver also stepped out of the taxi. He lifted a sleeve and checked his watch.

The time now is half past twelve, he said. I will give you five minutes.

Tori looked at him, confused. Eh?

For five minutes, he said, I will be waiting right here. It is all the time you will need to deposit your friend safely inside.

Tori stared at him. She could barely grasp at what the driver was trying to say. Where—where are we going?

To Sakyo Ward, said the driver. I believe that is where Kuramadera is.

Tori continued to stare at him, her mouth half-agape. Five minutes, she said.

Jing then slumped further against her side; she rubbed a hand over her own face, hardly able to stand on her own feet. Tori looked at her friend, unable to understand how she'd got like this. The driver let out a short whistle.

How about ten, he said.

Tori got in the passenger seat when she came back.

Oho! said the driver. I hope all is well with your friend.

She nodded. She's fine.

The driver laughed. Well done, miss. The Luckiest Girl in the World Must Also Make Great Haste.

The radio was playing at top volume now, as they sped out of Shinmachi. Tori glanced at the meter.

I haven't paid you, she said. How much—?

No, no, miss. This whole trip—all of it!—shall be on me.

The engine groaned as the driver stepped harder on the pedal. Tori held on to her seat belt; she clutched it, as though for life, as a song began to play on the radio.

You know it, miss? said the driver, to the sound of marimbas.

I don't! said Tori. She hadn't intended to shout at him—but the music was too loud.

It's a good one, miss. I love this song! said the driver. And Tori could only gawk as the driver sang along, joining in at the second verse: he knew every word, and every line of the song, it seemed, as every tooth in his fantastic smile shone bright alongside the melody—

While I walk, I look above!
Tearing as I count the stars!
Remembering! those summer days!
Tonight! is the night! I walk alone!

8

The macaque was a no-show when Isaac took his breakfast to the beach, though by the time he got there it might as well have been his lunch. He had a one-litre water bottle filled to the brim, kept on the side of his backpack; in a plastic bag he kept his curry bun, still warm from the bakery near Kōroen Station, as well as a banana from another 7-Eleven. All of the macaque's favourite things, he realised. Isaac walked down the river—the Shuku River, as it was known—down the avenue towards the sea.

He didn't go wandering down the beach this time. He sat along the sea wall, just as the macaque did the day before. It had rained overnight, and he could see patches of sand where the beach was still wet. Perhaps that was why there seemed to be fewer people today, fewer beachgoers. He was about to get started on the banana when he spied a woman, with an umbrella, looking through the same growth of weeds where he had found the leather purse. Instinct told Isaac to stand, and so he stood; it told him to walk over to her, and he did, causing the woman to turn towards him. She raised her umbrella, so she could reveal her face: it was the same face on the identity card, adorned by the same thinly-rimmed glasses too. Without exchanging a word he reached into his backpack and handed it to her, her coin purse. Her mouth hung open, shocked at the thing he had just placed in her hands.

The woman stuttered. She began to thank him, profusely, and Isaac quickly shook his hands, saying he didn't know Japanese. Ah, ah, said the woman—I speak English as well. She was a professor, she said, at Kobe University. She then thanked him once more. I was so, so worried, she said, with a light British accent. I went to the lifeguards, and the police station too, and they didn't say anything about a missing purse . . . She then smiled, and laughed. Thank you, really. You have no idea, no idea how grateful I am . . . The professor then told him her name, Hinata, and asked him for his. Ah, she said again—Isaac, as in, "he who laughs"? She asked if his parents were Christian, and he said that his mother was Catholic at one point in her life, before she was kicked out. Well, said the professor, her eyes widening at the fact. I was once a churchgoer myself.

And? asked Isaac.

Hinata smiled, adjusting her glasses, and looked down at the purse in her hands. I got divorced, she said. That made no one happy. And then more disappointments came my way, so well . . . you know how it goes. She looked up again, at Isaac, half-squinting at his face. She asked him where he was from, and he told her. She asked him what he was doing in Nishinomiya, and he said he was just a backpacker, going around Japan. The professor then asked if he had any plans for the day, and he said no, not really, all while his heart pumped harder, harder in his chest. He didn't know why. Hinata asked if he'd had lunch yet, and he held up his plastic bag, with the curry bun still inside.

That's all you're having? she said, mouth agape again. No, no, she said— that is unacceptable, really. She then turned around, and gestured for him to follow her. Let me treat you to lunch, she said.

Isaac nodded. He saw the professor walk towards a shopping trolley, which she had left along another section of the sea wall. I was meant to shop for groceries yesterday, she said to him, but a strange thought came over me, I don't know why. I just wanted to walk down the river, you know the one. So I went in the other direction and walked down Shukugawa, thinking it would be a short walk . . . but twenty minutes became thirty, became forty. I was already well past Kōroen-eki when I was shocked to remember—there was no beach, or rather, the beach wasn't where I thought it was, but further down. I kept on walking till I ended up, well, here. A new shore. Or maybe just new to me. The professor smiled at Isaac. By the time I got to the supermarket, I found that I didn't have my purse. And yet a part of me knew, even though I had walked a long way, that all I had to do was return to the beach, said Hinata. And now you and I are talking.

Isaac smiled back at her, though his heart continued to beat rather quickly. He was wrecked by the certainty that he was caught in the middle of something now, something important. Something inevitable. He asked her, softly, if she was intending to do her shopping today, now that she had her purse back. Oh yes, she said. Yes, absolutely. Right after lunch.

He followed her to the other end of the beach, where there was a restaurant, just a small one, wedged into the back of a narrow gap between two taller buildings. He noticed the poor state of the concrete, the grass that grew out of multiple cracks in the ground. But he could tell that the restaurant was well looked after, and packed: he could hear people inside it, chatting away, laughing. He could hear music too, jazz. I just found this place yesterday, said the professor, as she slid the main entrance open.

Does it have a name?

The professor shrugged. She pointed at a white T-shirt hung just above the doorway. This caught my eye though, she said, giggling almost. Isn't it so unique?

Soon they were brought to a table. There were all kinds of diners in the restaurant: beachgoers, salarymen, entire families. There were posters on the walls too, illustrated with large text and bold colours. Once their food arrived he found himself salivating: he'd never had this much food in his life before. He watched the server place a large bowl of boiling stock between them, already filled with sliced meat and cabbage. More plates of fish, prawns and other seafood appeared to the side.

Perfection, said Hinata. She had a small frame, the professor, but she also had a gleam in her eye; he felt like she could have the entire hot pot to herself if she wanted to.

Thank you, said Isaac, smiling at Hinata. You look so excited.

That's because I am! she said, handing him an empty bowl. You're young, aren't you? Eat as much as you want, Isaac.

He placed a piece of cabbage into his bowl, along with a spoonful of broth. He thought of the photo that she kept in her purse, the photo of the sandpit. You must take good care of your family, he said.

My what? asked the professor, with a hand behind an ear.

Your family, he said, as loud as he could over the noise—you must take very good care of them. And then he saw it, the pause: the professor's face almost seemed to spasm at his remark.

Ah, she said. Ah. She blinked, and nodded, turning back to the food. I do my best, yes, she said, before growing quiet. Isaac felt a chill as well, realising the mistake he'd made. Didn't she just reveal to him that she was divorced? I'm sorry, said Isaac to Hinata. I feel like I said something wrong.

The professor smiled again. It's okay, she said. I know what you meant. She then looked up at him, as though something had occurred to her. There's a special party happening this evening, in my neighbourhood, she said. Would you like to come?

Isaac looked at her, his chest now tight with the beating of his heart against his ribs. Can, he said. He asked her what they were celebrating tonight, and she told him that there was a comet in the sky.

A comet?

That's right. Comet Hyakutake, haven't you heard? Tonight's the one night we have clear enough skies, said the professor, except Isaac couldn't hear what she was saying any longer. Even the din of the restaurant grew muffled, indiscernible against the point of realisation he had been guided towards this whole time. He stared at the professor, blankly, knowing how close he was, to the moment. He was right on the brink of it.

Isaac quickly looked around him, the restaurant. He had to blink, turn back to his food; he still had some way to go.

*   *   *

The way back to the professor's home required two buses, followed by a walk. He watched the bustling downtown give way to a dense suburbia, an area populated by lavish-looking houses. One couldn't tell that any damage had taken place in the city here. Isaac kept mostly quiet during their journey, afraid of hurting the professor with another careless remark; he couldn't tell if it was a mistake or not, going through the contents of her purse. But Hinata seemed content to sit in the silence, with the same half-smile on her face. There was a difference, he knew, between the two faces of the same woman he'd seen—one who smiled now a faint sadness, and another who once smiled without restraint. There must have been a point in the professor's life that separated one from the other, he thought; there must have been a moment that led her from the before and into the after.

They walked down a narrow incline. Tall houses rose on either side, larger than even the ones he got to see back in Singapore, terraced houses and bungalows that he could only dream of living in. Eventually they came round to a kindergarten, in front of which stood a triangular park, with a playground set in the middle. He could already spot a few tables beneath the trees, laid over with dining mats. The professor waved hi to a pair of women, hauling a large cooler together to the side. The professor then made a gesture towards him, causing the women to nod and smile. When he smiled back at them they seemed to blush.

They think you are very handsome, said Hinata. Why don't you wait here while I head to the supermarket, all right? I won't be long, she quickly added, when Isaac appeared to protest. I'll get my husband to come out and keep you company.

Isaac felt confused. Husband? Before he could ask her anything else, she had already set off, heading towards the edge of the park with her trolley; he watched her walk towards a small gate of the house beside the kindergarten, a house obscured by well-placed hedges and a red-brick wall along the perimeter. She pressed a button on the intercom, and spoke a few words into it. Hinata then walked away, at a brisker pace, after waving goodbye at Isaac.

Isaac turned back to the women. The two smiled at him, attempted a bit of conversation. You, hungry? Sit, yes? Isaac could only smile, and nod; the women soon left him alone, and busied themselves with their other tasks.

At the corner of his eye appeared a middle-aged man, with a toy poodle on a leash. He had on a pair of frameless spectacles, as well as a head of white hair, neatly parted down the middle. The man was the father Isaac had seen on the photo.

Neo-san? he said. Isaac? He extended a hand towards him. I'm Shigeru, he said, Hinata's husband . . . This is Asimov, he added, referring to the poodle.

Isaac shook the man's hand. Asimov stood on its hind feet, panting as it pressed its paws into the front of Isaac's legs. Shigeru then pointed, to a bowl on the table behind Isaac. Would you like to feed him a slice . . . ? Isaac turned around, and found a bowl of sliced apples. Break it into smaller pieces if you can, Shigeru instructed, and Isaac did so by biting into one down the middle. The man laughed, and sat next to Isaac.

My wife says you found her purse, he said. We thank you for that . . . He then gestured towards the food and the drink, laid out on the benches. It was his idea, apparently, to have the party; he and a few other residents even managed to convince the local authorities to switch the lights in the park off tonight. A few colleagues from the university would also be coming down later, prompting Isaac to ask if it was the same university where Hinata taught. Yes, he said, Kobe University. It's how we met. Isaac then asked if he could clarify something for him: Your wife mentioned about being divorced, he said.

Oh, yes, said Shigeru. She told you that much . . . She's referring to her first husband, though their relationship didn't last very long, he said; she divorced him, just a year after they had a child together. She then married me three years later, said Shigeru, and we have been together ever since.

Shigeru then reached down, and brought the poodle up onto his lap. Out of incredible sadness comes happiness, he said. And then sadness rises once more, like waves on the beach, or leaves on a tree. Such is the natural order of things. He then turned back to Isaac, with sudden vigour in his eyes, and said: I was so proud, Isaac . . . so proud to learn that a Japanese man had discovered the comet—the Great Comet of 1996, of all things! Isaac then felt a wind pick up, rustling the trees that encircled the park, as Shigeru smiled at him. Isaac asked what was so great about it, the comet, to earn such a name, and the man told him that it's got the longest tail of any comet, stretching five hundred kilometres long. It's also the closest a comet has ever come to Earth in two hundred years. Any closer, he said, and it would hit the planet. And Asimov wouldn't want that, would he? said Shigeru, as he stroked the tip of his poodle's nose. The poodle then barked, and leapt off the man's lap.

Shigeru unhooked the leash on Asimov's collar, and they watched the dog go. And in the going Isaac found himself recalling that night in Kuala Lumpur, in the hotel room, with the TV on. He had heard these same facts before, weeks ago, he realised. And as another fact began to disturb him in the corner of his mind, he heard Shigeru speak again, about how he and his family had another dog before, a Labrador named Arthur. They lost him, alongside their son, in the earthquake last year. But we have a daughter too, said Shigeru, and we knew she had been in Kyoto at the time. We didn't know what had become of her, so we waited for a day, and then another day, and then a week, just to see if we would hear from her. When a month went by, we hired a private investigator, to ascertain if she was dead or alive. We had to know. And when we found out she was okay, we also knew, somehow, that there was a profound reason why she didn't tell us. Why she was ada- mant on never talking to us again, seeing us again. Why she even took on an entirely different job in the city. And so we let her be, hoping she would find other people to take care of her—not to love her, necessarily, said Shigeru, but to just be in her life. To have people in her life. And I like to think she is, you know, taken care of. Shigeru asked Isaac if he was plan- ning on heading to Kyoto anytime soon, and he said that he would, one day. He just didn't know when. Oh, that's good, said Shigeru, very good. And if you do, perhaps you could stay at this ryokan, please. The man then reached into the back pocket of his jeans, and took out his wallet. He gave Isaac a card, a business card, and it's a card that Isaac has as well, of the ryokan where Tori worked. My daughter's there, said Shigeru. I tell everyone I know to stay there if they can.

Isaac heard the dog, Asimov, bark again from a corner of the park. Hai, hai, said Shigeru, as he rose from the bench. A walk beckons, Neo-san—I will be back in a few! Isaac then watched him walk to the other side of the park, with Asimov's leash in his hand.

In the man's place sat the macaque, taking a sniff at its surroundings. I can never wrap my mind around it, it said. I detest canines.

Isaac smiled at the macaque; he smiled, even though he felt impossibly sad. I think I know now, he said, prompting the macaque to look at him, and only him. What do you know? asked the macaque, its voice soft.

We met three weeks ago.

And?

We were on a bus.

And?

The bus came to a stop.

Why?

Isaac paused; tears sprang to his eyes. What was he feeling precisely? Was it fear, or was it frustration? He then watched as the macaque extended its arms, and put them around him, pulling him into an embrace. He could feel his own heart hammer against the quick beating of the macaque's, could feel the animal place a hand on the back of his head. Isaac buried his face into the macaque's shoulder, taking in the sour, elemental smell of its fur. You were in a dream I had, he whispered to the macaque, and the macaque said no, Isaac. No. It was not a dream.

It was half past eight by the time Isaac returned to the ryokan.

He had expected to find Tori, only to be informed that she was out at the moment, having dinner with her friends. Isaac asked for a bed anyway, and was assigned to the same men-only room he'd stayed in the last time; he then headed down to the common kitchen, where he boiled a packet of pre-made curry from a nearby store. And he discovered he still had the banana, from the 7-Eleven that morning.

Eventually Tori returned, along with her friends. Jing was beautiful, of course, and he found it hard not to look at her. When he later watched them leave, he caught sight of Jing turning back to him, with a smile, before rolling her eyes at what she was doing. It made him smile back at her, even though Jing had reminded him, in that fraction of a second, of Sherry.

He recalled the intense feeling he had when he had first taken the bus from Golden Mile Centre into Malaysia: the burning. He headed back into the kitchen, hoping to drink a quick glass of water, only to ball his hand into a fist again. Later, after a quick shower at the bathhouse, Isaac sat in the lounge with his father's Walkman and switched the radio on, flipping through the channels every few minutes, all without attachment. He was in a foreign land, in a foreign world; he was a foreigner in this world.

The phone rang. It rang, then stopped, and then rang again. But the front desk was closed for the evening, with no one but him nearby. When the phone rang a third time, Isaac walked over to the counter and picked up the handset: it was an old woman, calling from Singapore. She was asking for Jing.

Hello, uh, I'm Isaac, he said. I don't work here, but I'm her friend. She left a while ago.

Left? said the woman. You mean she went out?

Yah, he said. She's out.

The woman sighed. She was her grandmother, apparently. That girl, she said, I don't know how she can—I don't understand what she's thinking sometimes.

He grew concerned. He asked her why, and what was wrong, and heard the woman swallow audibly over the line.

Isaac, she said, this is urgent. Can you . . . can you tell her to call me? Tomorrow, please. First thing in the morning?

Can, he said. First thing. He then asked if there was anything else she'd like to say, and she said no, no. Not at the moment. Instead she thanked him for picking up the phone, before hanging up. In the minutes that trailed after the call, he replayed in his mind the call he gave Tori, earlier in the afternoon, just before he left Nishinomiya for Kyoto.

Two calls in one day, she said. This has to be special. Tori asked him what was up, and he struggled to form a reply. He felt something akin to stage fright when he told her about this new joke that he had, one that he came up with a moment ago.

Knock knock, he said.

Who's there? said Tori.

I am.

I am who?

Isaac couldn't help but laugh. That's your problem, he said. Not mine.

Light flooded the ryokan from the street outside. Isaac held his hand up against the light, watching the backlit silhouettes of several figures emerging from a car: one of them looked at his watch, and seemed to pronounce the time.

The main entrance slid open. In came Tori, struggling to keep Jing on her feet. Tori looked relieved to find Isaac there, and got him to take her instead. Still up, are you? she said.

He nodded. I was waiting for you.

Tori blinked. You were?

Isaac nodded again—but Tori looked eager to head back out, to the man who was still waiting for her by the car. You got somewhere to go?

Tori was still breathless when she said, Yes, actually. I do. Still, he could count on his friend to sense when he had something important to say to her—something about why he was here now, in Kyoto, after his time spent in Nishinomiya. What is it? she asked.

Isaac shifted his weight; he had to tuck Jing's hair out of his face.

What is it? Tori asked again, and he blurted them out, the words, not knowing what else to say.

I've been talking to a monkey, said Isaac.

Tori stared at him. Her eyes bulged while her mouth opened and closed, like a fish. She then dashed back out of the ryokan, not before saying to him, finally: I understand.

9

July 1999. Barcelona.

Mateo would have a final meeting with the coordinator of the Artistic Department, at the Joan Miró Foundation. After working out the last details of his eighteen-month contract (as assistant curator, Public Programmes and Education), he would take a tour of the permanent gallery, located on the ground floor of the main building. Mateo would wander from piece to piece, familiar with most of the works on display, before chancing upon the one painting he longed most to see.

The painting was titled *L'esperança del condemnat a mort*, or: *The Hope of a Condemned Man*. The story, he believed, went like this: in February 1974, Joan Miró had begun work on a series of paintings, which he declared complete on the same day the Francoist regime had executed Salvador Puig Antich, the Catalan anarchist, for killing a policeman with a car bomb. What the painter had ended up with that day was a massive triptych, each frame two-and-a-half metres tall, three-and-a-half metres wide. Within the centre of each panel was a single splash of colour, and a solitary stroke of black.

That grief could span so wide a frame would come as no surprise to Mateo. That a person's hope could be just as wide, however, continued to astonish him.

Mateo stood in front of the triptych, his mouth dying for a smoke, even though he hadn't touched a cigarette in more than three years. He knew the itch, recognised it for what it really was. He could see the yearning that lay beneath it all. As a city, Barcelona held nothing but pain and sorrow for him, which of course made him wonder why he had even agreed to apply for the job. But everyone at the Foundation seemed to love him: they loved his credentials, his experience and apparently, his now rueful personality.

He began to entertain the idea that perhaps Barcelona wasn't so bad after all, until he heard Daniel's voice: from the corridor outside that linked the various rooms in the permanent gallery. And Mateo would not react, not immediately, even though every sense of his was pricked, on high alert: his memory of Daniel had followed him to weirder, more intense, more far-flung places before; being back in Barcelona, if anything, made easy game out of Mateo. But when he heard Daniel say his name again, he would not be able to help himself. Mateo would have to look over his shoulder now, somewhere over his right, just to be sure that this, this voice: it was just another trick of the mind. But what he saw before him that day was a Daniel he'd never envisioned before: an older Daniel, with streaks of silver dominating his neatly-cropped hair. Two severe lines cut down the sides of his mouth—smile lines, he was sure, caused probably by years of happiness, of a genuine joy. Mateo then noticed his leg next, his prosthetic: it's a new one. One he never thought Daniel would show off, not like this. Not even on a warm afternoon like that day's.

Mateo, Daniel would say again. I didn't . . . He took a few steps towards him, entering the room. He then gestured towards his companion, out on the corridor, about to step inside as well. This is, ah, Alfonso, he'd say. Aha. And Mateo, for reasons he couldn't fully grasp, would look up from Daniel's leg and find Alfonso's hand, and shake it. Oh dear, Mateo would say to himself: You fool. You pitiful, pitiful fool, he'd say to himself, as he uttered aloud the standard diatribes: good afternoon; I'm Mateo; it's a pleasure to meet you. Welcome to the Foundation. Even at the age of thirty, Mateo would continue to say the things he wished to feel, and not necessarily the words he wanted to say.

Three months into the relationship was when Mateo had introduced Daniel to his parents. And although Mateo's family was decidedly not a religious one, it was Daniel who had suggested, in the end, that they have a meal on the 12th of October, 1995: the Fiesta Nacional de España, the National Day of Spain, but also the feast day for Our Lady of the Pillar. Daniel had been affected, naturally, by the ETA bomb that nearly took Aznar out in April that year; the attack dogged him, followed him, for months and months. Whenever he heard about a bombing he'd think about the story, about the basilica in Zaragoza: about how three bombs had dropped on it, during the Spanish Civil War, but none had detonated. The basilica so happened to house an image of Our Lady of the Pillar, leading many to believe that it was a sign of her power, her protection over the people. It was a story that gave Daniel comfort like none other.

They arrived at La Latina, at the block where Mateo's parents lived. They lived on the top floor, the sixth, prompting Daniel to stare up the stairwell. He asked if there was a lift, and Mateo said no, there wasn't. Why? he said, his eyes darting immediately to his right leg. Are you not feeling okay?

Daniel's eyes darted to Mateo's. Hey, he said, I'm all right. I'll be okay. By the time they hit the third floor, however, Mateo turned to find Daniel slumped against the wall, sweating.

Daniel, said Mateo. Is it—? Before he could even answer the question, he immediately sprinted up the rest of the stairs, and quickly knocked on his parents' door. It swung open, revealing his mother. Get Papa, was all Mateo said, before heading back down to his lover.

Mateo's father dashed down to join the couple. Hello, Daniel, said Señor Calvo. It's so lovely to meet you, he added, prompting Daniel to laugh, and wince. It's so lovely to meet you too, señor. By the time the three reached the top, the ensuing commotion had already drawn out the neighbours on the second, third and fifth floors. What's going on? asked the old woman from the fifth floor, and Mateo heard his mother call back to the woman: It's nothing, Esperanza, nothing for you to see. You're better off watching Telecinco, please. Esperanza slinked back into her apartment as Mateo said, Thank you, Mama. Oh, oh, said his mother. Be careful, the three of you.

They crossed the topmost stair, and Mateo's father was the first to let go of Daniel. Are you okay? asked Mateo's mother, and none of the men knew whom she was addressing. She asked Mateo if Daniel had known about the lack of a lift, and he said no, Mama. Would you have got one installed, otherwise? Mateo then felt Daniel's hand on his arm.

It's okay, señora. In fact, I should be apologising, aha.

Mateo and his father hoisted Daniel across the final leg of the journey, from the front door to the dining table.

It's the joint, yes? It hurts? said his mother. Is there anything I can do to help?

Daniel shook his head. He was still chuckling, on and off, probably out of disbelief. I'm sorry it has to hurt today. I know I should replace the prosthetic soon, he said. But if you have any aspirin lying around . . .

Mateo's mother told him to wait. I've got some, in a cupboard, she said, and Mateo immediately left for the kitchen, he, his mother and his father, the entire family searching their various cabinets. And for a brief moment in time, it's just Daniel, all alone, removing his glasses. Seated at the table.

There were many things to give thanks for, Mateo said to himself, as he watched his father and mother ask Daniel a series of questions. They'd rehearsed this, surely: he could see his mother's hand in devising them, the questions, as well as the part his father played in editing them, to make them sound less affronting. They asked Daniel what he did for a living (an architect, he said, and an urban planner) and how he came into his line of work (he'd gone to Zurich years ago, to the Swiss Federal Institute of Technology, he said); they wanted to know which part of Catalonia he was from (Tarragona, by the sea), how he met his son (at MoMA, last July). Finally they asked Daniel how he felt about their son, and Daniel said, oh: he is my love, my soul. Mi amor, mi alma. I can't forget the day we first met.

Mateo turned bright red. So did his father, while his mother's eyebrows disappeared into her hairline. Silence reigned, before his mother asked Daniel another question.

Is Mateo your, ah—your first?

First?

Your first boyfriend, said his mother.

Ah, said Daniel. Yes.

His mother smiled. Same as my son then, she said. And may I ask, if it's not impolite, how old are you? This year?

I'm thirty-five.

She nodded. And do your parents know about . . . ?

Daniel worked up a smile. About?

About you and Mateo, she said.

He maintained his smile. No.

She nodded again. She looked around the table. Will they ever know, Daniel?

Someday.

Señora Morales put her hands together. Because of what, she said—religious concerns?

Mateo kicked his mother under the table. *Mama,* he said, causing her to go what, what, what? I've told you before, Mateo, don't kick me, I'm fragile. And I'm looking out for you, you ingrate, she said, before returning to Daniel. It's a legitimate question, I mean, look around: it's feast day, yes?

It is, said Daniel. And it's a necessary question, señora; I can see why you asked. It's just, well, it's not because of religion, aha.

No?

No, said Daniel. My father and mother are separated, you see.

Mateo's mother appeared confused. I don't want to come across as unsympathetic—but this complicates things how?

Daniel turned to Mateo: the first time they looked at one another, from the moment they'd sat down to eat. I'm going to tell your parents something I haven't told you yet, he said. I hope that's okay.

Mateo nodded. It's okay.

Daniel turned back to Señora Morales. He told her that he didn't have many memories of his father, and that was because he left the family when Daniel was eight, nearing nine; and yet it was the memories from his childhood that stood out most vividly to him, while his later life could only appear dull, imperfect, unvarnished by comparison . . . The clearest memory of his father took place on the afternoon he left them, in the only car they owned at the time. Daniel's mother, Señora Vilar, stood at the front gate of their residence in Tarragona, while her husband, Doctor Rovira, put his suitcase in the backseat of his car.

The month was August, the year, 1969; Daniel never really understood why his father had to leave, nor who the driver was, or why he was important that day. Years later, when Daniel was eighteen, her mother gave him the real story, just before he left for Switzerland.

Your father was in love with another man, she said to him. This man was also a surgeon, a colleague at the hospital . . . It was a matter of time before the two of them became close. But people around them were beginning to talk, so they had no choice. They had to hide, relocate. Nobody wanted them in trouble, and not especially in the galerías, she said. The señora then looked at Daniel. Naturally, I was never allowed to know where they had gone, she said. I still don't know where they are.

And then Daniel's story ended, with the clock on the wall striking ten. Mateo's mother waited for the clock to be done, before asking Daniel if that was why he hadn't come out yet. You're afraid of hurting your mother? she said, and Daniel said yes, that's why. Mateo's mother then asked what had happened to his father since that day, and Daniel told her that he was fine, and that they managed to reconnect, not long after he lost his leg, at the Hipercor bombing of 1987. He told her that he still went to a specialist in

Barcelona that his father referred him to, for all issues pertaining to his prosthetic.

But he didn't come back, said Daniel, to the table that evening. He didn't come back home. If that's what you wanted to know.

It was a quarter to eleven when Mateo and Daniel finally left. His mother offered his lover a second aspirin, saying it would help. Boosted by the painkiller, the two found themselves going down the stairway with relative ease, each step eliciting a slight groan from the old, wooden steps.

You okay?

Yes.

Are you sure?

Daniel nodded. The old woman from the fifth floor re-emerged from her apartment. Be careful! she shouted, just as they made their way past the fourth floor.

Mateo looked up at her, nervously. Puta, he thought, and said to Daniel, You—you have to tell me, please, if you aren't okay.

Daniel gritted his teeth. I will.

They pushed on, and they were out. Out, finally, into the crisp autumnal air. All the trees in La Latina, along Calle de la Ribera de Curtidores, had managed to retain their splendour, wondrous and golden. They had the effect of making everything fine again. That was nice, right? he said, turning back to Daniel.

Daniel nodded. It was, he said, before quickly putting a hand over his mouth. He then lurched forward, stumbling, scrambling towards the edge of the kerb, where he heaved. He threw up. He convulsed and choked as everything, every dish they just had for feast day, came spewing out in messy chunks. Chicken, sausages, potatoes, shiraz: all of it slapped onto the asphalt of the road, trickling and sliding down the incline. And all Mateo could do was stand behind him and stare. In that moment, neither of them knew when this, this sudden onset of horror, would end; it was also how they learnt the truth of who Mateo was, that night in La Latina: his inadequacy.

Four years later, Mateo would watch Daniel leave with Alfonso, through the main entrance of the Joan Miró Foundation. He'd wait an hour before he left as well, to the bus stop beside the car park, on the way back to his new apartment.

He found himself thinking back to the time he took a train here, to this very city, in January 1996. Daniel had been newly based in Barcelona at the time. Mateo remembered looking out the window, at the intervening country that passed him by that day: past Guadalajara, Brihuega, Serranía de Ronda; past the red mountains of Jaraba, and Calatayud, and the ancient city of Lleida. Past the Prades Mountains too, and Zaragoza, where he had sat up and thought about Daniel's story—the one about the basilica. As the train screeched and eased its way into Barcelona Sants, he wondered to himself if there was a saint for him, a saint for the very situation that Mateo was going to create that night. I am going to meet my boyfriend, he thought; I have not seen him in a month. I was unhappy, but I was free.

The walk took less than ten minutes from Diagonal station. There was a statue of a fat lion in front of the hotel, one that he had thought was a Botero at first, but turned out to be a statue cast by some other artist. Mateo remembered having half a mind to approach a porter from the hotel, to ask if they knew anything about the statue's provenance. Instead he caught sight of Daniel, walking out to fetch him from the cold.

Ah! he said. Mi amor. I thought you might have been lost . . .

Mateo mustered a quick smile. I'm not that bad, he said, as the two of them hugged, and kissed, and stepped inside. Even their feet had a similar rhythm, a natural synchronicity between their paces, as though they hadn't been separated the past month. Still, there was a nervous energy about Daniel, a slight fidgeting in his hands. You're wonderful, he said, as he gave

Mateo's elbow a squeeze. Thank you for coming all this way . . . And then the fantasy ended, just like that: with Daniel looking downwards, down at Mateo's hands.

Where are your things? he asked.

Mateo and Daniel looked at one another, an answer flashing between the two of them. A waiter soon approached Mateo, causing their connection to break. He asked him for his jacket.

Mateo was introduced to the following people seated at the table: Daniel's mother, Señora Vilar; Daniel's father, Doctor Rovira, and Doctor Rovira's partner, Juan—the driver that Daniel had seen in the car all those years ago. They had all materialised, like a story come to life, even though it was Mateo who had become the new object of fascination. In an uncanny reversal from feast day, he found himself subjected to Señora Vilar's questions, short but direct. He told the table about how the Movida had caught on in Madrid, and practically made up his entire childhood. He remembered, as a twelve-year-old, attending a private screening of Pedro Almodóvar's *Labyrinth of Passion*, held in the living room of a family friend. He remembered undergoing an epiphany, an awakening of sorts, via the sight of Antonio Banderas wearing nothing but faded blue briefs; by the age of eighteen he would fall in love with five, no, six men in total, of various ages and inclinations. The admission alone made Daniel's father chuckle, and caused Juan to laugh out loud, half scandalised and half in awe of the life this young man had led, so different from the life they both knew. And then Daniel spoke. He asked Juan who his first celebrity crush was, and Juan said in reply: I, I don't know what you mean, Daniel, celebrity crush . . . I never really had one. The time was nearly ten when Mateo had realised, a little belatedly, that there was perhaps a reason he'd been the subject of such consistent attention that night. He realised that Daniel's family had no desire at all to speak to one another, and that the family, so broken by years of mutual abandonment, had resorted to having someone else provide the conversation instead, even for this dinner, this rare reunion.

Mateo sipped on his wine. In the brief pause, Daniel leant forward in his chair and asked Juan how he was finding life now, now that he and his father had bought a home in Barcelona. How did the both of you know I was here, anyway? he asked, and that was when his father said it was his mother who'd told him, over the phone. So you guys, what—you guys talk? Regularly? said Daniel.

Yes, said Señora Vilar. We're husband and wife, she said—a sentence that caused Daniel to laugh. He laughed in a way that caused Juan to look at him with alarm.

Don't be rude, Juan said. That's your mother talking, you know.

And that was when Daniel purpled. Mateo could still remember this moment, the most dream-like moment of the entire sequence: his lover scowling, causing his face to crumple and expand, simultaneously.

And who are you? muttered Daniel. Who are you to speak to me? To sit with me, with us? What right do you—do you—? And Daniel sputtered, forcing himself into a state of silence. His father then sat up in his chair, laying his knife and fork back down on the table.

Was this a mistake? he asked, softly. Was this too soon, my boy?

Mateo looked at Daniel. Daniel, helpless, looked down at his plate. Let's go, he said. I'm done. He got up from his chair. I'll see you outside, Mateo.

Mateo watched him leave. He then felt a hand rest on top of his, a touch so discreetly made that it nearly caused him to jump. But it was only Daniel's mother.

Go, said the señora. Take care of him. Only you can do it now.

Mateo stepped outside, buttoning up his jacket. Daniel was standing beside the statue of the fat lion, shivering in the dry January cold. He had forgotten his own coat on the way out, and although Mateo was tempted to offer him his jacket, he quickly resisted the idea. He had his wallet in his jacket, his cigarettes, his lighter; he could not risk losing his card, at the very least, which would let him board at a cheap hotel for the night. He'd also need it to catch a train back to Madrid the following morning.

Look at me, Daniel said.

Mateo couldn't do it. He couldn't do what he said anymore, he thought. Daniel took one step closer towards Mateo, and Mateo flinched, automatically. Wha—? said Daniel, shaking. Where are your things? he asked. A few passers-by had turned their heads towards them, before quickly walking on; Daniel asked him the same question another time, his voice rising with every word: Where are your things, Mateo? I'm asking you. Your clothes, your underwear. Your toothbrush? You'll need that at least, Mateo. You hearing me?

Mateo kept quiet. He kept his hands in his pockets as the tears stemmed in his eyes. And Daniel began to laugh: he laughed as he demanded to know what the hell that was, in the restaurant, all of it. Was it bullshit? he said. Huh? Was all of it just, just—was it nonsense to you? Can you ever take anything seriously, Mateo?

Mateo tried to speak. But Daniel was still laughing to himself, shaking his head; he took his glasses off, holding onto them with one hand, as he looked away from him.

I knew this was a mistake, he said. I knew I shouldn't have—I shouldn't have moved here. I knew, I did. Oh god, aha. I knew your fucking heart would fucking change. Daniel then turned back to him, his face wet with snot, and tears.

Everybody leaves me, he said, the quietest he'd ever been. Everybody, he said. Even you, apparently.

Mateo tried to speak again. Once, he believed that it wasn't beyond him, the task; he believed he had it within him, to take care of someone so hurt, so morphed, so literally transformed by pain like Daniel. Loving was easy, wasn't it? Their love for one another should have been enough. But on that night, he told himself: he knows. He knows now. Love alone is not enough. This is as far as they will go for one another.

Mateo started to speak. He would say to Daniel what he had come all the way here to say, but Daniel wouldn't have it—he was already walking away, saying no, no. No, I . . . I can't look at you, was what Daniel said. You broke my heart the most today. He even managed to get into a taxi, speeding away, as Mateo said to him: I still love you. Mi amor, mi alma. Believe me.

He would report to work the following day, at the Joan Miró Foundation. And he would see Daniel again, in the café, much to his disbelief.

Mateo would stare at him, dumbstruck. Daniel's damn leg was out again, and it would make him want to burst into tears. He would want to shout at Daniel, to tell him to go back, go away. Instead he sat opposite his former lover, and asked him why he had returned to the Foundation. Are you based in Barcelona, again? he asked, and Daniel said no, he is not. I'm only here for a short vacation.

Mateo looked down at his hands. You know, he said: I should be the one chasing you back.

A soft laugh. Mateo looked up at Daniel again, and the fool already had tears in his eyes.

It must have been hard, he said, moving away from Madrid.

Mateo nodded, giving him a small smile in return. Silence threatened to settle over their conversation. In an ideal world, he thought, they wouldn't have to speak at all; they would merely have to look at one another, to understand. But there was one thing he needed Daniel to confirm.

Where's Alfonso?

He saw the change in Daniel's smile. Right now? he said. I'm not so sure.

Okay, said Mateo. But he knows where you are? he asked, and Daniel nodded, causing the tears in his eyes to fall. Alfonso knows where I am, he said to Mateo.

Mateo told Daniel that he would work till eight that night. It was his first day, he said, so there shouldn't be too much to do. At 8pm there Daniel was, in the same chair at the café, as though he never left.

Your place?

Mateo nodded. It's not too far from here.

Neither of them talked on the bus into the city. Neither of them talked when they transferred onto the tram. Mateo and Daniel simply held hands, their eyes towards the passing city, as the summer sun made its slow descent over the buildings, the roads, the trees, and over all of Barcelona's drifting people and passing cars. Neither of them would talk on the way up to Mateo's apartment, on the second floor of the building, until Daniel finally said: I love it. Mateo scoffed, and led Daniel to the small island in the kitchen, where he could sit on the one rickety stool that he had so far.

Are you hungry?

Daniel nodded.

I can boil pasta, said Mateo.

Daniel nodded again. Yum.

Mateo filled a pot with water, and set it on the stove. It was half past nine when they finally ate, aglio olio, the dish that Mateo had eaten for a week. He then poured them each a glass of white wine, something he had bought from the Carrefour around the road. Daniel picked up his fork, before quickly setting it back down.

Mateo.

Yes?

I've always loved you too. From the very first day we met. Tears came to his eyes again. Do you know that? he asked.

Mateo put his fork down too. That's nice.

Daniel paused. He blinked. And do you still love me? he asked, a little softly.

And Mateo said: I do. Of course.

Daniel's mouth opened, and closed. It was clear to him that something was still wrong, in spite of what they had just learnt about one another. What happened to you? he asked Mateo. What happened when I was gone?

Mateo looked at Daniel. Only he has the full story—the full story of what happened on that one night in Kyoto. There was a moment when Tori had known as well, shortly before she slipped away. Which left just him, he reminded himself; essentially him.

———

I wanted to get away, he said to Daniel. For three weeks I slept around, and smoked a lot, and drank a bunch too. That didn't change when I went to Kyoto, to see my friends. I would just wait for Jing to fall asleep, and then I would slip outside, walk around. Once Tori went out with me; that was nice, that was very kind of her, but at the time, I don't know—I found kindness to be cruel, you know. Every night I was in a different place, I burnt through so much cash. And for a few nights I was—I was seeing things too. I was seeing fireworks.

Fireworks?

Every night, said Mateo. I thought something, surely, was happening, like some kind of celebration, I suppose. They were really beautiful, and they broke my heart, you know? I just wanted to get as close as I could to something like that, something that could tear me apart and yet tell me it would be okay, even more than okay. Eventually I managed to track down where they were being fired from, which was this—this club. And while I could have gone alone I didn't want to. I was afraid. I saw a poster, you see.

What did it say?

I wasn't sure, he said. But there was the name of a collective printed on it, Dumb Type. Do you remember . . . ?

Daniel nodded. Teiji Furuhashi, he said, and Mateo said yes, bingo. The one at . . . ?

Daniel looked at him. At MoMA, he said: the day we first met. He then went quiet, and looked down at his glass of wine.

Was he there?

Yes, said Mateo, good job. How did you know?

He shrugged. It seemed like the story was heading in that direction.

Mateo paused. His mouth went dry, and he had to lick his lips. I met the artist that night, although, technically speaking, I shouldn't have been able to, he said. It should have been impossible.

Daniel looked at him again, frowning. Because you were seeing things?

Mateo shook his head. Because he was dead, he said. Teiji Furuhashi, the artist—he had AIDS, and it took his life in '95. He'd been dead for five months.

Daniel didn't speak for a while. And yet you say you met him, he said, the artist. In '96?

That's right, said Mateo. I even held his hand, Daniel. I had no idea he had passed away. Sometimes, though, I, I wonder—I wonder if it's possible to want something so much it appears before your eyes.

They looked at one another then. They kept quiet, studying the other's face, with something akin to disbelief.

Do you want me to continue? asked Mateo. With my story?

Daniel blinked; he removed his glasses, set them on the table. He then took his wine glass and drained it. Yes, he said. I want to know what happened.

What happened was this: dashing towards the end of the world, Mateo clung onto Teiji Furuhashi's hand, compelled by the strength in his companion's grip. Before he could even say goodbye to Jing, they ran out of the driveway, effectively leaving his friends behind. But he allowed it, of course; he wanted to see what the artist wanted him to see. Because this was what he wanted, no? To be wanted like this? To be summoned, made helpless? Oh, life, he thought: surely this place, the place that Teiji Furuhashi wanted to take him to—surely this place would be spectacular. Surely it would be filled with the same light that befell his companion, so that he too might bask in it, for just once in his stupid, godforsaken life.

They made a sudden right, towards the Ohashi Bridge, stretched across the Kamo River. The artist tugged on Mateo's hand and brought him down, down the ramp beneath the bridge, towards the bank of the dark river. Tei giggled, Tei ran, and so did Mateo, whooping and laughing as the city rose above their heads, the two going deeper into the shadows. There was a joggers' path at the end of the ramp, running parallel to the river in a straight and unbroken line, and it was there, further along, towards the river itself when Mateo said—What's that?

There was a disturbance, in the river. At the delta, where the two streams converged into one. But the artist paid no heed.

Come, he said—come! But Mateo remained rooted to the spot.

What's that? he asked again.

The artist smiled. A party, he said. A fabulous party. Come, my dear. And as the artist tugged on Mateo, something hit his shoulder from behind, knocking him off balance: it was two people, holding hands, pushing past them. Mateo watched the pair run down the joggers' path, with an eagerness that left him stunned. The artist pulled again on his hand.

It is time! he said. We do not want to be late.

Mateo kept his gaze on the strangers' backs, receding further into the distance as they sped away. There was another pair, two women, this time, emerging from a gap between two riverside buildings. They tumbled, down the slope of the embankment, narrowly avoiding a few of the planted trees; the four then leapt off the path and into the shallow basin of the river, the dark water splashing about their ankles, up to their knees as they kept on walking: closer and closer towards the commotion at the river delta.

Only then did it occur to Mateo that something was wrong. He strained his eyes to better see, though it was impossible, not without any light to help him. And still his companion pulled on his hand, even harder this time, all the time urging to him, Come, come—come see, at least! Be fun!

A few steps eventually broke into a run. What was he doing? Mateo thought, looking down at his legs. Did he—did he want this too? They ran down the path, closer and closer to the commotion. Mateo could feel his chest tightening into various knots as his breath quickened and thinned out into sharp intakes of air. Oh life, oh light—he felt them both slip away, the more Tei urged him to run, run better, run faster. He wanted Tei to slow down, only to be silenced, utterly, by the look of ecstasy that transformed his companion's face. Tei was laughing now, he was cheering, his eyes and his mouth wide open and overcome by wild delight. And still around him, more pairs just like theirs, dashing down to the Kamo River from all directions: Mateo found himself pulled into the water with Tei already ahead of him—he yelped and staggered as the cold stung and sloshed around his waist.

Tei! said Mateo. What are we doing! What are we going to do!

Come! was all Tei said to Mateo. Come closer! We are so near!

Mateo panted—he was still moving forwards, still compelling one leg to move in front of the other, wading ever closer towards the convergence in the river. Looking back, Mateo caught a glimpse of two men standing on the railing of the Ohashi Bridge, and then jumping—he had to look away, overcome by a fresh wave of horror, unable to tell what would happen should they hit the water. And yet Mateo kept moving, ever onward, his body now pushing forward with a will of its own, while his heart, his heart—it was desperate, it was: he wanted to take a good look at the gathering, the *party*, until he had to double backwards instead, shocked by the sight of people forcing their companions' heads under the water. It paralysed him, causing every joint in his bones to jam in an instant. He watched multiple bodies, submerged in water, struggle and then seize to a violent standstill, the last of their breaths emerging as a helpless stream of bubbles. No! he cried out, as a woman with a child lowered herself into the water, just barely lifting the baby above the surface, its arms and legs flailing in the cold air. And with his own body nearly chest-deep in the river he didn't know how else to look except towards the sky, where he caught sight of—of—

Of what? Daniel asked.

The comet, said Mateo. Hyakutake. Do you remember? The Great Comet of 1996?

Daniel frowned again. What's so important about it?

Mateo licked his lips. It made me realise something, that night. That there was a pattern.

A pattern?

To everything.

Daniel blinked. He shook his head. To what? What, Mateo? What's "everything"?

Mateo didn't answer. He kept quiet. His gaze began to drift.

All right, all right. Let's skip that, said Daniel. And then what, Mateo? The comet, and then what? What did you do?

Mateo looked back at him. I stopped, he said. And then I ran.

You ran?

Mateo nodded. I ran all night, he said to him. Tei howled the moment I tore my grip away from his hand. Tei howled when I pushed my way back through the river. I was forcing my way past dozens of people, who were now hurtling past me in the opposite direction. Come back, I heard Tei shout, behind me this time. This is the only way, I heard him say, all the while I said to myself no, no, I can't do this. I can't. I'm not brave enough for this. And when I finally clambered onto the bank I ran on the path, back to the ramp beneath the bridge. I ran up the ramp and then back towards the club, across the street, through this small neighbourhood, past even the supermarket where we had bought alcohol earlier, as though my entire night was rewinding in double-time. I ran and I ran and I ran, desperate to see my friends again, desperate to be rid of the water that still clung to— that still clung to my clothes and, and, and my *shoes*, running, and running, until I finally—I finally heard my own heart, telling me to stop, Mateo, you can stop now. And so I did. I did. I did, Daniel—I stopped.

Mateo and Daniel would spend the night together, after dinner.

While in bed they would talk. They would talk about the years they had spent without one another, about the men they had seen apart from one another, the jobs they had taken and the places they had seen.

It would be three, nearly four in the morning by the time they agreed to close their eyes. Just before he gave in to sleep, however, Daniel decided to ask Mateo one final question.

Did you check the news?

The what?

The next day, he said. March 23rd. Did the papers say anything about . . .

The river?

Yeah.

Mateo licked his lips. No, it didn't.

Daniel frowned. So . . . ah . . . how do you know it was real?

I don't, said Mateo.

You don't?

Mateo looked at him. His eyes are now wide open, unblinking. Sleep, once so near, felt far away again. But Daniel's eyes were still closed; he was just thinking aloud, thought Mateo. He was just trying to keep himself from falling asleep. I don't know, Daniel, said Mateo to his lover.

Another sentence would form on the verge of Mateo's lips. I'm not done with my story, he found himself wanting to say. This is not where the story ends. But the next part, he knew, would require another leap of faith. And it was a leap big enough for this thing to fail, this thing that they just managed to start again, the thing that they had spent three years apart for, healing and waiting. And so Mateo closed his eyes again. He would decide not to tell Daniel about Tori, about how she had appeared somehow, in the quiet morning, urging him to get into her taxi; he decided he wouldn't tell Daniel about Isaac either, and about how Tori had said to him: You are not alone, Mateo. You are not. Something strange is happening to him too.

10

And then, just like that: the year 2000.

Jing watched Isaac walk towards her, slowly. When they were finally close enough to touch one another, she reached out to him, hoping to hold his hand, only to have him put his hand on the small of her back instead. Happy new year to you, said Isaac, and she managed a smile at him.

Happy new year to you too. I caught you earlier, standing by the window, she said.

Oh, is it? said Isaac, casting his gaze downwards. He sounded like he'd been caught red-handed. How did I appear?

Jing nudged him lightly. You looked okay, she said. You looked like you. Isaac then smiled back at her, with something almost like gratitude, and for a moment it was just the two of them, regarding one another wordlessly, as confetti began to fall from the ceiling. Stage magic, she thought—why bother? Jing rolled her eyes, and she heard Isaac laugh at her reaction. He began to brush the glitter and the plastic away from her face, careful not to smudge any of her make-up. You're such a pro, said Jing, with something like adoration, and Isaac scoffed. Yah, he said, you bet. Jing then felt his hand rest on her chin: she found herself no longer looking at her husband's eyes, but at his lips.

Wanna see a real pro in action? he said, not in English, but in Mandarin, like he was in another TV show.

Jing rolled her eyes again; she laughed, they both did, and shook their heads at one another. It was possible, she thought, that he might try to get a proper kiss from her later, and it made her warm just thinking about what that kiss might lead to next. She then heard her phone ring, just as a person at the party began to approach Isaac: it was home calling, most likely her grandmother. When she turned to Isaac to ask if she could take the call, she saw that he was already gone, distracted, folded into a conversation with three or four others. Jing retreated to another corner of the clubhouse and answered the phone.

Happy new year, Ah Jing, said her grandmother. Just wanted to let you know that your son is asleep.

Oh, good, said Jing, letting out a quick sigh: the past couple of months had been the struggle of her life, trying to get Yong-he to self-soothe. Happy new year, Ah Ma; sorry I can't be there, she said. Her grandmother then tutted over the phone, telling her it was nothing. Please, she said, I am happy to do it, Ah Jing. You're already doing a far better job than your mother.

Jing felt a shrewd look cross over her own face. Don't be too confident, Ah Ma, she said. So do you have any wishes?

Wishes?

Or resolutions, she said. For the year 2000 and beyond.

Oh, said her grandmother, if we're projecting that far ahead . . . Well, my first wish is that I die quickly.

A jolt went through Jing's body. Ah Ma!

My second is that your grandfather dies quickly too. None of that cancer business, she said, none of it, no more. We wouldn't be able to bear it. Her grandmother then paused, for a few seconds. And if I get a third wish, well: it's for you.

For me?

Yes, said her grandmother. I just want you to be happy, Jing. No matter what happens to us or your family.

Her grandmother's words caused a cold to settle over her. The five of them lived together, in that house on Lorong Chuan: she, her husband and child, and her grandparents. She wanted to know if her grandmother sensed it too, the quiet lacking, the sense that something was still missing in the current arrangements of her life. She wanted to know if her grandmother had noticed it recently, or if it had always been there. Jing looked over her shoulder then, at the party, picking her husband out from the crowd; she found him turning to her too, in a moment of instinct, still smiling at the people around him. She felt tempted to leave him be.

Jing woke to a beeping sound, on the 23rd of March, 1996: it was the morning alarm, on Mateo's G-shock, sounding at nine.

She craned her head towards Mateo. He was on his side of the room, curled up in his futon, in the foetal position, pale against the sunlight that now streamed through their window. She could smell him too, something mineral; she couldn't tell if the smell was from his body or the pile of clothes, tossed into a corner of the room.

Jing got up. Mateo shuddered when she disabled the alarm on his watch. He felt cold, and didn't let go of his glasses, even when she tried to prise them out from his hands.

She then reached into his bag and took the Handycam, reviewing the previous days' footage. Filming herself shouldn't be so hard to do, she thought. But as she turned back to her things, she found a piece of paper beside her pillow, a note written by Isaac. *Call your grandmother*, it said. Later, when she made her way down to the first floor, she found him in the lounge, eating bread with a cup of coffee, his hair combed back and smelling of shampoo. Hey, he said—you got my note?

Jing held it up in her hand. You spoke to her last night?

He nodded. She got call a few times, he said. Jing gave him a weak thanks and asked the person at the front desk if she could use the phone. It took no more than a ring for her grandmother to pick up the phone.

Hi, Ah Ma. What's going on?

Her grandmother sounded desolate. I don't know, Ah Jing. We're very confused, she said. We need you to tell us what to do.

Jing didn't understand. Her grandmother explained that it had been around midnight when her grandfather had gone downstairs, to the kitchen, for a cup of water. It was peculiar, reported her grandfather: he'd expected some light in the living room, her mother still up and watching the TV. But it was dark, he said, no light. When he'd switched the light on in the kitchen, the resulting swathe cut into the living room, revealing the missing shape of her mother on the blanket. He then switched on the rest of the lights, in the living room, over the driveway, in the garden. He switched the lights on in the stairwell, and the second-floor corridor, followed by the rest of the rooms. That was how Jing's grandmother had woken up too, asking him what was going on, and he just shook his hands, indicating that he didn't know, he didn't know what had happened to Han. But no matter how hard they searched, she was gone, and when they checked what else was missing they discovered, rather quickly, that her wheelchair was gone too.

Jing didn't know what to say. And now, she said, she's—

Yes, said her grandmother, yes. Still gone. She began to cry, over the phone. You—you have to tell us what to do, Ah Jing. Just tell us.

Jing looked behind her: Isaac was observing her now, from across the corridor, his cup of coffee still in between his hands. Ah Ma, she said: you need to check her things this time. It was just as important to find clues, anything that might tell them about her mother's plans. Check her journals, her notebooks, everything, she said. Why, asked her grandmother—what are you thinking? Jing then told her it was nothing, she wasn't thinking of anything, even though she held the suspicion, the possibility, that her mother had chosen to send her away, to Kyoto, so that she would have one less person to evade when it was time to make her getaway. We'll have to call the police if she doesn't come back by dinnertime, said Jing. Okay? Ah Ma?

Okay, said her grandmother. Okay. We'll do what you say.

Jing placed the handset down. Isaac rose to his feet.

What happened? he asked. A couple other guests, seated at the table next to Isaac's, gave them a quick look as Jing took a step closer. She kept her voice low and asked if he had plans that day, and he lowered his voice too, saying no, he didn't. Why?

Great, said Jing, even though her mind had felt like a game of Tetris that morning, her brain going back and forth, left and right, trying, at every moment, to catch all the falling pieces. She asked if he knew how to work a camcorder.

They left the ryokan in half an hour, reaching Shijō-Ōmiya Station after a ten-minute walk. While waiting for the tram Isaac asked if Jing was hungry, pointing at a convenience store nearby, and she said no, she wasn't. Instead she stared at the Saturday crowd that gathered on the platform, and at the tram that soon screeched into the station. Once she got on board she quickly found a pair of seats: they sat, and Isaac opened his bag, handing her a slice of the milk bread he bought last evening.

Just eat, he said.

Jing looked at him still holding the slice out to her. She took it, and bit it, and was surprised to find that she could taste something, a mild sweetness.

You can tell me anything, he said. You can trust me.

She continued to chew on the bread, staring out the window. She found herself wondering if this was what her mother had seen too, this passing town and the backs of all of its houses, its many buildings. Tell me about you first, she said to Isaac, and she heard him say in return: What you want to know?

She wanted to know how he got to Japan, for one, and he said, By plane. Where did you land? she asked, and he said, Kansai International. Oh, how fun, said Jing, though without much enthusiasm. Did you know that it's built on an island of trash? And Isaac said no, he didn't know. Trash, really? he said, and Jing nodded, lifting what remained of the bread to her mouth. That's what I heard, she said, her mouth full.

The tram stopped; people were getting on board now, at Nishiōji-Sanjō Station, a simple platform with a few benches, a vending machine and a corrugated roof. Isaac asked if she wanted more bread, and she said no, no thanks, before turning back to him. You ran away, didn't you? You're a runaway, she said. You can't actually afford this, running around like this. And Isaac said yah, he was. He felt like his time was running out too, that and his money, for sure. And so Jing asked what it was that made him run, and he said that he was just angry. Angry at life. Angry at how things were turning out, at how things seemed to be getting worse for everyone at home. And so she asked him about his family next, and he showed her, the photo of them at the zoo. This you? she said, singling him out. So cute. He told her that this was the one time they'd ever gone out as a family: his father had won a prize playing TOTO that week, and had got a promotion too, at the car repair workshop where his father was employed. And so his dad bought everyone new clothes, treated them to McDonald's and took them to the zoo. Isaac then pointed to the monkey, asking if Jing knew what kind of monkey it was. She shook her head.

That's a snow monkey, he said. Nihonzaru. They're from here.

The tram stopped another time; it was slowing down at another station, passing through a large overhead structure that resembled a tunnel. In the brief darkness Jing asked how he met Tori exactly, and Isaac said she was sleepwalking. What? said Jing, and Isaac said, Yah. I found her near Kyoto Station, in the middle of the street. She told me she was having a bad dream. Isaac then paused, as though to word as best as he could what he was going to say next.

Something funny happened to me too, he said, when I was on a coach to Kyoto.

What? said Jing. Like what? The tram then began to move again, back out into the morning light: she could see the day pass over Isaac's face as he said, No lah. Nothing. It just—the bus took a break, at a rest stop, in the middle of the night. And when I woke up I felt really weird, like, really messed up. It felt like I was sleepwalking too, he said, it really felt like I was in the middle of a dream. Isaac then paused again, pretending to hold a microphone to Jing's face.

Okay, he said. Your turn.

Jing handed him the camcorder once they reached the end of the line. After walking through the main route within the bamboo grove, they managed to find it, the spot, or what felt like the spot her mother had stood on all those years ago. There was a smaller grove with narrower paths, laid out in a deliberately sinuous manner, so that the bamboo, surrounding the traveller on all sides, could take on a particularly labyrinthine feeling. She waited for Isaac to review Mateo's footage, with his eye against the viewfinder, just to get a feel of how they had shot the six previous tableaus. By the time he told her he was ready, she had already changed into her white blouse, buttoning up the front. Isaac took a final look at the *RANDEN* stills and said: Your mother's hair was really long.

Everyone says that, said Jing. She lost all of it, obviously.

Isaac didn't seem to understand, not at first. Oh, he later said, looking apologetic. Yah, right. He then held up the camcorder, putting his eye to the viewfinder again. Ready?

Jing turned her back to him. Ready, she said, even though her body had begun to shiver, to tremble. All morning she'd felt like she was on the precipice of something, of a great shift in her life. She asked herself what exactly she had to be ready for, as she heard Isaac say that the camcorder was now recording. In the forty seconds that led to the final scream, she wondered what else the universe was going to put her through, just as she felt like she might break out into a run. She had no idea.

They returned to the ryokan after lunch, the place quieter than usual. They walked up the stairs, stopping momentarily on the third floor. My room's here, said Isaac. Jing placed a hand on his shoulder, and she found herself looking not at him, but at the gesture, her hand placed on the mound of his shirt. Thank you, she said, and she found Isaac looking down at her hand too. Hey, he said. No problem.

Mateo was still there when she stepped into their room. The same mineral smell lingered in the stale air too. She placed her bag down and took the tape out of the Handycam, as Mateo finally stirred himself awake.

Ugh, he said. Apesta. The two then made eye contact, and exchanged a wry smile. It smells like a wet dog in here, said Jing.

Mateo chuckled, even though he looked like he'd aged overnight. Tori more or less said the same thing, he said. He then told Jing that Tori wanted to make them dinner, to commemorate their last night in the city, or something. She's probably out to the shops now, said Mateo, before he paused, and looked at the Handycam placed on the floor. I don't think I can be your cameraman today, he said, and Jing told him it was okay.

I've done it, don't worry. Isaac helped me.

A dark look passed over Mateo's eyes. Guess he's one of us now, he said.

Jing shrugged, avoiding the heat of her friend's gaze. She didn't know why he looked that way. He's nice, she said. Try talking to him later. She then heard a knock on the door: it was the person from the front desk, telling Jing she had a call.

Jing leapt down the stairs, two steps at a time. It was her grandmother again, telling her that she'd discovered a newspaper clipping, in one of her mother's sketchbooks. It was about an event called the Special Midnight Watch, organised by the Singapore Science Centre and the Astronomical Society of Singapore. It was held last night, her grandmother said, at the grounds of the Omni-Theatre. And as she recited the rest of the week-old article, a memory came to Jing, of a garden party held at her home a month ago, a week before her mother's laryngectomy: Jing had been at one of the tables, with faces both new and familiar, while her mother was being pushed around in her wheelchair, up and down the length of the garden, engaged in what would be her final conversations with her friends. And it was only now, hearing her grandmother over the phone, when Jing knew that they would have to call the police: they would have to report her mother missing, she thought, as she recalled the moment she heard someone speak to her, cutting though the haze of idle chat around their table. Jing, she'd heard a man say that night: would your mother be interested in catching a comet?

Jing walked back up the stairs of the ryokan. She gave a knock on the door, before sliding it open.

Hey, said Isaac. He was lying on his futon, to the sounds of a radio softly playing from a Walkman. He seemed to be reading a book too. Wanna come in?

Jing took a look around the room. It was much larger than the one she shared with Mateo upstairs, with room enough for eight futons in total. He appeared to be alone.

She stepped inside and sat down beside him. I'm going to lie down too, if you don't mind, she said, and she did so without waiting for him to respond. She then asked him what he was reading, and he said he wasn't sure. It was a book he'd found in another corner of the room, belonging to one of the other occupants, he said, though Jing wasn't really listening to him at this point. She said that she was going to tell him something, something she'd never told anyone else before, not even Tori or Mateo, and Isaac put the book away, turning down the volume on the Walkman too.

Jing said that it was possible that her mother had treated her coldly and at a remove, from the very beginning of her existence, because she resented her. And she said that although she had long suspected this, the thought only came into full bloom when she had come home one day, only to find two things on her desk: the first was a note, an inscription from her mother that simply said, *RECREATE RANDEN*; underneath that note was Mateo's postcard, letting her know that he was in Japan, a postcard she was sure her mother must have read. And while preparing for her trip to Kyoto she wondered why it had to be *RANDEN*, and why it had to be her, too. And the more she thought about it the more she found herself bumping against the thought that perhaps her mother had viewed her, not as an extension of her self, but as a conclusion of her self—that from the moment Jing was conceived, the artist had already envisioned the end of her self, so to speak, her individuated self, her singular self. That her mother might have resented Jing for making her who she was, a living reminder that she couldn't have achieved her life's biggest accomplishments on her own. Or perhaps the resentment ran deeper, to a more existential place—perhaps her mother resented her because Jing represented the one thing she couldn't resist, couldn't shape, couldn't mould under the exactness of her will. She had arrived without permission, like a counter against everything her mother had ever enacted in her life, a link she could never break. And in this new cycle of self-repeating scenes, the new *RANDEN* would come to feature not Han Aw, but Jing Aw, as though the thing that had lived inside Han Aw the first time had finally emerged, fully formed, shedding the artist off like moulted skin. A symbol not of new life, but as the final image in what must have been a long, long, terribly long process of dying. And did he know, said Jing to Isaac, that with every scream she made over the past couple of days, she felt—felt nothing? She felt utterly empty, hollowed out. She could feel her whole body ringing, shaking, like an empty glass after a hard tap. And as she said this to Isaac she could feel tears, falling down the side of her face, the droplets falling into her hair, her ears. Oh, she said, oh my god, wiping her face with her hands. She stared at the wet on her palms, bewildered by the sight of her own tears, her own sadness. Oh my god, Jing said again—what's happening to me? And as she said this she felt Isaac pull her towards him, next to him, into his arms as he said it's okay, it's okay, you don't have to be afraid. You have me now.

11

On the day of her departure, Tori would wake up at half past noon and review the events of the night before, certain of everything that had happened to her. She would then open her closet to look at her leather suitcase, propped open at the bottom, wondering if it could still fit everything she now owned.

It could, Tori thought. It still could. She got up and made her way to the topmost floor, and slid open the door to Jing and Mateo's room.

Jing wasn't there. Mateo was still sleeping, his face looking ashen, almost grey. Standing at the doorway, she recalled the look he'd given her earlier that morning, horrified and then utterly relieved, at the sight of her face through the window of her taxi. Get in, she said, and he did, sopping wet, with mud and grass stuck all over his pants, not bothering to question how she had found him in the first place. Instead he told her everything that just happened at Kamo River, and she told him that she understood, she did, he was not alone. Many strange things have been happening in Kyoto, she said to him in the taxi, stories about strange incidents taking place all over the city. In that moment she recalled what Jing had said over dinner too, about still being caught in the middle of a story; she took a look at the rear-view mirror, and found the driver's half-moon eyes, twinkling back at her. Something strange is happening to Isaac too, said Tori, and as she helped

Mateo take off his socks and shoes in the genkan of the ryokan, he said: What do you mean, strange? What's going on with that guy? And she said she wasn't sure—she said she'd still have to find out.

Tori stepped inside the room, and slid the door shut behind her. She knelt beside him, and squeezed his arm. Hey, she said, Mateo.

He stirred, just barely. Hmm?

She asked if he was thinking of leaving the ryokan today, and he mumbled out a no, never. In that case, said Tori—I was thinking of making everyone dinner tonight. For us three, she said, and Isaac too. Okay?

Mateo managed to peel open an eye. You sure?

She nodded, and wiggled her nose. Perhaps you should go to the sento, she said, causing Mateo to laugh weakly. Bitch, he said, fine, before curling himself back to sleep.

It would be nearly one by the time Tori headed to the ground floor. She had put on a white sweater under a pair of overalls, cash stuffed into one of its pockets. She said good morning to her colleague behind the front desk, and asked if she'd seen her friends around, the Singaporeans. Her colleague said that they'd left in the morning, around two hours ago.

Tori paused. Together?

Her colleague nodded. They seemed close, she said.

Tori would leave the ryokan with an umbrella and a shopping trolley, walking quickly towards Nishiki Market. She'd make her way east, towards Karasuma-dori, before making a right at Nishikikoji-dori, where the okonomiyaki diner was. As it would most likely be her final meal at the diner, she decided to order her favourite item, the negiyaki, a pancake containing a mass of chopped Kujo scallions. After paying her bill, Tori made her way down the remainder of the street, towards one of the entrances to Nishiki Market. The shopping arcade was in full swing that afternoon, and she had to be careful with her shopping trolley, lest she run its wheels over somebody's feet. She was about to make her way towards a fruits and vege-tables store when she heard the market's public address system, crackling and whining to life.

Heads turned around her. She caught sight of several people just exiting the market, swivelling their heads back to see what was going on too. Tori would keep her gaze upwards, towards the glass ceiling, staring at the panels that shone in their alternating rows of reds and yellows and greens; in the corner of her vision she noted the looks on more passers-by, some nervous, all curious, about what might be broadcasted through the system.

A voice came on. *Hey, did you know?* it said. *Everyone is made out of the same stuff as stars.*

A few shopkeepers stepped outside. They were staring at the ceiling too, in search of where the loudspeakers might be. But Tori could only close her eyes as a second voice spoke.

I'm not brave enough, it said. *Don't sound so surprised.*

Tori heard chuckling, from all around her. Eh, said someone to her left— what is this?

The first voice spoke again. *When we die,* it said, *we go back to the sun.*

The sun? replied the second.

Yes, the sun, responded the first. *It'll take us, reshape us, spit us back out. And then we'll be remade anew.*

There was another sound now, over the loudspeakers: like a microphone being dropped.

The dog's coming along, said the second voice.

Tori jumped; one of the shopkeepers behind her had laughed. Dogs now! he said, loud enough for everyone in the vicinity to hear. Is this the radio?

Another shopkeeper shouted at him, told him not to worry. It's just a routine check, she said, disaster preparedness, that sorta thing. Must have played the wrong recording.

Tori opened her eyes. Her face was wet, her nose blocked. She wanted to turn around, get out; she found the exit and was about to head for it, before the public address system came to life again, but with a song this time. She knew this song. She had heard it last night, in the taxi, on the way to Mount Kurama. Tori turned back to the two shopkeepers, the ones who had been talking earlier. She went up to them and asked if they knew this song.

If the shopkeepers had been startled by the sight of tears and snot, streaked all over Tori's face, they did their best to not show it. It's Kyu Sakamoto, isn't it? one of them asked.

Sounds like him, said the other. Too bad he died the way he did.

Tori nodded; nothing surprised her anymore. She asked them how he died, and one of them said: Plane crash, wasn't it? Took off from Haneda and crashed into the mountains somewhere . . . Tori then spotted something else at that moment, further into the market—a clearing amidst the Saturday crowd, around a curious opening of light. She walked towards it, looking up at the ceiling again, watching the colourful interplay of the glass panels above. She made her way deeper into the market until she chanced upon something else entirely: a single white thread, dangling before her eyes.

She stopped. She was directly beneath the thread right now. Tori fixed her eyes on it, and followed the line of it upwards, so thin, so barely there, that the thread itself seemed to disappear under the light—a light that was pouring through a missing panel in the ceiling. Tori stared at this opening, unable to figure out what had happened to the panel, and where the thread was being dangled from—or how it could remain so still.

Tori cast a quick glance around her, up and down the rows of shops: nobody, no one, seemed to mind the presence of this random thread. And as the song by Kyu Sakamoto continued to play over the public address system, she turned back around, nearly running this time, back to the ryokan. She stepped through the entrance, took off her shoes; her colleague remarked on the lack of items in her trolley, before asking where she'd been all day. What did you mean? Tori asked, and her colleague pointed to the clock behind her. It was nearly five somehow. She then heard voices, familiar voices, inside the kitchen down the corridor: it was just her friends, Jing, Mateo and Isaac, boiling a pot of tea. They were talking about the past apparently, the people they loved in the past, all while waiting for her to return.

Tori found herself back at the diner, but with her friends this time, seated in a booth together. Tori helped with everyone's orders before stepping outside, saying she needed to drop by a nearby pharmacy. But instead of going anywhere she stood outside the diner, and stared down the road, down the way into the entrance of Nishiki Market. It was a quarter past six, and the evening had just begun to settle over the scene: there were still remnants of daylight wherever she looked, even as tinges of purple began to colour everything in sight. She wondered if something, anything, might begin again, just as the door behind her opened.

It was Isaac. Hello, he said.

She smiled at him. She then pointed to the kerb. Shall we sit?

He nodded. They sat and stared, at the diners on the other side of the road. I don't think Mateo likes me, he said, and Tori asked him why. I dunno, he said; it's just the way he looks at me, I guess. Tori said that might be her fault actually, and she told him that thing she'd said to Mateo last night, about something strange that might be happening to him. Oh, said Isaac, with a faraway look in his eyes. No wonder.

Tori asked if he was mad. Nah, he said. Not at you. He then looked at her. Something's happening to you too, isn't it, he said, and she said yes. Yes, actually. How did you know?

Isaac appeared to think about it. Because you're still here, he said.

Tori nodded. She then asked him what made him say that. She asked if there was something he knew that she didn't, and she braced herself, ready to hear any number of possible things.

On the day we met, Isaac said—you still remember, yah? You said you had a bad dream.

Tori nodded again. Isaac smiled.

I had a bad dream too, he said. Can I tell you about it?

Tori took another look at him. The sun was in his face now, just across his eyes. She said sure.

I was on an overnight coach, said Isaac, from Osaka to Kyoto. I fell asleep and then woke up a few hours later, because I felt the bus had come to a stop. But there was no one on the bus when he opened his eyes. And the coach was not at Kyoto Station, but at the side of a highway, parked at what looked like a rest stop. When Isaac got off the coach he found that although it was dark, it was bright as well, caused by an object in the sky. Not the moon, he thought, but something else, like a giant orb, blue-green to the point of silver.

He told Tori about how he had walked towards the rest stop, in this dream, only to find that the glass entrances were smashed. Other windows too. He wandered around the cafeteria, in the semi-darkness; he wondered why everything was in such a mess, all of the tables and chairs in disarray, its shelves half-empty and ruined. He heard scurrying in a corner, and found a group of three dashing out of the building, fleeing into one of the cars in the parking lot. In the dream he watched the car screech out of sight and join the highway, amongst a multitude of other speeding vehicles. He then heard another noise, a lot nearer this time, and while Isaac hid he saw a woman smash open the lock to a refrigerator behind one of the food stalls. She opened a duffel bag, stuffing everything she could inside it, before running away as well.

Isaac rose. He looked around. He had a feeling that something was terribly wrong. The woman had left behind some fruits in the refrigerator, and he took an apple, followed by a second, just for good measure; he was about to take a third when he heard yet another noise, and jerked. There, at a corner of the cafeteria, sat what looked like the driver of his coach, lounging on a chair, watching the news on a television set. He recognised him for his uniform, and went up to him, though it wasn't till he stood by its side that he found the driver was not a man, but a macaque, dressed in a driver's uniform. All kinds of colours, flashing from the TV set, danced across the front of the animal's frame.

Take a seat, said the macaque, as it eyed the apples in Isaac's hands. Is that other one for me? it asked, and all he could do in his dream was nod, and hand one of them to it. Isaac then brought a chair over and sat next to the animal, the two now facing the TV, munching on their apples.

The announcement came at midnight, said the macaque; I heard it on the coach, over the radio. It then pointed at the television. Comet's coming for Earth.

At first he didn't understand. There on the screen was a live telecast of the night sky, lit up by the same object in the sky he saw outside, brighter than the moon itself. And then there was a cut to an infographic, depicting the solar system: between the moon and the planet Mars was a blue oval with a flashing label, causing the macaque to let out a hoot.

Comet Hyakutake, recited the animal. Everyone's panicking, of course.

Isaac went numb. He watched a red arrow on the TV trace the comet's collision course towards Earth, simulating various disaster scenarios should it hit land or water. In the dream he wondered when he heard about the comet before, and the macaque, reading his mind, said that the comet had always been reported to be passing by Earth. But the truth is a scarier thing. It's more likely that someone knew, it said: someone had always known about the reality of what was going to happen. They just neglected to inform the rest of the party.

Isaac put his hands behind his head. He didn't know what to think, what to feel. He wanted to cry, but he couldn't; he was too much in shock. Shit, he said. Shit. The macaque then turned to him, and held up the core of its apple, just as the realisation continued to wash over him.

Thank you, Isaac, said the macaque; the universe is indebted to you. It then leapt from its chair, towards one of the broken windows nearby. Shall we head back to the coach? it said to him, and Isaac again did not understand. He asked the macaque where it wanted to go, and the macaque coolly looked back at him, replying:

Out.

Isaac rose from his chair. Out where? he asked, and the macaque continued to leer at him.

Out of here, it said. To where you are needed more—more important than you can imagine. Where you can be of use! it exclaimed. You would like that, would you not?

Isaac shook his head; he didn't know what to say, in this part of the dream. He was truly speechless now. He then watched the macaque leap through the smashed window, out into the silver cast over the parking lot. He watched it dash towards the coach, and Isaac said, Wait! Wait! He ran out of the cafeteria, shouting: What if—what if I don't follow you! And the macaque screeched back at him from the vehicle, through the still-open door—Choose! it said. Choose another life! Or I'll be taking everything you own with me! And Isaac tossed the half-eaten apple aside and ran even more, towards the silver-lit vehicle, just as its headlights flickered on.

He managed to board the coach, at the end of this dream that he had. When he woke he found himself in the vehicle again, empty once more— but the bus was parked at the front of Kyoto Station this time. Isaac made sure he had everything in his backpack before disembarking. He checked the time.

Wait, said Tori. Can I guess?

Isaac nodded.

5.46, said Tori.

Isaac nodded again. And then I found you.

Tori paused. I asked you if you saw anything out of the ordinary.

Isaac nodded again. The snow monkey, he said, which caused Tori to chuckle. From the dream? she asked, and he said yes, it was. But the monkey said it wasn't a dream, but a memory; it said it happened to me, for real. And you believe it? Tori asked, and Isaac said yah, I have to. Why? asked Tori, and he pointed upwards, towards the sky, still overcast but clearing. Evening was upon them, now.

There's a comet, said Isaac. Same comet that was coming for me, three weeks ago. But here, he said, it's only coming now. Over here, in this version of the world—it's just passing by.

Tori didn't know what Isaac was saying, not at first. And then she felt it, the confluence, the common understanding. She suddenly recalled a story by Akutagawa, "The Spider's Thread", which she'd read years ago, the week after she turned fourteen: in it, Buddha dangles a thread into hell, offering its cursed souls a way out.

Here, said Tori. We're here.

Night descended. There was music on the street, all of a sudden. Tori and Isaac turned towards the entrance of Nishiki Market. Tori told Isaac to head back in, and he rose to his feet.

Is that for you?

She got up as well. I think so, she said.

Isaac looked down, at the hand he'd balled into a fist. He sounded hurt when he asked her: Do you have to go?

No.

His hand shook. Do you know where you're going?

Tori put her hand over his fist, to stop the shaking. I don't, she said. Did you?

He shook his head. I didn't.

There you go, said Tori, still holding on to her friend's hand. And you know, honestly—I cannot wait.

He looked up at her; he seemed stung, at first, before he nodded at her, and went back inside. As he did Tori wondered if she could have stopped him, bought them more time with one another, by telling him in return what had happened to her the night before. She could have told him about how the city had peeled away, all of its details hurtling past, as she sat in that taxi heading towards Mount Kurama. She could have told him about how she had listened to Emi speak over the radio, and how her taxi had stopped at the foot of the temple, and how the driver had told her to go, all the way up the mountain, just past the gate. She could have told Isaac how she had climbed its stone steps, up to the monorail station, where the slanted funicular carriage was already waiting for her, aglow on the platform on the second storey, ready to take her straight to the temple. When she had stepped inside she looked up towards the operator, and had seen that it was a giant fish, dressed in the uniform that a train operator would typically wear. The fish stood before a dashboard of buttons and levers, greeting her as she ascended the steps of the car.

Kurama-dera?

She nodded. She took the topmost seat.

What kind of fish are you? she asked.

The operator stared at her, unfazed. Isn't it obvious? it said. I am a tuna.

With its left fin the operator then pressed a button, securing both the top and bottom doors shut. Tori kept her gaze solely on the operator as the carriage began to move, shuddering as it inched its way up the tracks along the mountain. What kind of human are you? the tuna asked Tori in return, and Tori said, I'm a—I'm a girl.

The operator blinked, or rather, it would have blinked, if it had eyelids. It cocked its head to the side.

What kind of girl?

Tori cleared her throat. The operator looked rather imperious, the way it glared at her.

I'm the Luckiest Girl in the World, she said.

Indeed you are, said the operator. It raised a fin, and declared: The Luckiest Girl in the World Goes Wherever Her Heart Commands.

Tori looked out of the funicular. She could have told Isaac about how the carriage had crawled up the tracks like a submarine, casting its beams across the depths of the mountainside. And when she glanced behind her she gasped, at the sight of a group of people, crowding out the entire carriage. They sat and stood, not paying any attention to her, all staring at the surrounding forest; she got up, and went back down the steps, to the bottom of the carriage where the crowd seemed to part, revealing at first a dog and then its owner, both of them staring out the bottommost window. She could have told Isaac this: how the fur of the Labrador shone silver, as well as the hair on the top of its owner's head; silver did they look when she joined them at their side, by the window, gazing out at the scenery, at the sole image of a railway track receding down the mountainside, sliding out of reach of the carriage's light. And then her vision blurred, as tears filled her eyes, as she reached out to touch Hideo's pale, impassive face.

I'm sorry, she said. I'm so, so sorry. Tell me how I can stop grieving over you, Hideo. But Hideo didn't respond; Hideo continued to stare out the window. Tori then climbed the steps of the carriage once more, telling the operator to stop.

Stop? said the tuna. She nodded.

Stop, she said again. And then head back down.

Where?

Where I was, she said. At the bottom of the mountain.

The operator stared at her, silent for a few seconds. There is only one stop for you, it said.

Just one?

The operator didn't reply. Tori looked down at the dashboard. You have no say? she asked. You can't bring us back down?

Why would we ever do that? asked the operator.

Tori wanted to scream. Because I'm not done, she said. I still have things to do. Things to say, to talk about.

Like what? asked the operator.

She stared at it, and said: I need to pack.

The operator glared at her, silent. It then reached down with its fin and held up a walkie-talkie, just below its mouth. For ten seconds she heard nothing but static in an otherwise wordless conversation. The operator then placed the walkie-talkie back in its place.

The universe concurs, it said; it has acceded to your request.

It—it has?

Yes, said the operator. We will stop, and head back down the mountain.

The carriage ground to a halt, once the operator had cranked a lever. Every person in the carriage swayed, and then righted themselves, all of their motions seemingly in sync. The operator then pressed another button, and released the lever from its place. The carriage moved again, but in reverse this time, back down Mount Kurama.

The operator cocked its head towards Tori. The Luckiest Girl in the World indeed, it said.

Tori walked down the length of the shopping arcade. The song had started another time over the public announcement system, as though it'd been on a loop. And there it was, sure enough: her single white thread, lowered through a hole in the ceiling.

She still had so many questions, she thought. But it was impossible to fully understand the big picture: it was possible that she might never fully understand anything about this life, and how it worked. She thought about Mateo, and Isaac—and what about Jing? Why was she spared, or—or was she not? Again, again: too many questions, all of them coming to her, too late.

She's already here.

If anybody could see her face that evening—if anybody had to describe how Tori had looked that evening—they would say that she had been smiling, widely, wider than she had ever smiled before, just as the Kyu Sakamoto song had reached its final note; even as she reached a hand out, towards that single line.

12

Jing didn't know what to say to Mateo, not at first. It was just the two of them in the diner, while Tori and Isaac spoke outside.

Mateo had his eyes fixed on the corner of the table where Tori had sat. He saw the coins she'd left behind, caught in the condensation that pooled at the bottom of her glass. He then asked Jing how her day was.

Why? she asked. Are you asking about *RANDEN*?

He nodded. He asked what she was going to do next, now that the film was done. He asked what her mother might think of it.

A thing Jing realised was how much easier it became, each time one told a story. One would always find a way to flatten the story, shorten the story, make it more concise; each new telling became not so much a revision but a reduction of the story, a compression, until all that was left was a single phrase, a single feeling. The heart of the matter.

A friend came for her last night, she said. They haven't returned since.

Mateo's face seemed to crumple. His hand shuddered as he took off his glasses, and set them on the table. Do you know this friend? he asked, and Jing said yes. She had an inkling. Jing then asked Mateo if he wanted to tell her about what had happened last night, and he shook his head. Why not? she asked. Because I'm not Tori? Mateo shook his head again. She then asked if it was because it wasn't Teiji Furuhashi that they had met last night, and Mateo looked at her, confused. Why would you think that? he said. It's him, said Mateo, it's Teiji. And Jing said, Are you sure? Are you certain, Mateo? The actual artist had passed away, five months ago, said Jing, and he told her no, no. That can't be true. It was him, said Mateo. It was.

Jing watched him stare, once again, at the coins Tori had left behind on the table. He grabbed his drink and drained it, in a single gulp. He put a hand over his eyes.

Tell me everything else you know.

The three went back to the ryokan. I'm sure she's there, said Mateo. Where else can she be?

It was past nine at that point; the front desk was empty. But there was an old woman seated at the bottom of the staircase, whom Jing recognised as one of the cleaners at the ryokan.

Kocchi, said the woman, waving at the three of them. She then headed up the stairs.

Mateo had earlier insisted that they wait for Tori to return, until a waitress at the diner had asked if they still needed the table. And now the three were on the third floor of the ryokan, standing in the doorway to Isaac's room. Over his futon was an old leather suitcase with a Post-it stuck on the handle.

Mateo closed his eyes. Mierda, he said, turning away. Jing could only watch as Isaac went and picked up the Post-it.

What does it say? she asked.

Isaac held it up, for her to see. *Thank you for finding me*, it said. *Please take me home.*

———

Isaac had a dream that night: he was running across the parking lot of the rest stop, running after the bus. And then a silver light flooded and overwhelmed his vision, before he woke up, startled, caught in a mad rush of relief. He was happy to find that he was still here, in the ryokan, and not elsewhere.

He went downstairs, barefooted, to get a cup of water. He found Jing in the vestibule, seated on the small bench, keeping an eye on the main entrance. She had a mug of tea in her hands, which she then raised to him, almost as a toast.

Isaac sat beside her, their arms touching one another.

Mateo went to the nearby Lawson, she explained.

Is it?

She nodded. I just need him to come back. And then I'll be able to sleep.

Isaac reached over, and took her mug of tea; he sipped from it, and asked if she had her things packed.

I have, she said. Nearly. She then turned towards him, just as he set the mug of tea down. Please find me, she said. When you come back.

Can.

Whenever that happens.

He nodded. Can, he said again. Jing then placed her hand behind his ear, and ran her fingers through his hair. Isaac closed his eyes, and pressed his forehead against hers, wetting his lips, touching hers.

Both of them then turned.

Something bright was shining through the entrance of the ryokan. It was a brilliant white light, coming down the road outside. Jing and Isaac slid the entrance open, and squinted to find a taxi, driving towards them. They were barely able to spot her, Tori, seated upright in the backseat.

The taxi drove past their ryokan, further down the road, before abruptly braking. The door to the driver's seat popped open.

Isaac left the ryokan, still barefoot, telling Jing to stay inside. She remained by the entrance while he crept towards the vehicle, hoping to see who the driver might be. But it was just a man, he saw, rushing to the side of the street. The driver unbuckled his pants, and took a leak over a bed of flowers.

Tori! said Isaac, keeping to a whisper. Tori! But his friend didn't seem to notice, no matter what Isaac did to distract her. Nothing outside the taxi seemed to be any more of Tori's concern.

The driver shuddered, and buckled up his pants. He then turned around, towards Isaac, and gave him a wide smile. His eyes were perfectly semi-circular, Isaac thought, like two wedges of an orange. You have to excuse me, said the driver, but we really have to get going. It's a very busy night, all across the country.

Isaac asked what his name was, and the driver flashed a smile in his direction. Sakamoto, he said—Kyu Sakamoto. Isaac then asked where his taxi was headed, and Kyu turned back to him, saying he wasn't so sure. It's not up to me, sir, but the passenger, he said—and I have a feeling we might be travelling for a while. Kyu then tipped his hat towards him and slid back into the driver's seat, closing the door shut.

Isaac backed away from the car. Nothing could stop her, he realised; there was no stopping the leaving. And Isaac glanced at Tori, knowing that this was it, what they were witnessing—the inevitable. He went up to the window of the backseat, and pounded his fist on the glass, just as the taxi's engine returned to life. Take care, he said—take care, Tori. Thank you for being my friend. He then pressed his hand against the windowpane, in one final attempt, and felt his grip slip away from the glass.

The car drove into the distance, the illumination making one final turn into another street. He could almost hear himself panting, taking as many deep breaths as he could, as darkness quickly returned to the street.

PART II

HORVALLA

Isla Cristina, 2004

hola hola they shouted
how we laughed
looking up
how we laughed
till we cried
how we laughed

—Ho Poh Fun, "Thoughtscapes Singapore"

13

The Horvallan. Jing Aw. Flame of the Forest, Singapore, 2005.

The garden, 1996

This is a story about love.

But love is also just a story.

There comes a time, I suppose, when the truth becomes more than the truth: it becomes altered, transfigured, into an aspect of one's self. I say this, because at some point I began to wonder if I had made you up, after all. I wonder if we had ever met in the first place.

My mother was about to have a major procedure, at the time of our first encounter. She was due to have her larynx removed, an operation that would leave her unable to speak. And so, in true style, she asked her friends to come down to our house, to attend one final party at our garden. We substituted plates for ashtrays, and kept my grandparents inside their room; I supplied everyone with sotong fishballs from Old Chang Kee, and bottles of moscato from Carrefour. Joan Jett played, alongside the Ramones, Patti Smith, Haruomi Hosono and Lata Mangeshkar, while we kept the gate open, undiscriminating to whoever came in that night. Whoever wandered in would be welcome to join us.

As always, I am struggling to remember you from that night, even now as I attempt to write about you. You had a white shirt on, perhaps, with hair shaved down to a tight crew cut; you had large hands too, with long and knobbly fingers. You introduced yourself, and said you were a writer from Johor Bahru, a creator of science fiction. You were fond of stargazing, you said, and asked if we had read the papers that morning. You asked if we had heard about the comet, Comet Hyakutake—one that we wouldn't be able to see again in another 70,000 years.

You said my name then, in a moment when I had been distracted by my mother, by the sight of her being pushed around in her wheelchair. You asked if she might be interested, in catching the comet with you in March. And admittedly I can't remember what I had said to you in response; I can only remember thinking, just then, if my mother would still be around at that time.

My mother was reported missing on the 23rd of March, 1996.

I was in Kyoto. My grandfather had gone down for a glass of water the night before, only to find that she was gone. My grandmother searched through my mother's belongings, and chanced upon a newspaper clipping about the Special Midnight Watch, held at the Singapore Science Centre. We told everything we knew to the police.

The police came back to us two weeks later. They said that none of the security footage at the Science Centre had shown your or my mother's faces that night; they'd also spoken to guests of the garden party, who couldn't remember if you were there or not. For months I would see your face, attempt multiple recreations of your face, wondering if you were real, or if I needed you to be real. Even now it was hard to tell the difference.

And so imagine my surprise when I saw you, two years later, standing by the fence that ran around my home. I was on the second floor, cradling my newborn in my arms, trying to show him the moon. But you were lingering by the perimeter of my house, radiating an unnatural light all on your own. As soon as I spotted you, you saw me and waved, in an attempt to catch my attention—to confirm that it was you, indeed, standing at the edge of my home. And I could not help myself: I laid Yong-he back down into his crib, and treaded back to the window; I returned to my view of the fence that ran around the garden, and raised my hand in reply.

The playground, 1998

"A baby. Is it yours?"

I nodded. "Yes."

"Congratulations." You then paused for a while, unsure of what to say next. "Who's the father?"

"My husband."

You let out a laugh. "Who's the husband?"

I looked behind me. I took a few steps forward. I went as far as I could to the edge of the garden, and held aside the frond of a fern. "I thought you were gone."

"Gone?"

"Two years ago," I said. "With my mother."

"Right." You seemed unfazed, even amused, by my mother's missing status. "Well, I'm here now, if anything," was what you said. You then put your hand through the fence. "You can touch me, if you want, to see if I'm real."

I kept quiet. I stared at your hand, as large as I remembered it. I asked if you would still be around the following night, and you nodded, smiling. I cocked my head towards the main road.

"There's a playground, behind the gas station. The one across the street," I said. "You know it?"

You said that you did. "Same time tomorrow?"

I took a step back towards my house. "We'll talk."

We met at the foot of the slide. I crossed the street and walked towards the gas station, a Caltex, the largest one I know: it glows with a Ruscha-esque quality against the twilight, and then something more like Edward Hopper, deeper in the night. Beside it lay a field of grass that sloped down towards the playground; I was about halfway down the footpath when I saw you, waiting for me, signalling at me to hurry.

It was drizzling. You asked if we might sit under the slide, in case the rain got any worse. The sand was soft, and a little damp beneath the slide, while the perfume of the wet grass became rich and potent, rolling its way down the field towards us like a fog. And I could still see you, even in the dark, enough to confirm your place next to mine. When you asked if I still worked at the newspaper, and I said yes, our voices sounded muffled and yet close, too close to one another. I asked if you were still writing fiction, and you said no.

"No?"

You shook your head. "I haven't written anything new in years," you said. "But I have an idea that's been brewing for a while."

You said you were in town to work on a story. But it wasn't a novel you were hoping to create, per se, and it wasn't strictly fiction you were writing as well. I asked if this story might be about Singapore, and you said yes, I was right. It would be. But the story would also be about Johor Bahru, in the way every story of yours had always been about Johor Bahru. Later, when you said you had stopped publishing as well, I asked you why, and you said it was possible to circulate stories via other means. It was possible, you said, for stories to live not in text, but in memory; not in sentences, but in the images we leave behind with language. And then I wondered, in that instance, if that was how you had become friends with Han Aw: I imagined how a work of yours might land in her lap, in whatever form it took; it would have to go through an untold number of hands, up and down the length of Malaysia, before finally hitching a ride over the Causeway. And as the rain grew heavier I entreated you, finally, to tell me about my mother. And you kept quiet, quiet beneath the sound of the hard rain falling over us, over the playground; you said you didn't know what to say, and I told you that you had to find the words. Find them, I said, or we would never be free of one another. And you looked at me, almost pitifully, as you said—"Are you sure?"

"Of what?"

"Of wanting to be free of me."

I stared at you, incredulous. "Just tell me," I said. "What happened?"

Your eyes wide and tense now, hardly blinking. "She was there," you finally said. "Until she wasn't."

A painful pause ensued; we broke eye contact, and didn't manage to speak for a while. Under the cover of darkness another thought then came to me, irrational, fearful and totally contrarian to what I'd just said: I became afraid that I might lose you again, the only tangible link left to my mother; if you remained quiet any longer you might return to being a figment of my imagination once more. But then, like the twist of a knife, you added:

"I couldn't even find her wheelchair."

That night you shared with me the beginnings of a story you once shared with my mother. It was a story set in the far future, towards the end of the next millennium—but the larger story might be set across several futures, each one further into the beyond than the next; perhaps the story you wanted to tell might be situated across multiple millennia, spanning thousands and thousands of years, you said, the exact width and breadth of which remain unknown to you for now.

But your story would begin in 2989AD, at a hotel in Johor Bahru, Malaysia. You pictured a bar, populated by aliens, set at the topmost floor of the hotel.

Lush, here, is the dominant mood, as the bar overlooks the surrounding township of Iskandar. Only a dozen folk are present in this scene, chit-chatting amongst themselves: a seemingly random assembly of various sentient species, in all shapes and hues and sizes. This will be a common enough sight in any establishment in 2989AD, and no one would think to question it. In reality, however, the dozen or so present are there to attend an invite-only, top-secret meeting: armed bodyguards patrol every lobby of the hotel, while body scanners have been installed from the first to the thirty-fifth floors. Extraordinary measures have been put in place to prevent the wrong person stepping out of the wrong lift, out onto the wrong floor. This is a meeting in which the fate of not just humanity, but of all intergalactic life would be determined. It would be the beginning, you said, of a great movement of peoples, right here in this bar.

Central to this story is our heroine, you said, a Malaysian female, designated representative of all of Homo sapiens. You told me she had a certain resemblance to my mother, even though, from certain angles, you said our heroine looked rather more like me. She sits herself at a corner of the bar, with her tablet open and her blazer on. Our heroine orders herself a glass of mezcal, twenty minutes before the meeting officially begins, growing ever more curious about the presence of another human being. She takes a sip, and wonders if she is not the sole Homo sapiens representative, after all.

Our heroine thus approaches him, to better acquaint herself with this other human: a handsome but not intimidating male, somewhere between his early to mid-thirties. His hair is shaved down to a buzz cut, and his drink of choice is a frozen margarita, which he raises with a smile to our heroine. The diplomat manages to return the gesture, startled nonetheless; she has the nagging suspicion that he is oddly familiar to her somehow, that she might have interacted with him sometime in the past. But when? she asks herself—and where?

Our characters introduce themselves to one another. Quickly, you said, the man dispossesses the diplomat of her earlier assumptions. *I am not Homo sapiens,* he says to her—*however much I might look the part.* The man says he is a member of an entirely separate species, a species of immortal beings, of which he claims to be its last remaining member. And our heroine—up to date with every edition of the charter that catalogues every alien resettled on Earth—looks incredulously around the bar, refusing to hear what she has just been told. For one of the few comforts she holds onto is the fact that all life, surely, must come to an end. Death comes for us all. It is the only reason anybody can ever come to an agreement on anything, and why any party would demand a seat at the table. It is also why so many alien populations have fled to Earth, her planet, for a better shot at survival. To claim to be immortal while looking so much like a human, like a fellow mortal being, is a claim that our heroine cannot accept. *So what are you,* she asks, *if not human?*

I am a Horvallan, replies her companion. *The Horvallan.*

14

So, said Frankie. We got a problem.

They were in the garden, walking towards the tabebuia tree—the corner of the garden farthest from the house. Isaac could sense Jing's grandfather looking at them from the living room, pretending not to pay them any attention. Isaac asked if it had to do with why *8 Days* had cancelled their shoot that afternoon, and Frankie said yes, adjusting the folder he had tucked underneath an arm.

They're replacing you with Sherry, he said.

Sherry?

Frankie clapped Isaac on the shoulder. A win for her is still a win for you, he said. Agree?

Isaac nodded; he could see his point. Frankie was Sherry's manager too, had in fact been both of their managers from the very start. That, and Sherry hasn't appeared on the cover of *8 Days* or *i-Weekly* in ages. So what's the problem? he asked, eyeing the folder that was now in Frankie's hand.

He took out a photo, and handed it to Isaac. It's not super clear, but I think it's clear enough, he said. You see what's happening?

Isaac looked. The photo was small, pixellated; it must have been taken with the camera on someone's Nokia, he thought. Still, it's him, clearly him, fresh out of the gym and seated behind a sushi counter, slipping a tea mug into his shoe bag. The sight made him recoil, as though it were someone else, not him, doing the stealing in that restaurant. I got find it a bit weird lah, to be honest with you—it's just a small cup! said Frankie. Nothing you can't afford.

A cloud drifted overhead, causing the sunlight in the garden to dim. Anyway, continued Frankie—we received that in an MMS three weeks ago. Isaac watched his manager reach into the folder again, taking out two more photos. We got these last week, he said, before taking out a fourth item: a printout, this time, of what looked like security camera footage. It's Isaac, sure enough, walking around the desks at the SAFRA Radio office. That was yesterday, said his manager, which was the last straw for us, I guess.

Isaac bit on the tip of his thumb. He didn't want to think about who "us" had consisted of, bringing to mind the faces of various Mediacorp executives. He asked Frankie what he should do. Good question, said Frankie, as he placed the documents back into his folder. Just lay low, stay home. Do nothing. Be glad the drama is finally done. His manager then gave what he'd assumed was a smile of reassurance. We'll gao dim everything on our end, okay? You're not the only actor with a weird habit, he said.

Isaac nearly laughed. Weird habit indeed, like wearing clothes in nothing but bright colours, or having tea with an imaginary friend. He asked Frankie how long he should be lying low for, and Frankie said it would be best to wait until the drama airs. But only Sherry will be talking to the media, not you. Got it?

Got it.

Great, said Frankie, though he didn't look very relieved. You still got the Rolex commercial in Japan, so that's good.

Isaac bit on his thumb again. It was the first week of May 2004; they still had a month and a half till he was due to fly. Anything could happen, like a photo being leaked to the press instead. Frankie asked if Isaac was still planning to go to Spain after the gig in Japan, and he said yah, for sure. I have to. My friends are getting married, he said.

Frankie nodded; he looked distracted this time, making mental calculations in his head. Staying out of Singapore is good, he said. Take it as a long,

long break. His manager then turned, back to the house behind them. Does your wife know?

No.

Her grandfather?

Isaac scoffed; they haven't had the most cordial relationship, ever since Jing's grandmother had passed away. No idea.

Frankie waved the folder. You sure? he said. Now got all kinds of ways to record you, you know. He then asked where his son was, and Isaac said that Yong-he was still at the kindergarten.

Healthy?

Very healthy. Not a scratch or bruise on him, he said. Frankie then asked who usually picked the kid up, and Isaac jutted his chin towards the living room. His Ah Pa, he said.

Frankie narrowed his eyes. Maybe you pick him up today. Have people take nice pics of you instead. He paused. Can I ask one more thing?

Isaac waved his hand. Shoot.

Frankie looked like he already knew the answer, even before he had to ask. Were you the one? he said. Who stole Sherry's scarf on set? And Isaac didn't have to look at Frankie to know that now, all they had was the truth between one another. Yah, said Isaac. I stole it.

Frankie laughed, and shook his head. Siao, man, he said. That's another thing I'm never telling Sherry. He then patted Isaac's shoulder, and told him to take care. You know, arh, Isaac—I've liked you from the very start, he said. I consider myself very lucky to be your manager. Sometimes, right, when I look at you, I just think, like, wah, Huang Jialiang . . . Too good to be true. Frankie then walked back to his car, parked outside the main gate. Bye, uncle! he said, raising his hand at Jing's grandfather.

The old man nodded, before turning his gaze back to Isaac. The actor made sure to don his usual smile before heading back into the house, just as the sun re-emerged over the garden.

*　　*　　*

The assistant director of the Rolex commercial would spend a minute or two by himself, observing the passage of clouds across the sky every morning. Is he looking for rain? Isaac finally asked the interpreter, who doubled as his personal assistant on set. She nodded.

He's got nothing to worry lah, he said. It's been so sunny, really.

The interpreter shrugged, adjusting the rim of her baseball cap. She had a terse manner about her, which he secretly appreciated. It rains plenty in June, she said. Anything can happen, Mr Neo.

The shoot first took place at a seaside hotel, in Kamakura, before the cast and crew relocated to the prefecture of Fukui. Apart from the one morning they filmed at a stable, they spent most of their time beside anonymous fields of rice, with only two buildings standing in the distance, framed by green hills even further back into the horizon. Once in a while a car or a lorry would drive through the set with the windows rolled down, the driver's eyes wide open at the presence of cameras, cranes, light fixtures and other filming equipment amongst the farmland.

It was the final day of shooting. Isaac's task was to cycle towards a large automatic fan while several cameramen moved in tandem with him, trained on his body and the overly polished watch on his wrist. Once they were done they would celebrate with dinner, at a restaurant near their motel, followed by drinks along the river, to see if they observed any fireflies too. Isaac was securing the saddle on his bicycle when he caught the interpreter running towards him, his phone in her hand.

It's your wife. Do I pick up, or—oh, never mind. It stopped ringing, she said. I am so sorry, Mr Neo. The interpreter then turned back to him a few seconds later.

You have a message now, she said. Do I read it?

Isaac nodded.

Your wife says she just arrived at Isla Cristina: the hotel is nice, and so is the beach. She also hopes Japan isn't weird . . . The interpreter looked up at him, no doubt wondering why his wife would say such a thing. Shall I send a reply?

Isaac nodded again. Tell her that's nice, he said. I'll be there soon.

The interpreter blinked, before typing away on his Nokia. Sent, she said, pocketing his phone. She asked if there might be anything more from him, expecting to run back to her place behind the cameras. But Isaac did have a request, after all.

It's a separate matter, he said. I'll talk about it over dinner.

The interpreter's instructions were plain and easy to follow.

Isaac boarded a bullet train at Fukui Station, scheduled to arrive at Osaka two hours later. An hour and a half later, the train slid into Kyoto Station, causing Isaac to sit up in his chair and look around. He kept his eye peeled on the platform, unable to say, even to himself, what it was he was hoping to see. Isaac found himself unable to relax until the doors had finally closed again, and watched the platform slide past him. Everything returned to a reassuring blur as the train pulled away.

His last day in Kyoto had been a strange one. Jing had left after breakfast, to catch her flight back to Singapore, while Mateo was still in their room, no doubt contemplating when he ought to return to Spain. Isaac lay in his room one floor below Mateo, still staring at the suitcase that Tori had left behind, while two other guests chatted to one another in German.

The plan was to take the suitcase up to Mateo's room, for safekeeping, before delivering it back to Tori's parents. It was how Jing and Mateo had interpreted her Post-it: the guys would check out on Monday morning and take the train to Nishinomiya, to the address that Mateo still had. They'd leave the suitcase on the front steps, on a day they hoped her parents would be out at work.

But Isaac had other plans. He took it downstairs, where he found Tori's boss at the lounge, listlessly gazing at the register. Isaac passed the suitcase to him: he got him to hold on to it, and tuck it out of sight. He said he'd come back for it later, and Tori's boss merely nodded and acquiesced, and didn't a question a thing.

Isaac went up to the fourth floor. He stepped inside Mateo's room. He told Mateo he couldn't find her suitcase.

Mateo looked at him, frozen in the act of folding a pair of jeans. What are you saying?

Isaac didn't flinch; he kept his voice level. I dunno how, he said. But it's gone.

Panic flickered in Mateo's eyes. It's gone? he said. That too? And Isaac said yah, nodding along. It's nowhere.

Mateo looked away, and spoke nothing of it again. He resumed folding the pair of jeans. He then went downstairs, picked up the phone at the front desk and booked a seat on a flight back to Madrid. An hour later he left the city of Kyoto for good.

Isaac alighted at Kurakuen-guchi Station, after making a few transfers at Nishinomiya. He looked at the rough map the interpreter had drawn for him, and crossed the main intersection, walking down a narrow incline within a matter of minutes. He was on an unmarked road, but a familiar one nonetheless, flanked by tall houses on either side; not a single car or person passed him by as he downed a bottle of water, staring down the remaining length of road ahead of him.

Everything was just as he had remembered it, he told himself. Nothing seemed to have changed at all.

At some point the road plateaued, and the same small park revealed itself to him, bordered by a neatly trimmed hedge and a row of cherry trees. He recognised the playground too, installed in the very centre of the park. Isaac recalled the exact placement of the tables, at the Yamamotos' party eight years ago, and the bowls of sliced fruit that were laid about for eating. He could still recall the smell of the macaque's fur as they hugged one another, with the knowledge that had finally dawned on him that day: the comet, the coach, the crossing-over.

Isaac stood in front of the Yamamoto residence. A concrete wall ran around the property, with well-tended bushes along the perimeter. He pressed the doorbell, and waited; he heard a familiar bark, followed by the unlocking of a door. A middle-aged man with centre-parted hair slowly emerged from the house, while Asimov rushed out barking, repeatedly.

Neo-san, said the man. Isaac.

He nodded.

Shigeru unlatched the front gate, and extended his hand. The man was still staring at him, shaken, his voice laced with awe and confusion.

You just left, what—eight years ago, yes? It was eight?

Isaac took the man's hand. He felt a sudden, intense emotion collect behind his eyes. He had half expected the man to forget about him. He expected Shigeru to forget his name at the very least.

I'm really sorry, said Isaac. There was a place I really needed to go to.

A glimmer of understanding shone in Shigeru's eyes. What's the saying? he said. "Time waits for no man" . . . ? He chuckled. It is good to see you again, said Shigeru, before finally looking down at the worn leather suitcase, held in Isaac's other hand.

Oh my, he said. Oh, Neo-san . . . You found her after all.

The two men walked up the stairs, up to the very top of the house. Tori's old bedroom, used till the day she had left for university, occupied what had originally intended to be the attic. I remember she didn't want to take anything with her, barely anything, said Shigeru . . . It was bizarre to me, Isaac. Hinata practically forced Tori to take one of her suitcases, at the very least, and made sure to cram it with as many things as possible . . .

Shigeru's wife was attending a conference in Tokyo, it turned out. He then said he was glad, in a way, that she wouldn't be here to see this. I don't think she'd be able to take it, he said, though I'm sure, Isaac, she'd be glad to see you again.

They entered the attic. Tori's bedroom seemed to reclaim its original purpose, he thought: there were boxes now, placed on top of furniture Tori had once used in her youth.

It's hard to let things go, said Shigeru, as he looked at Isaac. He seemed to be holding a thought in his gaze, before he finally pointed at the suitcase. Could you . . . ?

Isaac nodded. He cleared the top of Tori's childhood bed, before setting the suitcase down on the mattress. As he did so, Shigeru took a metal rod and prised open the skylight, the room's sole window: the whole room seemed to gasp, letting in light and fresh air, the sky a perfect rectangle, clear and cobalt blue.

Tori must have spent a lot of time looking through the ceiling, thought Isaac; it made him want to ask what Tori was like as a child, and as a teen-ager. But Shigeru now had a shadow, permanently drawn across his profile, as he unbuckled the clasps on the old suitcase; it made it hard for Isaac to gauge the mood in the room as the man lifted the top shell of the suitcase.

The two ran their gaze over the topmost contents. Shigeru asked Isaac if he had ever seen any of this before. He said no.

Really . . . In all the time you had it?

Isaac shook his head. Why not? Shigeru asked, and Isaac shrugged.

She never told me I could, he said.

The man couldn't help but smile again, as he gave him that same, thoughtful look. You are a strange person, Neo-san, Shigeru said, as he began to unpack.

Isaac watched as he emptied the contents of the suitcase, setting aside one item at a time. Just clothes, he observed. Shigeru unzipped a pouch, revealing cases of long-expired make-up. Shigeru then unzipped a second bag, a leather clutch, which managed to elicit a sound of soft surprise.

Her passport, he said.

Shigeru held it out to him. Isaac took it, and flipped it open. It was her, all right. He looked at the date of issue, stamped along the bottom; he figured that this must be the passport she had used to fly to London, in 1994. In the photo he noticed that Tori also had a mole, just underneath her left eye. Isaac wondered if it had always been there, this mole, as Tori's stepfather lingered by his side.

Where do you think she could have gone? asked Shigeru. Without her . . . her passport?

Isaac looked at the old man. Her family must have told themselves that she had gone overseas. They must have imagined her on some remote continent, with intermittent access to reception, after more attempts to engage a private investigator. But Isaac had other ideas. For the past eight years, he had imagined her still in that taxi, cruising along a highway. Or else he imagined her on an overnight coach, sleeping, with her head against the window, waiting to be dropped off somewhere new. To her, the suitcase and its contents might have been a final abandonment, but to Isaac they were a vestige of his friend, the sole remnants of a life that's elsewhere now, somewhere new.

Soon there was nothing else left in the suitcase. Shigeru proceeded to leave the attic. I have to thank you, he said, for returning another belonging to us . . . He asked if Isaac had time to spare, and Isaac told him that he had the rest of the afternoon, at least. Good, said Shigeru, as Asimov skittered around their feet on the ground floor; I have to walk the dog.

Isaac stood in the foyer, watching the aged dog pace around the front door, sniffing at its hinges. While waiting for Shigeru to emerge from the back of the house, Isaac tried to look around the place, and see if he could find any photos of the family. There was just the one photo, a small one above the fireplace, taken, he had assumed, on the day of Tori's high school graduation. He found himself memorising her brother's face, the one who must have passed away during the Great Hanshin Earthquake; he found himself looking at Tori too, and at the same mole beneath her left eye, struck once again by the fallibility of his own memories.

Shigeru eventually reappeared. He fastened the leash onto the dog's collar, and stuffed a plastic bag into the pocket of his jeans.

Come on, he said, as he opened the door.

Together the two men left the house and crossed the road, walking towards the park. Already the poodle began to sniff at the trunk of a cherry tree, as Isaac found himself gazing, yet again, on the playground not too far away.

How was she? asked Shigeru. When you met her?

An image flashed through Isaac's mind, of Tori on all fours. I think she was in pain, he said. A lot of pain. I just didn't know why at the time. And while Shigeru began to nod, his eyes appeared to water, causing another image to come to Isaac. He pictured Tori getting up, and rising to her feet; he told Shigeru that she managed to let the pain go, in the end, causing hope to reappear in the old man's eyes.

Can you tell me? he asked. How . . . how you came to be in possession of her suitcase?

Isaac looked at him. He thought back to the ryokan once more, to that decision he had made for himself eight years ago. She left behind a note, he said.

Eh?

He nodded. He then hit a wall of sudden resistance, and forced himself to push past it: he reached into his wallet and took it out, the Post-it containing Tori's final words. And as Isaac watched the man read it, those two lines, he wondered if it could be just as easy too, to push past his desire to hold on to his things, to lose and let go of them all. What was the point of accruing all these objects, if they only failed to anchor his place in this new world?

Shigeru looked at Isaac, his cheeks wet, holding the Post-it in his hands like a precious, fragile thing.

You must have been a good friend to her, said the man. Right till the very end.

There was turbulence the following day, on his Japan Airlines flight from Tokyo to Madrid.

Seated next to him was Ana, a sometime resident of Madrid and seamstress of an atelier, whom Isaac had already befriended since the start of their flight. He watched her grip the armrests of her seat as the plane began to shake.

Ana, said Isaac. We'll be fine.

She looked at him, utterly unconvinced. Outside, through the open window, the plane was cruising through cloud and nothing else. He even heard the interpreter's voice in his brain, saying that it rained plenty in June. Ana fixed her gaze down at the messy stack of paper he kept on his lap, and asked him what he was reading. Oh, he said, quickly gathering it up in his hands—it's a script.

Ah, sí, said Ana. You did say you were an actor.

The plane continued to shake. It was shaking, frankly, to the point of being ridiculous. Even the very features of Ana's face had started to shudder, as she asked if he might be filming something in Spain. A big movie, or—or something like that?

Oh, said Isaac, I'm not. He realised that talking might be a way of allaying his companion's nerves as he added: This is strictly a holiday for me.

Ana attempted a smile. Still, he watched her eyes twitch towards a flight attendant, strapping himself down to a seat beside the emergency exit. Ana asked if he might be holidaying alone, and he said no. He has people waiting for him, friends and family already in Spain, he said. Isaac then told her about the wedding, Mateo and Daniel's, held at the Morales' beachside villa at Isla Cristina.

Ah lovely, said Ana. Very lovely. The new prime minister, Zapatero, she said—he's pushing for same-sex marriage to be legalised, did you know? And Isaac was about to say that he didn't, just as there was another shudder in the cabin, followed by a gravity-defying dip. He heard gasps, many of them, which lent him a strange comfort: he found that it didn't trouble him so much, to reckon with the prospect of a sudden, imminent death. And just as he was about to imagine it, the plane diving, or crashing, or perhaps even exploding, he caught sight of another flight attendant, inexplicably handing out drinks as she walked down the aisle.

There was a mole, right in the corner of the attendant's left eye. And Isaac's mind began to fill with a different noise, a wild static—he almost couldn't hear Ana ask what it was about, the script that he claimed to be reading on that flight; he found that he couldn't answer Ana's question, not till the attendant had turned around again, just so he could confirm that it was not whom he thought he was seeing.

It's about a relationship, Isaac said to Ana, as the plane continued to shudder. An affair.

15

The Horvallan. Jing Aw. Flame of the Forest, Singapore, 2005.

The playground, 1999

Same place, under the slide; a few months had passed since the last time we met. When I joined you, seated myself beside you, you said you had more time to work on your story, your not-a-novel, not-a-book. You were ready to reveal more of the plot you introduced to me, and my first instinct was to laugh. This is what you meant? I wanted to say. When you said, over the phone, "I have more things I want to tell you tonight"? And yet I found myself giving in, nonetheless, into the promise of your story: I wanted to hear more of the stories you might have fed my mother, up till the moment of her departure.

What I was afraid to admit: how much I wanted to revisit the bar in Iskandar. I was invested in our heroine, the diplomat, whose likeness you said was similar to mine; I also wanted to know what she would learn about the Horvallan, whose likeness you'd hinted was just like yours. But I suppose the deeper fear, really, was having to stay any longer in the house that night: another story, I'm telling myself now, for another time.

You told me to brace myself, before we could proceed. You said: "I don't want to lose you, but I'm thinking of making a jump forward in time." I asked you how much time we would be skipping ahead, and you said millennia, several millennia. Five, to be exact.

Five millennia, I thought: five thousand years. I couldn't fathom how I could remain in the story. "This is another storyline?" I asked, almost disbelievingly, and you said yes, another storyline, one that would run parallel to the first. It would be set in 7085AD.

"We're still using that?" I asked. "'Anno Domini'?"

"I'm sure."

"And the humans, we're—we're still around? We haven't grown, like, extra feelers?"

"No."

"Extra fingers?"

"No."

"Tails?"

You snorted. "Shut up. No." But genetic engineering does exist, in 7085AD.

I asked if I was still in the story, and you said I was. I asked you, "What am I, this time?" and you moved yourself closer towards me. "An oncologist," you said, which took me by surprise again.

"Cancer," I said. "Seriously?"

You nodded.

"We haven't cured it, by then?"

The question, you said, isn't about its treatment—the question instead lies ever more in its prevention. And as I thought about it, I found myself face-to-face with the hook of the story that must have ensnared my mother. I then felt your hand, placed on my ankle.

"You're on a spaceship as well," you said. "Somewhere between Earth and Mars."

I froze. I stared at him, kept my gaze on him. I did my best to distract myself from the heat of your hand on my foot.

"Outer space," I said. "Really."

You nodded again. "You still with me?"

*   *   *

And so, 7085AD: onboard the RSS *Ubin*. It is one and a half times the size of Singapore, built in Earth's orbit above the Sumatran Strait. It is the result of a joint effort of Southeast Asia and various alien species, housed in kelong-style settlements around the region. Construction of the space station took three-and-a-half centuries, consisting of materials harvested from cities sunken beneath the seas—a project led by Singaporeans, funded mainly by Singaporeans, one that inspired the leaders of other alliances to construct their own stations too. The demands of the *Ubin* reformed entire economies, and even inspired a fair number of new religious cults; political regimes rose and fell, while the world's space stations steadily grew in size with every year, sparking an exodus that cemented the collapse of the West.

The RSS *Ubin* owes its frog-like structure to a Javanese engineer of near-mythical repute, though it was her wife, a French scholar of Southeast Asian classics, who had given the space station its name. No one, not even the aliens, had objected to the decision; the meaning behind its name was not lost on anyone, not even in the year 7085AD. You then listed to me further examples of space stations' names, like the *Tianwen-XX* to *Tianwen-XXV*, numbered vessels of the Chinese fleet; the South American one is named *QUETZ*, after the Aztec god Quetzalcoatl; while the African space station, equal in size to the *Ubin*, is named the *Puikani*, after the Malawi folktale of the evening star. Your point was this: five thousand years into the future, we have forgotten neither our gods nor our myths. Some might even say that we will have more gods and myths than ever before. Our stories have prevailed, in some shape or manner, and that, you say, is a kind of miracle too.

You then informed me that our second heroine, the oncologist, is also a Malaysian female. It's uncanny, you said, with a hint of a smile, how identical she is to our heroine of 2989AD. And I told you I remained surprised while my heart began to ache, with a pain I could equate with pleasure. "Tell me more about her, please," I said.

*　　*　　*

The oncologist is well-liked within the Medical Wing. She is triple-board-certified, and a well-respected leader in the field of photon laser surgery, a technology that relies on the annihilation between matter and antimatter particles. You said it was imperative I understood how important this technology has become: in the year 7085AD, matter-antimatter annihilation has been used to erase tumours, power the Martian colonies, and thrust civilisations across outer space; the technology has become proof of our progress, the common vision we share as a species, a testament to all of life's collective will to survive. It's something our heroine doesn't take for granted as she lingers along the famous corridor that stretches between the Residential and Medical Wings of the RSS *Ubin*. It has a marvellous window that spans its entire length, a popular destination for couples and families on board the space station, eager to take a long and deep drink of outer space.

Our heroine often comes here, alone, wearing her white doctor's coat over the day's grey scrubs. She's often looking out at Mars, a planet she has never seen in person before. It's her first tour on board the RSS *Ubin*, having left Earth for good just ten weeks ago; the space station is due to enter Mars's orbit in fourteen days, approaching as close as it can to the Annie Cave until the wardens down below send their signal to the *Ubin* to stop. And then our heroine will remain on board while a dozen ships leave from their many hangars, travelling to and fro the *Ubin* and the Southeast Asian colonies, taking with them people, assorted cargo, energy supplies, waste. It's a process that can take between three and six weeks, depending on the total volume of deliveries to be made. And when that is done the *Ubin* will reverse itself, charting another three-month course back to Earth, where it will park itself somewhere within the exosphere, some place between the planet and the moon, just so that an army of ships might leave it yet again, loading and unloading whatever is needed on either planet.

The oncologist will soon be able to witness this entire process, you said. She is prepared to witness this process repeat itself, for years and years and years, until she is eventually awarded a home on the Malaysian colony, a unit on the sixteenth floor of a high-rise multiplex, boasting gorgeous views of the Arsia Mons. And she would share this unit with her brother's family, also consigned to a life on the *Ubin* with her: her brother and sister-in-law are senior pilots of the RSS, serving their fifty-second and forty-fifth tours, respectively, while their only child, Xian, goes to primary school in the Academic Wing, with no need to keep track of the time she's spent in space. Our heroine's niece is a member of Generation Glass, born in vitro and raised on the *Ubin*. She's eight.

The oncologist heads towards the Medical Wing, greeting the nurses who are there on shift. She then greets some of the patients too, the ones she has already become acquainted with. There's the New Filipino chef, for instance, here to enquire on the state of his lungs, while K'weyu sits beside him, the six-eyed Veroniss merchant, a hypochondriac with a perfectly fine abdomen whom she will have to dismiss in time. But there's her niece, of course, a regular at her clinic, patiently waiting for her in the reception.

The oncologist and her niece trade little smiles the moment they catch one another's eyes. Xian has had a hard time fighting bacteria, viruses, even the more minute effects of space radiation lately; she's the major reason our heroine has chosen to serve on board the *Ubin*, while medical scholarship on Generation Glass is still underway. The oncologist asks one of the nurses what her schedule is like for the morning, and asks if she is seeing Xian first.

Sorry, boss, says the nurse. *Everyone's being pushed back by an hour.* He then cocks his head towards the door of her office. *I'm not supposed to say anything, apparently.*

The oncologist leaves the counter and enters her office, feeling more annoyed than perplexed. It's the first time she has ever had her schedule hijacked like this, without even a message or a notification on her tablet to update her. When the door slides open, she finds a man there, already seated before her desk.

Our heroine walks up to him. She takes a good look at his face, and flinches, unable to understand why this man might be seated in her clinic.

She's seen him in books, music videos, research papers, essays. She's seen merchandise of the man too, smelled perfume named after his home planet, delivered injections over tattoos where his face would have been.

I know you, don't I? she says to her patient.

The man blinks, and nods at her, unable to speak. He's also taking note of her face, unbeknownst to our heroine—a face which he has not seen in a very long time. He's reaching far into his memory, back across thousands of years by now, just to retrieve images of a bar and a glass of mezcal. He can feel his chest constrict, the longer the Horvallan looks at the oncologist's face; it's as if he can feel his heart literally break into two as he replies: *In some way.*

Wow, mouths the oncologist, as she attempts to bring up his chart on the tablet. She scans his ID, only to encounter rows upon rows of biodata that are restricted from her access. She does get a glance at his date of boarding (ten weeks ago, just like hers) and then at his date of departure, a mere thirteen days from now. The man's on a one-way trip to Mars, and to the Singaporean colony, of course. She puts her tablet back down on her table.

You're really the Horvallan, she says. *The immortal, in my very clinic.*

Our hero nods another time. It seems like she doesn't know him, after all, not in the way he knows about her. The oncologist asks why he's here, out of all of the places in the RSS, and the Horvallan cannot help but smile as he says to her: *I finally have reason to think I am dying.*

The accident, 1999

The memory of it remains vivid in my mind, even as I am writing about it now. But my curiosity nevertheless takes me to Bugis, to the National Library, a literal tower beside the neighbouring Bras Basah Complex. When I look at the two, side by side, I cannot help but wonder if one is meant to be a relic now, of what we used to be, while the other gets to be this amalgamation of our desires, our hopes and our dreams, our vision for what all of society will look like one day. I even find myself wondering how fast the lifts would be on the RSS *Ubin* as I make my way up to the eleventh floor, home to a complete archive of Singapore's periodicals. I'm asking myself how many storeys a space station would even have.

I tell the librarian at the counter that I'd like to browse *The New Paper* please. She asks me which date in particular, and I say the 21st of September, 1999, the day after my son's first birthday. The librarian opens a cabinet and hands me a roll of film, on which I find, sure enough, a tiny catalogue of our night-time accident. I suppose I should feel grateful, for the little press the event had caused, even for a tabloid like *The New Paper*. Suffice to say it still contains my name, as well as my husband's, followed by yours too, printed in the following sentence; I find myself pausing, at the sight of the three of us together, your name shining, literally, from the lamplight that's passing through the negative.

The accident unfolded like this: a car made a left at the end of Ang Mo Kio Avenue One, hoping to enter the lane at Lorong Chuan. Instead it got rammed by another car, a second car, whose driver had just sped past a major intersection of four roads.

The first car was yours, a rental from Johor Bahru, a Honda Accord 1991 sedan. It was painted red, borderline maroon, containing your travel documents, a rucksack full of your clothes, and a backseat piled with reference books. You sustained several bruises and abrasions along the right side of your body, injuries that you'd heal from in a matter of weeks.

The second car was mine, or rather, my husband's. He'd paid for it, and also laid claim to it in a particular way, habitually referring to it as his girl. This fact might surprise some people, but his car (his girl) was nothing overly glamorous: a second-hand Lexus, touched up with a new coat of black paint, so that it reclaimed its potential to gleam. On a hot day the air-conditioning was absolutely necessary, as the seats would soon start to smell; on a cool one we'd switch it off to save on fuel, and roll down the windows to let in the wind, as though we were both in a movie.

I liked being in the passenger seat, while my husband allowed himself certain liberties on the road. An amber light was a test, an empty expressway an invitation to race. Even parking would present itself as a puzzle to him. All of it was some version of a game, and it didn't occur to me back then that my husband might be changing, that the addition of a car in his life could prove to be more chemical than arithmetical. He didn't have road rage, but I could see it in his eyes, a quiet seething that unsettled me at times.

He had to rest in the hospital, for three days in total, having complained of a pain in his back. I would suffer from a bad knee, one that would remind me of this night for weeks, for months—for years to come, in fact.

I can only assume that you had recognised me, in the same way I had recognised you too. Perhaps that was how the accident had happened: two acquaintances, in two separate cars, sharing a glimpse of one another through the windows. The glimpse then becomes a gaze, held for too long of a second: me, safe in my passenger's seat, while your foot had failed to hit the brake in time.

Everything unfolded very quickly, but also minutely, in a way that suggested time was slowing down. My husband howled as he held desperately onto the wheel; I might have screamed as well, in that moment of temporary suspension, unclear as to why we suddenly seemed to be adrift. But my husband would later tell me that I hadn't uttered a sound, while our son's birthday cake turned to smithereens. And there your car would go, careening somewhere behind us before finally crashing into a tree.

My husband and I were fine. His car though, the Lexus, had spun a hundred and eighty degrees, the tyres screeching and then steaming as the rubber skidded over the narrow lanes. By the time Isaac and I could emerge from the vehicle, a traffic jam had already started to form, though the pile-up was certainly the least of my concerns. People ran down the road from the Caltex to see what had happened; Isaac, in turn, started walking towards the crowd, insisting we were okay. "We're good!" I heard him say, his voice trailing further and further away from me. "There's no need!" he said again, in Mandarin this time, while I, stumbling somewhat, found myself making my way towards your car, traversing the wreckage and the debris that had shattered all over the road. When I finally watched you emerge from your car, more or less okay but visibly shaken, I wanted to shout. I wanted to scream, for real this time. "Damn it," I said, under my breath. "What the fuck were you doing here?"

You knelt down beside me, with fear in your eyes. "It was just the two of you, right? You and your husband?"

I stared at you, bewildered: again, months had passed since our last encounter. "It's just us," I said. "My kid's at home."

"Okay," you said. "Shit. I'm so sorry. I, I—I fucked up." You then looked up, at the sight of my husband walking towards us both. "Is that him?"

I looked over my shoulder. It was him, all right.

"Someone's going to call for an ambulance," I said. "And then the police as well."

Your eyes grew wide. Surely you were thinking what I was thinking too: that neither of us wanted you implicated again, for the part you played in my mother's disappearance.

"We are total strangers, you and I. You understand?"

"I do."

"We never met before."

"No."

"We never—we *never* met before."

"Agreed."

I looked over my shoulder again. I couldn't imagine how or when we'd ever meet again as I saw Isaac heading towards me with strangers in tow. Extras, I thought, calefare—everybody loves a goddamn tragedy.

"Did you see anything?" you asked.

I made sure to act as though I hadn't heard you. "What?"

"You know," you said. "You're meant to see something, apparently. At a near-death experience."

I wanted to curse at you, I thought. Of all the things to ask! "I saw nothing," I said. "Did you?"

You seemed relieved. "No," you said. "I saw nothing either."

Chomp Chomp, 2000

I was dazed and in mourning, the fifth time we met. My grandmother had passed away a fortnight ago; she slipped on a wet tile and smacked her head against a wall. My grandfather was the one who found her.

Allow me to take this opportunity to talk about my grandparents. They were the ones who raised me, while my mother fell short of her duties. They were the ones who taught me the value of keeping a home, of doing my homework, of reading my books. But it was a relationship that comprised mostly of gestures, as opposed to words, which they thought were more of my mother's responsibility, I suppose. Love, as I knew it, was expressed as a generous portion of rice; disappointment, on the other hand, was a sudden desire to tend to the garden. A squabble between them, or between us, would mean that the clothes might be left in the washbasin for a week. Stories would not be told, but preserved in photographs, kept in albums shelved away in the storeroom. That I would spend my entire life not knowing my grandparents' names—having called them nothing but Ah Pa and Ah Ma—would not be an issue for me. Not till it was time to take them to hospital, at least, or to fill out the form for an obituary.

Her name, officially: Aw Bin. She was born in Taiwan, in the year 1925. She came to Singapore at the age of six, having been given up to an uncle who worked here, a merchant with a passion for reading fin de siècle

American literature, a passion he managed to pass down to her. And then a long blur, a whirlwind of colour, before she passed away at the age of 75. She had many kids, and grandkids too. I was just the one she never stopped raising.

Her funeral, suitably, had been crowded with mourners. We had a way of making every death an affair, the Aw family.

I found you with another woman. I remember the scene very well: you, her and a plate of carrot cake, with a cup of sugar cane juice each.

I was at Chomp Chomp getting a bag of grilled chicken wings for supper. Yong-he was going through a phase of craving savoury foods, and so was my grandfather apparently; I had just placed an order at my usual stall when you and I managed to lock eyes, even through the steam that permeated the hawker centre. It was very unromantic, and very public. And I remember my right knee wincing in pain, almost like a warning, a radar.

I looked away. My face burnt with shame, and humiliation. I was shocked, I think, by the realisation that I could be hurt, even jealous. All of this lay on top of the assumption that I'd never see you again, least of all here, back here, in my neighbourhood.

Later that night, in your phone call to me, you said that the woman you were with was nothing more than an old friend. She was an arts programmer, at the Singapore Art Museum. I would have recognised her, in fact, had I taken the opportunity to say hi instead of run away. I would have recognised her from that party in my garden, in February 1996.

"Oh," I said. "I must have forgotten." I asked if she was there, then, at the Science Centre with my mother. You said no.

"Who was there, actually? Apart from you and my mother."

"It was just us."

"Just the two of you?"

"Yes," you said. "No one else was interested."

"Huh," I said. "Not even your old friend?"

You sighed. "I just told you, no." You then asked if we might meet again, the following night, at Chomp Chomp. "Or we could meet at the playground, if you want."

I felt a tiny spark then, a spark of triumph that could very well lead to a flame. "Let's eat," I said, before hanging up.

It was half past eleven when we met. Yong-he and my grandfather had already gone to bed. Isaac was out, on the set of yet another television drama, filming a slate of night-time scenes. He told me he wouldn't be back home till the next day.

You looked nice that evening. You wore a shirt, another white one, with the sleeves rolled halfway up your forearms. It made you sweat, though you didn't seem to mind. And your hair was in a crew cut again, which gave me a prominent sense of déjà vu, of my memory of you back in '96. You asked me how I was doing, and I said I was fine. I said I was the same. "And are you?" I asked. "The same?" You said you were all right.

There was a long pause. We sat at either end of the table, with a plate of carrot cake between us and a cup of sugar cane juice each. It was the exact same set-up as yours the other night, except this time neither person was smiling, and neither person was eating. It was probably the unhappiest scene that Chomp Chomp had ever had to witness.

"I missed you," you said.

"You did?"

You nodded. "Do you believe me?"

I picked at the carrot cake. "I don't know."

A second pause. You asked if I wanted to leave. "Let's go for a walk," you said.

We avoided the road where my place was, and trekked the hilly road up Chartwell Drive instead. Because the evening remained hot, the air full of moisture, I soon found myself sweating too. But there was a wind, a strong one, that rustled the leaves in the roadside trees. And we passed by houses, many houses, until finally you stopped and pointed one out to me, an overachiever, three storeys tall with a roof garden at the top. It was here where you asked if we might sit, and rest, and talk for a while. Again I acquiesced, and waited for you to speak.

It was here when you said you were in town, for just a few days, to attend an exhibition at the Singapore Art Museum. That was how you had met the other woman one afternoon, while walking inside one of the galleries. You asked if I knew that my mother's work was being exhibited there, and I told you that I did. I said I was now the guarantor of my mother's estate. And had I seen it yet, in the museum, where it stood between Lee Wen and Melati Suryodarmo? I told him I had not.

Later, you found a way to revisit your story. It's been a year, you said, and the plot has now taken on considerable size and shape. You had three storylines now, still set in parallel to one another. There was the diplomat, in the year 2989AD, and the oncologist, in the year 7085AD. The third storyline would be set even later, in the year 68525AD, you said.

I could barely even imagine what the world must look like by then. I could only trust you to tell me what you thought. "And our heroine?" I asked. "What is she now?"

You looked at me, sadly, and with some measure of pity.

"A ghost," you replied.

We find the Horvallan back on Earth, utterly alone. The weather has become ruthless, the world hardly habitable, in 68525AD. Singapore is now a land of perpetual, unceasing rain, and it is where the Horvallan has chosen to spend his final years.

It's impossible to tell that this country was once a city. He is the only fully sentient creature on the island, which has been otherwise overridden by small animals, reptiles, plant life and insects. He lives in a shed of his own making, one that he has to regularly repair due to degradation from the ever-changing elements. He spends his days taking shelter from the sun, and ventures out only during the night: he uses that time to distil his reserve of rainwater, and to harvest various fruits and vegetables for sustenance and the occasional topical remedy. It is a simple life, one that the Horvallan has found himself able to endure, as he goes through his days with an almost monastic predictability. He has memories of poisonous weeds, and rough encounters with feral creatures, conflicts over territory with armies of red ants. But his shed is located in the heart of several angsana trees, prone to shedding their leaves like golden dust; on the numerous ponds and streams, formed by the constant rain, the leaves would clump and form blankets of gold, roiling and shimmering over the many surfaces of water.

That life becomes disrupted, however, when buildings somehow repopulate the city. First came the housing estates, followed by partial networks of roads and expressways; then came the shopping malls, from various eras of Singaporean life. By the time the condominiums return, many of the other buildings fall once again into ruin, without any people around to tend and care for them.

The Horvallan thought they were hallucinations, at first, before he stepped into one of the buildings—a building, he is sure, that must have originated from his earlier years on Earth. He then takes everything in the shed into a penthouse at the top of a condominium, overlooking what used to be Orchard Road. He raids the other units as well, the ones he can get into at least, as well as the malls, all covered in vines and weeds. The road itself has been swallowed up and sunk underwater, the whole boulevard now part city, part swamp.

Something is wrong, of course. None of these buildings are appearing without a reason. There are nights, you said, when he looks up into the sky, and sees a grateful parting in the clouds. There are times when he manages to see the moon, diffusing its light in a clear circle across the sky. There are times too when he gets to see the stars, another thing that he has learnt to be grateful for in this life. And then one night, on one fateful evening, the

Horvallan would see another gap in the sky above. Our hero doesn't see the moon or the stars, but something else altogether.

"He sees a comet."

"No. A comet?"

You nodded. "It's the brightest thing he has ever seen. Brighter than the moon. Its radiance casts everything beneath it in a pale, unearthly silver."

"And his life changes?"

"It does. He knows, from this point forward, that something catastrophic is about to happen. Something he won't be able to outlive or outrun this time."

"So it's the end," I said.

"It is," you said. "But he won't be alone."

"No?"

"No," you said. "Days pass, you see; nights as well. The Horvallan continues to scavenge for food, distilling and purifying his containers of rainwater. He does his best to live his life, all while the comet continues to pierce through the night sky."

"It's bad?" I asked.

You nodded again. "There are nights when he can't do it—nights when he fails to see the point of it. There are nights when he puts on his clothes, clothes that he has learnt to fabricate himself, and he feels like tearing it all off. There are nights when he doesn't see the need for him to continue, a need that eventually grows into a want."

"And then?"

"He hears something, a sound he hasn't heard in a while. It's coming from the floor below, the abrupt knocking of a door."

I smirked. "Damn."

"The Horvallan pauses. Or rather: he is frozen on the spot. He nearly forgets to breathe. The only person left in the world doesn't move, not a limb, until he hears the knocking on the door once again.

"The Horvallan walks down the stairs of his penthouse suite, one step at a time. It is pitch black, you see, save for the moonlight that's beaming through the windows; he crosses the minor expanse of the living room towards the front door, his heart hammering harder in his chest the longer the knocks continue. And instead of opening the door, or peering through the peephole, the Horvallan stands at some remove from it instead, in the middle of his reclaimed home. He uses his voice for the first time in God knows when."

Who are you? he says—but the words come out imperfectly, forcing him to clear his throat. *Who are you!* he says again, louder this time.

And then the knocking stops. He hears the door open, slowly, as though this were a horror film. The Horvallan's body shakes out of fear—

He hears a voice, still shrouded in darkness. *It's me*, it says, as a person steps forward.

A shaft of moonlight rests upon her countenance. The person is wearing a doctor's coat, thrown over a pair of grey scrubs.

A ghost, thinks the Horvallan—a spectre.

Our heroine.

16

Isaac watched the Andalusian country roll by from his view on the bus. His eyes wandered over the dry grass and patches of dirt, at the speckling of native bushes and eucalyptus trees. Spain reminded him more of Australia, so far, more than any other image he had of European life.

After his flight had landed at Madrid-Barajas, Isaac transferred to a domestic flight that took him south to Seville; Ana, his momentary companion, had given him advice on where to go and what to see if he had the chance to spend a day in the city, speaking at length about Giralda, Alcazar and the Plaza de España, sights and attractions that he could see over the span of a single afternoon. But when his Iberia flight landed in Seville, he took a bus directly to the transit station, at Plaza de Armas, where he had no desire whatsoever to see the sights. Isaac stayed within the station, where he purchased his ticket on a westward coach to Isla Cristina.

Fifteen euros, said the person behind the counter. Gracias.

Not running away, then, but heading towards: this was his life now, though he had a lot less money when he had returned to Singapore eight years ago. All he had then were the things in his backpack, and the suitcase that Tori had left behind. At Narita International he had been advised to check it in, the suitcase, and with a mild wave of anxiety he watched it trundle away on the conveyer belt, tagged with a label that said it was his. It is in good hands, Mr Neo, said the woman behind the counter. Isaac remembered thanking her as he left for the boarding gates.

He had known where to go, at Changi. He took a bus to Bishan, to Junction 8, and made his way to the photocopying shop where Sherry's mother worked. It was hot that day, the sun blistering on his neck; even the little breeze that fluttered beneath his shirt felt warm, as perspiration beaded at the back of his knees. He was half-soaked with sweat by the time he showed up at the store, and when he stepped inside he found quick relief from the air-con, as well as the shop's familiar sounds and odours.

Hello, leng zai, said Mrs Wong, standing behind the counter. She asked how she might help him.

Hi, auntie, said Isaac. He watched the way her eyes rested upon his, at the blankness that came with a lack of recognition. Do you, uh—do you know where Sherry is? he asked.

Mrs Wong sharpened her eyes. Sherry? she said, turning to her staff, the aunties looking back at her with amusement, confusion. By the time Mrs Wong turned back to Isaac, he was already thinking to himself: It's too much. It's all too much. This is actually happening.

You mean, my daughter? she asked.

He nodded.

Mrs Wong frowned. How you know my girl?

Isaac tried to speak; but the woman now snickered, pitying him, in a way. Is it you know her from poly? asked Mrs Wong. Or are you a new friend . . . ?

Isaac shook his head. No, he said. I—I'm uh, I'm sorry. He then turned and walked right out of the shop, back into the sunlight. When he took one last look at the door, he felt the sun's glare in his eyes, stinging.

He looked around the terminal. There was a roundabout, just outside, as well as a row of fig trees and white stucco houses. Isaac then found a sign for the taxi stand, pointing him instead towards the opposite end of the terminal, where he finally heard the loud honk of a car, a jolting sound in an otherwise dead quiet town.

He exclaimed: Daniel! My man. They first met a year ago, when Mateo had invited his family to stay at their apartment for a week; Isaac and Daniel had fast developed a friendship since, corresponding periodically over an email chain. He knew that Daniel had taken up running, and was thinking of training for an upcoming marathon, looking to get his prosthetic upgraded soon. Isaac put his things down, and the two men hugged one another.

Congratulations, man.

Thank you, Isaac.

I'm so proud of you, Daniel.

He laughed. I am proud of me too.

They broke the hug; Daniel unlocked the boot, and watched Isaac place his luggage inside. How was Japan? Daniel asked, and received a simple shrug from Isaac. He said that it was okay, that it was just work. And his friend looked incredulous, like he wanted to laugh and punch him at the same time.

A commercial for a luxury watch, aha—that's just everyday business for you? Okay.

The car Daniel drove was an old Volkswagen that Mateo's mother bought in the late nineties, rather impulsively at a dealership in Huelva. She used it to drive the family down to Isla Cristina, where it hadn't left the area since. The car's sole purpose was to ferry people and run errands around the main town, where there were plenty of taxis, and not much else in terms of public transport. Cycling was fine, but barely tolerable. And walking, according to the Morales women, was nobody's idea of a good time.

Isaac asked if the villa was nearby. About ten minutes by car, Daniel said, though he had been told to steer clear of the casa. Isaac asked if it was due to wedding preparations, to which Daniel replied, Sí. And too many relatives, aha. All they ever do is talk and talk and talk . . . now I know where Mateo gets his tongue from, he said.

The Volkswagen rattled as it wound down the uneven roads, the Carreras River bright and blue-grey to the left, dotted by a plenitude of pleasure boats. Isaac asked if Daniel's family was here too, and he said yes, aha. They are at the same hotel, added Daniel, which made Isaac ask if they were expecting many people. Quite, he said, with a slight cringe. I don't think there are any remaining rooms at the hotel.

Isaac smiled; he felt happy, actually happy, as the car continued to course down a tree-lined road. He found himself remembering his and Jing's own wedding, and how much smaller it had been in comparison. Did you know Mateo was our maid of honour? he asked, and Daniel began to smile, too. Funny enough, he said—your wife also brought it up today.

He raised his eyebrows. She did?

Daniel nodded. But you know what's funnier? he said. Mateo never told me about this.

Isaac's voice dropped this time. Oh.

Daniel gave him a quick, sympathetic look. He told Isaac about the period that they didn't talk about any longer, from 1996 to 1999: basically the three years they had spent apart from one another. We *used* to talk about it, but only when we first got back together. But now, aha—not so much, I guess, said Daniel.

He soon parked the car, in a tree-shaded lot behind the Hotel Sol Y Mar. It was a single, square building that stood on the beachfront, wonderfully white and pristine on all sides, each room furnished with a private ocean-view balcony of its own. It had a large terrace too that connected directly to the sand, occupied by a restaurant and bar, so that it was always filled with people, eating and drinking, on two dozen circular tables draped with white linen. It was where Isaac found his family, seated together with their backs against the beach, more tanned than he had ever seen in his life.

His son let out a scream, and careened towards Isaac, causing the adults around the table to rise from their chairs: Jing, Mateo and a few older women he'd come to learn were Mateo's and Daniel's mothers. Isaac kissed his son on the top of his head and approached their table, noticing quickly the near-anomalous presence of his wife's laptop, half-open beside a drained cup of coffee. Were you writing? he asked, and Jing looked at him like he was silly. Yah, she said, of course. There's always something to write. Isaac then hugged Mateo, though with Mateo he sensed the same reservation, a qualm and an unease that contrasted against his partner's relative keenness, as well as the winsomeness of the setting itself, the sun and the sand and the sound of waves crashing only a short distance away.

Hey, handsome, said Mateo. Glad you could make it, in the end.

Isaac nodded, and found himself saying what Shigeru said to him too: Time waits for no one, am I right? The group then decided to have Yong-he stay with the Spaniards, while Isaac followed Jing up to their room. The Neos were at the end of the third floor, where they had both the balcony and a window to the side, looking out onto the trees and the boardwalk that stretched the length of the beach. Placed before this window was a desk, on which Jing set her laptop down, strewn otherwise with pens, the peel of an orange, another half-empty cup of coffee; there was a plate too, presumably from the restaurant downstairs, filled with sand and an assortment of seashells. Is this Yong-he? Isaac asked, and Jing said yeah, he's obsessed. He's a hoarder, I think.

Isaac put his bags down. There was their bed, queen-sized, as well as a smaller makeshift one for their son to the side. The very room seemed to shrink, now that he and his things were inside it. Jing jutted her chin towards the shower: You can freshen up, if you want, and he said he was fine, for now. She then asked if she could help him unpack, and he told her that was okay too. The two then looked at one another, in the quiet of the room, with Jing by the desk and Isaac now seated on the edge of the bed. Jing softened her voice, and asked what Isaac was thinking about, giving him the impression that she was very far away. He asked if she remembered their wedding, now that they were about to attend Mateo and Daniel's, and with a distant look in her eyes she said:

I'm remembering it all the time, Isaac.

Cool, said Isaac. Same. They got married seven years ago, in November 1997: just family, and the few friends they had at the time, under the tabebuia tree in Jing's garden. Frankie was his best man. Isaac had hoped that married life would represent a kind of horizontal slate, a prevailing, unchanging state of affairs, when truthfully it felt more like a cycle, a pendulum that swung between fulfilment on one end, one that gave him a sense of camaraderie with his wife, while a sheer and cold ambivalence lay squarely on the other. Things were good in the beginning, especially when Jing had confirmed she was pregnant with Yong-he, but then it got bad anyway, so bad they had that car accident on Lorong Chuan. After that their relationship seemed to improve, before it worsened yet again, sending them into a rut, one they had yet to emerge from and of course followed them now, here inside this hotel room in Isla Cristina. As Isaac looked at Jing, and at the plate of their son's seashells beside her on the desk, he thought it was no wonder, really, that he'd started stealing again this year. It's what he did whenever he felt he was losing a sense of control. What scared him more was the fact that he was okay, even willing, to be benched because of his habit, to have his little crimes become the start of a larger undoing. One that he couldn't take back.

I ask you, he said. Were we too quick to marry? Do you think we should have been a bit slower about things?

Jing crossed her arms; he didn't need to look at her to know that it was something she thought about too. Truthfully? she said, causing a new chill to run over Isaac's body. Yah, he said, truthfully.

She tucked a hair behind her ear. I think we could have, she said. Slowed down. Jing then paused another time, and he caught her eyes glazing over, her focus seemingly adrift amongst the words that she was still weighing, and considering, and ultimately holding back from uttering out loud. But oh well, Jing replied—nobody asked you to propose to me. And I still remember how *that* happened, she added, with a gentle laugh this time.

Isaac smiled, an effect his wife's laugh always had on him. They were on the MRT, he remembered, on the way home from The Substation: there was a speed to life back then, coursing along a straight line; he felt like anything could happen, even though there was only one destination that he held in his mind. And he remembered too, the way he had opened his wallet, and showed her the ring he had kept, there in the compartment where he kept his coins.

You did say yes, he wanted to say to her; nobody asked you to say yes to me too. But of course, on second thought—it was him, all right. It was him who was doing just that, the asking.

The Morales family had made dinner reservations that night, down at one of the restaurants within the puerto. But the marina was in the west, along the mouth of the Carreras River, while the hotel was in the east, near the villas, cloistered from the hubbub of river life. They drove, with Isaac and his family in the backseat of the Volkswagen, while Mateo and Daniel sat at the front. Yong-he spoke up immediately, from the moment the car got going, excited to be in midst of his adult friends; he asked Mateo where they were going, and Mateo turned around, his eyes bright, happy to play along. And while the two spoke Isaac found himself looking at Jing, staring out the open window, wondering what she might be thinking. He thought about the time she had picked him up, at Chinatown, in '96, in her grandfather's Mercedes Benz; he got in, amazed that she knew how to drive.

I didn't have a choice, she'd said to him. I had to send my mother to hospital all the time.

Isaac remembered watching Jalan Minyak recede into the distance. He had made sure to leave Tori's suitcase behind, at the eleventh-to-twelfth floor staircase landing in the building where he used to live; it was the only place he knew where trash could accumulate, without being moved. It was the only place he knew where the suitcase would be secure.

Jing didn't speak, not till they had left Chinatown behind entirely. So Mateo flew back to Spain? After the suitcase disappeared?

He nodded. Jing, on the other hand, seemed to be holding her breath.

And you're not going back home, she said. Even though you're here.

Isaac looked down at his lap, at the backpack between his legs. No, he said. I'm not.

Jing then paused, possibly wondering what he was going to do now, with no friends, no money, no will to keep adventuring. He felt like he could shrink to nothing in the interior of her grandfather's car.

All right, he heard her say, words he now wondered if she'd ever regretted saying. We'll figure something out.

The car wound down the long slope of Ang Mo Kio Avenue One. Jing lived in an old but well-maintained semi-detached house, located at the corner of a road that branched off from Lorong Chuan. Night quickly descended over the garden as various people were at work, it seemed, setting up a screen alongside various pieces of tech. Isaac looked at Jing, confused.

They're friends, she said, as she killed the car's engine. Welcome to my mother's memorial.

They got out. Jing led him past the front door, past a portrait of her mother, her face smiling and garlanded by leaves and flowers. She brought Isaac upstairs, to her grandparents' bedroom. The old couple appeared not so much unbothered by the activity, but more resigned to the artist's mysterious ways, even when they seemed to be conducted from beyond the grave. Or perhaps they suspected that all this was a charade, and that Han Aw couldn't possibly be dead, not in the way that the artist herself seemed to be insisting. Their youngest daughter was just missing, they must have thought; she could always come back.

Jing introduced him to her grandparents. In reality, however, it was just Jing's grandmother Isaac was speaking to, as she sat in her reading chair in the corner. Her grandfather remained by the window, gazing down at the furniture being set up in the garden.

A distinct scent of jasmine and lemongrass wafted about the room. Her grandmother didn't blink when Jing suggested that Isaac stay at their house for the time being. You don't have a place, right? said Jing. You don't even have a bed?

Isaac looked between her and her grandmother, and nodded. He was afraid that one of the Aws would ask him why, afraid that one of them might enquire about the state of his family. But while he braced himself, anticipating how he might explain that things were different here, in more ways than he could understand, Jing's grandmother placed a hand on his forearm.

We spoke before, right? she said.

Isaac nodded again. He thought back to the ryokan, to Friday night, when he had picked up the phone behind the front desk.

And that's all you have? she asked. Just your bag?

He nodded a third time. The sum of his whole life, he thought. That's it, he said.

Jing's grandfather cleared his throat just then. Isaac noticed how the window, from his point of view, revealed nothing but the sight of the tabebuia tree outside. I'm sure there's food, the old man said, before falling quiet once again. Outside, Jing would say that her mother's room was vacant for now, had technically been unoccupied for nearly half a year at that point. But perhaps you can stay in my room first, said Jing, and Isaac said okay, before taking her hand into his. Thank you.

He had waited till Friday night to retrieve the suitcase. He knew Jing would be busy, with a special screening of *RANDEN* being arranged at the garden that night. It would have a two-channel set-up, with one screen in the living room playing the original *RANDEN*, while the screen in the garden would play Jing's remake of the film. The footage had already been edited by a friend of a friend, used to time-urgent projects; her mother had apparently written to him weeks ago, and told him to be on standby for Jing's return from Kyoto.

Isaac remembered slipping out a few minutes before six. As he sat in the Volkswagen, now minutes away from the puerto, he recalled making his way back to Chinatown, to Jalan Minyak, for what he knew would be the last time. He had returned to the twelfth floor, watching the lights flicker on, one by one in the block. Tori's suitcase was still there, on that landing, amidst the same mound of trash. He remembered squatting before the suitcase, unable to bring himself to touch it, not without looking at the thing for a damn minute.

What else was there to say that he hadn't already told himself that day, or for the years to come, in fact? As he now held his son's waist, making sure he would stand steady in the middle of the old car, Isaac found himself wondering, yet again, which was more difficult: to be the thing that vanishes, without rhyme or reason, or the thing that is left behind, or wait, better yet—to be the thing that arrives, unwelcome, to a world he would have to make his own. It was the same thought that guided him, on that day in 1996, to finally pick up the suitcase and look up the remainder of the stairs. It compelled him to walk down the twelfth-floor corridor, towards the unit he once lived in. He reached towards the grilles of the bedroom window and slid the windows open with his fingers.

There, he thought, was the reason he wasn't friends with Sherry in this world. It was him, his face, propped up on a pillow on the bed beneath the window. But it was caked with drool, the mouth and teeth all brown and jagged, while his hands were clenched together into something like claws. But he knew that their eyes had met, were meeting one another's in that moment, even though it was hard for Isaac to tell: the light of the public corridor had caused him to cast a shadow into the room, over his double, over him. Another version of him.

Isaac held onto the grille of the bedroom window, tears collecting fast in his eyes. He couldn't even find any trace of his sister there in that room that evening. He then laughed while he cried, sobbing while shaking with laughter, as he suddenly recalled an old joke, a really bad one.

Knock knock.

Who's there?

No one.

No one who?

No one but you, said Tori.

Another me?

Yes, she'd said, *another you: walking away, never to return.*

Isaac soon returned to Jing's house. There was already a throng of people gathered around a screen, paused on the image of Jing's back.

He was anxious to avoid Jing in her own home, fully aware of the risk he was taking. But he knew her house well enough by now to know what to do, and where to walk, as he climbed the stairs, two steps at a time, passing by strangers while maintaining the smile of someone who now belonged here, who now lived here. He didn't even allow himself to let out his breath when he entered Han Aw's bedroom, and saw it was empty; instead he grabbed a stool and opened the topmost drawer of one of the closets, containing an assortment of coats, jackets, gloves, scarves. He hoisted Tori's suitcase up and made it fit into a space that he had already cleared the day before, and packed more of the late artist's winter wear around its sides. Isaac then shut the closet and set aside the stool, before finally sinking down onto the parquet floor, his heart beating in a chest that already felt so frail, so ready to burst and smoulder at any moment. As he lay on the floor he thought back to what Jing had said to him, back at the ryokan—to be at the end of something, yes, but to also be at the start of something new. It was a wonder he hadn't turned to ash yet, he thought, as he heard the first scream issue from the garden, a feeling he felt then and a feeling he felt now, seated inside a Volkswagen beside the new family he had since made. He ought to burn.

17

The Horvallan. Jing Aw. Flame of the Forest, Singapore, 2005.

The bridge, 2000

You continued to tell me the story of our heroine, as we faced the house with the roof garden at Chartwell Drive. By some wonder of the world she has reappeared, looking just the same as we had last seen her, on board a space station many millennia ago. Now she is here again, years later, leaving the Horvallan understandably confused, as am I.

The first question he wants to ask is whether she is real—but he already knows she's not real, and so chooses to skip it. His second question is concerned with what she is then, exactly, especially when she can touch things, move things and knock on things like doors. But the Horvallan stops himself again, perhaps out of loneliness, or the fear of cruel, needless heartbreak—or perhaps it's because he has been through this before, the visions, the inexplicable reappearance of things; he has practically found shelter in one of them right now, forcing himself to understand the difference between what is real and what is truthful. And as he looks at the oncologist—at the spectre of the oncologist—he can feel it too, the closing in, of hope on one end and despair on the other; he knows that if this is indeed a dream, he really ought to let it be. And he will, he tells himself—he must.

*   *   *

"So what does he do?" I asked. "What's his next step?"

"He approaches her," you said, "and she moves towards him. Over the course of many seconds, our hero, the Horvallan, finds new opportunities to doubt what he is seeing." Lightning then flashes behind him—it fills the entire room with light, you said, gesturing with your hands and your arms—eliminating all doubt, none whatsoever, over the person who has just walked through the door.

"The oncologist," I said. "She looks fine?"

"Yes."

"And she is there."

"Yes."

"But she is not real."

You nodded once more. "Not in the way we understand the word."

I took in a quick breath. "Will the Horvallan resume speaking at some point?"

You coughed. "Touché."

Because our hero is at a loss for words, and because I felt like we were in dire need of some exposition, I took it upon myself to ask you some basic questions of my own. I asked you if this story was about civilisation, about several of them, about the co-existence of mankind with extraterrestrial life. I asked if this was about the end of the world instead, about a comet that would strike Earth, 70,000 years into the future—or if it was about phenomena, strange phenomena, giving rise to houses, ghosts, and the appearances and disappearances of things. And while you remained quiet and thoughtful, I asked you if this was a love story, a question which finally forced you to respond.

"Between?"

"The Horvallan," I said. "And our heroine."

"With all our heroines?"

"Across time," I said.

You looked into my eyes. You asked me if that was the story I would like to hear.

No, I told you. You asked me why not.

"I can't trust them," I said. "I hate love stories."

You let out a laugh. And then we grinned, like idiots in a movie, conspiratorial in some way.

"This story I'm trying to tell," you said: "It's about all of these things, yes. But it's primarily about a place, a very faraway place. Farther than you or I can imagine." And that was all I ever heard you say on the subject, not for a few more years, at least. That's the game we're playing here.

The Horvallan *does* speak again, at some point.

He is bewildered, you said, agitated, but also immensely grateful. He is filled with the gratitude of having company, at long last, as well as the joy of seeing her face again, a joy so singular he felt he might immolate. He asks the spectre, first of all, if she is who she seems to be. And the spectre smiles and says, *Yes, that is me. I am who you say I am.* To this he says that he has missed her, and that he has longed for her, in ways he has learnt to forget.

Do you remember how we parted? she asks.

Yes, he says. *Of course I remember.*

We were in the hangar, she says; *you were on the other side of the airlock.*

He chokes up. *Yes.*

A look of pity crosses her face. *I had to go.*

The Horvallan is able to recall the scene immediately. He remembers looking through the window, at the sight of her face turned towards his, saying her last words to him.

I told you we would see each other again.

The Horvallan nods. *Yes.*

She smiles again at him. *And now I am here,* she says.

The Horvallan steps towards her. He puts his hands on her shoulders, before running them down her arms. He feels the fine fabric of her coat against the calluses of his palms, hardened by years and years of survival. He hears his voice break again as he tells her, gasping—*Yes.*

The spectre rests a hand on the side of his face. *I have to thank you as well,* she says. *For taking Xian with you.*

The Horvallan then takes her hand—he leads her up the stairs, towards the loft, where there are drawings of flora and fauna, all on the wall that faces the bed. All done by Xian.

The both of you lived here, she says. *When the two of you returned?*

He nods again. He then directs the spectre's attention to a series of markings, meticulously made in a corner; she quickly adds them all up, numbering the total. Forty-three.

The spectre turns to him, eyes wide and fearful. *Days?*

The Horvallan shakes his head. He smiles as his face wets with tears. *Years.*

The spectre asks what his plans are for the night. The Horvallan stammers, telling her he needs to forage. *For what?* she asks, and he says, *For mushrooms.* The spectre then asks him where, and he tells her there is a hilly forest some distance away, over what was once known as Thomson. *That's where the mushrooms are.*

The spectre looks at him, as though she were assessing him again, analysing his condition on board the space station. *Would you like some company?*

The Horvallan breaks eye contact. *Sure,* he says. *It's quite a walk.* But the spectre only shrugs, and says: *I have all night.*

The Horvallan grabs his hiking gear. He has hiking boots, and socks, and a waterproof poncho; he also has a bucket hat, a face mask and a pair of large diving goggles. He takes with him his backpack, an empty rucksack, as well as a lantern, with thirteen hours' worth of solar-powered battery life. The spectre takes the lantern and rests a finger on the logo of the RSS *Ubin,* embossed onto its silicone frame.

How do you still have these? she asks.

The Horvallan casts his eyes over the marble floors, the high ceiling, the induction cookers over the kitchen island. *They came with the place,* he said, as she hands back the lantern to him.

You must have many questions.

He nearly laughs. *Oh yeah.*

She offers him a smile. *I promise I'll explain,* she says, *once we are done foraging for mushrooms.*

The Horvallan nods. He then takes a look at her: at her scrubs, her sneakers, her hands now in her pocket. *I assume you don't need anything?* he asks, and the spectre shrugs again, saying she's fine, she's all set, all in a way that causes his heart to grow larger, tenderer.

Our hero leaves the penthouse with the spectre. She watches as he closes the door behind them, and asks him why that is necessary. He tells her about the canines that also live on the third floor, as well as the amphibious lizards, active in the night-time. As they scale down the stairs, the Horvallan points towards several metres of water, waiting for them at the ground floor. There is a wooden boat, tied by rope to a rusty railing, bobbing rather invitingly.

During the daytime, the Horvallan says to the spectre, *the water is infested with sleeping lizards.*

A look of alarm crosses the spectre's face. *And where the hell are they now?* she asks.

God only knows, he says.

The Horvallan gets into the boat. He watches the spectre clamber, seating herself on the other end. He feels the addition of her weight as he steers with his oars, the boat drifting out of the stairwell and into the flooded lobby, carpeted by flowering creepers and the skeletal remnants of chandeliers, half-studded with plastic diamonds that have long lost their lustre. One of the chandeliers, the Horvallan says to the spectre, is now even a beehive.

The spectre asks when might be a good time to turn on the lantern.

Maybe in a bit, he says to her.

She nods. *Okay.*

Their boat glides out of the condo. A fine rain pitter-patters over their clothes and the boat. Flashes of lightning provide momentary illumination, revealing to the spectre the world that the Horvallan has made his home: a garden city, now more jungle than garden, the air filled with the smell of pollen and spores and other dust-like allergens, while the constant activity of insects have combined to form something like a distant, high-pitched, bird-like scream. The boat continues to sail down the river that was once known as Orchard Road, filled now with lily pads, and lotus plants, and the criss-crossings of giant dragonflies and the croaking of bullfrogs. Thankfully the lizards remain nowhere to be seen.

We keep rowing like this for an hour, says the Horvallan. *You can take over and help if you want.*

Sure. The spectre smirks. *And then what?*

We disembark at the MacRitchie Viaduct, he says. *And hike.*

The two of them row until the boat hits asphalt. The Horvallan takes the rope and ties it securely against a rusted railing. The MacRitchie Viaduct rises before them out of the water, an expressway on which they will have to travel by foot; the Horvallan treads carefully while the spectre remains carefree, the lantern now shining and back in her hand, casting an iridescence over the road under the constant activity of rain. She asks when the Viaduct had reappeared in Singapore, and he tells her he couldn't remember when, exactly. It was one of the first things, however, that led him to discover the mushrooms.

The spectre then asks what the mushrooms are for. The Horvallan chooses his next words carefully.

They're for sleeping, he says. *That's always hard to do during the daytime.*

And what about dreaming? asks the spectre. *Do they help with that too?*

The Horvallan avoids her gaze, as he says they can.

Our hero and the spectre walk down the expressway: two people and a moving globe of golden light, while an immense jungle surrounds them on either side, rich with the muddy and grassy smells of a marsh. Its silence is punctured by the occasional shriek of warring primates, while clouds of bioluminescence flare like the sparks of a forest fire, at times orange and then a more haunting blue. A sudden break in the clouds prompts the spectre to switch off the lantern, to take advantage of the momentary moonlight—and it is now when everything is awash in a hue of chalky white that the spectre says to the Horvallan, with an uncharacteristically empty look on her face: *I don't have the need to dream anymore.*

They pause for a moment, and so does the rain. The look on the Horvallan's face remains invisible, hidden beneath his mask and his large diving goggles, items on an ever-growing list of things he is grateful for that night.

You and I left the house soon after, leaving Chartwell Drive behind. You asked if I was familiar with this part of the neighbourhood. "Quite," I said; I went on long walks as a child, up and down these hills. These walks of mine would be so long that they would tire my grandparents out. And they were all so utterly spontaneous, so unplanned and led by instinct, that we'd often find ourselves lost in the place we called home.

And then I asked about you. I asked you what your childhood was like. You said you stayed at home a lot.

"Reading?"

"Yes," you said. "Lots of reading." You said you were a big nerd, and I said, "I figured."

You let out another laugh. Every laugh of yours sounded like a boom, like a volley, with the ability to trace wide arcs across an expanse. Later you asked what inspired these long walks, these arduous journeys I forced my grandparents to take with me, and in reply I said I was looking for my mother. As a child I thought that she was probably around somewhere, somewhere nearby, just out of sight. But this was a sensitive topic, missing mothers: you and I kept quiet, keen to avoid eye contact for a bit, focussed again on our own aimless walk.

I lost track of the time at some point. We had gone past a church, followed by a school; we became stranded around the Li Hwan area, filled with houses I no longer recognised. Still I managed to point out a tree, a particularly tall pine that towered over the immediate area. We spent a good minute, you and I, wondering how old the tree might be.

"A hundred years old," you said.

"Two hundred?" I ventured.

"Three hundred," you offered. "Four?"

It didn't matter. At some point you decided to take my hand, and I allowed it. You led me to an alley between two houses, an alley where no light could reach, and I allowed that too. With my mouth against your ear, I asked if you knew that there was no coming back from this. And with your mouth against mine you said that you did.

"Do you want this?" you asked.

Yes.

"Say that you want it."

I want it.

"Say."

"I want it."

"Do you need it?"

I rolled my eyes.

You repeated yourself: "Do you need it?"

"I don't."

"Oh, really?"

I kept my gaze elsewhere. "Oh, yes."

The Horvallan and the spectre eventually come to the end of the Viaduct. An hour's walk has led them to the edge of a forest, where the asphalt abruptly disappears into the soil.

The mushrooms are in there, says the Horvallan, even though the spectre bears a look of apprehension.

You hear that too, right? she says, referring to the once-ambient noise of the insects. Their bird-like cacophony is sharper, more intense, omnidirectional this time; he takes the lantern from the spectre now, and switches it back on.

Everything thickens the more they step inside: foliage, flies, the shadows. The available light is too scant, in spite of the lantern, to help mark the trees that surround them. And because the foundation of the forest is asphalt, not soil, they find themselves walking on a network of exposed roots, toughened over tens of thousands of years, the two extra careful not to trip over anything untoward.

The buzzing, says the spectre. *It's insane.*

I know.

And the smell.

That too.

The Horvallan raises his lantern above his head. He looks up this time, hoping the golden light might penetrate into the higher reaches of the forest. The spectre asks him what he is looking for.

Primates, he says.

What about them?

They rule the forests, he says. *They have clans now, tribes.*

They can self-organise? says the spectre. *Can they use tools too?* She then pauses, just for a second. *Have they discovered—*

Fire? Yes.

Incredible, says the spectre. She has turned her gaze upwards as well, just like the Horvallan. They can barely see the sky through the canopy. *I wonder if they've developed a faith. Or maybe even a culture,* she says. *Are you looking out for sentries?*

He nods. *They seem to be absent.*

The spectre continues to scan the forest. *Perhaps we're not the source of danger here.*

And so the two advance, a little quicker this time: their confidence grows the more they adjust to their surroundings. They can also feel the moss over the ground becoming thicker and spongier, more carpet-like beneath their feet. The spectre's eyes water from the worsening odour, the metallic screech of the insects intensifying to no end; eventually they halt, arrested by the sight of an animal's limb, resting at the edge of their pool of light. An additional step forward causes an entire cloud of flies to part, dramatically revealing the rotting carcass of a chimpanzee, with what seems like an arrow struck through its strong but bloody chest.

An intruder? the spectre asks.

Possibly, says the Horvallan.

From a rival clan? The spectre squats before the carcass and takes the arrow out of the corpse, noting how the end has been shaved to a point— rudimentary, but effective. She wonders how it's been glued together as well, before asking how much farther the mushrooms are. *We're nearby,* says the Horvallan.

Soon they find a second primate, its corpse slung over a tree branch, two arrows struck through its head. More bodies show up, killed in increasingly various ways: puncture wounds caused by bullet-like pellets, and gut-spilling gouges made by knife-like tools. The spectre asks if this is not so much an intrusion, but an organised invasion; she asks if it is possible to tell the primates apart, to see if the corpses belong to a single tribe, or several ones at war. The Horvallan says the tribes are organised not according to species, but according to some other affiliation he has yet to discern. *Strength, perhaps? Intelligence?* the spectre offers. *Values, if any?* She then comments on how marvellous it is, how remarkably similar their style of warfare is to the human race's. She wonders aloud if it's a matter of imitation, or a matter of evolution. She wonders if the cycle of violence never truly ends, but merely repeats itself elsewhere, wherever it may manifest.

Eventually they reach a clearing in the forest. The moonlight falls in a perfect circle, gently over a bed of flourishing fungi. They grow as delicate white fingers, out of the exposed roots of the trees. But amidst them stands a single primate, no taller than a metre: it is poised with a bow and arrow at the ready, which forces both the Horvallan and the spectre to freeze. The primate shifts the aim of its arrow, quickly and expertly between the two of them, indicating that it can shoot either one of them at any time. Both of them raise their arms in surrender.

The primate begins to grunt. It's a red-faced macaque, with blonde fur that shines nearly silver under the moonlight. It licks its lips, and fixes its aim on the Horvallan, nudging with its head towards the ground.

Lower the lantern, the spectre says.

The Horvallan lowers his arm—the macaque takes a step forward, letting out a shriek in protest.

Okay, okay! says the spectre. *Wrong move.* She quickly glances at the Horvallan. *Lower your mask.*

What?

Do it.

The Horvallan takes it off with his free hand. The macaque, quivering under the strain of maintaining its pose, continues to glare at the Horvallan, breath quickening.

Now your goggles.

He pulls the goggles down his face, beneath his jaw, allowing them to rest around his neck. Bugs smack against his mouth, but he resists the urge to twitch too much. The macaque takes a second step forward, its eyes widening with wonder as it looks into the Horvallan's. The macaque seems to have recognised the man somehow, relaxing its stance and bending its back, leaning over a cluster of white mushrooms. It wrests a handful free from the ground, the sight of which causes the spectre to gasp: the mushrooms don't grow from the roots of trees, nor from the moss that covers the ground. They grow from the bodies of primates instead, arranged over one another into an indiscernible pattern, gathered into a pile where they might collectively face the sky. The spectre quickly shifts her weight from one foot to the next, feeling a limb crack into two beneath her.

The spectre remains in silent observation as the macaque skips forward towards the Horvallan, offering the mushrooms to him; under the glow of the lantern, it becomes evident that the macaque has fought hard in whatever conflict that just took place, its face and torso gleaming with fresh blood. The Horvallan squats before the primate and takes the mushrooms from its hand.

Thank you, he says, in a low voice. The Horvallan then reaches into his rucksack, and holds out in exchange a handful of fruit.

The macaque grunts again in reply. Ka seems to be the word: *Ka.* It snatches the fruit from the Horvallan's hands and resorts to hand signals, using an uncannily human-like gesture to tell the Horvallan to leave. It then raises an arrow upward, up towards the sky, prompting our characters to look: at the comet that now greets them, here in the clearing, much larger than it was a week ago. It shines like a single diamond, radiant enough to light the land on which they currently stand.

Ka, says the primate again: it retreats back towards the centre of the clearing, careful to avoid stepping on any of the mushrooms, drawing its bow and arrow once again. The Horvallan secures the buckles on his rucksack, before strapping his goggles and his mask back on.

We have to leave, he says, his voice muffled once more. Our heroine follows him out without saying a word.

It was three in the morning. We stood at the cliff edge of Li Hwan Close, where the long thread of Ang Mo Kio Avenue One lay down below, distant like a river at the bottom of a valley. An overhead bridge spanned across the entire road, with an old, iron roof and hexagonal windows, connecting the Li Hwan area with Golden Hill on the other end.

"That story about you and your grandparents, walking all over this neighbourhood—you weren't just looking for your mother, was it?" you said.

I looked at you. I told you I didn't understand.

"Your mother has a story about this bridge," you said. "A story she told me before, in exchange for the one that I was telling her. She said there was one time your father came to Singapore, just to see you, and how you were doing. She said the three of you spent an afternoon together, walking through this neighbourhood, only to end up here, at this bridge, a newly constructed one at the time. You must have been five or six, and you wanted to be held, so you might look down onto the road below. And even though you were too big to be carried, your father picked you up anyway, the two of you looking at the cars for a few minutes. In your mother's mind, however, she had only pity for you, for the both of you, eyes focussed on the cars of all things, when it's the closest you two have ever been with one another." You paused. "She knew that you and her would never see this man again, after that day. That it was possible to reappear in one's life momentarily, even if just to make a mark, a small one. She knew he would disappear once more, back into the place where he'd come from, wherever."

We turned back towards the bridge. It was as though the lights had formed a golden beam, a brilliant passageway across the night. I tried to imagine how we might have looked, me and this man I had never met in my life, and I wondered how I might have been altered, irreparably, from this incident I couldn't even remember. And I couldn't recall if I had ever walked the full length of this bridge—if I had seen with my own eyes what kind of neighbourhood might lie at the other end.

"We should cross," I said.

"Let's do it," you said.

We began to make our way. It was impossible to shake away the story you just told me, but I tried in vain anyway. I asked you what the deal was with the primate, the macaque, and the mushrooms it seemed to be protecting. You said that the mushrooms most likely hold a particular significance for the primates of the forest—especially since they have been emerging from the bodies of past companions. It is possible, you said, that the mushrooms are a form of afterlife for the primates. That they might even be regarded as a rebirth.

"And so the place is sacred."

"Yes."

"Worth protecting?" I asked. "Worth dying for?"

"To those who believe so, yes."

"And the mushrooms," I said. "They induce sleep and . . . ?"

"Dreams," you said. "Vivid ones, filled with sensory detail." The dreams, you said, were enough to make one feel as though they were reliving the past, or some form of past life. "They allow you to revisit your most beloved memories," you said.

We reached the middle of the bridge, you and I. It was amazing how I still had zero compulsion, none whatsoever, to cross the remaining length of this golden bridge. Even now I can't really articulate what was holding me back that morning.

"The macaque," I said. "It knew the Horvallan?"

"In a way," you said.

I continued to stare at the traffic. "So what happened?" I asked. "On board the space station? Between the Horvallan and—"

"The oncologist?"

"Yes," I said. "When the spectre was alive."

You turned to me with a smile. You asked if you could tell me the next time we met, and I asked, in return, how much later that time would be. You shrugged.

"Say you want me. Say you want me back soon."

I shook my head. "I can't."

You chuckled. "I know." You began to walk away, down the length of the bridge I couldn't cross. "It'll only be a while," you said, and I knew, one way or another, that it was just a matter of waiting. I would have to head back home, while the new day had yet to break, wondering when you would deign to reappear.

18

Isaac could hear the water lapping against the deck. It was half past eight by the time they arrived at the parking lot of the puerto, and made their slow way towards the marina, where the sky remained a rich blue, the sun barely setting over the yachts. The restaurant, La Boccana, laid several tables for them out on the deck, where they could bask in the panorama of the mouth of the Carreras River. The marshes formed a dark line at the horizon, over which the sky was just beginning to blush, while the pier lay in the shorter distance, coming from both sides to form a small bay.

Across the table were Jing and their son, with Mateo seated on Yong-he's other side. On Isaac's side was Daniel, taking pictures of the evening with a digital camera, while Mateo's parents occupied the remaining seats. Señor Calvo was tall and pale, with striking blue eyes, while Señora Morales most closely resembled Mateo, with a defined nose and thin lips, and brown, tousled hair. Isaac also noticed how mother and son would frequently exchange glances across the table, not so much to communicate but to guess what was going through the other's head, a game they must be used to playing with one another.

A waiter came and took their table's orders. He served the adults sangria, prompting a quick round of cheers while Yong-he sipped from a glass of orange juice. Mateo's mother asked how Isaac was settling in, and he said he was great, and that the location was beautiful. He couldn't think of a better time and place to hold a wedding. You didn't come here, last time? she asked, and Daniel said no, they remained in Barcelona last year. Daniel then said that there were celebrations for San Juan last night, with bonfires lit along the beach. Isaac asked the table what they did, during the festivities, and Jing said that she was writing at the terrace of the Hotel Sol Y Mar; Yong-he had stayed up as best as he could, until he had to be carried up the stairs to their room.

The table murmured with laughter. You carried him? he said to Jing. Mateo then said no, he did.

Oh, said Isaac. Thanks, man.

Mateo smiled. It felt forced, as usual. But Mateo sounded genuine when he said he'd do anything for the boy. He attempted a playful jab in Yong-he's side, prompting both Isaac's wife and son to swat Mateo's pesky hand away. Isaac asked Daniel what the schedule was like over the rest of the week, and Mateo's mother spoke up at this, saying there was a barbecue the next day, at the villa, followed by movie screenings in the evening.

And then the wedding, said Daniel, on Saturday. Everyone we've invited should be here by then.

Isaac nodded, recalling something that Ana had said to him, on the flight to Madrid. He asked about their new prime minister, Zapatero—was he making marriage legal between gay people? Was it legal, already? And Daniel said no, not yet. It's on his agenda, yes, but no one has any idea when that will actually happen. But you don't want to wait, said Isaac, and Daniel brightened up at this. It's like you said earlier, Daniel said to Isaac: time waits for nobody? Aha.

There was a pleasant pause, as Mateo continued to play with Yong-he. Jing took a quick sip of her sangria. Mateo's father then said something, in Spanish, prompting Mateo's mother to translate. He wants to know about you, she said to Isaac. You're an actor, yes?

He was, yes, said Isaac, prompting a quick back-and-forth between the señor and señora. Now he wants to know, said Mateo's mother, if you might be considered famous? In Singapore?

Isaac laughed; he glanced at Jing, with the usual, shy pleasure he had while explaining his career to other people, only to be thrown, somewhat, by the way she looked back at him askance. I, uh, I guess, he said, I get recognised quite a bit, and while Daniel laughed along, and patted Isaac's arm (You're being humble, my friend! said Daniel), Señora Morales then asked, in turn, if there might be a way for her or her husband to watch some of Isaac's work. Is it on tape, she asked, or perhaps on disc? But before he could answer, he heard Jing say instead, It was okay, really. They didn't have to bother.

Mateo's mother appeared both affronted and amused. But why, my dear? We're so curious! she said. Isaac watched as Jing shrugged, and said that it was just, well—how do I put it? She then looked at Isaac another time, before quickly turning away again, as though he were to blame for putting her in this position. And he found himself relishing it almost, when Jing said: I'm not saying it's not good work. Isaac is very good at his job. But it's just, I mean—it's entertainment. Señora Morales threw up her hands: she said that she and her husband can watch anything these days, causing Daniel to shake his head while Mateo said, Nop, Mama, nones. Now you're just lying. You're just trying to impress the handsome man at the table.

And Isaac laughed again, though he was also simmering this time, as Daniel clasped him reassuringly on the shoulder. He found it unbearable to look at his own wife, even by the time the first dishes arrived, with plates of seafood, black rice and croquetas to share. While everyone began to help themselves Mateo's father spoke up again, urging Mateo's mother to ask if there was a role Isaac was particularly proud to play, or a television show that made him especially happy. And while Jing topped up their son's plate with food, he said he could think of three television shows: the first was *Star Search*, in 1997, when he was a contestant, and had been crowned Male Champion; the second was a drama he shot in 1999, when he got to play the part of a policeman that won him his first acting award, for Best Supporting Actor; the third was a show he completed recently, just this year in fact, shot from February to April. He played the young owner of a family-run restaurant this time, in direct competition with a rival restaurant whose owners lived on the same floor. And as he told Mateo's mother all of this he knew what he was doing: he knew he was making Jing simmer too. In fact, he could see proof of Jing's anger when Daniel asked if it was ever strange to see Isaac on TV. She said it was, admittedly, at first; but she had a busy life too, as an editor and columnist for *The Straits Times*. Isaac's dramas would air when she'd still be working, and once she missed an episode it was always impossible to keep up. Plus, she said: it's not really my thing.

TV, you mean? said Daniel.

Sure, said Jing, handing Yong-he a croqueta. You can say that.

But it's your husband, said Mateo's mother—your husband on the silver screen! And although the señora said this cheerfully, encouragingly, Jing's manner of speaking seemed almost sour when she said she'd beg to differ. It's not really my husband, is it. It's just a version of him.

Isaac scoffed; he drained the rest of his sangria. Daniel beside him grew quiet too, chewing on a spoonful of black rice, while Mateo and his mother exchanged another surreptitious glance, raising their eyebrows in unison. It provoked a sudden silence, one that confused Mateo's father, and coerced him into eating as well. Isaac could barely taste his own food when he heard Mateo remind Jing to eat, as though he were playing the part of Jing's partner, now that Isaac was far from willing to do it himself. As Isaac raised his hand, requesting another glass of sangria, he found the sky ablaze, this time, with lashings of marigold and vermillion, as though the setting sun were vindicating his displeasure, his disappointment. At some point Mateo's mother spoke up again, and asked Isaac about his time in Japan—Did you really film a commercial for Rolex? It made Isaac blink, and look around the table again, reminded that this dinner, in fact, was partially held to welcome him, for finally making his long way here, to this corner of the southwest of Spain. It made him feel reckless as well to find Jing and Mateo now staring at him, no longer eating, waiting for him to answer the señora's question.

He said that's right, he did. He filmed a commercial for the brand, yes. And after he told the señora about the various locations the shoot was held, he told her also about this errand he had to do, once shooting for the commercial was wrapped up. He told her it was an errand he meant to do eight years ago, when a friend of his had disappeared. By the time he told her about how he had taken the train to Nishinomiya, to personally hand Tori's suitcase back to her stepfather, he wasn't so much talking to the señora anymore, but to her son, staring back at him now with a pain that twisted his features, his eyes red and filling with tears behind his glasses.

So you lied to me, said Mateo. When you said it was gone?

Isaac nodded; he told himself to maintain eye contact with him. He didn't want to look at Jing anymore, now that she knew that he had lied to her too.

Why? Mateo asked. Why not tell me the truth?

Nobody ate anymore. Isaac didn't know how to reply; telling him the truth would be tantamount to unravelling everything about him, the reality of who he was. He told Mateo that he had a problem, one that he most likely had before he even met Tori, and Daniel spoke up just then, asking who this Tori was.

You don't know? said Jing. Mateo never told you? But Mateo paid neither Jing nor Daniel any mind as he asked Isaac if he knew what he had done, not to Tori but to him, him specifically. He said that Isaac didn't just steal her suitcase, he had stolen his friend away from him too. Isaac had somehow managed to rob Mateo of any final interactions he could have had with Tori, right before she vanished. She was *my* friend, Mateo said, his hand now a single point, jabbed repeatedly into his own chest—*my* friend, Isaac, he said. I don't know who the fuck you think you are, but all I know is *you* showed up one day, and then *Tori* is the one who's fucking *gone* in twenty-four hours. He then asked if Isaac knew any of that, any of the misery he's had to live with over the past eight years. *Do* you? he said, slamming that same hand on the table, and for a moment it was as though the whole world had shaken, had flinched, had come to a sudden standstill. And then there was a whimper, a cry, and Isaac knew immediately that it was his son, cowering against his wife, away from the man who was now visibly transformed into something else, something no one at the table could recognise.

And as Mateo rose from his chair, Daniel got to his feet as well, saying, Cálmate, Mateo, por favor—Isaac watched the two hurry out of the marina while Mateo's father looked graven, shell-shocked at what had just taken place, while Señora Morales had her hands over her mouth and her chest, muttering solemnly to herself.

Isaac watched his wife tighten her arms around Yong-he. She kissed the top of his head, and told him it was okay. She then looked at Isaac, and said they ought to head back. And by the time they did, Isaac could only watch, from the doorway of the bathroom, as Jing showered the boy, and towelled the boy, and pulled the sheets over him in his bed. The boy was still whimpering, his body shuddering as an aftereffect of all his crying, distraught and anguished over something he couldn't understand, could possibly never understand.

Try and sleep, okay? she said. Mummy is going to talk with Daddy downstairs. She then kissed Yong-he on his forehead, gently rubbing her thumbs over the corners of his eyes. I'm sorry we hurt you, honey.

The terrace of the Hotel Sol Y Mar was a strange place to be, at this time of day. It felt like being in an aquarium, a tank full of light, as he and his wife sat at a table. It felt like a shelter from the mercurial darkness, the night languishing in its own tumult on the other side of a glass barrier, the beach and the boardwalk and the palm trees all appearing to howl. He could only imagine how a bonfire would look like now, there on the beach; he wished he could feel the heat of the inferno as he said, I'm sorry.

Jing's voice sounded distant again. For what? she asked.

For doing that, he said. I knew what I was doing.

Jing ran a finger over her mouth. That's okay, she said, which surprised him. She said it was bound to happen, sooner or later. She said it was a mystery, really, how they had managed to spend their lives so far not mentioning Tori even once; not even when they were in Barcelona, last year, when they had spent that whole week together, five of them in that apartment.

Everyone acted like nothing had happened, back in '96. Jing shifted in her chair. I wonder if you've also noticed, she added—but Mateo's been a little on edge the whole time.

Isaac sighed. Because he hates me, no?

Jing smirked. No lah, she said. Don't flatter yourself. She then paused, and told him what they had talked about the night before, here in the terrace away from the San Juan festivities. Mateo told her that he had been caught in 11-M that year, in the Madrid bombings in March. He was awake at the time, and in Madrid as well, for reasons he hadn't disclosed to her; he was about to pass through the ticket gates of a metro station when the bombs went off, all ten of them, a sound that knocked him back, making him momentarily deaf. And then, well, Jing said—a really selfish thought went through my mind.

What? said Isaac. And Jing smirked at him again, but with a sadness in her eyes this time.

It made me think that this wedding, really, is just a response to what happened in Madrid, she said. It made me wonder if their marriage is going to be just like ours.

Isaac's hand curled into a fist against his teeth. He asked his wife if she still loved him, and Jing nodded, afraid as though by his need to even ask. Of course, she said. Of course I do. And as she reached her hand out to him, he found that he had to unclench his fist, in order to take her hand. Once he did that she brought him in, the two embracing one another, holding one another, faces pressed into one another's necks as he began to cry. He cried, even as relief coursed through him, with the understanding that things wouldn't turn out so bad after all. Things could always be better, so long as they remembered that they still wanted to be in each other's lives.

Isaac asked if she might want to walk, down to the beach with him. Jing said okay, and they rose from their chairs and left, leaving behind the sanctuary of light that was the terrace. They felt almost giddy, crossing over the threshold into the coastal summer night, where things weren't as dark as it had seemed back at their table; they could still make out the grass, and the footpath, and the foam on the waves, crashing by the shoreline. There was still a rouge tint in the sky too, while the sand remained grey and soft beneath his feet. And as they walked he could feel the magnitude of their problems lessen, reduce, shrink in size: he wanted to ask Jing, for instance, about how she might still be grieving the loss of her mother, or about how she felt now about the way that Tori had disappeared; instead he felt as though they now carried a film of the light they just left behind, wrapped around themselves like a divine shroud against the wind, the very elements that buffeted against their very selves as they linked their arms together, still making their slow way across the beach.

But it was Jing who'd ask Isaac about the problem he alluded to earlier, back at the puerto. She asked him about his stealing, and he told her, a summary, of the conversation he had with Frankie more than a month ago. He told her that the reason he'd been freer lately was not because he was in between projects, but because he was being made to stay quiet, keep a low profile, avoid all interactions with the media. She then asked if there had been a notable resurgence in his habit this year, and he said yes, it's true, there might be. She asked if it might have started around April, to be exact, and he said yes, yes. It was possible. It was when the shooting for his latest drama was coming to an end. It's Sherry, isn't it, said Jing, and Isaac knew, really, that there was no point in denying it. And she said it was okay, she'd already suspected as much, that filming with Sherry again was always complicated, difficult. I saw the article, she said—about her dating that businessman from Hong Kong. And as Jing said this, Isaac couldn't tell if the light they had managed to enshroud themselves in was finally tearing away or not. He felt someone approaching them from behind, and it was Daniel, just Daniel, walking towards them from the hotel.

Hola, he said, to the two of them. I saw you from my room, aha.

Isaac looked back again at hotel, wondering if he might see Mateo too, somewhere. Daniel placed a hand on his shoulder, and asked Jing if he could speak with her husband for a while.

Jing nodded; he made sure to kiss her on the cheek, before she went away. Even her footprints in the sand felt luminous to him.

So you're still invited to the wedding, said Daniel.

Isaac nodded. Okay.

And you're still my friend, Isaac. Let's not forget that.

He blushed. Can, he said. Thanks.

Daniel smiled. He then looked out at the ocean, at the Gulf of Cádiz; they were seated on the sand, the waves only a metre or so from their feet, seashells around them exposed from the low tide.

Did Jing tell you what happened to Mateo?

He told him she did. He told him he's really sorry to hear that too, that someone in their lives had to go through something like that. Isaac told Daniel that when the attack had happened, he admittedly didn't think much of them; the incident felt so far away from him, from where he was in Singapore. It shocked him, yes, but the shock was a dull one in the country he lived in, as though living in Singapore had inoculated him from the rest of the world, from the dangers that resided in those parts. He didn't even think to ask Daniel about the Madrid bombings, considering how they were now based in Barcelona. He asked what Mateo was doing there, back in Madrid; Daniel told him that their relationship had been in a rough patch, that they had been on the verge of breaking up again.

Isaac felt surprised, genuinely surprised. How come? he asked. You guys looked so happy when we visited you last year. And Daniel said it was precisely that, their happiness, that prompted him to propose to Mateo, only to have Mateo reject him that year, not because he didn't love him, but because he couldn't see the point of marriage, not while Aznar was still in charge of the country. And so the two entered a sort of impasse, with emotion on one hand and politics on the other, wearing and tearing away at them, their relationship.

And then one day, said Daniel: Mateo got a job offer, back in Madrid. A former boss of his had become the new head of a museum, and wanted Mateo to interview for a position he was opening up. And so you told him to go? Isaac asked, and Daniel said, Of course I did, aha. He flew to Madrid the following week. The two friends then sat on the shore, content to stay in the silence for a while.

Daniel asked who Tori was eventually. Isaac told him what he had told Shigeru: that she was someone in pain, and that she was also someone who wanted to be lifted out of that pain. She was his only friend when he was just a loser, with no clue what to do with his life, after he had run away from home. Tori was how he got to meet Jing and Mateo too, in the kitchen of the ryokan where Tori worked. When Isaac told Daniel what she had left behind, Daniel asked why it took him eight years to return it, the suitcase.

Isaac said he wanted to make amends, before it was too late. Before what was too late? asked Daniel. Isaac then brought his hands together, as though in prayer, as he said:

I started stealing again.

Why? asked Daniel.

Isaac replied: There was an accident. A really terrible accident in Singapore. He told him that there was a tunnel being built, for a new train station located deeper underground than usual; the tunnel fell, and it caused an entire section of road to collapse, six lanes wide and thirty metres deep. Isaac asked Daniel if he had heard about it, the collapse of the Nicoll Highway, and Daniel shook his head, causing Isaac to nod, and think—Of course not.

He then told his friend that on the day of the incident, he was filming the last scene of his latest drama; the actors were piled into a small room on set, assistants steam-ironing the actors' clothes and touching up their make-up. And then the news started to play, from a small TV plugged into the corner: it displayed an aerial shot of a giant hole, a massive crater in the middle of the highway. And when the cast and crew stared, aghast, at something they'd never witnessed in Singapore before, Isaac found himself reminded of things he'd long forgotten, bringing him back not just to his friend, to Tori, and the story of what she had gone through during the Great Hanshin Earthquake, but also back to that time, in the flat he used to live in, listening to the radio describe the earthquake. He remembered imagining, wishing, for Singapore to experience something like that too. And as he thought about this he stared at his co-star, the actress Sherry Wong, convinced somehow that the collapse of the Nicoll Highway had been an incident of his own making—that what he had wished for in the past had fired like a bullet, one that he had shot into the air and was careening, finally, back down towards the earth after a span of eight years. And as he looked at what it had cost, at the destruction he had caused, just by wishing for something like this as a young man, he became afraid of himself, of what he was capable of, and deathly afraid too of losing everything he had as a consequence of his actions. And so he took it, a scarf, as though to compensate for any future losses he might sustain; it was the first thing he'd taken in a long, long time, and when the cast and crew finally tore their eyes away from the news, it was too late—the scarf was already missing. Nobody knew where it had gone, while the stealing, the taking—it would only go on, unabated, until life finally told him: it had enough.

19

The Horvallan. Jing Aw. Flame of the Forest, Singapore, 2005.

Joan Miró Foundation, 2003

My family and I flew to Barcelona that year to celebrate a milestone in our friend's life. Mateo Calvo Morales, a curator at the Joan Miró Foundation, had finally moved in with his partner into a brand-new apartment in Barcelona. He would be turning thirty-four as well, on the 30th of May, which made that weekend the perfect excuse to party, he said to us in his email.

Mateo has been in my life for a long time; we've been friends for ten years, to be exact. I got to know him in my final year in London, when I, relatively friendless, became his roommate in a flat in Russel Square. Since London, however, I have only managed to see Mateo twice: once in Japan, in 1996, and then briefly the following year, in Singapore, when he was the maid of honour at my wedding. We were supposed to see him again, in 2000, when we learnt that his partner was turning forty that year, but the passing away of my grandmother forced us to reconsider. And then 9/11 happened, eliminating all talk about our visiting him again, not till 2003, when he sent us a livid email (the subject line reading: "I'm older than Jesus will ever be, you bastard??") that made us decide it was finally time to fly. And Yong-he would come along too, to see this legendary "Uncle Matey", who had only ever appeared as photographs in our periodic emails to one another. There were moments when Uncle Matey too had become an imaginary friend for Yong-he.

At this point, I have to admit: I didn't think I'd ever see you again. And while the thought did haunt me from time to time, it might have spurred me, in a way, to focus on my family. Something must have changed in me, ever since you told me that story, about me and my father on the bridge: you handed not a key to me, but a beacon, one that shone light over a chapter of my own history I was still struggling to understand.

Which is not to say that things were perfect, of course, between me and my husband. By May 2003, Isaac would have won seven prizes at the annual Star Awards: two for acting, five for popularity, a true prince of Caldecott Hill, second only to Li Nanxing. By the time we left for Barcelona, Isaac would have long emerged as the breadwinner of the family, having bought and sold three increasingly expensive cars. He paid for renovation works throughout a house he slept in less and less, overhauling the electrical wiring, the light fixtures, and all of the bathrooms, a process that excluded and ultimately alienated my grandfather from his own home. And although he and I became busier and busier with our respective responsibilities, it ensured that whatever time we had left together would be spent cordially and politely, for the sake of our son, with no energy left to pick unnecessary fights. It was as though we were moving through a strange, dissociative fugue, happy to let time pass through us rather than what I thought should be the other way round: to make full use of the time we still had together. To push against the passing of time, to insist, in our own way, on some method of living more authentically, more meaningfully in the present. All while my heart—wherever it may be—became ripe with longing for an alternative future.

I'd received photos of their new apartment before, a west-facing unit that occupied the fourth storey of a short but handsome building, situated discreetly along Rambla de Catalunya. But I never truly grasped the true extent of its splendour till my family and I stepped foot inside it, on the morning of the 25th of May. It glowed bright green with the leaves of lime trees, planted in neat rows up and down the length of the gorgeous avenue.

It was Mateo's birthday that Friday, the couple about to leave for dinner reservations; Isaac himself was preparing a curry for the three of us, with Yong-he as his garlic-peeling assistant. I found myself wandering into their study, after several days of aggressive sightseeing around the city. I could hold my arm up against the light in the room, just to see how it dappled on my skin. The shadows of the lime trees played over all of their books too, mostly on art and architecture, with a few novels and memoirs scattered about. I also managed to find an entire row of old LPs and cassette tapes, and even a large case of floppy discs. And I suppose that was how I eventually stumbled upon a photograph that intrigued me, hung on a small, bare section of a wall. Quickly the photograph made the hair on my arms stand; it made me wonder if I had imagined it, or if it was just another trick of the light. It made me walk out of the study, where I managed to find Daniel, in the living room, watching CNN while Isaac continued to cook.

"Where's Mateo?" I asked. Daniel turned towards me.

"Probably still getting dressed," he said. "You know how he is."

Mateo spoke in Spanish when I knocked on the door of the master bedroom; I told him it was me, and he promptly opened the door. "I was just about to spritz myself," he said. He then beckoned me to come in, and I did, seating myself at the edge of their bed. Mateo disappeared into the en-suite bathroom while I said: "I was just in your study."

"Ah," came his reply. "It's really more Daniel's room than mine, to be honest." He asked if anything caught my eye, and I said yes, in fact. I told him I was intrigued by a photograph, framed and in black and white. Mateo said the photograph I was describing was a gift from the artist herself.

"I love it," he said. "Almost abstract, is it not, for a photograph?"

I got up from the bed. I lingered by the entrance to the bathroom, watching Mateo put on contact lenses for the evening. I told him I was intrigued by the title; I told him I'd seen it, scribbled at the corner of the frame, right underneath the signature. "I'm wondering if the title's in Spanish?" I asked.

It was, said Mateo; he told me it was both a portmanteau and a corruption of two Spanish words. "In English it would read as *hour-fence or time-fence. I suppose the most elegant way of putting it would be a fence in time.*"

"'Fence'?" I said. "As in boundary?"

"As in a marker," said Mateo. "Of where two places meet, intersect."

I asked Mateo if it was the title of a series of photographic works; the numbering in the label seemed to indicate this aspect of the artwork. Mateo nodded again, and said I might get to meet the photographer tomorrow, Deepika Rai, the Foundation's artist-in-residence this season. He had invited her to the party, and was keen to introduce her to his circle in Barcelona. Mateo then said that it might be a good idea to visit his workplace if I was so intrigued by the series of photographs: it was all being displayed as an installation at the Foundation. I told him I'd like to be there, first thing tomorrow morning.

"Miss Singapore," said Mateo, stepping out of the bathroom. "Ever on a mission." He asked if Isaac and Yong-he might tag along as well.

"I'll ask them," I said. "Thanks, Mateo."

After Mateo and Daniel left, I found my husband and child still in the kitchen, Isaac stirring his curry in the pot. I told him that Mateo was planning to take me to the Foundation the next morning, and Isaac didn't seem to mind.

"Daniel offered to take us to Barceloneta Beach," he said. My husband then suggested taking Yong-he with him, when I failed to say that I would.

I slipped back into the study, closing the door behind me. I looked at the photograph once more, an abstractly-rendered photograph, with multiple layers of images superimposed over one another. One of the few, clearer images within the photograph was that of a paper boat, or was it a paper aeroplane? It remained hard to tell. More importantly, in the corner, was the label that said:

"Orpheus bound for love"
Horvalla (No. 16)
edn. 3/8

"Fuck me," I said. It took all my effort to remain calm. It took everything in me to rejoin my husband and my son, saying that dinner was ready to be served.

The next day, Mateo and I took the metro from Passeig de Gràcia station down to Paral·lel, where we took a tram in the southwest direction, alighting a stop later in the midst of the majestic Parc de Montjuïc. It was a three-minute walk, about two hundred metres or so, surrounded by expertly-trimmed hedges and the smell of freshly cut leaves. The Joan Miró Foundation, nestled within the park, was itself a large complex of curiously designed buildings, resembling blocks that stacked on top of one another. This complex was also painted entirely in white, betraying a kind of intense purity, set against the backdrop of luscious, copious greens.

Mateo showed me around the building, including his office. But first he brought me to the upper floor, where Deepika Rai's photographs might be found. And there were plenty of them, too many of them, some might say, arranged in a mosaic-like pattern over the walls of a single circular room. The overall effect was disorienting, dizzying; every glimpse of a face, every sketch of a scene, every trace of an object, every altered image already layered on top of one another, threatening ever more still to flow out of their individual frames and merge with those beside them, as though to render even the very boundaries of the medium illusory.

This was Horvalla, I thought—and there, you were.

*   *   *

We didn't speak until an hour later, back down on the ground floor with the permanent exhibit. Standing next to one another, I was at once stunned and numb to the fact that you looked just the way as I remembered you, with a white shirt over a pair of trousers, but with the addition of sunglasses, clipped over an open collar.

"I had a free admission ticket," you said to me. "I had to come."

I asked if Deepika Rai knew about your current project. I felt a pang of jealousy when you said that she did, and that she was part of a small group that knew of your stories about the Horvallan.

"So it's done?"

"No," you said. "It isn't."

"And yet you've started, what—circulating it to others?"

You shrugged. "That's out of my control. And I am close to the end, anyway: the end of the story."

You led me to the cafeteria, where we ordered a cup of café con hielo each. For some reason, I found that I had zero compulsion to ask you anything personal, as the two of us sat opposite one another. I had no desire to know anything specific about your life. I didn't want to know what you were going to do that day, or when your time in Spain would come to an end; a part of me knew none of those things mattered, and that neither of us wanted to waste the other's time.

"You said you would tell me what happened on board the space station."

"Between the Horvallan and the oncologist."

"Yes," I said. "In 7085AD."

You nodded. That we hadn't seen one another in three years meant nothing to you, it seemed. For what were three years, after all, compared to a thousand? You said:

"The Horvallan is seated before the oncologist, inside her clinic within the RSS *Ubin*. He says to her: 'I finally have reason to think I am dying."

Our heroine asks him why. *The only thing that can put you in harm's way is some kind of irreparable trauma,* she says. *Even the most advanced virus would have a tough fight against you.* She quickly looks at him, up and down, to size him up. *Are you sick?* she asks. *Are you in pain?*

The Horvallan doesn't stir. *I think I am seeing things,* he says instead, and she asks him what that means. He replies:

I see things that are not meant to be here. Things that cannot . . . possibly be on the space station. I'm wondering if I'm losing my mind.

Our heroine now looks the Horvallan squarely in the eyes. She knows that he played an important part in shaping human history; she knows that he was instrumental, to say the least, in guiding Earthlings and its aliens towards the collective colonisation of Mars. She simply hadn't anticipated that the Horvallan might be going mad as well. If her brief rotation on psych has taught her anything, it's that you never tell a person that they are in the midst of a psychotic break—especially if that person has a following of cult-like devotees.

I can call in a neuro consult, our heroine says. *Would you like that?*

He shakes his head. *Let's keep this between us for now,* he says, though the oncologist remains naturally hesitant.

You are aware my specialty is in cancer, she says, and he nods, saying, *Of course.*

The oncologist rises from her chair, and directs the Horvallan over to an adjacent room. She tells him that there are well-documented cases of brain cancers that induce hallucinations, though it is very rare, of course, for cancers to ever reach that stage these days. She then pauses, and asks if that was why he cut her queue, and the Horvallan smiles bashfully. His security clearance is amazing, and it comes with certain privileges, he says. *I might have abused them in this instance,* he adds.

Our heroine makes sure to flash him a neutral smile in return, even as she says: *Quite right.* She then points to her scanner, a chamber no larger than a closet, with a glowing tile on both the floor and ceiling. *I'm going to put you through a quick scan, okay?*

The Horvallan does as he is told. He changes into scrubs, and steps into the scanner. Our heroine takes quick note of a scar he has, across the right of his torso; she then presses a button on the screen of her tablet, which seals the chamber shut. The oncologist holds her tablet out for him to see, through a window in the door that only reveals his face.

You see all this red here? she says via the intercom. *Top secret, everything. Every single one of your past scans.* The oncologist then brings up the operating system for the scanner, and shows him the button at the corner of the interface. *Once I press this, however, I'll know everything about your body in less than sixty seconds, with analysis in less than ninety minutes, maybe two hours, tops.* She asks if doing this will get her into any trouble, and the Horvallan shrugs and says they'll have to see. The oncologist's jaw drops.

First you cut my queue, she says—*now you're holding me hostage?*

The Horvallan blinks. *What?*

If the Singaporeans pulverise me in my sleep, she says, *I'm going to be very, very upset with you.*

The Horvallan lets out a laugh; his breath causes the window between them to mist up for a moment.

They're not going to pulverise you, he says.

Drug me, then. Wipe my memory? Whatever happens, says the oncologist—*I'll come back, I swear, because I'm not expected to die for another sixty years. I'll haunt you good,* she adds, words that have a strange effect on the Horvallan this time. He looks unable to decide if he might laugh or cry.

I guess it's a race then, he says. *To see who actually perishes first.*

The oncologist purses her lips, and looks down at her tablet. Nothing about this morning has gone according to plan. She presses the button, and her tablet glows a shade of green, indicating that the scanner is now extracting the Horvallan's biometrics. *You're really keeping your shit together by the way,* she says, *for someone who's seeing things for no reason.* A low chuckle emerges from the Horvallan.

There isn't much else I can do, he says.

The green glow fades: his data pops up on her interface, which she manages to access with no resistance. She tells him it's done, hoping that her excitement isn't too obvious. She unlocks the chamber of the scanner. She asks the Horvallan what his schedule is like for the day, to go over his data once the analysis is complete, and the Horvallan tells our heroine that he has a fair number of people to meet over the afternoon. But he would be free to talk over dinner, says the Horvallan. *Would that idea appeal to you at all?* he asks.

The oncologist nods, and blinks, unable to figure out the sudden blushing in his ears. *I'll be right here,* she says.

Draining the last of your coffee, you said: "There is nothing wrong with the Horvallan."

"Not even a brain tumour," I said.

No, you replied: our hero is perfectly healthy. "He's been healthy for thousands of years."

I crossed my arms. "So there's another reason he's hallucinating."

"Yes."

"And will I find out that reason today?"

"Not right now," you said, "but tonight, perhaps." That was when I saw Mateo coming towards the cafeteria—and that was when you said you'd be at the housewarming that night, as Deepika Rai's plus-one.

It was half past nine. You appeared, dressed for the occasion, with a navy blazer worn over a striped T-shirt. You looked charming, I had to admit, now that you were out of your usual uniform. But what I realised next was that all the people I ever loved could now be found in a single room; all of their paths had converged somehow, at the very same point in space and time, and my first response to the fact was to leave it.

I once had a friend, you see, many years ago: she never liked to stay at any one place for too long, and who was a lot like my mother in that final respect. And I never understood either of their compulsions until then, there in that place that Mateo called home, where I could see that it was possible to be loved, and to be surrounded by love in a way we know we do not deserve. If you are big enough of a monster, you just know. And if you are good enough of a person, you will not settle for simply knowing the fact. You will also walk away.

But I didn't walk away, of course; I didn't say I was a good person. Instead I stayed in that apartment, carrying Yong-he around, introducing him to people. I fed him carrot sticks, which he loved for their sweetness, and I would dip them in many sauces too, just to fool him into thinking he wasn't eating the same thing constantly. I did my best to remain with the boy until I couldn't resist it any longer, the pull you had over me, and handed Yong-he over to Isaac. I then walked over to where you stood, in the kitchen, where you were pouring yourself a glass of sangria.

"I don't think your husband remembers me," you said.

"What do you mean?" I asked.

"From the car accident. Four years ago."

"Right," I said. I nearly forgot about it myself, that night. I asked if you had spoken to him yet, to Isaac, and you said no.

"Haven't you heard? I'm playing a game," you said. "It involves not being noticed by your husband for as long as possible."

I smirked. "How do you win?" I asked, and you laughed and said: "Time with you." Later you asked if I had spoken to Deepika Rai yet, and I said that I hadn't; we went in search for her, and managed to find her, the artist, seated on the floor of the study. Daniel was there too, standing in a corner of the room, taking what seemed like a photo album out from one of the shelves.

"My sweet," said the artist, reaching out to hold your hand. "Sit beside me."

I took my place beside you two, and introduced myself. She raised her glass.

"Are you the mother?"

I laughed, and so did Daniel, who came over to sit with us too. "I am the mother, yes," I said to her. Later I asked where Mateo was, and Daniel said he didn't know. I then asked what he was doing with the album, and Daniel said that he wanted to show Deepika something: a photo of himself, taken as a child in Tarragona, his hometown, a port city situated by the Mediterranean Sea.

"Here it is," he said, pulling the photo out from its sleeve. "That is little me."

"And that's the cathedral?" said the artist, smiling as she fixed a look at you and then at me, her large earrings swinging and glinting in the light as she did so. Deepika said she was fascinated with buildings such as the Cathedral of Tarragona, buildings that curiously combined two very different architectural styles, which in this case was the Romanesque and the Gothic. "A building constructed over the course of two centuries," she explained, "straddling two eras, two worlds, two modes of being— embodied and resultant in a single, marvellous creation." Deepika then smiled at us again, with the pleasure of hearing herself speak; she pointed to a detail in another photograph, this time taken in the interior of the building.

"Look at the windows," she said. "They are a great example of what I am talking about: Romanesque in shape, with these curiously curved mould- ings. But the windows are stained, which are totally Gothic in style." You then reached over, and pointed Daniel out in both pictures, sporting glasses of the thickest frames.

"You were short-sighted, even as a child?"

"Oh, yes," said Daniel, "of course. I read too many books, at too young an age. That was entirely my fault."

Deepika chuckled at the exchange between the two men. I asked her how she was finding the residency, and the artist smiled as she tilted her head back, as though to savour what was she was about to say. "Fabulous," she replied. "I owe a great, great debt to the Foundation. And to this man, of course," she added, placing a hand on your forearm.

"Because of Horvalla?" I asked, eyeing the gesture. "The word?" I pointed towards the framed photograph, hanging on the wall behind Deepika; the artist looked over her shoulder and said yes, exactly that, unsurprised by how I came to know the exactness of their connection. "How did you come up with the name?" I asked, to you this time, and you shrugged, saying that you didn't know.

"To be completely honest," you said: "It just came to me."

Daniel held up a hand. "I feel like I am missing something here," he said. "You are the one who gave her the title?"

You nodded, and said Deepika took it, more like.

"And what do you do?" Daniel asked. "Are you also an artist?" You smiled at him, and said you were a writer, to which he responded, "Aha—like Jing?"

"Not quite," you said. "She is a journalist, a columnist. I write science fiction."

"Aha," said Daniel again, eyes wide with excitement. "And so Horvalla is . . . ?"

You and I looked at one another.

"A place," you said.

"In one of your stories?" said Daniel.

"In a large story I am working on, yes."

"Is it a planet?" asked Daniel. "Horvalla, hmm—it *sounds* like a planet. Maybe I am wrong, but it feels like one, I mean. Is Horvalla where the book is set?"

You looked at Daniel, very intently. You appeared to mull over the question. But it was the artist, Deepika, who answered the question instead.

"It's *somewhere*," she said. "An in-between sort of place. Which might not make it much of a place at all: a place that isn't bounded, but is located in between the bounds. Am I close?"

You had your hand on your chin, and slowly nodded at her. "Are we losing the two of you?" you then asked, to me and Daniel both, and all we could do was laugh.

"I'm okay. Maybe not drunk enough," said Daniel. "Do you get it, Jing?" he asked, and I said I was trying to. I asked Deepika how she had allowed the word, *Horvalla*, to shape her photographic output, her current exhibition at the Foundation. She said it all boiled down to the very nature of light.

"My whole life, I've been working on a thesis," she said: "That light is a measure of time. You might have heard this from somewhere before: the filmmaker, Andrei Tarkovsky, once said that cinema is a *mosaic* in time. No?" She turned to Daniel. "Has Mateo, your darling, ever mentioned this to you?"

He shook his head. "No," he said. "Unfamiliar."

"I see," said Deepika. "Well. Throughout my career I had to always ask myself some important questions. Questions like, when I take a photograph, what am I *recording*, exactly? What am I measuring, or rather—what am I *proving*? That things exist? That people exist? That this happened? Which is to say, what—the truth? But what would be the point of any of that, if, like Jeff Wall, I reveal that my subject is in fact a model or a group of actors I paid to pose for me? Can we still say that the photograph captures the truth?" Deepika paused then, smiling at the three of us. "It would be naive to think that anything in a photograph is a hundred per cent true. Because even the truth itself shifts, no? Is ever-changing?" she said. "But the world persists in thinking otherwise. The world persists in believing that there is an absolute truth. That the photograph can only stand for the truth. But the *only* thing that is true—in any photograph anybody takes—is that it was taken in a moment in time. Time is the only truth that remains," she declared to the room: "The light that burns on a piece of film is the instance in time in which everything, really, is made to hang in the balance. And so light, to me—it's not just a measure of time. It's a mark in time as well."

The study fell quiet; the only sounds we could hear then were from the party outside. "So you've proven that time exists," I eventually said to Deepika. "So what? Everyone knows that too." And the artist, luminous as she was in the study that evening, remained undaunted by my challenge.

"Of course we do," she said. "But our grasp on the idea of time remains terribly . . . insufficient. Because what does it mean to say that we exist in time? To exist within a temporality?" She turned to everyone. "It is to acknowledge that our planet is in constant, continual motion. Isn't it? And because the planet is constantly moving forward, so shall all the life that presides within it. So will death, then: not as a pause, but as a step forward, ever onward, in tandem with the pace of our lives. And so how does the photograph fit into this scheme of things?" she asked. "What good does it do, for *me*, if the photograph renders something mobile—immobile? Wouldn't you say that's inauthentic to how life actually works? Do you see what the dilemma is now?"

"I think so," I said. The best I could figure was this: to Deepika, an artist, this was both a practical and a conceptual concern, bordering even on the existential. To her, the photograph ultimately captures time in a way that isn't reflective of how time operates. It is an inherently flawed enterprise in capturing the world. And so I looked up at the photograph once more: at *"Orpheus bound for love"—Horvalla (No. 16)*. "When you layer multiple images over one another, like you do in the *Horvalla* series, are you attempting to, I don't know—give movement back to the photograph? To free the image from being static? So that it can more closely resemble our reality?"

Here Deepika smiled at me, although somewhat sadly. "That would be impossible," she said. "Look at it now: is it in fact moving, right before your eyes?"

I shook my head.

"So I'm cheating death," she said. "When I freeze time, multiple temporalities even—I'm forestalling the prospect. But even that is just an illusion, of course, for I can't actually stop time. And I can't actually stop death. Not if I only have ink on paper." She then brought her hands together. "Can you see how the photograph falls into a self-made cycle? One that it can't free itself from? How it suggests one thing while reinforcing the opposite idea?"

You looked at me then. I looked at Daniel. He looked at Deepika.

"And so all of us," he said: "we're trapped. There is no freedom."

"Yes," said Deepika.

"Not from time."

"Yes."

"Not from death."

"Yes, yes."

"But we do all we can to escape this trap."

Deepika nodded. "But we can't. Let me remind you: time is a cruel thing, something that we can never escape. And yet isn't it so human?" she said, to everyone in the study. "To think that we might? To say we shall try, at least, even against the odds? Because all we want is to be free, to liberate our-selves—against all suffering, yes?" She smiled at us once more. "That is what breaks my heart," she said. "And that is what has kept it beating till now."

It was midnight. I had barely seen the birthday boy, Mateo, all evening. Isaac and I had just put Yong-he to bed, in the guest room, when Deepika asked if I might want to walk with her, for just a bit.

"Wait," I said. "What about our dear friend?" I asked if you had already left.

"Oh I think so," she said. It was not really your style, she said, to make proper goodbyes.

I told Isaac I would be out for a bit. I then headed down to the foot of the building, where I found her, the artist, standing over the roots of a lime tree.

"Where would you like to go?" I asked.

"I'm not sure," she said. "But I'm okay with that."

And so the two of us started walking, in some general direction along Rambla de Catalunya. It was chillier at night, hovering around fifteen degrees Celsius, but neither of us seemed to mind. I asked Deepika where she was from, and she said she was from Uttar Pradesh, in northern India.

"You're not Malaysian, are you? You're from that other place—you're Singaporean."

I nodded.

"Does being Singaporean mean anything to you?" she asked. It was a question nobody had asked me before. I told her I didn't understand.

Deepika smiled. "I just wanted to know," she said. "Whenever people ask me where I'm from, I always tell them. I tell them everything they want to know except the fact that the question's not really important, not to me at least. It's probably more meaningful, more interesting, to ask where we are going *to*. Do you disagree?"

I scoffed at her; we were still walking down the Rambla. "Well, I did ask you," I said. "And you literally just said you weren't sure."

"Yes!" said Deepika, bursting into laughter. "And I made sure to clarify that I was okay with that, didn't I?"

Eventually we hit an intersection. Deepika turned to a rather upscale and crowded bar that stood at the corner, and asked if she could buy me a drink. She then led me to sit at the one available table they had on the sidewalk, and ordered a glass of white wine each, along with some tomatoes on toasted bread.

"Who do you think the Horvallan really is?" was the first question she asked me. I told her I wasn't so sure myself, and that all I knew was that he is immortal. "He presents himself as more or less human," I said, "and that he is presumably from a place named, well—Horvalla."

Deepika nodded. "To be perfectly honest, I don't even know what Horvalla is. I can only guess so much from how the word was put together."

"'A fence in time'?"

She nodded again. She asked me: "What do you think it means, to have a fence in time? I want to know what you think."

I told her I've been trying to figure it out all day. "Typically, a fence functions as a border, or a boundary," I said, recalling what Mateo said to me the day before. "It marks the bounds of any given territory."

"Yes, sure. But this is *time* we are talking about," said Deepika. "A *temporality*. A fence, if you think about it, marks the presence of at least two territories; it clearly marks where two lands, two properties have chosen to co-exist, side by side. Is our friend saying that there are two *times*, then? Two temporalities? That it was possible to exist *between* these two things?"

"I suppose that's why you called it an 'in-between' place," I said. "Earlier, back in the study."

"Yes," said Deepika. "That I did." She then appeared to be distracted, gazing off into the road before us. "Have you ever heard of the saying?" she asked. "'Death is a clock with no hands'?"

I shook my head. I told her that was the first time I ever heard it. And that was how her smile came back: her knowing, sad, beatific smile.

"I was in despair once," she said. "A long time ago. The despair, how do I describe it . . . It felt as though someone had reached into the most intimate, innermost part of me, and ripped out all the light I ever had, my soul. And then for a period of time I was totally adrift. I was lost, wandering." She took a sip of her wine. "When you wander for too long, everything, even time itself, blurs in a way that will make you think: maybe this is it. This is forever." She then let out a laugh, as though she was ashamed of what she was saying. "Maybe I will never stop hurting, you start to think."

I told her I was sorry. I asked her what had changed. She told me to guess.

"You met someone," I said.

"I did. Our dear friend, as you so put it," said Deepika. "We met by chance, and he told me a story . . . A story he is telling *you* right now. A story that showed me that time, time—it's not what we think it is. It's not uniform, or neat. Not even the stories we tell one another. Life follows a line, yes, but that line is messy. It's scrambled, intertwined. From a distance, that line might even resemble something like a web, a circuit. Perhaps even a circle."

She laid a hand on our table. "He saved me, is what he did. With just this story," she said. "It's how I found it."

"The light?"

"No," she said. "The love, darling. I found love. A pure love, the kind of love one needs in order to tell a true story, a truthful story. I know I can tell you this, because I know you found it too."

I looked at her. Deepika never stopped smiling at me that night, there at the bar. Neither of us managed to notice that our food had yet to arrive.

"He suggested that I tell you the next part of the story," Deepika said to me. "But I won't. I'm sorry. It's he whom I am in love with, not you. And so I am going to be selfish this time. You're just going to have to stay stranded on the RSS for now."

I leant back against my chair. I felt winded, blindsided; I told her I already knew the Horvallan's going to be fine. "There's nothing wrong with him," I said.

Deepika snorted. "Woman!" she said. "There's something wrong with all of us. You just have to lean in and look." She scratched her collarbone absentmindedly, before she spoke up again.

"Would it be okay if I never said a word to you again? Would that be fine with you?" said Deepika. "The wine and the toast, it's all on me, so—would that serve as my apology? Or my price?" She now had both hands over her chest. "Please," she said to me, still smiling. "For fuck's sake."

20

The barbecue began at noon, as planned. From the deck on the rooftop, perennially strewn with sand, Mateo managed to spy on the Neos, sauntering their way through the maze of dirt paths leading to the front gate. Lines of sun-warmed linen and the day's assortment of beach towels flapped beside him as he watched Yong-he dash towards the other children in the courtyard, target clearly locked, embroiling himself immediately into an intense game of tag.

Jing and Isaac remained arm in arm, still walking into the villa. Mateo managed to catch Daniel's voice, raised in greeting to the couple. Where's Mateo? he heard Jing say, while Daniel replied: I'm not sure.

He didn't know when Deepika had arrived, but he could hear her voice anyway, echoing up the staircase behind him. My sweet Mateo, she said: what a lovely casa this is. And as he looked over his shoulder, taking note of the artist's new haircut and her mustard yellow summer dress, he found himself back at that bar, at the end of Rambla de Catalunya, on the night of the 31st of May, 2003. But first, they had to hug; he commented on how fabulous she smelled, causing the artist to demur, saying that she just arrived from Amsterdam. Deepika then congratulated him, for marrying the man after all; she said she was nonetheless surprised, considering how things went the last time.

I distinctly recall some resistance to the idea, said Deepika.

It was how Mateo knew that the artist was thinking of that same night as well, the night he and Daniel held their housewarming party: Mateo had chosen to slip out of the apartment and grab a glass of Prosecco instead, at the nice, crowded bar at the end of the street. It was a place he took note of immediately, when he and Daniel had agreed to buy the apartment; it was a place where he felt he could be alone, but not alone, a phrase he remembered Tori once saying to him. A glass however became a bottle, became two bottles and a half; and then Jing appeared with Deepika somehow, at a few minutes past midnight, the two taking the one table left by the sidewalk. And then Jing left too, prompting Mateo to get up and take her place, the chair still warm with the remnants of her presence. Oh! said Deepika. Like magic! And Mateo cackled, planting his bottle of Prosecco on the table. A fucking fairy, that's what I am, he declared, and as the artist narrowed her eyes at him, he said oh, oh dear. I know that look. I know exactly what you're thinking.

Deepika raised an eyebrow. Do you? she said. Enlighten me, please.

Mateo bit his lip; a server came, bearing a plate of pan con tomate. He knew that he and the artist shared a professional relationship, but it didn't change the fact that they had become friends as well. And so he told her that he might have fucked up last night, and Deepika asked him how so. Wasn't it your birthday? she asked, and he said yes, it was: Daniel had taken him to Casa Sayrach last night, to La Dama, the famed restaurant. He said the topic of marriage came up somehow, after the truffled paté, the lettuce hearts and their plate of bay scallops au gratin had arrived; it came up when it was revealed that Daniel would be taking Isaac and his son to Barceloneta Beach the following morning, while Jing had asked to be taken to the Foundation instead. I like Isaac, said Daniel—I might prefer him, actually, over Jing. And as Daniel divided the paté, he said that their son was beautiful too, a very sweet child. I think Yong-he has his mother's brains, but his father's heart, aha.

He told Deepika, spurred by the Prosecco, about how he gave Daniel a weak smile, one with no words. What? asked Daniel, and Mateo said nothing at first, focussed on his scallop. He then said the same thing he just said to Deepika: I know what you're thinking. And Daniel asked if he was sure, if Mateo actually knew what was going through his mind right now, and Mateo had responded: You're feeling inspired.

Deepika chortled at this point of the story. She took a bite of the pan con tomate, and asked Mateo what Daniel did next, wiping away the crumbs from her fingers. And Mateo said that Daniel had laughed as well, albeit uncertainly. He wanted to know what was so wrong about that.

Because we can't, replied Mateo.

We can't?

Not under Aznar, he said. Not with the unión de hecho. I know you're supportive, but—

Darling, said Daniel, cutting him off: this is not about whether I like the prime minister.

No? said Mateo. You don't see how this issue is political?

And Daniel said no, but yes, but then not in the way it has to be, clearly incensed by Mateo's question. He said that he didn't need to ask the government's permission for Mateo to live with him. He said he didn't need its permission either for them to spend their lives together, or to include him in his will, his insurance policies, whatever. That would be pathetic, right? You agree? he said, hands shaking as he adjusted his glasses. Only when the shaking stopped did Daniel add: The world doesn't have to make sense, Mateo.

Mateo shook his head. No.

Everything is upside down.

Sure.

Mateo watched Daniel place his hand across the table. So all we have left is love, he said. To put everything right again, no?

Mateo stared at him. He looked down at Daniel's hand, still pleading. Take it, please, his partner said, and Mateo did. The two men held hands at La Dama, not speaking for a minute; Mateo then said he was sorry, to forget what he said. And Deepika, pouring more Prosecco for herself in the bar along Rambla de Catalunya, asked how Daniel had responded to that. With regret in his voice, he told her: "What if I don't want to?"

So what changed since then? asked Deepika, on the deck of the rooftop beside him. Mateo continued to look down onto the courtyard, and at the trail of smoke that now wafted from the barbecue pits.

Do you remember how I sent you off, that night?

Deepika looked perplexed, like she had to hold back a laugh. Not really, she said. Should I?

Mateo neither nodded nor shook his head; instead he continued to fix his gaze on the scene down below, where he could see Isaac and Jing now, trying to feed their son some lunch.

You said: "You know, I worry for the child, instinctually." You remember this? asked Mateo. You then gave me this whole speech about your first divorce, and how you knew that you were deliberately hurting your child. I asked you what that had to do with Jing; I asked if it had anything to do with what you were talking about that evening. You then said you could tell how a couple was doing, not by the time they spent together, but by the time they spent apart. The artist had then drained her glass right after that; he remembered how she had asked Mateo to be a dear, and help her get a taxi. I'm going to float away any moment now, she'd said.

Mateo then told Deepika about an image he'd seen, once he managed to flag a taxi down for her. The car came, and screeched, and in the night appeared momentarily silver, lustrous and blinding; he told her about how he'd seen an image like this, many years ago in Japan, while coming back from a convenience store to his lodgings. He told her about how he had kept to the side of the road, and hid in the shadows, aghast by what he was seeing and hearing; he told her how he had managed to live with this image, an image that has frankly haunted him for many years, one that he managed to beat back into a dark corner of his mind when he reunited with Daniel. But the image managed to return to him that night, there at the bar on Rambla de Catalunya: it made him begin to dream of it, the memory, walking down that same road in Kyoto every other night, seeing that same car, and the people in that car. It made Mateo drink again, the way he used to in his turbulent twenties, and even resort to sleeping pills; but the dreams kept returning, he said to Deepika, kept forcing him to relive that moment, even on the morning when he was back in Madrid, three months ago, on the 11th of March, 2004. He woke and left his old bedroom, in his parents' apartment in La Latina; he went on a walk, through the city, cold and still asleep. Mateo told Deepika about how strange the city had looked, so desolate at that time of day, like a planet with no people. He remembered walking towards the nearby mercado, hoping to get himself some fruit, an early breakfast, but it was still closed, of course. And so Mateo continued to walk, up and down the hilly, cobbled slopes of Madrid, till he had ended up at the Reina Sofía, hours before a job interview of his was supposed to take place. He stumbled onto the large plaza and sat on one of the stone benches at the farthest corner of the square, farthest away from the museum.

He then asked Deepika if she knew about this triptych, by Joan Miró, titled *The Hope of a Condemned Man*. Deepika, serious now, told him that she did, of course; it was a work she made sure to see every time she found herself in the Foundation. And he said that the painting always gave him clarity, guidance; it provided him a sense of purpose, an understanding of his place in the world. He told her about how, over the past year, he had assumed that the black streaks across the paintings might be comets, a motif that might stand for the lives of promising young men, men like Salvador Puig Antich. He told her that this impression had changed, somehow, and that when he saw the painting now, he saw not hope, but the end of hope. All he saw were the failed orbits of these young men, spinning out of gravity's grasp, destined in the end to be cast astray: lives made lovelier, by some silly notion of art, of beauty, of the illusion beautiful things might continue to cast over them, only to be made undone, made lonelier, cast aside by life itself in their eventual confrontation with death.

It was something he thought about, he said, sitting in the plaza of the Reina Sofía. He told Deepika about how his phone then rang, with a call from Daniel, asking him where he was. Daniel said that his parents couldn't find him, and that he'd left the door to the apartment wide open. Mateo then told him where he was, and Daniel said—Isn't your interview at eleven? That's three hours from now, Mateo. He said he knew, he knew; he said he had a dream. What dream? Daniel asked, and Mateo began to say he was sorry. Why are you sorry? asked Daniel, and Mateo said it was because he couldn't tell him, he couldn't say what the dream was about. Daniel asked if it was a dream about Japan, and Mateo said yes, it was; he told Daniel that he was drinking again, trying to knock himself out every night so he might not dream about the place any longer. Don't scold me, please, I'm broken, said Mateo; some things about myself, I cannot help, he added. And Daniel told him to calm down, and that he wasn't going to scold him, no. I didn't know you thought so harshly of me. And Mateo said, I think you are very harsh; you are the meanest person I know. And then Daniel laughed, over the phone. He said: Mateo, my darling. You don't want to work at the Reina Sofía, do you? Make haste, he said next. Come back home.

Eventually we hung up, he said to Deepika. I told him I'd head back to La Latina, to my parents. You now have to imagine me, a grown man, wiping my face with the sleeve of my hoodie as I make my way to Atocha Station. Mateo then said he was reminded of what a friend once observed about him before: about how he only feels valued when he is desired. But was that so bad, he thought, to know that he was wanted? To know that he could still be wanted, in spite of his inadequacies? Couldn't that be a source of strength, one he could use against the cruelties of life? Little did he know, of course, that the first of four trains, leaving the Alcalá de Henares station at 7.01am, would carry with it three deadly explosives; he didn't know, he said to Deepika, that the first train would pull into Atocha Station, at 7.37am, and that the explosives would detonate, right then, and that it would go off again, for a second and then a third time. He had already stepped through the ticket gates, determined to return home, only to hear the bombs first, and then feel them second. His eardrums popped, and his knees buckled, as the air and the earth both rippled, and vibrated.

Deepika had one hand over her mouth, and another over Mateo's shoulder, as he described to her the way he had slowly crawled out of the station on the morning of 11-M. He told her about the deafness he'd experienced, and how his phone had become signal-jammed too. When the police and the ambulatory services finally descended onto the scene, he was slumped against a streetlamp, being asked how he was, though he couldn't hear them at the time. He almost couldn't see them either. All he could do was gasp, and gulp for air, all while being confronted with the absoluteness of his self, the very finitude of his self, still standing, somehow, on the edge of life. To die would be to enter this extreme loneliness, and to live would be to prepare for this, to be faced with this, not with the horror that wrecked him now, but with a confidence that would allow him to confront the chasm. He knew that now, he said to Deepika: that he'd have to be lifted up, rather than drawn away, towards that eventuality.

The daylight receded; the only lights that were on at this time were the ones in the courtyard, and the ones along the staircase. Mateo sat next to Daniel, feeling his partner's breath upon his neck, while Señor Calvo started a movie on the old VHS player. Everyone he had ever known, everyone he had ever cared for, was gathered in the living room to watch his favourite film by Almodóvar. And it didn't even matter if they knew Spanish or not: a young Antonio Banderas appeared on the screen, wearing nothing but a pair of cotton baby blue briefs, and it worked every time. He felt his heart break yet again, his own eyes filling with tears, as he thought about how so much was catching up with him that day.

Once *Labyrinth of Passion* was over, Mateo's father popped the tape out and played a DVD of *Cinema Paradiso*, Daniel's favourite film, using the option to flash subtitles in English this time. It was a film Mateo had seen only once, in the cinema as a nineteen-year-old, on a date with a much older man; as he watched it again, in the villa he stayed in every summer of his youth, he found himself aching, trembling, with the knowledge of how old he'd become. And there's one particular scene, in which a blind Alfredo tells Toto a story, about a soldier who pines after a princess: he promises to wait under her window for a hundred nights, only to bail on the ninety-ninth, to protect himself from the knowledge of the princess's final decision. Soon after that is a brief montage, in which the passionate Toto similarly pines for a girl named Elena: he waits under her window for an equally long time, marking out the days on his calendar, only to find his love unrequited on the night of New Year's Eve. The young man walks away, dejected by the sight of his beloved's closed window, while the town around him fills with the sounds of cheering, and laughing, and the shattering of plates and dishes, thrown out onto the cobbled streets. And then the sky soon fills with light, with the splendour of fireworks, silver, pink, blue, red—Mateo had to close his eyes, before forcing himself to reopen them, and take a slow look around the living room. In the twilight of the summer evening, he saw members of his family, and Daniel's family, and old friends from his colegio days. He found Deepika on the stairs, her face peeking through the banisters, her summer dress unmistakable to anyone. And he managed to find Isaac too, seated on a couch farther away, with Yong-he fast asleep on his lap.

But Jing was nowhere. She wasn't in the villa. He whispered into Daniel's ear, asking if he'd seen her around. Mateo then left for the kitchen, and poured himself a glass of water, watching the film play on in the living room; he left through the door that led into the courtyard, and left the villa too, down the dirt path that led towards the beach. Mateo walked down the boardwalk towards the Hotel Sol Y Mar, where Mateo finally found her, at one of tables in the terrace, alone with her laptop open, writing.

Hey, girl.

Hey, you, she said, still typing—I thought you were avoiding us. She looked up at him. Excited for tomorrow?

Mateo smiled at her; he distinctly saw the words "Bestari Heights, 2004" on the top of her screen, the filename of her Word document. Something on your mind? he asked.

Jing turned back to the screen, her hands now hovering above the keyboard. She quickly saved her document, and lowered the screen shut. Are the movies over? she asked.

Mateo sat on the chair next to Jing's. He made sure to speak slowly as he said: Let's play a game. Okay? I ask you one question, and you have to answer it truthfully, honestly. Is that a deal?

Jing began to frown at him. Sure, she said. Only if I get to ask you a question too.

Mateo nodded; it unnerved him to see how straightforwardly Jing could react to a provocation like that. Of course, he said. That's only fair.

Jing set her laptop aside, and took a quick drink from her cup of coffee. Why don't I go first? she said, as she offered him a tentative smile. Do you remember those rumours? Tori's rumours? About the things she said were happening in Kyoto?

Mateo nodded again. I asked you to tell me about them, he said, in the diner.

That's right, said Jing. She wanted to know if Mateo thought they could be real. She wanted to know if, over the month of March, something strange was actually happening, not to everyone, but to some people, while Comet Hyakutake was approaching nearer and nearer to the planet. She wanted to know if he believed in the things that people were seeing.

Mateo nodded a third time. I think they're real, he said. Of course they're real.

Jing's frown only deepened; he saw the fear as well, shooting through her eyes. Why?

Mateo didn't understand. Why was she afraid now? Mateo thought as he asked: What do you mean, why?

Jing's fear turned to bafflement; they were both baffled, at one another's reactions. Jing said that she had seen what had happened, and what could happen too, when people allowed themselves to believe in things that just didn't make sense. They go missing, she said, they leave other people's lives; they do irresponsible things, irreparable harm. They will find themselves capable of destroying everything that's good in their lives.

Her words gave Mateo pause. Bitch, he wanted to say, trust me: I'm fully aware of all of this. He then looked at her laptop, at her hand placed over her laptop, and wondered if she too was trapped in a story of her own making.

Okay, he said. My turn. On the scale of every day, I guess, to not at all— how often do you think about where Tori is?

Jing balked. What? What did you say?

You heard me, said Mateo. Because as far as I know, today was the first day I've ever heard you say her name. And then the time before that was, what, eight years ago? In '96? And Mateo now caught an anger flash through Jing's eyes as she said: Truthfully? Honestly? I used to think about her quite often. But then my mother also disappeared, in case *you* haven't forgotten. So now, I dunno, Mateo—I go for long, long stretches of time, I suppose, until I come across something that reminds me of her. You can't blame me for that, she said. You can't judge me for that either. And Mateo said no, he couldn't. Not for that. So you're saying, every time you look at your husband's face—you don't think of her?

Jing looked stumped this time. Excuse me?

Now he wanted to laugh. It's amazing to him, how capable this woman was, in moving past the one thing that had thwarted his entire life. Jing, he said: Isaac was her friend. That's how we even met him. Without her, Isaac would never have been in our lives in the first place. And Jing said yes, that's right. That's true, Mateo. She asked him why he's bringing up either of them, then, and he said—So you never thought about it?

About *what*? Jing asked.

About his *arrival*, said Mateo. About the *nature* of his arrival.

Jing's mouth hung wide open; he watched her hands slide off the table, into her lap. No, she said. I, I never—I don't understand what you're implying, she said. And for a while Mateo didn't respond, prompting Jing to clap her hands, and shout at him. *Say* something, Mateo! And Mateo then sat up, as though he had whiplash. It's not that simple, Jing, he said. You see, I think—I think there is a place that some people have gone to, a place that—a place we've never seen or heard of before, or even managed to *think* of before. But it might also be a place that Tori has gone to, willingly: a place that is so far, far beyond our ability to comprehend, that to approach it would be as good as to disappear, Jing. That's as far as I've got so far. But if there *is* a place, a place that Tori has gone to—then surely there must also be a place where other people can come from too, except to do so would be akin to a summoning, an appearance as opposed to a disappearance. Now, I don't have a name for this place, said Mateo, and I don't know if you still understand me, but, but I, I just—I just don't think we properly know about where Isaac has come from, Jing, in the same way we don't know enough about where Tori has gone to either. But we have him, at least, he's the one that we get to have, right now, and for all we know he could have just come out of nowhere. And I don't mean that as a manner of speech, Jing, said Mateo—I mean that as a fucking *fact*. And as Jing's face began to harden, her mouth setting into a single, straight line, the sound of the waves, still some distance away from the terrace, now seemed so near, so loud, it was as though they were seated by the very shoreline instead. It thundered around them, crashing like falling plates. They were right in the water, it sounded like, as he said, softly:

You were there. You and him. You were both there when Tori's taxi came around.

Jing didn't move; she continued to stare at him, her gaze turned to steel. You saw it?

I did. I saw it, saw everything, he said, while walking back from the Lawson that night. I heard everything too.

You were hiding?

He nodded. You know, I was inside the car myself.

She blinked. You were?

He nodded again. I'm pretty sure it was the same taxi, yes. Mateo then told her that he had also been mulling over Tori's Post-it for the longest time: "Thank you for finding me," she'd written to Isaac. He then told her that when he saw Isaac that night, standing by the taxi, he couldn't help but wonder about the part that Isaac might have played, in sending Tori away. Didn't she first disappear at the diner? said Mateo to Jing. Not long after Isaac went out as well, and talked to her? Right after he came back in?

Mateo then asked if she had ever wondered who Tori's driver was that night. The taxi driver? Jing asked, and Mateo said yes, the man with the eyes that also smiled. You managed to hear his name also, no? he asked, and Jing said yes, she did. She had managed to hear it too, that night.

Mateo bit on his lip. And you haven't, what—you never bothered to look into it, Jing? The *name*?

Jing closed her eyes. And this is the part that Mateo would never know: that she too must have been in the same taxi; that she'd been asleep in it, in fact, on the way back to the ryokan, hearing snatches of Japanese spoken between Tori and the taxi driver. I don't—I, I just—

Christ, said Mateo, wow. You forgot the name, didn't you? The name of the one guy who was with Tori, at the very, very end.

Jing kept her eyes closed, while she began to shake her head. Mateo—

The name is Kyu Sakamoto, Mateo said to Jing. It is the name of a singer who passed away in 1985, on a flight from Tokyo to Osaka. It got into the air and immediately crashed into the mountains, somewhere in Gunma prefecture. The plane had only been airborne for forty-five minutes.

Jing opened her eyes this time, red and pooling with tears.

Mateo went on. The night before, when we went to Prismatic—you remember meeting the artist, yes?

Jing nodded.

He passed away in October 1995. You told me this. Didn't you?

Jing nodded again; a tear fell now, into her lap. Tori and I, we thought—we thought he was just—

An imposter, he said. Someone pretending to be him? Mateo then dragged his chair closer to Jing's: he reached out to her, with both of his hands, holding them in her lap.

You feel this?

Yes.

I'm real.

Okay.

This is real.

Okay, she said again.

He then held her hands even tighter, and pressed them against his cheek. You held his hand, too, didn't you? he said. Felt him? Spoke with him? Teiji Furuhashi?

She nodded again.

So you know, don't you? What I really think about this? What *you* really think about this? said Mateo. What you really, truly believe?

Yes, she said. Yes, she said again, I know. And then poor Jing began to plead with him, as she told him about how Isaac had saved her life. He's a good person too. I don't know if you see that, Mateo. And he never, never—Isaac never did a bad thing, not to me or my son, Jing said. He's always been good to us, in the grand scheme of things, she added. And Mateo had to bring their foreheads together, while the sound of water continued to surge around the terrace, his knees now wet with the falling of his friend's tears. The grand scheme of things, Mateo now thought: how grand are we talking, Miss Singapore? When will we ever know how large, how truly large, this life can actually be? Oh honey, he said, I'm sorry. I don't think any of that matters anymore.

21

The Horvallan. Jing Aw. Flame of the Forest, Singapore, 2005.

East Coast Park, 2003

I began to write the story of us about a week after I returned from Barcelona. To be clear I always had it in me, this impulse to record our time in words, except then (and even now, perhaps) I no longer had the heart to fight it. That was Deepika Rai's gift to me, I suppose: I take out all my planners, my schedulers, eager to piece together when you and I met and where. And then I let the words come to me, sketching out our story over notebooks.

"We tell ourselves stories in order to live," Joan Didion once famously wrote. You tell stories to map the future, while I write mine compulsively, perhaps to my own detriment, eager to preserve the past; but it is the very present, this whole business of waiting, I find, that nobody can really bear to go through. Not even in the writing.

Where is the present, then? the reader might ask. It is here, at East Coast Park, whose unfailing pleasantness I hate. I'm irritated by the mown grass, and the perfect, winding paths; I detest the colour of that faded blue sea, and that perfect horizon of ships even more.

It was my husband's idea to come here, the week our son was turning five. He'd been five years old as well when his own father brought him to the park, to learn how to ride a bike. And so while we made plans to teach Yong-he how to cycle, I thought about how we were orphans, basically, and what he and I were passing to our child. But such things can become frightening, if one were to dwell too long on the subject, like peering down into the bottom of a well; even Isaac's own parents remained an enigma to me, having never met them over the course of our marriage.

He did show me a photograph once, many years ago on a train—of his father, his mother and his sister, too. I'm constantly reliving that day, to remind myself how we found each other in the first place. I'm wondering, in fact, where that photograph is now.

Isaac wanted to know how we'd continue to teach cycling to our son. "We can take turns," he said, the night before our first lesson. "You and then me, and then you again." He said we'd do it together, of course, if we so happened to be free at the same time, and I told him that would be nice. I told him I'd prefer that, actually. "Now he sees his father more on the television than in real life," I said.

Isaac shot me a look. "You know I'm already doing my best here, Jing."

I observed him, that night, tucking Yong-he into bed. I stood in the corridor, outside the door that was once my mother's bedroom; we still had some of her things, whatever we couldn't relinquish or thought we might reuse, set aside now into a single closet.

Yong-he asked Isaac if he'd see his Ah Ma again. I held my breath, sure that my husband's had caught at the question too. "No," he said. "It's been three years, you know. Have you been waiting all this time?"

I didn't get to hear my son's reply to the question. Instead he told Isaac that his great-grandfather was scary, and I began to chuckle to myself while my husband played along: "Scary? Ah Pa? Yah, right, Ah Pa a bit scary . . ." Yong-he giggled; he told Isaac about how, in kindergarten, he had been asked to draw a family tree. He told him he'd made a mistake, thinking that my grandparents were his. Yong-he then asked Isaac what his father and mother were like, and I held my breath again, eager to hear what my husband would say.

"My father was a mechanic. He loved us very much. But he wasn't very good with money," said Isaac. "And my mother, well . . . She also loved us very much. But I think the more she loved us, the sadder she became."

Yong-he wanted to know why; he said he didn't get it. Isaac said he didn't get it either, it's just like that for some people. Yong-he then asked if he loved me, and he said that he did, and that I saved him, actually, for without me he would be nothing. And without Mummy there would be no you, he said. Daddy loves Mummy very much, Isaac said again. Yong-he then asked, in the midst of my husband's pause, if that was the reason he was crying right now.

My husband drove us down to the park, on the 20th of September, 2003. He went to one of the rental kiosks and got Yong-he a tricycle, which our son took to brilliantly, exceedingly so. We wanted him to be the fastest, the swiftest, the bravest out of the three of us; Isaac was right behind him the whole time, goading the boy on while I remained at the back, feeling as hateful as ever towards the park, at the spell it seemed to cast over us that day. For I knew the magic wasn't made to last: I would have to be careful about the crumbling, and would have to catch the gossamer once it fell away. My own son leered at me when I told him that his father couldn't join us the following week. "You have to be faster," he said, as though he were issuing me a warning. "Be fast, like Daddy, or you will lose me."

Saturday came, and my plan was to rent a bicycle, just the one. But Yong-he soon kicked up a fuss, insisting that he wanted the tricycle; I told him he was already way too good for that one, and that it was this one, the one with two wheels that would excite him more. But my son continued to complain, unwilling to admit that he might risk a fall, or make a mistake in front of his own mother, while I did wonder, for a good minute or two, if I ought to relent to my son's request.

I was determined, unfortunately, to break the spell; I never quite know why I am like this sometimes, ever eager to rid people of their illusions. I told him we would never return to the park if he didn't get on the bicycle, and that Daddy and Mummy would never take him back because he's unwilling to learn. "It seems to me like you don't want to try," I said, "even though I told you, you would like it, this bicycle I got for you." I then asked if he would trust me, a question he was too terrified to answer.

"Tell me you will listen."

He nodded.

"And you will try?"

He nodded again.

"Good," I said. "You don't want to fall, right, Yong-he?"

He shook his head. "I don't want to," he said. I put both hands on his shoulders.

"It will happen," I said. "But the falling will teach you. This is how you learn, okay?"

Yong-he whined; but I was glad to feel his courage now, and imagined his still-tiny heart hammering away as he put one leg over the saddle. I now held the bicycle from the front while he placed one foot on a pedal.

"You gotta push now," I said.

"I don't want," he cried, while I inexplicably broke out into a smile.

"You can do it!" I said to him. "Push!"

He let out a wail: "I'm scared!" And yet he pushed anyway, with his remaining foot. And I swore on my life that afternoon that I would never let him fall; he would never know what it meant to have his elbows or knees scrape against the asphalt path, not if I could ever help it. Whenever my boy screamed I screamed as well, and whenever he made a turn I'd turn with him, never mind if it meant the bicycle would scrape against my legs. And then you called me on my mobile, a Malaysian number flashing on the screen—you called me right at the moment Yong-he got the hang of it, and was actually urging me to let go of the handles. "I want to try!" the boy said.

"Please, Mummy, now!" Instead I instructed Yong-he to stop, to bring his bike over to the grass, the both of us sweating while I attended to your call.

You asked me where I was. I told you.

"That's a big place," you said. "Where exactly?"

I looked around. "I'm not entirely sure. I think you'll have to find me, somehow."

"All right," you said. "I'll do that." You then asked if I was with my son, and I asked how you knew.

"You're panting," you said. "You sound glad."

We were at one of the stand-alone restaurants at the park, with a wooden deck to dine al fresco on, where we could also enjoy an up-close view of a Frisbee match. For a while I did nothing but watch the kids, the teenagers, tossing the yellow plastic disc at one another.

"Hey, pal," I heard you say. "You like chicken wings?"

Yong-he nodded at you. I said he deserved them. You then asked the child if he was happy, and the child nodded, which made me smile.

"I win," I said.

You winked at me. "If you say so."

I couldn't read your face at that moment. I then looked at Yong-he again, watching the Frisbee match go by, with a chicken wing in his greasy, oily hands. I wondered if this was how I discounted every good thing I did that day, just by allowing you to eat with us.

Eventually I told you about my chat with Deepika. "She told me nothing," I said. She left me stranded on the RSS *Ubin*, to use her words. You said that was disappointing to hear, which made me want to laugh.

"You really hurt her," I said. "You know that, don't you?"

"I do."

"Do you know she's in love with you?"

"In a way."

"And yet you still go to parties together. Meet up in foreign countries together. Hang out and tell long stories to one another."

"That we do."

I nodded. "We really are the worst," I said.

You smiled. "We're horrible people," you said.

I looked at my son once more. I watched him walk over to the table, put the bones in his hand down, and pick up another wing. He then went back to his corner, where he could watch the kids play Frisbee, enacting the kind of ridiculously carefree picture of what being a teenager could look like, all while dusk spilled over us, bleeding pink and purple over the park, the kids on the grass continuing to laugh, and scream, and run, and throw. It's possible they might never stop.

"I want to hear the whole story," I said.

"Okay," you said.

"I don't care how long it takes."

"Okay," you said again.

I told you that you would have to continue, pick up from where we last stopped. You said: "Naturally."

7085AD. The RSS *Ubin*. After the Horvallan leaves her clinic, the oncologist gets her nurses to update her again on the day's scheduled appointments. She decides to see Nakarin first, the chef from Thailand, and do a more focussed scan of his lungs. She gives K'weyu a scan as well, another routine one, which she will definitely charge him credits for. She looks into all six of his eyes when she tells him that it's not her he needs, but a psychiatrist.

K'weyu's abdomen flashes in protest. Her own tablet flashes too, as it sends the alien a translation of her message: *I mean it!*

Finally, there's Xian, her last patient for the morning. *You want to grab lunch with your auntie later?* the oncologist asks. Her niece nods, as eagerly as she can, before coughing up a thick wad of phlegm. The oncologist encourages her niece to spit into her glove, all of it, and gently pats her back with her other hand.

Oh, Xian, she says. *It's okay. What's wrong with you now . . .*

Our heroine later accompanies Xian back to the Pilots' Wing, where her niece resides with her parents. The two walk to the end of the Medical Wing, where the tram will pick them up and ferry them across the *Ubin;* while waiting, Xian asks who the man was earlier, the one who had dropped by the clinic and cut the queue.

That was the Horvallan, says the oncologist, eager to see the look on her niece's face. But Xian remains characteristically nonplussed.

That was really him?

Yes. He's very special, the oncologist says, trying to wow her niece. *The Head Pilot could come to the clinic and I'd still tell her to wait in line. But not him.*

Xian nods. She still looks terribly unimpressed, tempting our heroine to ask if the Horvallan had personally offended her or something. Instead she asks Xian what it is they learn about him exactly, in their history classes, and Xian tells her the story that practically everyone else in the universe knows by now: that he was once on a faraway planet, but not too far, home to an advanced civilisation that invested its efforts into genetic and cellular re-engineering, into unlocking the secret of immortal life. In fact, the oncologist recalls watching a movie as a child, one that illustrated how the Horvallans lived for hundreds and thousands of years: science and religion consequently intertwined, resulting in a prevailing theocracy over the planet while death cults propagated on the fringes. Horvallan society thus panicked when news of an incoming comet broke, threatening to destroy their beliefs along with their world. The fringes reformed into military factions, while theocratic society split into radical groups. The Horvallans waged war over ideology, over precious resources, even their plans for the comet; they were fighting, essentially, over the future of their species, one that inevitably tore life apart on the planet. Horvalla was as good as gone, their immortality laid to waste; it did not matter if the comet would actually strike the planet or not upon its scheduled arrival.

The Horvallan was just a child when he went on board a defectors' space-ship. He gazed through its windows as it shuddered through the atmos-phere, propelled as though by the explosions that erupted below him. He and the other minors were then made to go to sleep, in cryogenic chambers installed at the basement of the main deck; when he eventually woke up, and began his physiotherapy, he came to realise that only a third of the ship's crew was present around him.

Is everybody else asleep?

No, they said.

Where are they, then?

Far away, they said. Some had chosen to return to Horvalla, while others had chosen to leave, to chart their own path across space. They left and they left, one group after the other, until the final group took the last of their escape pods.

But where can they go? asked the Horvallan, and his seniors said they didn't know. He then asked them where their ship was headed towards. A new home, they said—a faraway home. Its inhabitants have named it Earth, according to a radio signal they decoded. Earth has already welcomed a handful of other refugee species, from other nearby parts of the galaxy. It is the only known planet to do such a thing, an actual paradise, in all of the cosmos: a planet not of single-minded unity, but a planet that has learnt to embrace difference, to celebrate difference, they said. That's where they have chosen to go to.

But this is where the story of the Horvallan, our Horvallan, ends: it ends with him, alone, the only crew member left on the spaceship, hurtling towards the very image of Earth. Years would have passed since the time of his awakening, you said: he would have seen person after person, in moments of noble self-sacrifice, eject themselves into space, just so they might preserve whatever resources the ship would still need to keep flying. Parts of the ship would have to be ejected as well, just so that their species might make it to Earth one day. And they did, they finally did, or rather—he did. The spacecraft burnt up and crashed into smithereens, somewhere on the coast of Singapore, an island nation along the equatorial line of the planet. And the Horvallan then emerged, gasping, alive, as the one sole member of his immortal kind.

The oncologist and her niece are now on board the tram, bound for the Pilots' Wing at the end of the line. Because the Wing is at the frontmost end of the *Ubin*, while the Medical Wing is located towards the rear, the two of them find themselves riding the full, thirty-minute journey across the length of the space station.

This is the most the oncologist has ever been away from her clinic in a while, and so she takes the opportunity to be a tourist for once. With every stop the tram makes, she looks through the windows, eager to take in whatever new worlds she has yet to familiarise herself with: worlds like the common canteen and the food processing centre, or the sports and entertainment complexes, and even the civil service offices, housing the justice and legal departments.

But it is the people, getting on and off the tram, that surprise her the most. It's rare when she notices more than a quarter of any crowd sick, visibly unwell and straining to function; in fact, the oncologist herself doesn't feel entirely okay when the tram passes through the heart of the space station, where its core engine is known to reside. She feels light-headed, nauseous almost. *I know how you feel*, Xian says to the oncologist. *It's normal, apparently. The engine is meant to do that to you.*

When they reach the Pilots' Wing, they encounter a number of complicated security procedures, which is to be expected. But because Xian is a child of two pilots, and because the oncologist is a direct relative of the people they intend to see, the security personnel let them through at every scan, every escalator, every checkpoint, until they finally emerge in the reception hall, which is at once luxe to the eye and also strikingly plain. A door slides open, and the oncologist sees her sister-in-law coming towards them and greeting them both.

Did you have a good journey? she asks.

Somewhat, says the oncologist, ignoring the lingering queasiness in her gut. After a few more pleasantries, she tells her sister-in-law that she will need to talk to her, in private, about Xian's health.

She's not doing so good, she says to her, taking out her tablet from the inner pocket of her coat. *Her vitals are somehow worsening,* the oncologist says, pointing out Xian's blood pressure, her white cell count, her thyroid hormone levels. The pilot puts a hand on her forehead and swears. *Damn it,* she says. *I don't understand. I don't know what to do.*

The oncologist looks at her sister-in-law with concern. *Xian will be fine. I'm here, after all,* she says. *I'll do everything I can to make her feel better.* She is about to bring up the possibility of relocating Xian—of allowing her to live in the Annie Colony ahead of schedule, or maybe even back on Earth. Instead she notices the colour of her sister-in-law's skin, causing the oncologist to feel alarmed once again. She asks if she might like to drop by the clinic one day, and her sister-in-law tells her no, she's fine. *I'm just over-worked, that's all.*

The image of the Horvallan comes to mind just then. *Is it him?* asks the oncologist. *He's making you busy, and all that?* And the pilot says ah, followed by yes. There are always meals to be had, meetings to be had, and all just to talk; she says that people can't get enough of him, not even the ones who technically wield greater power and authority than he does. *You can practically see the religious fervour in their eyes,* she says to our heroine.

The oncologist smiles, encouraged by her sense of humour. But she takes another hard look at her anyway, and opens up her tablet. She tells her she has a free hour next Thursday, and that she's putting her and her husband's names down on her calendar. *Doctor's orders,* she says, tapping the confirmation button. *Now you both have an excuse to slip out of work, while I finally get a chance to see my brother's face.*

Her sister-in-law lets out a sigh, staring down at the calendar on her screen. *You know what,* she says—*that's a good plan.* She turns around. *Thank you for being such a good aunt.*

The pilot wishes our heroine godspeed, and leaves. The oncologist turns and exits the hall, bracing her stomach for the ride back home.

I asked you if something was wrong with the engine. You nodded.

"Possibly a leak," you said. "That's the risk with antimatter engines: from the leak comes a certain amount of uncontainable radiation, which can spread across the entire station if left unchecked . . . " You imagined it would be tolerable at first, and hardly anything worth noticing; all would be good for a while, until it is not. "And that's when a health crisis will emerge," you said.

I clicked my tongue: it sounded just like any other disaster on Earth. "Do you understand anything?" I asked my boy, and he shook his head; he was sitting next to us now, content to drink his orange soda and listen to you, the same way I did and have always done. "Nope," said Yong-he, almost cheerfully, causing you to laugh.

"Huh!" you said. "That's a shame. I hope you do, one day." You looked at me. "Do you see why the Horvallan is nervous?" you asked.

I made a face. The time was 8pm, the Frisbee-playing teenagers long gone; only the sound of the sea remained, as well as the light of the lamps in East Coast Park, shining like individual points in a constellation. "Seeing things would be a particularly bad symptom," I said, "whether it's caused by radiation or not."

But you seemed to disagree. "I actually wonder," you said. "Anyway."

The Horvallan can't concentrate, you said. Celebrity, honorary diplomat, patron saint of the Martian enterprise; the Horvallan can encounter the slimiest, most Scrooge-like, most blatantly Machiavellian of Very Important People on board the space station, man or alien, and his nerves would still be nothing compared to the ones he has now, alighting from the tram, walking down the long corridor from the Residential to the Medical Wing . . . All day long he has had to ask himself to think back, to reach back more than four millennia, to the moment he had last seen the face he saw that morning. For now it stands out to him with a clarity so surprising he genuinely cannot believe it: to find that the memory of a person could still be there, stored beneath layers and layers of information, and that the feelings too have remained, within a heart that should have worn out so long ago.

So the year is 2989AD once again, top floor of a hotel—the Horvallan is seated in a bar with a killer view, one that overlooks the prosperous and ever-bustling town of Iskandar, Johor Bahru, Malaysia. He is there because the Singaporeans have sent him there, and also because, not too surprisingly, they own the hotel and many others beside it. More importantly, the Horvallan is there because he has something to share, a message he needs to deliver to some of the highest-appointed designates of every sentient lifeform on the planet, to every Earthling and alien, refugee and resettler, here on the same biosphere they will eventually have to vacate. He has to tell them that this planet, this beautiful paradise of a planet, will also become under threat.

And they will argue with him no doubt.

Hasn't climate change been fixed? they would say to the Horvallan. Hasn't it finally been reversed, with the collective will of the people? Bolstered by the support of all of our alien friends, who have brought with them story upon story of total ecological collapse—all under Singaporean leadership, no less! What threat is left that still persists on this Earth, except for a virus or two, accidents that arise from human error, a random natural disaster—the occasional act of God? And then the Horvallan will tell the story of who he is, the story of his own planet, of Horvalla: the story that will end up being told for millennia to come.

He will tell them about the comet, and how his world had thought it would strike the planet, tearing it apart in other insidious ways.

He will tell them how, a thousand years ago, this same comet had headed for Earth's way as well, only to miss the planet by 0.1 astronomical units.

But it will come back, the Horvallan says to everyone. And when it does, it will strike your world, the same way it was thought to strike mine. And unlike my people, who were ill-prepared for the disaster, your people—all of the peoples!—will have years and years to prepare for it: 65,536 years, to be precise. And nobody will have to die this time.

Not a living being present in the meeting will know how to speak. *What—what comet is this?* one of the alien representatives will finally demand. *Why haven't we heard of this thing before?* And the Horvallan will say he is not sure. He will implore all with intergalactic scanners to search for the object in the sky, to calculate and chart its trajectory, to prove that he isn't telling a lie. He will then turn towards our heroine, the diplomat, seated right beside him.

The diplomat has remained silent, all throughout the Horvallan's speech. She has been caught in a state of shock but also jolted into a flurry of total competency. Her phone, for example, has transcribed his words into written text, wired in real time to her aide via a secure line between their devices; she has sent her aide instructions too, to explore every possible means of destroying the comet, anything that might steer humankind away from reversing nuclear disarmament. The diplomat does all of this, all while maintaining impeccable eye contact with the Horvallan as he says to her:

Its official designation on Earth is C/1996 B2.

She doesn't even bother to ask the Horvallan how he knows. *Thank you?* is what she says, which makes him smile.

But your people would have given it a proper name, of course.

The comet's name then appears on the diplomat's screen, just as the Horvallan utters it with his own lips:

Hyakutake.

22

Jing said she would head back to the hotel, shortly after Yong-he was fed. Would that be okay? she asked. I need to work for a bit.

Isaac set their son's plate away. You sure? he said, as he now glanced at Yong-he, rejoining the game of tag. One of the parents reminded the kids to be careful, and told them to stay clear from the barbecue; Isaac then looked at Daniel, still flipping cuts of meat and capsicum over the grill, telling the kids to keep on playing. You haven't even seen Mateo yet, Isaac added, to which Jing gave him a quick shrug. Mateo's not gonna miss me, she said, and the work is not going to write itself. She told him she'd come back to the villa, as soon as she ran out of words that day.

Isaac looked around the courtyard, and then behind him into the living room; there were so many people he didn't know. He was about to ask if she could stay a while longer, keep him company for the next hour at least, when his phone began to ring: it was Sherry, according to the caller ID, and he quickly rejected the call while his mind began to scramble for a place where he might call her back.

Jing's eyes darted between his face and his phone. Shall I go? she said, and Isaac said yes, all right. I can leave the boy with you too? she said, and Isaac said to her, Can, can. Don't work too hard, Jing.

He retreated to the second floor, and called Sherry back. So you are in Spain, she said to him, and he said yah, he was. Sherry wanted to know when he would be coming back, and he wanted to know if this meant she had forgiven him. Wow, said Sherry. What kind of person do you think I am? She was angry, yah, but not the type to hold a grudge. Isaac then asked if she knew what kind of a man he was, a question she realised she was somehow meant to answer. You're a good man lah, she said to him, if not a little bit of a coward.

Isaac winced; he wondered if that might be true. Sherry asked him again when he was coming back, and he told her that he had a Singapore-bound ticket for the end of the month.

So you're still coming to the dinner? she asked. I won't have to give your seat to someone else?

I am, said Isaac. I'll be there. I know what will happen to me if I'm not, he added, an answer he knew would make her smile, even though he was too far across the world to tell.

Oh, for sure, Sherry later said. You don't get to run away from me. Her reply made him want to smile too.

In the world that he now lived in—in this version of the world he now inhabited—Isaac and Sherry would never become lovers, just colleagues, and then friends much later on in their careers. They would meet for the first time, not at the polytechnic as teenagers, but as adults in their early twenties, at the 1997 edition of *Star Search*, when the finalised contestants convened for the first time at a rehearsal studio in TCS.

But it was hardly a conducive place for them to form a meaningful connection. Every hello was met with a cursory look; every question was followed with a non-committal phrase. Any attempt to know one another was thwarted, continually, by a wave of indifference. And while their non-existent relationship continued to unravel, a story had begun to spin, in plenty of Chinese media, about how a potential romance was brewing between the two young stars, bizarre to everyone involved. But the more Isaac insisted that he already had a girlfriend, and that he was living with her, in fact, the more he became convinced that he and Sherry were destined never to be. If anything, it confirmed to him that the Sherry in this world was still the Sherry in the other one, committed to the life she was determined to build for herself, and nobody else. Sherry's number one priority would always be Sherry.

He still remembered the moment, however, when they were both crowned champions. He remembered the applause, and the confetti that fell from the ceiling; he hadn't heard either of their names, but he felt the repeated clapping on his back, his fellow contestants cheering as they pushed him forward to accept his trophy. And when he did, he couldn't help but smile at her, at Sherry, both of them winners at last. And that was the moment too, when she finally fixed her eyes with his, her lips curling in a way that betrayed nothing but resolve; he remembered the way her eyes had shone at him, with the certainty that she was always going to win, and that the winning, really, was always a matter of when. Sherry had entered the competition a hundred per cent sure that she would come out on top, and Isaac, how lucky of him, just so happened to be there when she reached for her destiny, and took it.

After the win, Isaac and Sherry led separate lives for a while, starring as supporting characters in separate shows; they remained connected nonetheless by Frankie, their manager, who got them to be cast in the same forty-episode 9pm drama two years later, in the breakout roles of a policeman and policewoman who finally fall in love in the penultimate episode. Isaac's character is fatally stabbed, in an attempt to protect Sherry's from the knife of a serial burglar, and while fifteen minutes of screen time are devoted to cremating the body of Isaac's character, securing his eventual nomination and win for Best Supporting Actor at the Star Awards, the rumours rekindled, fuelling speculation that an affair must certainly exist between the two actors, rumours that Frankie now took full advantage of. The two became increasingly touted as a pair, to market whatever potential they might have between them to the public. They scored a Daikin commercial, in which Isaac and Sherry played the parents of an adorable girl, letting out sighs of relief amidst a fantastical vision of the South Pole. They became close to starring in another drama too, as the lead actor and actress this time, only to have the part reassigned to Florence Tan weeks before shooting commenced.

Isaac asked Frankie what had happened. Frankie showed him a copy of the Chinese papers, stashed in a drawer beneath his desk; the papers were dated just over a month and a half ago, on the 21st of September, 1999.

Isaac knew the date immediately: it was his first day at the hospital, after the car accident he and Jing had on Lorong Chuan. He scanned the article, thinking he might see a photo of the wreckage, only to find an image of his younger self instead, holding up a trophy. It's *Star Search 1997*, the night of their respective wins—Isaac is looking at Sherry in the photo, his adoration plain for everyone to see. Sherry is turned towards the audience instead, a gaze of confidence that was now circled over and then magnified, in an article that sought to set the two actors apart. Isaac was a family man, a team player, an actor destined for greatness, it said, while Sherry was unfriendly, unapproachable and an uncooperative shrew—traits that should have been evident to all from the very start, according to a paragraph. Didn't everyone know she was a star? she was reported to have said, on the set of the show they just starred in together. Sherry Wong was no longer the well-deserved Female Champion, the starlet tipped for future glory: now she was just the bitch that won.

Isaac was aghast; neither Jing nor Frankie had shown him the article while he had recuperated in the hospital that day. He told Frankie that Sherry had never said anything like that on set, that thing about being a star.

Frankie put the newspaper back into his drawer. We wanted Sherry to sue, he said. But she told us she didn't have that kind of money.

And so his and Sherry's paths would fail to meet, for several more years, all while Isaac's reputation as a golden child steadily grew. He was loyal too, during a particularly tense period in broadcasting history, rejecting multiple lucrative deals to jump ship, to SPH MediaWorks, the new rival network at one point. This resulted in a power he didn't even know he had, a power he remained unaware of until Frankie sat him down one afternoon, in the back of a company van parked just off the set of a variety show.

They want you for another drama, he said. Thirty-five eps, male lead, confirm.

Isaac smiled at him. Good script?

Good enough, said Frankie.

Got title?

Still thinking about it. But there is something the producers want to know, something you'll need to decide for us, he said. His manager then reached into a folder and took out five photographs, laying them out on the cushioned seat between them.

The female lead, said Frankie, stating the name of each actress, as he tapped a finger on each face: Phyllis Quek. Florence Tan. Vivian Lai. Yvonne Lim. And finally—

Sherry Wong, said Isaac.

Frankie nodded. Yep.

His mouth went dry: it was already disorienting enough, to know that he had the ability to make such a call. And he knew the risk he was about to take, the possibility that everything would explode in his face, all for a person who wanted nothing to do with him any longer. He found himself craving to see what would happen as he said: I want Sherry.

Frankie's mouth nearly twitched into a smile, even as he got Isaac to double-check if he was certain. He went so far as to say that Sherry was the backup really, she was the producers' last choice. But Isaac didn't care.

Tell them to cast her, he said.

———

Sherry Wong's side of the story began at the age of six, at Ghim Moh Market, when she visited her uncle's bak chor mee stall for the first time. She looked at her uncle, serving her a bowl of fishball noodles, with more of the chilli sauce she loved but didn't know he made. Her mother handed her a pair of chopsticks.

It's your uncle's turn now, she said, now that your Gong Gong has passed on.

After their noodles, mother and daughter made a trip to the nearby hospice, where she would see her father in a wheelchair, motionless and still, staring into nothing as usual. Because she had already seen him like this, had already accustomed herself to his being like this, she found herself distracted, instead, by the lingering sensation on her lips, still stinging from the extra dose of the family's chilli sauce. It was a sensation that hurt her in a way that pleased her too, a sensation she wouldn't know if she wanted more or less of in her life from then on. Later, from the ages of nine to twelve, when an early-onset growth spurt would make her the tallest girl in primary school, Sherry felt like she finally knew the answer to that question. For Sherry wasn't just tall, nor was she simply beautiful: she was sexy, a fact that alarmed the girls, horrified her teachers and deeply confused the boys. But Sherry didn't care; none of it mattered to her. All Sherry knew was that she needed bigger shoes each year, as well as a longer and longer skirt: things she was afraid to ask for every stupid, shitty year, which meant that her answer, in essence, was no answer. She would no longer confuse the luxuries she managed to enjoy in her life with the luxury of having choices.

It was only when her and her uncle's family moved into a five-room flat—when sister and brother-in-law finally decided to live together, to pool their resources—when a more traditional arc to her story emerged, one in which Sherry would make a series of important decisions for herself. Her mother would open her photocopying store, using the payout they got from her father's insurance to start the business, while Sherry, now in charge of taking care of her two younger cousins, would exercise her decision to end it with her first boyfriend. He only ever wanted her for her looks anyway, and her long legs too. The day she lost her virginity to him was the day she knew that this, this love that they kept claiming to have, was just a teenager's idea of love: her boyfriend shot her a look, wondering if she was somehow disgusted by him, and Sherry would grit her teeth and smile as he poked his cock inside her; she would allow their first, truly honest moment together as a couple to sail out of sight, welcoming their relationship's demise two weeks later.

At poly, Sherry chose Media & Communications, the only topic on the list that appealed to her in any sort of way. But because she was prettier than ever, and surrounded by more hormonally active boys than ever, Sherry Wong would spend half her time rejecting and avoiding these boys, her suitors, unaware of how inadequate they were. She couldn't imagine any of them following her, for instance, to her mother's store after school, talking shop with her and her employees, all of them aunties who lived in the same block. Sherry could only squirm in embarrassment when some of the boys, the ones who were hardcore in love with her, turned up at the store every now and then, leaving it to her mother to show them the door, before the aunties erupted with laughter and applause.

Life would only truly start for her, dramatically, at the age of twenty-two. She was in the shop with the other aunties—Auntie Anitha, Auntie Swee Lin and Auntie Indranee, photocopying the previous years' PSLE prelim papers for English by Anglo-Chinese School (Junior)—when the first episode of *The Golden Pillow* aired, and she was hooked. No: educated; no: rearranged. She came to feel love for a stranger, for the very first time in her life, and it was not even an actual person. It was Xiao Dan, played wonderfully and earnestly by Zoe Tay. Like Sherry, Xiao Dan too is busy fielding away the courtship of a man she barely has time to consider; instead she goes about her day, looking after her childhood friend, this rugged, tanned-skin, honest-looking fellow, with eyes that glint like marbles and who expects nothing at all from Xiao Dan. But better still: Zoe was being seen, by thousands and thousands of people, both in Singapore and (possibly!) abroad. And it was not even she whom they get to look at. It's Xiao Dan, or rather: it's Xiao Dan, the heroine. An actual heroine.

The age of twenty-four was when the story of Sherry Wong would end. Henceforth she'd be known by her Chinese name instead, Huang Huiying: the Female Champion of *Star Search 1997*.

But Sherry would insist on being called Sherry, to whomever she met in show business. Huang Huiying could be the bitch for all she cared, the ungrateful vixen in wait for her comeuppance, scowling as the husband-stealing villainess in every photo, while Sherry Wong could be the young ingénue, glad to receive any work at all. On the rare occasion she bumped into Zoe Tay, at a media event or on Caldecott Hill, Sherry would look the other way and turn, aware that she was not worthy. With every bit part and supporting role she continued to get, Sherry would tell herself that she would be an inspiration too, to whichever young girl watching her on the screen, desperate to change her life. It was more or less the only thing that allowed her to keep being Huang Huiying, Mediacorp artiste, the bona fide xue gong zhu of Channel 8.

And then Frankie called one day, in the final quarter of 2003, to give her a piece of unexpected news. This is it, he told her. This is fucking it, Sherry, your first leading role. Who else is starring? she asked her manager, her voice shaken by the news, and he told her all of the names he knew so far, starting with the director, the scriptwriter, and each one of the producers, followed by every actor and actress that filled the supporting cast. But Frankie always loved to save the best titbit for last. He told her who her co-lead was. It's Isaac Neo, he said.

Sherry's stomach threatened to flip. She felt her scalp prick with sweat. She told her manager that she was not going to do it, she's not doing the show, while Frankie swore at her, asking her why the hell not.

She repeated herself. She repeated herself another time, before adding, I can't. And then she hung up on him, knowing without a doubt that she'd do the show anyway.

The drama, according to Isaac, was about a man and a woman from two rival families, living on the opposite ends of a common corridor.

The premise was quite exciting, and partly fantastical. Both characters realise that their rooms somehow connect to one another, for exactly half an hour after midnight, resulting in a number of comedic and romantic hijinks: one character comes back from the toilet, and stumbles into the other's bedroom by accident; both end up finding opportunities to sneak into one another's places, to avoid getting caught by their respective family members, while multiple items become displaced and found inside the other's home.

Oh, and the drama, Isaac added, is named *Door to Your Heart.* Sounds great, yah.

Sherry could only look at Isaac as he told her this—all of it. The month was November, a Thursday afternoon; production for the drama would have to start in five weeks. This was the first proper conversation they had had in the six years they'd known one another as colleagues.

I don't get it, she said to him. You can't get another actress, is it?

She noted the effect her words had on him, the way he flinched when she refused to play nice. Still, he said to her: it has to be you, Sherry.

Why? she asked. Or maybe you don't like Florence anymore? I recall the two of you being very buddy-buddy together, back in *Star Search.* Always hanging out with the rest, eating supper at Chomp Chomp. You're still good friends with her, right?

Isaac put his hands together; he looked like he was begging her now. I considered Florence, he said; she was my second pick. I was going to go with her when you said no, but that was before I read the script. But I've read it, he said, and now I know for sure. I know there is no other woman for the part but you.

What is this? thought Sherry. What is this charade? She scowled at him, to the point she thought she might shed tears instead. You really lost it, horh, she said to him. You're insane, you know that or not?

Isaac shook his head. I'm the one who doesn't get it. I don't get why you hate me so much, he said, getting agitated. I never even do anything to you, I only—I only want the best for you, Sherry. That's it.

Sherry's lip quivered. There was one day, she said. Years ago, during one of the *Star Search* rehearsals. You were showing everyone what you kept in your wallet. You remember?

Isaac frowned; it's clear he didn't know what she was referring to.

It was a flyer, she said to him. Right? But more like, a *photocopy* of a flyer. Correct? And there's a huge typo, big as fuck. Can you tell me what it is?

Isaac blinked; his eyes widened.

It said—it said 1996, when it should have been—

'97, said Sherry. You know how I know about the typo?

No, said Isaac, and so she told him: a production assistant at TCS, on her way home from work, had dropped by her mother's photocopying store one day, in 1996. She said she needed to make thirty copies of the flyer, A5, black and white, for her superiors to vet the next day. Sherry made two copies of the flyer before she pointed out the most glaring mistake to the assistant, who had managed to blush and curse at the same time. The next one is '97, correct? she'd said. *Star Search* is mei ge liang nian, right? Sherry remembered this incident, because she remembered demanding the ten cents shortly after, to pay for the copies she had already printed. The production assistant promptly handed her the coin and stormed out of the store that evening, never to return. Sherry, on the other hand, thought it was a sign.

So you know what I end up doing? Sherry said to Isaac. Instead of throwing both copies away, I keep one of them instead. Inside my purse, as a message to myself: Maybe I'll get to act one day. You want to see?

Isaac said nothing. Sherry opened her purse up anyway. She unfolded it for him, the photocopied flyer, seven years old by now. It still managed to say: *Star Search 1996.*

So tell me, she said to him: how the hell do you have the other copy?

Isaac stared at her. For the longest time, that's all they did, staring at one another in a café, while Sherry was unable to figure out what was going through the man's mind. And then he told her: he told her what happened to him that year, in 1996. His story would begin at Golden Mile, and then pass through Kuala Lumpur, Malaysia, before he ended up in Kyoto, Japan, where the craziest thing had happened to him.

*   *   *

Here is where their friendship finally began. Sherry agreed to sign on to the drama, and got assigned the first leading role of her life. She was thrilled, elated; she had to smack herself half the time, to tell herself to come to her senses. She would have to be professional but friendly, personable but not personal. Whenever she and Isaac shared a scene, they would greet one another, and promise to have a meal afterwards, and it was over the course of those meals when Sherry learnt that Isaac didn't have much to say about his personal life. A part of her wondered if it was because he couldn't spend much time with either his wife or his child; another part wondered if he was simply unwilling, because it was her that he was talking to. And so, to fill the silence, she told him the story of Sherry Wong instead, and how that Sherry had to become Huang Huiying. Huang Huiying, if he'd like to know, was being courted by a businessman, a man from Shenzhen based in Hong Kong: they had met at one of those fancy dinners actors and actresses tended to have, at a seafood restaurant in East Coast Park. And this man was somehow determined, more so than she was, to allow her mother and her uncle the retirement they'd always deserved. He wanted to marry her, and better yet: he wanted to make her family happy, to give them a chance to step back from their businesses. All this moved Huang Huiying, but more importantly—it deeply impressed Sherry Wong.

But do you actually love him? Isaac asked. Sherry nearly laughed at this.

I guess so, she said. I guess I actually do love this man.

Isaac appeared bewildered, if not indignant. And he loves you too, right? This businessman?

He calls himself Carl.

Carl, said Isaac. You don't mind being married to this guy? And Sherry looked at him like he was stupid as she said, It's really not an issue for me, Isaac. Isaac then asked if she believed in soulmates. Do *you*? asked Sherry, so casually once again, so one hundred per cent Huang Huiying that she managed to wound him, the award-winning actor Isaac Neo.

I think we're soulmates, he said. You and I.

Sherry did not laugh at this; she pitied him instead. I'm not in love with you, she said. That's just what the media wants us to think. We're not actually in love, Isaac.

But Isaac didn't waver. I never said we had to be, he said, and Sherry finally laughed. She clapped her hands, guffawing. Wah, she said. Isaac. Always surprising me leh, you know. And this, they knew, this laugh: it's a hundred per cent Sherry Wong.

Afterwards she told him the story of the scarf, in more or less the same mode. She reminded him about the scarf that her character's mother will come to wear, in *Door to Your Heart*, when her mother's cancer is introduced later in the series. It's a scarf that Isaac's character gives to Sherry's, as a sign of his secret love for her. But in a moment of character development, in a sudden dramatic reversal, Sherry's character passes the scarf on to her mother, to use as a wrap around her increasing baldness. Now the scarf becomes a symbol of her loyalty, signifying where her character ultimately stands.

Sherry asked Isaac if he knew where the scarf came from. Is it from Carl? he said, and Sherry nodded and said yes, so smart. When I saw the scarf that the costume department wanted to use, I thought it looked like nothing, got no character, so I showed them the scarf that Carl got me instead. Sherry then stopped talking, smiling to herself now.

They said it was perfect, she said. And then I called Carl, and asked if he minded. No, he said, he didn't mind at all . . . He was glad I thought of him, of his gift. He never expected me to use it, actually. Now his gift, an actual piece of him—it gets to be on TV, said Sherry, before falling into another pause of contentment. Isn't that wonderful of Carl? You don't think that is a measure of love? she asked.

Isaac looked away, probably thinking about what an actress she could be. He can always buy you another one, he said. *I* can always buy you another one. He's not the only you qian ren here, okay?

Sherry nearly laughed at Isaac again. Instead she smiled at him, pitying him even more as she said: I guess so. She then paused for a third time, just for a second, before dropping her voice an octave lower, her smile now completely wiped away. She was glaring at him as she said to him, in Mandarin, in this lowered voice of hers:

I am going to marry him—*Carl*. I am going to marry Carl, Isaac, because he loves me more than I love myself. And I need it, you know? I need it to live. And you, Isaac, my dear, fucked up, so-called soulmate: I know you, okay? I know you up and down, inside out. I know what you eat, and I know what comes out of your ass. Better yet: I know your real story hor. I know who you are, I know what you did, and I know what you left behind. So you better listen to me when I say, okay: you don't get to act like you are innocent. You don't get to act like you are any different from me. You don't get to pretend you got yourself married for any other reason than that. You don't get to shit on me for finding a way to survive.

———

Isaac heard Daniel coming down from the rooftop, the weight of one foot heavier than the other. I'm sorry, he said. He still doesn't want to see you.

Isaac nodded; what else could he do? he thought. It's okay, man, he said. I understand. He told Daniel, somewhat bitterly, about how his own wife would rather write than keep him company. He then felt Daniel's finger, poking against his hand—a hand, he saw now, that was clenched into a fist.

Daniel let out a whistle. Let's walk.

They sat on the sand again. It must have been two or three in the afternoon, the beach full of revellers and holidaymakers. Daniel made sure to put a socket cover over his prosthetic, to protect it from the sand, before he bit on the flesh of a grilled chicken wing.

So were you always this angry? he asked.

I guess, said Isaac.

Daniel paused; he dropped the bones onto the plate beside him. You ever hit Jing?

No.

Yong-he?

Hey, said Isaac. I don't hit anybody.

Daniel raised his hands, waved them around. So you just, what—imagine things? Utter chaos and destruction? That is your outlet?

Isaac made a face. Perhaps.

Daniel licked the grease on his fingertips. I'm not belittling you, Isaac, he said. I just think you feel lonely. You must feel like you're the only person in the world who understands what you're going through. Daniel then asked if he felt like Tori had abandoned him. He asked if Isaac felt like he had to be happy for her, because abandoning him was part of what Tori wanted to do, in a way.

Isaac nodded. Yeah, he said. Maybe.

Daniel jutted his chin towards his prosthetic. He asked if Isaac knew about the Hipercor attack, the reason behind his lost leg. Isaac nodded. But I never told you how? said Daniel.

Isaac shook his head. Okay, Daniel said, picking up another chicken wing. I'll tell you now, aha. Same story that got Mateo to marry me in the end.

You serious? said Isaac, and Daniel nodded, chewing. He told him about how, on the 20th of March that year, Mateo had come home via a six-hour car ride from Madrid to Barcelona, with Señor Calvo and Señora Morales taking turns at the wheel. When they arrived, they let Mateo rest, and take a shower, while he and Mateo's parents discussed matters at the front door. And while they did they placed their hands on his shoulders.

I hope you're okay too, said Mateo's father. You must be traumatised as well, Daniel.

Daniel had waited a minute, upon closing the front door. He returned to the bedroom, and found Mateo sitting up in the bed they shared, looking at him, smiling. That was a morbid conversation, he said, as Daniel sat on the mattress, not far from his partner. He was already prying his prosthetic off. You heard everything? Daniel asked. Mateo replied, My family, you know. We're very dramatic.

Daniel set his leg aside. Yeah? he said, his voice choking up. I think so, too, Mateo. He then took his glasses off, just in time, the two already in one another's arms. Later he'd tell Mateo the same story he was telling Isaac on the beach: the story of how he was twenty-seven, and barely an architect, living in a small studio apartment in Sant Andreu.

I was nothing, he said: no responsibilities, just tasks, at this great but demanding agency. It was a Friday, but I had a half-day off. I was getting groceries, you see, for this dinner I was going to make. What dinner? asked Isaac, and Daniel said: A dinner for my girlfriend, a woman I was going to propose to that night. Isaac wanted to know how Mateo had responded, upon hearing this part of the story; "hot" was what Mateo had said, causing a laugh to burst out of Daniel's chest that day. He told Isaac about the way Mateo's head had bobbed on his chest, up and down as they laughed together, holding one another.

Poor woman, said Isaac, amused as well. Daniel sighed and said, I know, I know. I hated my life, if you had to know. I hated every part of it, he said, as he watched a family before them place a beach towel over the sand. For one, I didn't know why I was thinking of proposing to this girl, said Daniel. And I knew I was only staying in the city because of my father, knowing he was in there, somewhere ... But I think you tell yourself, at some point, that the things in your life would always unfold in two ways: either because it's just the way that things will go, or because it's the way you have always wanted things to go. It's either totally natural and expected of you, your life, or it's going to be something magical, fantastical, as though the world had read your mind. And I don't know what to make of it, he said to Isaac: I don't know why it feels like these are our only choices, sometimes.

Daniel's eyes were still fixed on the people that thronged the beach that afternoon. He said that his father had finally reached out to him, after the bomb went off at the supermarket. And it was such a tragedy, Isaac: too many people had died, people who shouldn't have died at all, he said. The authorities had apparently known that the bomb was going to be placed there, which meant that people could have lived, and I wouldn't have lost my leg. And my mother cried, kept crying, is all I remember of that time . . . She tells me, all the time, that it was the saddest day of her life, and that the days of her life would continue to be sad. Daniel then paused, and looked at him, at this particular point in the story; Isaac could feel his friend's old grief, reaching out to touch him now, like a wet stain on a piece of fabric.

But then the attack gave me other things too, he said. I met my father, you know? I got to see him again. And we spoke, and laid eyes on one another, for the first time in nearly twenty years. And then I left the girl, of course, telling her it was a mistake, added Daniel, as a laugh left through his nose. It should make no sense, really, that something good can come from something so tragic. But that's what I am trying to say, Daniel said: I think about that all the time, every time I am reminded that I have this damn leg. And sometimes, when I look at you, I think you're able to understand what I'm saying. Because it's true, he said; it took me many years, but it's true. Things are actually good now, and for real. There is a beauty that can arise from the pain.

Isaac nodded. He asked if that was how he got Mateo to marry him. Did you use the same speech?

Daniel shrugged. More or less, aha. But first we kissed.

Ah.

For a very long time, said Daniel, with a cheeky smile. I then told him that I loved him, and that I needed him, and he said he felt the same way too. He said, You know we can't get married, and I said I know, I did. It's not legal, said Mateo, it might never be, and I said again that I knew, I knew. I knew all of this. But it might, yeah? said Mateo. One day. And as I felt my face cupped between my lover's hands, he said to me: We could just have a ceremony. A fucking big one, in a really small, really intimate place. And I couldn't stop nodding, I was so in love with him, aha. It was crazy how in love I was with him that day.

Isaac was lying down now, with his face towards the sky. It frightened him, to see how clear it was; it took him back to Japan again, to the patch of sky he'd seen through the skylight in Tori's old bedroom.

Can I tell you something? said Isaac.

If you want to, said Daniel.

Okay, said Isaac, frightened now by what he was going to say. I think Jing is cheating on me.

The expression on Daniel's face began to darken. How do you—?

Isaac held a hand up. I'm not innocent either, he said, as he told him about Sherry, and the media's unwavering perception about the two of them. He told Daniel about how working with her had made his marriage suffer, the first time. He said he knew what he was getting himself into when they were cast in another series this year.

I was barely home at all, busy shooting the drama, he said. That was when Jing began to travel too, more than she usually would. Isaac then told Daniel about how his wife was in Malaysia, at one point, in Johor Bahru: she said she was there to cover a story, and he took the opportunity to go elsewhere too.

Where did you go? Daniel asked.

Malaysia, said Isaac. Not JB though, Penang.

A completely different city.

Isaac nodded. I spent one night there.

One night to do what?

To see Sherry, said Isaac. One last time.

Daniel paused. He was now staring at the sea, his expression serious but beseeching. So you were in love with her? he asked.

Once, said Isaac. Before we were even actors. When we were just kids.

Daniel turned back to look at him, surprised. And now?

I'm not so sure, said Isaac. He felt the truth of this fill him up from the inside. I feel the difference all the time; the difference between now and then, he added.

———

The story of Huang Huiying, finally, culminated in the day she announced her engagement to Carl Lim, to the cast and crew of *Door to Your Heart*.

Congratulations piled in the direction of the once-scorned actress: everyone was delighted for her, happy to celebrate the life of a woman they'd been led by the media to misunderstand. On the final day of filming, the 20th of April, 2004, the make-up artists presented a bouquet of flowers to her, and to Isaac Neo as well, for anchoring the production with their time, their talent, their hard work. The crew then converted a room on set into a dressing room, urging the actors to settle into their chairs. Huang Huiying, already crying, apologised to her assistant for ruining the mascara, while Sherry Wong, in rare synchronicity, felt more or less the same.

And then the inexplicable happened: breaking news aired from the TV in the corner, showcasing footage of the collapse at Nicoll Highway; life in the dressing room halted to a standstill, only to resume, eventually, with an episode that needed to be finished. A member of the crew turned around, however, and said the scarf was gone. And so the director yelled at the crew—he had always known that this would happen, from the moment they turned the set into a dressing room on a whim; nobody in this room, not one person, has learnt to value anything in their lives it seemed. Sherry felt that the director had gone too far. Dao yan, she said. If they cannot find it, they cannot find it! We'll have to make do with another scarf, she said, a suggestion that the director found ridiculous.

No filming would be done that day, he said to everyone on set—not till they find the fucking thing.

Shooting was postponed. The mood on set worsened, in a way that has never worsened before. And they never found the scarf again, forcing the scriptwriter to rewrite a few scenes from an earlier part of the episode. At the end of the ordeal, two weeks after they should have been done with the show, the costume department apologised to Sherry, saying they should have taken better care of it. They knew it was a loan, and that it was a gift from Sherry's fiancé, no less. Sherry assured them that it was okay, saying that it was nothing. Carl understands, she said.

There was a post-production party, scheduled to take place over the first weekend of June. Sherry sent an email to the cast and crew explaining why she couldn't attend it. She said that Carl was in Penang, for a business trip, and that he had bought tickets for her to join him, the first time they had seen one another since shooting for the drama began. And the replies soon came on the email thread, telling her to go and not think of them, to go and be in love. And Sherry did go, the moment June arrived: she thought that she might truly be in love too, when she got on her flight to Penang Airport, where her fiancé, Carl, was waiting for her.

The couple stayed in a lovely room, at one of the top floors of a new hotel, overlooking the coast of Georgetown. Their time together was very pleasant: their conversation, their sex, even their occasional silence—all of it was pleasant. It was the first time she had ever been in Penang, and everything she had seen managed to make her happy. While in the hotel, she typed out a second email to the cast and crew of *Door to Your Heart*, inviting them all to her engagement party in early July. And as she sent the email, hearing the whooshing sound her laptop made, she could feel her own heart, no, both of her hearts, hammering in one sudden, singular alignment.

They were at the pasar malam one evening, just down the road that ran along the coast. They made the short walk from their hotel, smelling the swamp and the salty surf, mixed with the exhaust from the cars that rumbled past them. And the pasar malam itself was particularly crowded, full of standing people, queuing for food or scouting for available seats. Carl, capable as he was, somehow found seats for them both; but when Sherry came over to his side, she was stumped, even a little horrified, to find Isaac Neo also seated at the table. They stared at one another while Carl said to Sherry, in Cantonese: This nice fella told me we can sit with him. And then Carl left, to get dinner for the two of them, while Sherry seated herself opposite the man. Isaac zipped open the sling bag he had brought with him, and took out a scarf, all too familiar.

So you found it, said Sherry.

No, said Isaac. I took it.

She asked him why he took it. He told her he didn't know. She said she would tell Frankie. Why? asked Isaac. Why do you have to tell anyone? She told him it was the right thing to do. What he did, she said to him, had cost the drama a lot of time and money. Isaac then told her he was sorry. He then told her he didn't care.

Sherry grew agitated. Why not? she asked him. Why don't you care? Isaac told her again that he did not know. And so Sherry abandoned her line of enquiry, and looked around the pasar malam. You are really alone? she asked Isaac. Your wife is where? Isaac said it did not matter.

Why not? said Sherry again. Why not, Isaac?

He did not say a thing.

Sherry's fiancé returned with the food. He had ordered rojak, and wanton noodles, as well as satay and popiah and sugar cane juice. Carl asked Isaac, in his heavily-accented English, if he was going to order food as well, or if he might possibly like to share. I got order too much, I think, he said to the table, and his friendliness managed to surprise both actors.

Isaac turned to Sherry for approval. She gave it to him: she passed him a pair of chopsticks. We spoke a bit, she said to Carl. He's Singaporean. He's all alone.

Ah, well, hello, he said. I am Carl.

I'm Zach, said Isaac.

Hey, Zach, said Carl. Got any plans tonight?

Isaac shook his head.

Well, that's awesome. I was thinking of going for a swim, after this meal. A quick dip in a pool, he said. You wanna join us, Zach? Sherry, would that be okay?

Sherry nodded. Isaac nodded as well. Carl smiled. In Cantonese, he said: Eat up.

Later, towards the end of their meal, just as the sun was fully setting over the scene, drenching everything at the seaside in an intense, burning pomegranate light, Isaac decided to thank Carl for his generosity. You look very happy, he said to him, which caused Carl to smile again. Of course I am, he said to Isaac. I'm getting married to this beautiful woman, after all.

Sherry beamed. She turned to Isaac. She noted the way he was looking at her, and she knew, in an instant, what the hell this fella was trying to do right now. It's an act-off, a dramatic showdown: champion versus champion. Except the camera, this time, was a human being. It was her husband-to-be. And she wasn't that interested in acting any longer.

We're very happy, she said.

———

We went to the swimming pool, Isaac said to Daniel, both of them still at the beach. He told him about how he had sat at the edge, with his feet in the water. He told him about how Sherry had lit herself a cigarette while Carl swam naked in the pool, his clothes on the deck chair behind them.

Lucky no one's around, said Isaac to Sherry.

Pretty much, she replied.

Isaac knew she was furious. And still the three of them remained that way, undisturbed for a few precious minutes, the night sky growing darker and deeper above them all, like a piece of paper soaking in ink. One by one the stars came out, as Sherry began to smoke.

Do you hate me? he asked.

A bit, she said.

Do you want me to go?

She shrugged. Haven't decided yet.

Are you still going to tell Frankie?

Oh, I am, she said. I know now, for sure. I won't be changing my mind on that.

Isaac remained still. Well, you won't have to tell Frankie, he said. Because he knows.

Oh? said Sherry, though the look in her eyes had failed to soften. Isaac did not move.

I told Frankie, he said, a few weeks ago. By then I'd taken a lot of things too, things other than your scarf. Isaac then told Sherry about the photos of him, taken on people's phones. He told her about Frankie cancelling all his media appointments too, prompting Sherry to ask if that was how she had got the *8 Days* cover. It was you, right, she asked, at first? And Isaac told her no, to not ever think that way. It was meant to be you and me, he said to Sherry. But I fucked that up.

There was a short pause. Isaac looked at the image of his feet, dancing and rippling in the water of the pool. He said:

I was afraid of losing you, at first.

And now?

Not so much, said Isaac. I think it would be okay.

Sherry shook her head, tipping the end of her cigarette. The ambers fell, only to be quickly put out.

Of course it's okay. It *should* be okay, she said. You got an actual family now, a great career. Correct? Look at the world you have, Isaac. The one you have right now.

Isaac nodded. He thought, in that moment, that there might be no difference between this and any of the other worlds he's in. It's possible that in every version of this, in every timeline of the world the Isaacs all share: he loses her. He will lose her, Sherry Wong. Every single time.

Suddenly he heard Carl's voice. Come in! he said to Sherry, and she did. She stubbed out her cigarette, and took off her shirt. She unclipped her bra, revealing her breasts to Isaac, the shape of them limned by the lights in the water. He had a vision then, of the last time he saw them bared like this, so long ago—and then she jumped, wildly into the pool, leaving her clothes behind in a small pile next to him. And it was true, what he had earlier said to Carl, and what Sherry later said to him, and what he would in turn say to Daniel, seated on a beach in Isla Cristina: the two looked so very, very happy.

23

The Horvallan. Jing Aw. Flame of the Forest, Singapore, 2005.

The playground, 2004

While my husband was away, shooting scenes for his new drama, you told me about the reports that pour in, after the meeting at the bar is concluded: the diplomat's laptop is alight with data and the interpretations of those data, all from the nearest space observatory she can command, situated atop the Cameron Highlands. All of it screams at her one thing: that the comet is, indeed, headed straight for Earth, in a closer approximate of sixty-five thousand years. The chances of it striking the planet stand at forty-five to sixty per cent, with a twelve to seventeen per cent chance of the comet striking water instead of land. The chances of Hyakutake hitting nothing at all stand at less than five per cent, even after allowing for further gravitational pulls from planets like Jupiter or Saturn once the comet reenters the solar system.

But nothing can account for the planet of Horvalla. It doesn't exist, as far as anybody or any alien is aware of. For a society so technologically advanced, there are no radio signals, no broadcasts of any kind, transmitting information of any sort that would pinpoint the existence of such a planet. When she attempts to contact any of her counterparts in Singapore, enquiring about the existence of Horvalla—its size, its coordinates, its geography, even the etymology of its name—she is met, unsurprisingly, with total silence.

All she has is this story. His story. Which she has to believe somehow, she and the rest of the intergalactic co-operative. She turns to her aide, cross-legged on the floor, staring into his laptop.

See if you can get me the Horvallan's room number, the diplomat says. She then dismisses him, and tells him to go home. Her aide asks if she is sure.

I can stay, read more data. I don't mind.

The diplomat knows he's doing his best; he's just like her, wrestling with worst-case scenarios, already forcing himself to rise to the challenge. He has already raised a number of solutions to her, including the crazy plan of expanding existing outposts on Mars. But the diplomat insists that he must go. *I need you back here, alert, tomorrow morning,* she says. *Leave tonight to me.*

After her aide departs, the diplomat leaves her room, and takes the lift down two storeys. All she has is her personal phone. She finds the room number and knocks on the door. It swings open, and it's him, the Horvallan, in a T-shirt and a pair of jeans. Her eyes fall on a pair of sneakers too, which somehow infuriates her.

Tell me when you arrived on Earth, she says.

The Horvallan doesn't say a word.

I just need a date. Or maybe even a year.

The Horvallan remains silent.

Fine, says the diplomat. *At least tell me what happened to your spaceship. The one from your planet. Did the Singaporeans keep it? Is it locked away? Taken apart in some kind of lab? Is it buried in the ground, in the sea? Is it incinerated? Where is it?*

Nothing. His lips remain shut.

You need to tell me something, she says. *Anything. How did you pick up our language? How have you managed to speak like a native? Actually, scrap that—how old are you even? How can you prove to me that you are immortal?*

The Horvallan's eyes bore into hers, causing the diplomat to grow from restless to indignant, her mind racing with a dozen more questions. And then she finally asks him the one thing, in fact the first thing, that has bugged her since before the meeting even began.

Tell me how I know you, she says to him. *Can you tell me that, at least? Tell me how I have seen your face before.*

The Horvallan blinks, finally—and the act alone is enough to shake her. She doesn't even know how tightly she has crossed her arms until she finds him tugging, on one of her hands, trying to wrest it free. She lets it sit in the Horvallan's own palm.

Are you hungry? he asks.

No, she says. *Though I haven't had dinner.*

He asks if she would like to eat with him. She says okay. He asks if she would like to eat in the hotel, or if she'd prefer somewhere outside instead, out in the town of Iskandar. She feels a prick behind her ears, the sudden onset of sweat; she can feel more of it collect around the wedding band on her finger, which is also when she chooses to finally free her hand from his.

Let's head out, she says.

"What's Iskandar like, in 2989AD?"

"Beautiful. Sprawling. An immense but low-lying city, unlike any you've ever seen before. Only a few buildings, like the hotel they are in, are allowed to reach as high as it stands."

"And the food?"

"Sedap."

"And the streets?"

"Wide. Well-paved."

"The weather?"

"Pleasant enough."

"The people?"

"Gorgeous," you said. "They are gorgeous, Jing. As cantik as the town they live in."

*   *   *

The diplomat and the Horvallan hop on a hover-bike, parked at the front of the hotel. The Horvallan takes his phone and slots it into the dock between the handles. Automated and driverless, the hover-bike lights up, and the hum of its engine is kicked up a notch, ready to go at any moment.

And then they take off, the vehicle shifting its own gears. The diplomat, more accustomed to armoured limousines and the occasional helicopter, reminds herself to breathe as they wind their way through the township, alive and illuminated, full of colour in the busy night. When she peers through the windows of the buildings they pass by, she sees people, many of them, eating and drinking and talking, gazing out onto the street they are on. They must look like anyone right now; she must look like any other girl, riding on a bike behind some other boy. They are anonymous tonight, and they disappear into the frame. It's astounding to her that this, that any of this, won't somehow last forever.

The hover-bike is about to make a turn; her centre of gravity shifts. She feels weightless, untethered; she wants to raise her arms, and scream, as they make one loop around the major roundabout. The hover-bike then takes an exit, taking them down a street that the diplomat knows; she shoots the Horvallan a look, before turning towards the holographic sign-board atop the diner.

You know what it says? asks the Horvallan. He looks totally innocent, but the diplomat doesn't buy it.

Don't fuck with me, she says. *You know it too.*

The street is drenched in a different colour, every time the signboard flashes a different letter: not in English or in Malay, but in Japanese, in katakana. Together, the letters spell,

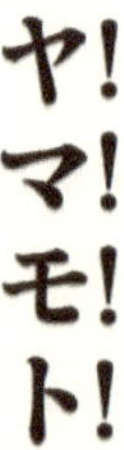

"Yamamoto."

"Yeah."

I said it again: "Yamamoto."

"That's right," you said.

I stared at you. I told you about a friend I once had, a friend with the same surname, a friend I hadn't seen in eight years. You asked if something had happened to her, and I told you I wasn't so sure. "She left us, got on a taxi, didn't tell us where," I said. All she had left behind was a note and a suitcase for us to discover.

"What did the note say?" you asked.

"'Thank you for finding me. Please take me home.' Nothing more, nothing less," I said. Later you asked me what the suitcase had contained, and I told you I didn't know. It seemed impossible, to me, that the sum of her life could fit inside that one thing.

The comment gave you pause. "It must have been very small," you replied, "a very small life." I said I didn't know that, at the time; I said knowing that now made me envious, somehow.

The diplomat chooses a booth next to the window, one that looks out into the street. The Horvallan sits across from her, their feet nearly touching. The whole of YA!MA!MO!TO! is like this, with booths like these, and griddles installed on all of the tabletops. She asks if he knows how to make okonomiyaki, and he says that he thinks so. She suggests they order one each, though she is also happy to cook his order.

That's very kind of you, says the Horvallan.

I'm being diplomatic, says our heroine. *But I am also a pro at this.*

The Horvallan shrugs. *You'd have to be. Especially if your family owns the place.*

His remark gives the diplomat a keen sense of defeat. You know me more than I know you, she says, and the Horvallan now smiles, sympathetically.

There's not much to know about me, he says. *I've told everyone what they need to know.*

Their waitress comes along. She doesn't recognise our heroine, but she does recognise the card that she flashes at her, as well as the surname that's clearly printed beside her photo. The diplomat says she'll get the prawn, oblivious to the waitress's mounting anxiety, while the Horvallan says he'll have the ham and cheese; the waitress leaves, only to scoot back to their booth a few seconds later, realising she had forgotten to ask about their drinks. The diplomat orders them two beers.

That means we won't be able to hover-bike, says the Horvallan.

The diplomat shrugs. *There's always the taxi.*

Their okonomiyaki mixes arrive promptly in their bowls. The diplomat dispenses the oil, and waits for it to sizzle, before pouring the mixtures into two perfect mounds; she fries them both at the same time while the griddle lights up from red to green, indicating how cooked the batter is. Nothing has changed for her since the age of sixteen: she can still fry up a mean pancake like it's nothing. The Horvallan, content with watching the diplomat cook, doesn't say a word.

She asks him what he's thinking about, and the Horvallan's smile turns somewhat bashful. *I'm wondering how I should convince you,* he says. *That I am who I say I am.*

The diplomat ponders about this for a moment. *If I took one of your arms and forced it onto the griddle—would it hurt?*

My skin would tear from my flesh, he says, *so yes.*

But you would heal.

Yes, he says. *How it would do that would depend on the kind of treatment I receive. But it would heal.*

Completely?

Most likely.

What would happen, then, if I took some samples from you? Like your saliva, your skin, your blood? What would I find? she asks. *What would the lab say?*

That I'm quite extraordinary, says the Horvallan.

The diplomat waits for the chill to run through her body—but it does not. She waits an additional second before flipping her own okonomiyaki. She then flips the Horvallan's, and it's perfect, both times.

You like scallions?

I'm okay.

Bonito flakes?

Love.

The diplomat nods again. *Can't live without the sauce, though.*

That you can't.

The diplomat finally looks away from the griddle, and into the Horvallan's eyes. She feels once again the onset of time, bearing its weight upon her shoulders.

Tell me something.

Yes?

Tell me why, she says—*why I can't get away from this feeling.*

What feeling? the Horvallan asks. The diplomat takes a quick breath.

I keep thinking that I've been through this before, she says. *That we've sat here before, you and I. That we've ridden on that hover-bike too, at some point in the past.* She asks if she is the only one who feels this way, and the Horvallan shakes his head.

Maybe we met as kids, he says.

Maybe, says the diplomat. She leans back in her seat. *I still can't believe that a comet is coming for us. Even though I won't be here, really, by the time that thing is.*

The Horvallan apologises, even though it's an apology she doesn't need to hear. The diplomat places their okonomiyaki on separate plates, feeling that same sense of defeat again. But her ears pick up on an old piece of music, now playing from the speakers as if on cue.

Maybe I had a crush on you, she says to him. *Maybe you broke my heart here, right in this very restaurant.*

The Horvallan nods again. *Maybe,* he says, before they eat.

Hotel Atlet Century Park, Jakarta, 2004

It is that exact scene that the Horvallan recalls—that scene in the diner, between him and the diplomat—when he sits down in the oncologist's clinic. She asks if he is feeling peckish after a long day of meetings.

I could really chow on something right now, she says.

The Horvallan asks the oncologist if she would like to head to the canteen, to take advantage of his special access. Her stomach clenches, however, the moment she thinks about getting on the tram again. She tells him they'll order in, which is the thing she usually does anyway. She shows him the menu on her ever wondrous tablet.

I always go for A-2, she says. *The whole set.*

The Horvallan frowns. *Isn't that just a nutrient block?*

The oncologist shrugs. *Beggars can't be choosers,* she says, *a phrase which is still around, of course.*

In a way, the Hotel Atlet Century Park embodied many of the characteristics that defined its city. It was large, larger than most buildings I ever saw in Singapore; the place could also be tremendously busy in one moment and then completely desolate the next. But an air of solitude would pervade, no matter where I went in the hotel, which was also how it felt for me in many parts of the wider city. That was Jakarta for you; that was the Hotel Atlet Century Park.

The first morning at the hotel, I asked you how long you would take, being at this festival.

"You don't want to come?"

"I'm not into literary things," I said. "Perhaps tomorrow."

"Okay," you said. "I'll be back in the evening."

We promised that we would text, even though texting, strictly speaking, was a thing we never did very well with one another. The moment you left I lay on our bed, contemplating how I might spend my time. I could go swimming, though I didn't bring my swimming suit; I could use the gym, or play tennis, but I didn't bring the right clothes either. There was that final option, of course, the one where I would leave. I would walk out of the hotel, and get into a cab. I would tell the driver to take me anywhere he or she wanted, and disappear. I could disappear.

Instead I continued lying on the bed. Our bed. This was our world for now, with barely anything to be found in it. In that moment, I frankly couldn't tell if that was delightful or thoroughly, irrevocably reprehensible. Now, I thought, was a good time to feel guilty.

Outside the window I saw only trees, and a single building.

A good person would leave.

The Horvallan and the oncologist relocate to the corridor for their dinner. Two green arrows, dimly flashing on the ceiling, indicate the number of metres remaining, in front and behind them, to the lobbies of the Residential and Medical Wings.

The Horvallan bites on the corner of Set A-3. *Let me try A-2,* he says, and realises that the Sichuan option is hardly any better than the Moroccan one. *You eat this every day?*

Oh yes, says the oncologist. *Sometimes twice.* She asks him what they serve instead in the VIP section of the canteen. He lists a number of things she longs for instantly, things like sausages, potatoes, fruit salad, cake. Once in a while fried chicken comes along, he says, which causes her to moan involuntarily. *Damn it,* she says.

He looks out the window, grinning. The best view of Mars, indeed. He asks if this is how and where she tells her patients that they are dying, our heroine begins to choke on her block.

You're not dying, she finally says.

I'm not?

She shakes her head. Scans show up nothing, she says to the Horvallan. *Nothing in your brain, your heart, your liver. All your vitals lie within a normal, acceptable range. Your metabolic age, irritatingly enough, is somehow thirty-six.* She then asks him about his visions. She asks him when they began.

Fifth day on the Ubin, says the Horvallan. The oncologist asks him what he's seen, and he tells her, showing her a list he has made on his tablet, all relics of the twenty-first century somehow. He has seen iPods, and newer things named iPhones and iPads, scattered around his room; a brochure from the Chinati-Bing Foundation, dated 2065, slotted into the inner pocket of a suit; two Pokémon, a Nidorino and a Gengar, engaged in battle in a corridor; a tortoise, flapping its fins on the floor of his shower, with a plastic straw stuck into one of its nostrils; a video clip, on one of the iPhones he found, showing Kim Jong-un and Donald Trump, hugging one another; a second video clip, this time of a tsunami, washing over a coastal village; the voice of a spoken word artist, informing him he needs to update an app on his phone; a third video clip, on his own tablet this time, of a volcano erupting in Yellowstone National Park.

Gosh, is all the oncologist can say in response. *How does it feel to be fallible, my dear Horvallan?*

He tells her it feels new.

The oncologist recommends he sees a psychiatrist again, as they begin their walk back to the Residential Wing. She tells him she won't tell anyone about their conversation either, and that she can delete his biodata if he wants. *I'm intensely private,* he says to her, *so I'm glad I can trust you, doctor.* The two then discard the wrappers that came with their nutrient blocks once they manage to reach the lobby.

Goodnight, doctor.

Goodnight, you.

He nods. *I'll see you again, if I can't find a psychiatrist.*

The oncologist tells him to do that, please. *Though there are too many of them, I think, on board this station.*

He smiles at her. She smiles at him. They continue to smile at one another, as they stand in the lobby.

Take care, he says. *You too,* she replies, before she is whisked away.

"The days pass," you said, on our final night at the hotel: "The Horvallan shows up at the clinic, again and again. He becomes a fixture at the clinic, and therefore a fixture of the oncologist's life. They spend evenings together, awash in the coppery light of their favourite corridor, as the planet of Mars soon fills the entire span of the window. Even their very skin takes on a bloodstained hue, as two figures in the back of every photo taken there, standing side by side before the sight of a red world."

They discuss their move to the colony. He asks the oncologist when her contract will end.

I'm not sure, she says. *When it's time to retire, I suppose.*

The Horvallan then looks at her, sadly, his face aglow with a new light, reflected off the surface of a new planet. He looks at her in a way that confirms to her, our heroine, what she's been guessing all along: that he has feelings for her. That he might very well have fallen in love with her, and that she might feel the same for him as well. But the two have less than a week before it's time for the Horvallan to disembark, even as he continues to experience new visions, you said. A drag queen appears to ask if he would like more water in his glass; five voice actors from the three thousandth episode of *The Simpsons* recite lines to one another on his bed; he sees the volcano again, the one on Yellowstone National Park, erupting on the surface of Mars this time, through the window of his own guest suite in the Pilots' Wing. As a large plume of ash spews from the crater, the Horvallan blinks, and turns, and focusses his sight on the door of his room. He heads towards our heroine's clinic, where the doctor, however, is nowhere to be seen.

She's at the Intensive Care Unit, according to the nurse at the reception. *She's now tending to Xian, her niece.*

The Horvallan heads down two storeys and arrives at the ICU, startling all of the nurses there. He asks them to take him to the oncologist, while the nurses insist that the Horvallan gowns up first. And as he walks through the ICU he finds himself scrutinising the other wards, the other patients, all floating in liquid canisters, chambers designed to simulate womb-like conditions.

It's crowded, he says, as the nurses beside him glance nervously at one another.

Xian's ward: the Horvallan looks inside, and the girl is in one of six canisters, with a tube through her mouth and a smaller one in her side. The oncologist is standing before her canister, tapping on her tablet. The Horvallan stares at Xian's parents, and manages to recognise one of them: her father is one of the RSS *Ubin's* most senior pilots, the rank on his sleeve confirming that he is only a rung or two away from the very top of command. They've even had a few lunches together, over the time the Horvallan has spent on board the station, and he is the first to spot him too, standing outside the ward. Xian's father steps out to greet him, followed soon after by the oncologist.

Sir, he says. *To what do I owe the pleasure?*

Oh, says the Horvallan. *I'm here for*—He awkwardly waves at the oncologist. *I'm here for your sister.*

The pilot turns towards her, with a look of recognition in his eyes. *I've been told you are seeing one another,* he says, and the oncologist tells her brother not to be creepy. She then gestures towards Xian's canister.

I'm a little caught up in this situation, she says.

The Horvallan asks them what happened. The oncologist says that her niece was found on the tram, en route to the clinic, weak and unable to breathe. *It's radiation poisoning, clear as day,* she says.

But what's the source? the Horvallan asks, glancing at the girl's father. The pilot appears unperturbed, if not a little annoyed by the question.

There is a rumour, he says, *floating around the station. Some are suggesting that there is a leak in the engine, a containment fault, and that the engine is the reason everyone is getting sick.*

The Horvallan asks how sure he is, that the rumour is simply a rumour. *Can you confirm if there really has been a leak?*

A vein twinges in the side of the pilot's forehead. *I can,* he says, *though I don't necessarily have to, sir. I need to attend to my daughter,* the pilot quickly adds, before heading back inside the ward. Husband and wife begin muttering questions to one another now, careful not to be lip-read through the viewing glass.

They know something, he says, as the oncologist puts a hand around his arm. He feels it tighten around his elbow.

You need to find out what it is, she says.

Bestari Heights, 2004

We were getting greedy, at this point. We decided to see each other again, on the first weekend of June; you called me, telling me to meet you, on a Friday morning at Tuas Second Link. Some distant cousin of yours was finally getting married, and you said it would be nice if I was there.

"As a date?" I asked, and you said, "Yes, as a date." I asked you where next, and you said the wedding would be held in JB, of course.

"It's in, well—it's in Iskandar, actually. You might have heard of this place," you said.

On the morning of the 4th of June, 2004, you showed up in a rented car, at the Caltex across the street. You asked me to get in, and I closed the door, and kissed you on the lips. You readily kissed me back.

We took off. Over the highway and over the strait we entered Malaysia, and eventually found our way into Iskandar, in the southwestern area of Johor Bahru. We drove around a roundabout, the largest one I've ever seen, and I had a brief vision of the Horvallan and the diplomat, riding together on a hover-bike, our heroine tempted to let out a scream. We exited onto a smaller, sleepier section of the neighbourhood, with dirt crunching audibly underneath the wheels of the rental, as we made our way between a row of shophouses and the side of a large shopping mall still under construction. We then drove over a gully, crowded with all sorts of bushes and weeds, and then down a long street, bordered by tall trees on either side, so that their leaves had formed a canopy over our heads. At the end stood a gated community of terraced houses, rows and rows of them, all identical too.

"This is where I live," you said: "Bestari Heights."

That we were able to occupy an entire unit, an entire house all to ourselves, continues to boggle me now.

The house was yours, but barely furnished: all you had was a couch and a table downstairs, and a bed and mattress in one of the four rooms upstairs. There was hardly anything in the kitchen too, while the garden needed something more than mere pruning. Sometimes during the day, in the thick silence of Bestari Heights, a rhythmic, metallic sound would pierce through the haze, something between a squeak and a screech: I stepped outside, determined to know what the source of that sound was, and saw that it was just an unlatched gate, swinging back and forth, presumably from an unoccupied unit across the street.

We drove to a mamak eatery, at one of the shophouses nearby, for lunch. We got roti and briyani, and a cold glass of teh limau each. When we headed back I found myself re-encountering the same sights again—the short bridge over the gully, the trees along the road, the rows and rows of identical houses—all striking me anew. I guess I couldn't believe I was lodging in a place like this, a place so obviously new and excessive, but with a totally barren spirit. Come nightfall we walked around, just to amuse ourselves, just to find something other than fucking to do. We walked up and down the streets, past one empty abode after another; I was unable to process how many empty homes there could be in a single space, which conversely made me curious about the people who chose to live here. I asked you what prompted you to get a unit in Bestari Heights, and you said it was a bid to stake a claim in Iskandar, in a place that had inspired you so much.

"Plus I love it here," you said: "a place where you can actually disappear into."

It rained that night, a classic thunderstorm. You and I held one another, on the one mattress upstairs, with nothing but a thin sheet over our bodies. I was addicted to the pointed touches of your body, your sweet and sour smell; it was like drowning from the inside, having sex with you, while the sound of raindrops smattered all over the surfaces of your house.

You said it would rain like this, would begin to storm like this, the moment the Horvallan and the spectre emerged from the forest.

68525AD: The spectre looks over her shoulder, certain that they are still being watched. She can't imagine that the primates would let them leave like this, with a rucksack full of treasure. But she can't find any of the creatures, from any of the warring tribes, in any of the trees they've left behind.

Lightning, again—several bolts forking and streaking across the sky; the resulting thunder volleys over their heads, sooner than she appreciates. The forest behind them rustles and shivers now, in a great chitter-chattering of trees, while rain skitters off the worn tarmac of the MacRitchie Viaduct. The Horvallan picks up the pace as best as he can; the spectre hurries along, following close behind. A pack of giant lizards scamper across the leaf-strewn lanes, slithering into whatever cover from the impending storm they have found, presumably beneath the Viaduct. And then a magnificent chorus, the constant shrieking of primates, cascades in ripples and then in waves across the electrified air, their cries crashing over them like an avalanche of sound.

The Horvallan takes one glance at the comet. It's behind the clouds, a fuzzy spot of light, looking twice as big. The rain then starts to pour, falling in hard and battering sheets. *Be careful,* he says to the spectre, the moment they reach the water, rising up fast over the end of the Viaduct—he passes her the lantern, followed by his rucksack, while he hastily climbs on board their boat. The spectre follows suit, swinging the lantern about, realising it's even harder now to discern their way back to the penthouse.

We need to find shelter, she shouts, and he agrees. He says that if they keep pushing forward, he is certain they will hit a building soon.

And if we don't? asks the spectre. *If nothing were to appear?*

Then the boat will flood, he says. *And then we sink!*

But of course they find it, shelter, in less than fifteen minutes: their boat sails straight into a neighbourhood of terraced houses, an enclave quite like Bestari Heights, one that the Horvallan has never seen materialise till now. But the Horvallan doesn't have time to marvel at the miracle: he swiftly guides their boat through an open gate into the living room of an empty house, steering it straight towards the staircase, where it bumps against a tiled step. There they disembark, and quickly tip the boat, unloading all the rainwater it has collected so far; then they haul it up to the second floor, tying it to the railing via a cord while the water continues to rise from the first floor.

The spectre quickly casts the lantern about, shining light into each of the four rooms, checking for the presence of unwanted animals. The Horvallan then urges the spectre to come into one of them, a room shaped a lot like ours, you said, large and rectangular, and with a balcony that faces the surrounding neighbourhood. You then pointed to me the windows that the Horvallan now proceeds to shut.

The spectre sets the lantern down. The windowpanes shudder against the storm outside, while all they can do is pant and stare as the wind whistles sharply through a crack into the room. The spectre's coat squelches awkwardly as she peels it off her body, prompting the Horvallan to remove his goggles, his mask, his poncho. She squeezes the water out of her hair, and asks if they can make a fire, somehow. The Horvallan extracts a lighter, a tin can, and a block of fuel from his backpack—more items, he says, that also came with the penthouse. Later she asks what else he's got in there, and the Horvallan can't help but smile when he reaches in and shows her: a nutrient block.

I couldn't find A-2, he says.

The spectre doesn't seem as amused as he is. She passes the rucksack of mushrooms back to him.

What are you trying to do with them? she asks, the question she's been meaning to ask the whole night. The Horvallan opens up the rucksack, and runs his hands through the haul, just to see how they've held up over the journey.

I'm making a soup, he says. *A really nice one.* He tells her he's going to use everything he has inside the rucksack.

That's a lot, says the spectre. *Some would say it's too much.*

He neither agrees nor disagrees. *Should be enough for me,* he says.

The spectre looks at him, lit by the small fire he's made in the room. He's done it, somehow, growing older; he has bags under his eyes, and wrinkles too. She even appreciates the added weight in his movements, which she has observed while in the forest. She asks him when he is going to make and drink this soup, and he tells her that he'll do so when the right time comes.

You mean the comet, says the spectre. *You mean, when the comet comes.*

The Horvallan nods. *That's what I meant to say.*

You and I went, the following afternoon, to the hotel where the wedding was located. It was nice, I thought. When we went into the lobby, and took the lift up to the banquet hall, I asked if this was the same hotel where the Horvallan and the diplomat first met, in 2989AD. You asked me if I were truly that keen to be part of a story.

Later, over dinner, I became surprisingly at ease with questions about who I was. My name is Jing, yes, Jing Aw, I said. I am an editor and columnist for *The Straits Times*, I told one of his relatives. Yes, I said, I'm Singaporean, yes. I am thirty-four, yes—and it's about time we thought about it, yes. So charming, he is. Yes. We met at a party, at my place, actually, for he was a friend of my mother's. Oh, my mother? My mother's gone, actually. She, well, she passed away; it's how we connected, actually, yes.

After the wedding we left, tipsy, blasting the radio in your car. We were wicked. We kept laughing, like we just got away with a crime, a grand heist. We went around the main roundabout multiple times, round and round as though it were a game, although truth be told it was because we kept missing our exit. And when we finally made it, it was nothing short of a release, and when we sped over the gully towards Bestari Heights, I screamed, we screamed, because you had nearly hit one of the streetlights. And when we both stumbled out of the car we were laughing some more, outside your unit. I don't know how, I don't know when, but at some point your house began to feel like my house too.

You then pointed out the hotel to me, the hotel where we just came from: the tallest building in all of Iskandar, standing proudly over the treetops. You would tell me to look at its signboard, displayed at the top: seven bright letters, all in white, shining over the canopy.

INSPIRE, was the word. We howled.

The storm continues. The spectre turns to the Horvallan. The gaze she gives him then is a gaze of love, pure love.

I'm sure you've wondered, she says. *I'm sure you've had plenty of time to ask yourself this question.*

He looks at her, seated before him, a figure within a living dream. *What question?* he asks, as the spectre begins to smile.

What you've accomplished, she says, *what you've done with your life. What the point of your life must be.*

The Horvallan trembles. He knows it's not simply from the cold of the rain. He trembles as the spectre begins to tell him a story.

Once, when I was much younger, I found myself in conversation with an accomplished author, she says. *At the end of our chat together, the author asked: "What do you think a character should feel, when they have finally reached the end of their story? Do they or do they not wish they could change anything about their past?"*

The spectre then asks the Horvallan to guess what her answer had been back then. Our hero blinks, unsure of what to say.

They wouldn't change a thing?

The spectre nods. *That's exactly what I said. But the author shook her head at me, and told me I was wrong,* she says: *"Your character must always wish that there was something they could change, something they could do better, if they were granted the ability to turn back time." That is what makes a story meaningful, the author said to me. What use is a story, my dear, if it is a story without mistakes?*

The spectre continues to smile at him. She then moves closer to the Horvallan, and he can barely shrink, can't even cower, as she places her hands around his face.

There is a place, she says. *A place I have gone. A place that exists outside of everything we know, or understand. It is a wondrous place, I tell you, a spectacular place, a land of absolute purity. A place that only knows peace, a place filled with people like me, and people like you, people who understand what it means when I say that life—it's suffering. It's pain. Life is a whirlpool and it sucks you in, down the spiral towards its lonely centre, a centre I chose not to resist, any longer.*

She pauses again. The Horvallan can't respond, not when he is still caught within her enthralling gaze.

I'm saying you have a choice. The same way I had a choice too, the spectre says. *You can leave with me, you've earned it—you can take off right now, if you want. You can come with me—you can let me take you—off to the place where there is no suffering, no pain. No more loss, no hurt. No fear, no failure—no death, not even birth. Not even us, just you, the essence of you, spread across an unlimited expanse, in a constant state of heightened being. Wouldn't that be better?* the spectre asks, as her smile grows ever wider. *Wouldn't that be everything?*

24

Once upon a time, a king gave a feast, with the most beautiful princess of the realm in attendance . . . A soldier, standing guard, watched the king's daughter go by . . .

The villa was dark, with just the TV on, playing Daniel's favourite film; but even in the darkness the sound was immense, louder than the very film itself, even as Alfredo tells Toto the story of the soldier: the sound of two dozen people crowded together in that one living room, all breathing, all murmuring, drinking out of cups and glasses of wine. Isaac could hear them wandering too, fidgeting, making their way in and out of the room, their feet creaking on the floor tiles as they headed towards the toilet or the kitchen. Some escaped into the courtyard too, the soles of their sandals scraping against the sand over the terracotta floor tiles, the ends of their cigarettes like fireflies against the darkening night.

His son's head, placed on his lap, felt like a piece of a coal. He was fast asleep. And Isaac could sense the same thought turning itself over in Mateo's mind as he glanced in Isaac's direction, the voice that said that his wife was nowhere to be seen.

Fireworks erupted, all over the TV. Mateo got up and left for the kitchen; he could sense every eye on the man's figure as he wove his way through the bodies in the room. Isaac then managed to see Mateo's shadow dart across the courtyard and then through the open gate. He turned back to the couch where he and Daniel had sat, and saw both of the grooms' mothers turn to ask Daniel something; Daniel could only shrug, and jut his chin towards the television, while the movie and its music played on towards their heartbreaking conclusion.

Only later, after Señor Calvo popped out the DVD and switched off the TV, did the woman on the staircase finally come down to speak to Isaac. The lights in the villa were still flickering back on as she asked if she could sit next to them on the couch. Isaac nodded, and brought more of his son's body up onto his lap, so that now the boy's head could lie on his collarbone instead.

Do you remember me? the woman asked. We might have met briefly last year. Isaac nodded and said, Very briefly, causing the woman, Deepika, to sigh as though to say, I understand. I've been meaning to ask you a great number of questions, actually, the artist said, and the actor began to steel himself against the prospect. Deepika asked if he knew where his wife was, and he said yes, he did. She's at the hotel, he said. You think Mateo's there too? Deepika asked, and he said yes, he probably was. She wanted to know what they could be talking about now, and this time Isaac said he didn't know. It was impossible to know.

Deepika sighed a second time. He says he's been dreaming, she said, about a silver taxi. Do you know what *that* is about? she asked, and although Isaac didn't reply, Deepika took his silence as a yes.

You know she's working on a story, she said.

Isaac dared himself not to say it, but he did anyway. He couldn't be entirely powerless in this conversation. *The Horvallan*, he said.

A smile crept over the artist's lips. It's really not my place to tell anyone what they can or cannot do, said Deepika—but what your wife is doing right now, it's problematic.

Problematic, he thought; he didn't quite know what she meant by that. And yet he still found himself defending her, protecting her dignity in the face of others. It's her life, he began to say, only to have the artist cut him off and say no, it is not. It is not "her life", Isaac—it is Milton's work, she said. And Isaac could feel the flames begin to lick against his very bones as he said, Milton? That's the man's name? And Deepika scoffed at him, shaking her head. There's so much you know, and yet so little, really, she said. Finally, she asked him how he had known about the story in the first place. Did your wife tell you? About everything they've done together?

He shook his head. He could still feel the flames, licking the back of his eyes and nose this time. I found them, he said, her notebooks.

The artist clapped her hands, and nearly tumbled off the couch. She seemed mad with glee, and exclaimed in a way that nearly stirred Yong-he awake. Tell me, dear Isaac—where did she keep them? she asked. And Isaac thought now of the closet in Han Aw's room, the room that was now their son's: it was a wonder that they had managed to leave it alone, even after they had handed so many of Han Aw's other items to the conservators, the archivists, the collectors and the curators; even after they had proceeded to convert the room into a nursery for Yong-he, and then eventually into his bedroom.

Top of a closet, he said to Deepika. Hidden beside all of her missing mother's things.

Isaac carried Yong-he back to the hotel. The palms that lined the boardwalk seemed to flatten against the wind, while more sand began to drift from the beach; he made sure to turn his son's head away from the sea, while he made his way slowly back to the Hotel Sol Y Mar.

It was on the 5th of September, 1997, when Isaac had asked for Jing's hand in marriage. He had ordered the ring a week before, after discreetly measuring the width of her ring finger while she slept; he got the call that morning, to collect it from the store, and had planned to propose four days later, on the night of her 27th birthday.

Jing took Isaac to The Substation that evening, for what he understood to be a retrospective of her mother's life and work. They arrived after an early dinner and a quick drink of iced kopi at the nearby S11, sure that they would need it for the night's barrage of smiling, greeting and shoulder-rubbing; instead they found the affair sombre, the mood serious, as they were ushered into The Substation gallery. The first thing they saw was Jing's re-enactment of *RANDEN*, playing on the wall next to the double doors; once inside they found a makeshift altar too, a creative response to Han Aw's work constructed by another artist, the candles dripping red wax onto the concrete floors. Installed in the centre of the altar was not a figurine of the Goddess of Mercy, but a miniature of Han Aw herself, cross-legged and palms together, her long hair braided around her body.

Good god, said Jing, gripping Isaac's hand even tighter. Don't you dare leave my side tonight.

At some point, however, it was Jing who had to leave him alone, as a number of people began to discuss with her the contents of the following event: a panel about the legacy of Han Aw, moderated by Lee Weng Choy inside The Substation theatre. And as Isaac dutifully slunk away, unsure of what to do with himself, he heard a young voice say hello to him, a gallery-sitter, handing him a pamphlet whose header said:

HAN AW:
1944—PRESENT

Isaac thanked the gallery-sitter; she was just a girl, no older than a teen-ager, blushing as she said, You're welcome. Before she left, he asked if she could show him around, maybe even show him her favourite piece inside the space. The girl blushed again, and said she could do just that. She brought him to a black-and-white photograph, about the size of a large poster: Han Aw, the artist, is kneeling in the middle of a large room, much like the one they were in, writing something on the floor with a black marker.

The gallery-sitter asked Isaac if the room looked familiar to him. He quickly read the label—*A STORY* (1995), premiered at The Substation gallery. The gallery-sitter told him that the spot they were standing on was approximately where the artist was kneeling too, in the photograph; the artist had made a request that they empty the space and have a technician lay a special varnish over the floor, one that would allow her to write on it with a marker, edge to edge. Isaac asked the gallery-sitter what Han Aw was writing about, and the girl said that she was writing about her life, or rather the story of it, which then grew to describe what her mission in life was, in a way. Isaac looked at the photograph once more, and read what he could on the floor. *I am going to live,* was what the picture had managed to capture: *I am going to claim life . . . I will love, and hate, and weep . . . I will, I will, I will . . . I will reclaim everything, all of my lost lands, from the waters lapping at the edges of myself . . . I will . . .*

Legend went that Han Aw was only a metre away from the doors of the gallery when her marker had run out of ink. And that's when she got up and left, said the gallery-sitter.

She left? said Isaac. And then?

The girl smiled. She fiercely went on with the rest of her life, she said.

Later, at the panel, Isaac remained in the final row of the theatre while Lee Weng Choy, the moderator, introduced their final speaker of the day. He began by asking Jing how she felt that evening, earlier in the gallery. Lonely, was the reply Isaac still remembered: lonely, but not alone in the feeling. He then brought up her mother's memorial service, one that Han Aw had planned and even invited people to, all without Jing or her grandparents' knowledge; he asked Jing about the *RANDEN* re-enactment, the one that was still playing on loop on the corridor outside. I understand that your mother went missing while you were still in the midst of finishing the film, said Weng Choy, and Jing said yes, that's true. A friend had come, a man based in Malaysia; he came to our place, and put her in her wheelchair.

And then they were gone?

Gone.

Never to be seen again?

No, said Jing, while the audience seemed to hold their breath. The moderator asked if she still misses her, her mother, and Jing said yes, but also no. I do and I don't, she said. How does one miss a presence, if that presence had always been a hole? Jing shrugged. All I can do is cope, she said, to find new ways of dealing with the absence—words that confirmed to Isaac that she was not just the one, but the only one, for him. They would be the only ones for one another.

The stairs of the hotel creaked under their combined weight; he had yet to reach the top when the door to their room swung open, causing an unusual, bluish light to spill all over the corridor.

I thought it might be you, said Jing. Hand him to me.

He followed her back into the room, admiring the way she could still carry their son, even though Yong-he was at the age and weight that should have made the boy impossible to carry by now. As Jing put Yong-he to bed, Isaac found his attention turning to the desk again, the one by the window, his wife's laptop still open, but to an empty Word document. He was practically basking in the white-blue light of the computer when he heard the door close, and found his wife's hand on his back, urging him to take a seat.

What? he said, almost spluttering. What—what are you doing?

Jing held a finger up to her lips, before nudging her head in their sleeping son's direction. She then got him to scoot over, to make space for her to sit on the chair too. Isaac could only watch as she brought her hands over the keyboard; he felt his own mind go as blank as the document as she typed the words: MATEO SPOKE TO ME EARLIER. ABOUT KYOTO, 1996. She then hit the backspace button, the words disappearing off the screen of her laptop as she now typed, with shaking hands—

WHERE DID TORI GO?

She sat back in the chair. He could still feel his wife shaking, shivering, as their sides pressed into one another's. Isaac reached a single hand and typed, slowly:

i dunno

Jing bit her lip. ARE YOU LYING TO ME?

Isaac replied, more forcefully: no

Jing then typed out another question, with greater speed—HOW DID YOU COME TO KYOTO? And his wife had to put another shaking hand over her mouth, keeping her stare on the screen of her laptop, her eyes nonetheless betraying all of her anguish, fear, confusion. He typed now, slow again:

wrong question

Jing shook her head as she began to tear up. WHERE DID YOU COME FROM? she typed now, and Isaac was about to reply as she added: I STILL LOVE YOU, NO MATTER WHAT YOU SAY YOU ARE. Jing then turned to him, pointing her still-trembling hands at their son. We are your family, she mouthed to him; we will still love you. And Isaac found himself profoundly moved, as though she had just severed a chain within him, setting free an anchor that had weighed him down for the past eight years; he's seeing her too, back on the North-South Line, taking the train home after that night at The Substation. He's watching himself show Jing the ring in his wallet again, feeling himself hurtle through a tunnel in the earth, as Isaac begins to write out the story of who he is.

25

The Horvallan. Jing Aw. Flame of the Forest, Singapore, 2005.

Lovina, 2004

We spent one last time together in Indonesia, in Bali, in October that year. You told me that you would be there for a week, to attend a writers' conference at Ganesha University. I asked if that meant you would like me to be there, even with the knowledge that it would have to be the last time we ever saw one another.

"Of course," you said. "I wouldn't call you, otherwise."

I told you to give me the dates, so that I might see if I could take the time off from work. I then asked if I could come with you, to some of the events at the writers' conference, a request that must have surprised you. You asked if you should introduce me as your girlfriend again, and I laughed. "I'm over it," I said. "And I'm not your girlfriend, please. Just say I'm a writer."

"Oh yeah?"

"Your muse, if they insist."

You chuckled; it was an awfully cringeworthy thing for me to say. "I can do that," you said nevertheless, and I promised I would message you soon.

I found not you, but our driver, at the airport in Bali, a stern-looking uncle whose name he never gave me, even though he clearly knew mine. *Jing Aw,* he had written, on a small whiteboard that he owned; "Ching" was how he had pronounced my name—"You Ching?" The uncle then asked if I had water to drink, and maybe a snack, for the journey ahead. I asked him if there was anything I should be concerned about, and he said, "Mountain, big mountain. Gunung besar." When I merely looked at him with confusion, and perhaps a tiny bit of alarm, it seemed obvious that I would not be getting any water or snacks for our ride across Bali. The uncle then gestured me to follow him, to the minivan that he'd parked just ahead, and said nothing more to me that day.

I should have done more research, it turned out. I ought to have looked at a map and checked where our villa was, where Lovina was, in relation to the airport. Because the uncle had been right to warn me that day: I couldn't have recalled a longer, bumpier, more precarious ride on a vehicle. After emerging out of the expressway and into the main town, where most of the tourists in Bali would stay, the uncle continued onwards, until the roads got narrower and the cars less common. I would look at my watch, wondering how the minutes could stretch into an hour, and then two hours, as the pressure in my ears began to build. The buildings grew sparser, although the stray dogs and the playing children remained aplenty.

The sun set: evening was pitch black in these parts. I saw nothing but a dirt road, lit by the bright but limited swathe of our headlights, illuminating only the few metres ahead. Every time there was an oncoming car, my chest would tighten, and my heart would seize; the darkness was absolute, so absolute I swore I could feel it as a physical substance, inside and outside of me. If I opened my window, I thought, I could reach out and feel it, the darkness, grazing across my skin. I would feel it slide between my fingers, trace amounts of it catching beneath my nails.

And then we were out of the mountain. My ears felt clear again. We were back on proper roads, on clear, demarcated lanes, in a town full of cars and the people inside them. We then drove past a series of plains, before heading down the narrow paths of a neighbourhood, full of large and domineering houses. At the end of it was a magisterial gate, made out of carved wood, which opened and revealed to us the sight of a gorgeous villa and a long, illuminated pool. The uncle parked the van and held open the door. He only had three words for me, after all that time we spent together.

"Welcome to Lovina."

You did what you said you would, the following morning. At the conference you introduced me as Jing Aw, a fellow writer, born and based in Singapore. You said I was an essayist, and a journalist; you even defended me when someone asked if journalists actually existed in Singapore, a question which I paid no heed to. Later I even laughed out loud, when a fourth person asked how exactly we knew one another. "She's a very, very special friend," you said. "She's practically my muse."

We sat together in one of the lecture halls, at Ganesha University, for what the programme said was the opening keynote. But the person speaking was Australian, which automatically meant that we were bored.

"Can we go?" you asked. It had been barely twenty minutes.

"Why, yes," I said. "Spirit me away."

We made our way down towards the campus quadrangle, where tables and chairs had already been set up for the conference attendees. Caterers were busy setting up the buffet. You grabbed us a cup of instant coffee each and sat at one of the tables. You asked if I would mind listening to you instead, now that we'd bought ourselves some time.

"You know my answer," I said.

There is a blackout on board the RSS *Ubin*. It happens two days later, after Xian had been admitted to the Intensive Care Unit; it takes place three days before the station is scheduled to arrive at Mars, ready to dispatch its ships down to the Annie Cave. But the blackout only lasts for four minutes—four minutes and twenty-six seconds.

During those four minutes the Horvallan is in the Pilots' Wing, having tea with a small number of intergalactic delegates: all of them fall into a nervous silence when the darkness descends, the only thing alight was the small flame burning beneath their steamboat. Meanwhile the oncologist is in her office, telling K'weyu, the Veroniss hypochondriac, to stay calm while he is stuck within the scanner. *You are not going to die under my care,* she says to him. *The backup generator will be up and running soon.* When all of the lights in the *Ubin* blink back to life, the oncologist lets out a sigh of relief, while the Horvallan is frowning, deep in thought. He's got proof now, and many, many witnesses: something is wrong with the engine. The only matter left is deciding who should be blamed for it.

That evening, bulletin boards all over the *Ubin* report that a joint statement is to be expected, from both the Pilots' and Engineering Wings. But soon a story is passed, from one mouth to the other, about how a patient had passed away—a patient from the ICU, an Asesanian priest from the Clan of the West Mahdar, on life support when the blackout had happened; his body had struggled to breathe, six seconds into the power outage, and passed away in less than two minutes, the scales on his body fading from light purple to blue.

The Horvallan hears all this as fact from the oncologist herself, via a voice message she has sent to him. He asks her where she is, and she says she's at the clinic, of course.

I'm heading over now, his message says.

He leaves his VIP suite in the Pilots' Wing, and boards the tram. It sends him to the end of the line, and he realises that the tram is awfully, unusually empty. No one except for a few climb onboard, only to quickly disembark. The Horvallan doesn't take a seat; he stands, holding on to one of the straps, eager to alight as soon as possible. And he runs when he does, sprinting towards the clinic. He finds the oncologist behind the counter at reception.

Where are the nurses? he says.

They've left, she says.

The Horvallan asks her where.

The oncologist shakes her head. *I don't know. But look around: I've got no patients either.*

The Horvallan joins her behind the counter. He asks what she's doing on the computer, and she says she's looking up protocol, to relearn what she has to do in case another blackout happens.

The Horvallan places a hand on her back. *People are panicking,* he says. *And for good reason, I think. But we need to stay calm.*

She looks up at him. *I'm calm,* she says. *Though a little worried.* The Horvallan uses his hand to bring her closer towards him.

A little bit of worry is good. It means you'll fight, if you have to, he says.

The oncologist frowns. *Are you panicking, right now? Is that what's happening?*

He tries to smile. *Possibly,* he says. *I just need you safe.*

Our heroine puts her hand beneath the Horvallan's chin, and brings his head down for a kiss, just one. She asks if he is still doing what he can to find out what's wrong with the station. He says he is, bolstered by the look of confidence that the oncologist gives him.

That's the only thing that matters right now, she says.

Evening arrives, and the bulletin boards flash nothing: the joint statement does not arrive as promised. The Horvallan steps out of his suite the following morning, walking down the corridor. He discovers that the rest of the rooms are empty. The other VIPs, delegates and top-security personnel en route to Mars—all of them are gone.

When he arrives at the canteen, ready to partake of his breakfast, there are many people, hundreds of them, talking urgently over their food.

The VIP section, however, is empty as well.

The Horvallan packs his bags in a hurry the next day. The bulletin boards now announce that the *Ubin* will be arriving at Mars sooner than planned. When he checks the current speed of the *Ubin* he sees that the information has been blacked out.

The Horvallan decides to pay the cockpit a visit. It's the heart of command, the only place aboard the station that he has no access to, but he is going to try anyway. When he steps out of the lift though, a second blackout happens, and the darkness is total. He raises his hands, and takes a few steps forward, hoping to run into a wall, or a button, anything. He finds himself just as helpless, just as panicked, when the directional arrows come to life. He doesn't know what is going on anymore, but there is a smell, a smell that can only be identified as smoke. And then he hears it, a hissing—something is about to explode, thinks the Horvallan.

But no, he realises—he thought wrong. It's a lot more sinister than that. It's another vision instead, right there in the lobby where he stands. He knows this because his foot has come into contact with something hot, something rubbery, something out of place. His eyes adjust to the sight.

It's a relic; another relic, from an earlier century. But it's also a relic from an earlier life, his youth. It's a bike, and it is smouldering. It's in smithereens.

Pain ripples through his body—it shoots across his torso, and spikes across his old scar on the right—

The Horvallan collapses.

A party took place at our villa, somehow, on the second night of the conference. All of the writers brought their own booze; everyone was in the pool or in the living room, ordering food or getting more alcohol from the kitchen.

At one point several guests demanded that a reading take place. It was a conference of writers, after all. Some of the poets immediately offered to read, in front of all of the guests wading in the pool, standing atop one of the poolside chairs. And your name came up eventually: people wanted to hear your stories, and pulled you out of the kitchen, where we'd both been hiding. I sat on the deck chair next to yours while you gladly obliged the audience.

"This story," you said, "is set in 2989AD, at a hotel in Johor Bahru, Malaysia." You smiled. "I want you to picture a bar, populated by aliens, set at the topmost floor of the hotel. It overlooks the surrounding township of Iskandar."

I didn't know what to feel as you told them the same story you told me, so many years ago. And I had to keep one hand over my mouth, my face, while you related to them what you took years and years to tell me: how the diplomat sat herself beside the Horvallan; how the Horvallan told everyone in the room about the comet; how the diplomat later met the Horvallan in his room. Everyone appeared enraptured, delighted when you described how the two of them got on the hover-bike, and drove, all the while levitating, towards the diner named YA!MA!MO!TO!. Everyone appeared charmed by the way you relayed our characters' conversation, line by line, the same lines of dialogue you'd once relayed to me:

Tell me something.

Yes?

Tell me why—why I can't get away from this feeling.

After they are done eating, you said, the diplomat and the Horvallan step out of the diner. They order a taxi back to the hotel, driverless and automated, just like their hover-bike earlier. They get in.

The Horvallan is the first to speak. *We're complacent,* he says. *We've been nothing but lucky. We're the luckiest people in the universe.*

The diplomat scratches at a mole, just above her left cheek. She notes the Horvallan's use of the collective pronoun and says: *Quite true. We've achieved world peace, re-stabilised our climate. I'm sure that was all down to luck.*

The Horvallan pauses. *That—that's not what I'm saying. You know that.*

The diplomat delights a little, upon sight of his frustration. *I get what you mean, though,* she says. *I do. Aliens kill themselves, literally, trying to get themselves to Earth. Those of us already here can't help but think we're special.*

But we're not, says the Horvallan. *Earth is doomed. We can't afford to think like that anymore.*

The diplomat looks out of the window. Iskandar shines its multicoloured fancy across her face. Even now, in the taxi, her phone is still buzzing, notifications flashing across her screen with emails, messages, updates to important documents. It never ends.

It will take years, she says. *Centuries, even. And a fuck ton of money, more resources than anyone can imagine. More unity, more—more coordination that nobody is prepared to handle, or accept. More advancements in tech, to lift an entire civilisation. To take many of them, all of them, all off the ground, including all of our supplies and resources. And we can't do any of that without convincing the taxpayers first. It's possible I might not achieve anything in my lifetime,* she adds. She then turns to the Horvallan.

For how long more will you get to live?

I don't know.

Centuries? Ten of them? Twenty? That's two thousand years on Earth.

The Horvallan doesn't say. He simply gazes at her, from across the back-seat. *I don't know,* he says again.

She gazes back at him.

Who's the oldest Horvallan you know?

He repeats himself. *I don't know.*

Come on, she says. *What do you actually know?*

And again, he repeats himself: *I don't know.*

Her eyes are wet. She understands, now. She understands what it is she needs to accept.

I have a husband, she says. *And kids. Two girls and a boy.*

That's lovely.

A tear falls across her face. It shines yellow and green and red, as the taxi cruises across town.

We couldn't have met as kids. I thought I should just correct you on that, she says. Because I never—I never learnt how to ride a bike, actually. How did you learn to ride one yourself?

The Horvallan smiles. It's a beneficent smile, a smile of recognition.

My parents, he says. *A long time ago.*

The diplomat continues to look at him. She looks at him for a full minute, knowing what is at stake; she knows that is what they'll need, in order to ensure that the rest will come in time.

Your planet was at war, she says to him. *Even in its final moments.*

The Horvallan doesn't blink. He lets the diplomat keep on talking.

You escaped on a spaceship, she continues to say. *You had hoped to avoid the conflict that was ravaging your planet. You and your crew—all of you just wanted to survive.*

The Horvallan nods: *Yes.*

You were soon put to sleep—you and the other children, she says. *And when you awoke, you realised you are far from home, farther than anybody had initially planned. Because the crew has given itself a new mission.*

They have abandoned Horvalla, he says.

She nods. *They had no choice. The only alternative was—was Earth.*

Yes.

But your crew shrinks, she says. *Tragically so. Because the journey is too far.*

Yes.

It's far too important.

Yes.

They do what they need to ensure that one—at least one of them—will always remain, she says.

He nods back. *That's me.*

The diplomat smiles. She tells herself to take a breath; she inhales and exhales, shakily so. Everything will be okay, the diplomat says to herself, as long as they have the details.

That's right, she says. *That's you.*

"The following day," you said, "the diplomat erases all traces of what she did that night: nothing on camera, nothing on audio. She gets her aide to find the taxi they took back to the hotel and delete all footage it would have recorded of them. Her aide brings up a programme without question and executes her commands, everything expunged in less than three minutes. She then gets him to put together a list of possible outcomes, should the comet eventually strike the planet.

"Everyone re-convenes," you said. "They re-assemble at the bar, at the top of the hotel. Every representative from every race, ready with more doubts and questions for the Horvallan. But only the diplomat has something to say, to tell everyone present in the room." And then you stood on your feet, before me and everyone else at the pool that night, the same way you imagined the diplomat might stand.

"'The time has come, or rather: the time has passed. After the age of miracles, we entered the age of reason. And now we shall put that age behind. This, in fact, will be the age of faith. *This* is the age we find ourselves in now. We need it, now more than ever: in ourselves; in one another; in what all of us have stood for, and will come to stand for, in a time few of us will be privileged to see through. Those prospects will terrify anyone, anyone who cares to believe in this, and it terrifies me, even now as I speak. I cannot predict what will become of us in a thousand, two thousand, much less ten thousand years, but it is in the unknown in which we shall find hope. It is the unknown from which we shall draw our courage. And it is towards this very unknown that I shall strive, a place that all of us will need to go, again and again and again. For our future.'"

7085AD: The second blackout, the vision—the Horvallan wakes up.

Nothing has changed; the power has not restored itself. But there is a wash of red light, an orange hue, cast across his body. The door to the cockpit is wide open too, and he realises that he is looking down at Mars, directly at the colony in Annie Cave: a glittering metropolis, still in the midst of being built, encased in multiple bubble-like spheres. The Horvallan next realises that the cockpit is empty, save for two people: the oncologist's brother and sister-in-law. But the Horvallan doesn't approach them. He doesn't even want to talk to them. He knows what they are doing.

They're trying to steer the *Ubin* manually.

The Horvallan feels his mouth go dry. His heart plummets, his stomach shrinks. He finds himself admiring them for their arrogance almost. He takes a step back, stumbling over his feet, and the sound of it causes Xian's mother to look over her shoulder.

What are you doing here! she shouts.

The Horvallan stutters. *I—I just—*

Find her! she yells. *Find them both!*

Okay, says the Horvallan. *I will—*

Go! Now! she says. *Get them off the ship!*

He does what he is told—he's got no time to think otherwise. He turns and races towards the lift, only to realise that it isn't working. He looks at the directional signs, and finds his way to the emergency stairwell. His eyes adjust to the lack of lighting, and pick up the vaguest detail: the glint of broken glass; the smell of something scorched; shouts from several people, asking for help. The Horvallan races down the stairs, one step at a time, and only flinches, once, when he steps on something soft, unwilling to confirm if it is an arm or a leg.

When he finally reaches the main lobby, he runs into a wall of bodies: security personnel, defending the stairwell against a mob, demanding to be let in, demanding to be given answers. The civilians are wielding torch-lights too, criss-crossing beams of light over their aggressors' vision, but the Horvallan still manages to find an opening, ducks out of sight; he squeezes past the mob while hiding his face, desperate to leave the wing in one piece. He then dashes, as fast as he can, down the corridors towards the tram: he pushes his way past the crowd, the only one heading in the other direction. The only person.

On the last day of the conference, you and I said our farewells to the few friends we made at the event. We were standing by the main porch of Ganesha University, outside the doors to the main foyer, when you received a call from the villa. You turned towards me.

"They're saying that our driver's unavailable," you said. "He's on the other side of Bali."

"Oh," I said. "How will we go back then?"

You paused. "They're saying—the manager is suggesting she come pick us up herself."

I felt confused. I knew the manager of the villa; she stayed in the annex built beside the main gate, in charge of making sure all our needs were met. Her husband and two kids lived there as well. I asked you how she would come get us.

"By scooter," you said. "I'm going to say yes."

"Oh, you are?"

You smiled at me. "Why? You scared?"

I stuttered. I told you I had never ridden a scooter or a motorcycle, or anything like it before.

"Well, you're going to ride one soon," you said. "In fifteen minutes, actually."

The manager arrived in ten. She was followed soon by a second scooter, driven by her husband. Standing in front of each of them, with their feet on the platform and their hands on the handles, were their kids, a tall and slim girl and a shorter, fatter, younger boy. All I could do was stare at the boy, standing beside his mother's scooter, while the manager passed you a helmet.

"You with me," she said. "You, miss—with my husband."

In a mix of Bahasa and English, you told the manager I'd never ridden a scooter before. The manager laughed.

"Never?" she asked.

I had to regain use of my voice. "No."

"It's very easy," she said. "Just sit tight, can already."

"Really?" Her husband passed me a helmet, gave me a thumbs-up. "Just like that, can?"

"Yes, yes," she said. The manager then restarted her scooter, prompting you to hop on behind her. She then got her daughter to stand in front of her instead of her son, causing a look of confusion to pass over the boy's face. He was being swapped, he realised, and he didn't like it at all. Large tears trembled in his eyes when you and the manager took off.

The manager's husband restarted his own scooter. I secured my helmet and hopped on, knowing I had no choice in the matter. And I yelped when the poor and confused boy obeyed his father's commands, riding with the parent he didn't prefer. He screamed, at the top of his voice, the moment we took off; he didn't stop screaming, even when we left the university compound, joining the main traffic. He kept on crying, during which I envisioned a situation where the boy would throw an actual tantrum, the final stage in his outcry and protest, causing the three of us to be thrown off balance—we'd be flung to the side of the road, bleeding at various parts of our body, mangled by the wreckage of the scooter. It's not like I hadn't been in a vehicular accident before.

"It's okay," I kept saying, reaching past my driver's waist to massage the boy's shoulder. "Please stop," I begged. It was so pathetic I could hear fellow motorists laughing at our situation.

Eventually we caught up to the manager's scooter, at a red light at an intersection, on the left side of a major four-lane road. There were other motorists too, in front and behind us, who had clearly noticed the boy's incessant screaming. I looked at you, terrified.

"He won't stop!" I said.

You let out a laugh—one of your great fantastic laughs. The manager shook her head. She then parted a leg: her daughter stepped off the scooter, and walked towards me. They were switching places, the children, there in the middle of the road; the boy promptly slipped off my bike and quickly joined his mother.

"Look at that," I heard you say. "World peace."

I stared at the boy. The boy stared back at me. The abandonment was total, and delightful; it was brutal. And the boy broke into the most ridiculous smile, just as the light turned green.

The platform for the tram is packed with people: the Horvallan notes the look of rage, etched on all of their faces. They are running in waves down the tracks of the railway, leaping up onto the platform. The carriage itself is nowhere to be seen.

The Horvallan leaps down onto the track. The way is harsher and crueller, the beams from the occasional torchlights shining directly into his eyes. There are moments when he is granted an incredible distance, and then others when he is just bumping, constantly, into the torso of another person. And then the crowd stops, finally; there is no one else in the tunnel.

The Horvallan sticks to the side of the track; he runs until he picks up a stray torchlight, and he runs some more until he is finally confronted with the carriage of the tram itself, doors wide open. He steps inside, and flips open a panel of buttons. He tries to use the intercom. He finds no way of getting it to work again, not without power.

And then everything goes sideways: he falls forward, aware that the space station has somehow shifted course. The Horvallan slides down the floor and collides into the base of one of the carriage's poles; he holds on to it as the tram itself slides forward, all while his side continues to sting from the cold impact against the pole. The tram then becomes a bullet—it speeds, down the length of the space station, past places now empty and dark. And when the station rights itself again, the tram continues to move at full speed, slamming headfirst into the very end of the line. The Horvallan braces himself; he yells under the impact, his arms straining under the immense effort to maintain his hold, his balance. But he doesn't stop; he gets to his feet again; he switches on his torchlight and runs past the lobby of the Residential Wing, down the corridor, ignoring the view of Mars, of its many cliffs and valleys, of the beautiful rim that forms the circumference around the Annie Cave, coming into starker and starker detail the more the space station hurtles towards the colony. He ignores the sight of the Ubin's own shadow, cast across the glittering metropolis that he—that everyone— was meant to emigrate to. At the Medical Wing he takes the stairs down towards the ICU, where the light is dim but still more than enough for his eyes. And there the oncologist is, shoving into a duffle bag medical supplies from a toppled and smashed open cupboard, the floor wet and sticky with fluid.

Oh god! she says. *You're here!* She barely even has time to make eye contact with him; instead she abandons the cupboard, and zips up her bag; she grabs hold of one of his wrists and dashes towards the end of the corridor, where there is another stairwell, leading to another storey below.

You're going to escape, she says, as they race down the stairs. *With Xian.*

How? says the Horvallan.

Ambulatory hangar, she says. *There are only two shuttle pods left.*

The oncologist brings him to one of them, where the Horvallan can spot Xian, eyes closed, her body caked with jelly and laid across a stretcher. She lifts the door to the pilot's seat and throws the bag in, before shoving the Horvallan in as well. His eyes widen when the oncologist pulls the seat belt over his body; she reactivates the dashboard, and plants his palm on the scanner. She's registering him as its pilot.

What are you doing?

Head back to Earth, she says. *I've already set the route and destination.*

But what—?

Don't bother going to the other Martian colonies, says the oncologist, as she sets the other controls. *Xian needs to be on Earth, she needs the air, the sun, the gravity—she needs this, you understand? She deserves to have a proper life.*

The dashboard in front of the Horvallan lights up with new commands. His seat belt then tightens into a final click; he jams the button multiple times, but it won't unlock. Not without her authority. When he looks at the dashboard again, he sees a pre-planned route indeed, plotting a path back to a coordinate on Earth: Singapore. He looks away and glares at the oncologist, already climbing out of the shuttle.

You take care of her! he shouts. *She's your fucking blood. Don't you dare leave her!*

The oncologist only looks back at him, staring right at him, through the window of the closing door.

It's doomed, she says. *The Martian enterprise.* She pauses. *And they are my blood too.*

The door closes. The Horvallan doesn't know how to tell her that it's impossible. The station's gone, which means her brother and sister-in-law will also be gone. She just doesn't know it, the Horvallan wants to say, but his voice can't seem to start; he can't find a way to tell her. He's stuck in the damn thing, and can only watch as the oncologist runs over and pulls on a giant lever on a wall: the doors to the airlock rise from the ceiling and the floor, like two sets of teeth, ready to gnash. And this is when he realises it, that it's the end of them, of her, forced to end when it had barely begun, now when he can barely see the oncologist's face, through a small plate of glass on either door of the airlock. He doesn't even want to look at Xian, lying somewhere prostrate behind him, as he slams his own hands on his chest, pulling on his seat belt, the tears falling hot and fast over his face. An animal-like noise, a desperate groan, leaves his throat as he shakes his head. He can barely form the word *no.*

And then he hears her voice, for what he thought would be the last time. It crackles to life through the intercom.

Don't cry like that, she says. *You're the hero of the world, you know? You brought us all this far.*

All he can do is close his eyes. *No,* he manages to say, finally. Through the intercom, somewhere in the background, he hears a second voice: *Airlock sequence complete in 8, 7, 6 . . .*

He forces himself to open his eyes. He can still barely make out her face on the other side of the hangar. Our heroine now has a hand on the glass, while the other is placed over the microphone.

We'll be right behind you, she says. *All of us. I'll see you soon.*

A light on his dashboard flashes a second, imminent countdown; he keeps saying no, no, no. *Please, no.*

The pod ejects out of the RSS *Ubin.*

The sight of her face reduces to a single point.

———

It was sundown when we left the villa. We loaded our bags onto the minivan; the driver, the same uncle again, nodded at us when we settled down into our seats. "Airport?" he said. "Airport," you said. When we left, we waved goodbye to the manager and her family, standing by the gate. Her son hid behind her legs, eager perhaps for us to leave; I kept on waving anyway, until we settled into a silence, a mutual silence, one that held us both hostage in the minivan. You then said it was getting dark, as soon as we got back on the mountain again.

I got you to tell me the final chapter of your story, knowing that this would be our last time together. Without turning to me, you said it was 68525AD: "The waters subside, and they row back home. The spectre can only watch as the Horvallan prepares his final brew.

"She asks him if he is sure. He tells her that he is, unfortunately. But you will die this way, she says to him, feeling the need to state the obvious. You won't ever be the same again, the spectre says, and the Horvallan will tell her that that truly means the world to him."

Our minivan shook over a bump in the road. "Eventually the comet arrives," you said: "It will take up the whole sky, now ablaze into a brilliant silver. Havoc begins to wreak, as the tides now rise to extraordinary levels. The spectre can practically smell the sea, the moment she opens the windows.

"The Horvallan will take his brew, and go into a deep sleep; he will see his entire life, his whole and immense life, flash before his eyes. And oh," you said to me: "what a life. The Horvallan will see the spectre of the oncologist, standing by his side; he will see Xian breathe again, and live till her final days, come at the age of forty-three.

"He will see other images too, such as the *Ubin* again, flames erupting over flame-coloured soil.

"He will see the diplomat again, and her single tear, at the back of a driverless taxi.

"Towards the end of his visions, he'll wonder: maybe it's there too, his family, the sight of them next. The sight of all of them, everyone, as young people again, coursing down a path on their bicycles."

I felt a stab in my knee as the minivan shook and rattled, over the coarse road that cut through the forest. "What's wrong?" you asked, noticing the way my leg had flinched.

"It's an old injury," I said.

"From the accident?" you asked.

"Yes," I said. "The accident." I found myself back in the car again, recalling the yell that came out of Isaac's mouth. "It was my fault, I think, why our two cars had crashed that day."

The minivan shook again. Outside the windows, nothing but dark. Nothing but the glare of the headlights, shining from the front. I felt compelled to keep on speaking, as I began to stare at the silhouette of the old driver's face.

"We were arguing," I said, "inside the car. Some brand wanted Isaac and another actress to endorse them for another year. I told him I didn't like that at all."

"Was it good money?" you asked. I said it was. "So what was the problem?" you asked me next, a retort that made me smirk. I said those were Isaac's same words to me, as we drove our way back home; he said he didn't know what I could be upset about.

"And so I told him that I had been upset the whole year," I said. "I told him I couldn't stand it, that my pride couldn't stand it; I told him that if he wanted to be a good man, and a good father to Yong-he, he would stop being involved with the actress altogether. Isaac then told me that it was an unreasonable demand; he said that these situations were often out of his control." I suppose we had been so distracted by our fight, so insistent on deciding who was right or wrong, that we hadn't paid enough attention to the road: he crossed a traffic light, and neglected to look out for the other cars at the junction. I told you that I could have done those things for him instead, but I had also been distracted by something else.

You asked me what that matter was, in the darkness of the minivan. I told you I was struggling, in that moment, with whether I should tell Isaac what I had done that same day.

You asked me what that might be. "I was at the office," I said, "wrapping up some work." When I was done I had walked over to a former colleague of mine, now working for the Chinese papers, covering the arts and entertainment beat.

You asked me what it was that I did.

"I planted a story," I said. "I told my ex-colleague that I had some rumours to share, rumours that I had heard by virtue of being the actor's wife. I said this actress was difficult, and hard to work with on set; I said she was jealous of me too, of my early marriage to Isaac." I told you as well about the photo I suggested to my former colleague, a photo that would mark both the start and the end of the actress's career.

"And that's how he wrote the story."

I nodded. "He said it could work."

"And was it published?" you asked.

I nodded again. "The very next day."

You asked me if I was that afraid of the actress. I said I was, in fact. She was an old flame of his, in the life they had lived before they became famous. "Before I came along," I said.

You then asked if I got to tell Isaac about this in the end, and I shook my head.

"The indecision lasted for a second or two, at best," I said. "And then our cars had crashed."

The minivan shook another time. I had to clasp a hand round my knee. You paused, for a bit, before you said you needed to tell me something.

"I know what you're thinking, Jing. About the story I've told you. But it's . . . it's not that, I'm afraid. It's not what I've led you to believe."

I did my best to remain calm. I asked you what you meant.

"I'm not the Horvallan," you said.

I said I knew.

"You do?"

I nodded. "It's Isaac."

You shook your head. "I'm sorry," you said. "Good guess. I can see why you'd think that, but no." You then looked away from me. "And you're not— you're not our heroine either."

The darkness felt truly solid at that point. "No?" I asked, as the minivan shuddered.

You stared at me. "It's not about either of us," you said.

I felt the urge to speak, back then. But the minivan had come to a sudden stop, you and me thrown forward in our respective seats: we had hit something, apparently, up in the mountain.

I felt cold all over, as our uncle began to yell. I glanced through the windows, and figured that we had emerged from the forest, and had begun driving through one of the villages in the mountainside.

You quickly opened the door, and stepped out. I followed you, went after you, towards the front of the minivan. It was the body of a stray dog, trapped beneath a wheel, still breathing and still whining, so clearly in pain while children began to scream at the van.

"We need to get help," I heard you say. But when I looked up to see you, standing on the other side of the vehicle, I became blinded instead by the beams from the headlights. I had to squint as I rose to my feet, swayed by the spots and flares still floating about in my vision. "We need to get help," I heard you say again, "from somewhere in the village." And I could barely watch as you ran away, further into darkness, into a place I could not see. You were gone.

26

Isaac found himself thinking back to his own wedding, in 1997, as he and his family found their table at Mateo and Daniel's convite. He and Jing had got married in November that year, on the 16th, when the weather was balmy to the point where they knew, come evening, that the sunset would be particularly glorious. After the tea ceremony that afternoon, offered to Jing's side of the family, they hosted a simple solemnisation in the garden under the tabebuia tree, whose white flowers took on an otherworldly lustre under a stunning pink sky.

He had vowed to love his wife, and cherish his wife, for the rest of his strange, new life, words that had more or less come from a script but he remembered meaning nonetheless. He found himself reaffirming those words, to both his wife and child this time, as Mateo and Daniel and their respective parents took their seats by the head table in the courtyard. And as Mateo pressed on a pocket square and gave a warm smile to everyone present, he recalled the way Mateo had given him and Jing a toast, during the small, catered dinner they had provided together seven years ago, with chairs strewn all over the living room and the garden. We welcomed you, he'd said to Isaac; we folded you into our love. Isaac knew, from the moment he had picked Mateo up from the airport that afternoon, that he had no intention of staying in Singapore any longer than he had to; he knew there would always be a difficulty in their relationship in the years to come, something he would have to endure, and maybe even overcome, like all the other things he had to overcome so that he could arrive at this moment. Later that evening, just before Mateo had to take a taxi back to Changi Airport, Isaac would hear Mateo tell him and his wife the good news. He was inspired by them, by him and Jing, and their wonderful ability to move on in life, said Mateo: he had decided that he would move on from Daniel too, his ex-boyfriend, and that he was finally, finally going to start a new life altogether. But do you still have feelings for him? Jing had asked Mateo, and Mateo responded, Ugh—who cares, Jing? It doesn't matter. Love alone is nothing without a will.

The reception eventually began: Isaac found the dusk to be settling grandly over the villa too, as Mateo's father, Señor Calvo, gave a short toast to everyone seated in the courtyard, the living room, and farther out on the driveway. Salud! he said, at the end of his speech—Salud! His laughter soared over all the guests, just as they raised their glasses, the very air seeming to sparkle as a round of mass tinkling commenced. Isaac then watched as the grooms rose to their feet to embrace Señor Calvo. More laughter then burst forth from Daniel's parents, after Señora Vilar downed her glass in a single, surprising take; Doctor Rovira and Juan clapped while their faces turned bright red.

And then Daniel was the next man to stand. He had his hand on his tie, a nervous gesture, as he asked for everybody's attention. He said yes, he was aware, nobody usually makes speeches at the convite. But he told everyone that he had something to say anyway, as Mateo bowed his head, and closed his eyes.

I have been thinking a lot about alignments. Las alineaciones, he said. I've been thinking about what it takes to have a coincidence become something more like providence, because we were not supposed to get married like this. In many ways, Mateo and I were not supposed to get married at all. No one would love me, I thought, either because of the leg or because . . . because I didn't love myself. So I want to thank you, Mateo, for agreeing to be my husband. Thank you for being here. Thank you for being alive, for my sake. You were the first person I ever fell in love with, and I hope you will be my last. I can't imagine loving anyone else.

Mateo nodded, with his hand over his own heart. Daniel then turned back, smiling, to the rest of the guests.

I think you have to live a life openly, and willingly, he said. You have to live a life that allows for a kind of possibility, a miraculous one, to occur between you and another person. When I think back to the time Mateo and I first met, I cannot help but wonder, surely: surely there must be another world out there, with another me who never said hello to Mateo. Who chose to be in another room, or another museum, instead of the one I met Mateo in . . . He paused. When I think back to that Daniel, that Daniel of 1995, I think: wow. Wow. You have no idea, aha. You have no idea how happy you're going to be, and how sad. How heartbroken. And yet so loved, so cherished. And so, so, so lucky, he said.

He then gave a quick laugh, right after a light cough; Mateo had taken Daniel's pocket square and pressed it into his face. Daniel continued to smile as he wiped his face.

Being loved by someone is so special, he said. It sounds so silly and so corny, but it is true. Because being loved is one thing, but being brought together, being allowed to encounter one another—*that* is the wonder to me. It makes me feel like I can do anything, anything at all. So I just want to say, to everyone hearing this now, that my heart—my heart is filled with thankfulness. Thank you, all of you. Thank you, everyone, for being here, for coming all this way. Thank you for being a part of my life, and for staying in it too. I give special thanks to my mother, and my father, and to Juan; I give thanks to everyone, even the ones who are not here, and even the ones who have hurt us, who broke our hearts . . . I give thanks to God too, for being so kind to us. To all of us. I'm so happy we're safe, for now, and I've never been happier in my life. Thank you, truly. Aha.

Mummy is crying, he heard his boy say to him. Isaac turned, to look over his shoulder, and saw that it was true.

Damn, said Jing. You caught me.

Isaac could feel his very heart reach for her, as he placed his hand on his wife's cheek. It was a gesture that seemed to surprise her for a second, before she gave in to it anyway, smiling as he wiped a tear from an eye. She asked Isaac which drama he had learnt that move from, and he told her it was a film, not a television series, a fact she should have known. Jing rolled her eyes and dried her face with a napkin.

God, she said. My eyes physically hurt. I've been crying so much lately.

Another memory came to Isaac in that moment: he saw Tori again, on the ground, a street away from Kyoto Station. I'm sure Tori would have loved to be here, he said.

His wife nodded. She put her napkin aside. Do you remember the diner? she said. The place that served okonomiyaki?

Yes, he said.

Jing told him about the coins Tori had left behind, at her corner of the table. Exact change, Jing said, for everything she had ordered: 627 yen. Tori knew what she was going to do when she brought us to that diner.

Isaac nodded. Yeah, he said. That's right.

Jing's eyes teared up again. You had quite a friendship with her though, didn't you?

He nodded again; he thought back to Tori and her passport photo, the one she had to take for her time abroad in London. I only knew her for a month, said Isaac, causing Jing to shake her head.

Don't do that, she said. Don't discount what you had with Tori. Jing then paused again, while the guests began to collect their food from the kitchen. Can I ask you something? she said.

Ask me what? said Isaac.

Jing paused. Where did you keep it? she asked. Her suitcase?

Isaac could feel his fingernails dig into his palm, hand clenched yet again under the table; he had to ignore his son blindly repeating the word "suitcase". What do you mean?

Tori's suitcase, Jing said, while resting a hand on Yong-he's back. You held onto it, for eight years, so—where did you keep it? she asked. Jing frowned and tilted her head to the side, practically speaking to herself as she added: It had to be in the house; it had to be in a place no one ever checked.

And then her eyes grew bigger. For a moment she didn't say anything, while the convite continued around them. People ate, and talked, and passed dishes to one another. She placed her hand on their son's head, and ran her fingers through the boy's hair. You know what? Don't tell me, she said. It doesn't matter anymore, Jing insisted, in a tone of voice that reminded Isaac of Mateo at their wedding again, telling the couple his grand theory about love.

Later everyone began to clear the courtyard, to make way for music, for dancing. The guitar players, strumming through the reception, laid their instruments down while Señor Calvo plugged an iPod into the speakers.

Jing told Isaac that she would take Yong-he back to the hotel, to get him showered and ready for his nap.

I'm about to finish a piece, anyway, she said. Don't stay out too late.

Isaac nodded. I won't, he said, his hand now hurting, swollen, as he gathered up their plates.

He didn't dance that night. Instead he waited, for an hour, while he watched people drink, and cheer, and clap their hands to the music. Mateo and Daniel spun on the spot, virtually in a world of their own making.

The air smelt of wine and smoke. It smelt also of perfume and sweat. And he began to smell the salt and the sea when he left the villa behind, and finally made his way back towards the hotel.

The room was quiet when he opened the door.

He saw his son, asleep on their bed, face turned away from his. His wife sat beside him, seated on the bed too, one hand stroking the top of his back.

She angled her face towards him, a face strewn with fresh tears. He then saw one of his bags, open on one of the chairs; he saw the thick stack of paper, placed directly over her lap: photocopies of her notebooks, her scattered jottings, a rough but thorough account of her affair.

No, was what he wanted to say: it doesn't matter, anymore. It's just a story, was what he said instead.

She smiled. She then closed her eyes, as though she couldn't bear to look at him, to not even see his face in their final moment together.

But it's mine, she said.

Isaac took a step forward. He hadn't even closed the door. We're both, he started saying. (Both what? he asked himself.) We're both—

No, said Jing. Not anymore. She paused. You're a good guy, Isaac.

He shook his head. He believed it when he told her: I'm not. I'm not.

But you are, she said. You are good. You've always been good. She then took the bundle of papers, and held it up. She held it out to him, as though they were actually his, not hers.

A good person would walk away, she said. They are the ones who get to go.

Isaac shook his head again. It was the last thing he wanted to do.

I love you, he said, as he watched her face crumple.

Just go.

Isaac dragged his suitcase out of the bus terminal. He only had a few hours in Seville.

He recalled just the one thing, the Plaza de España, that Ana had suggested to him to see in the city. Isaac found a map, the moment he got off the bus from Isla Cristina; he plotted a simple route, walking down a network of connected roads. He headed south on Calle Torneo, towards Puente del Cristo de la Expiración el Cachorro; he continued on to Calle Arjona, and then Paseo de Cristóbal Colón and Paseo de las Delicias. Isaac then turned left onto Calle la Rábida, and then right onto Avenue de Chile, and then left again onto Avenue de Mariá Luisa, on the very edge of a large park. He then made another right, onto Avenue Conde de Urbina, which cut through the park into its very heart, where the Plaza finally, rightfully lay.

Isaac had dragged his suitcase behind him, from the terminal to Plaza de España, the suitcase's poor wheels rattling over the many cobbled streets. For a few hours he was just a man—the one with a loud suitcase—the loudest, surely, in all of Seville: a city he now had the heart to see.

Isaac dragged his things with him, to the centre of the Plaza. Nobody knew who he was; nobody cared about how he got there. The building was larger, and grander, and most unlike anything he'd ever seen in his life.

Here he was no one, he thought; he had no one, he thought next.

It took his breath away.

PART III

PARADISE

Iskandar, 2015

Perhaps in a concluding dream, I may
cross the brink of myself, no longer
lover, son or brother, and enter
a vast field of nothingness.

—Cyril Wong, *Oneiros*

27

Isaac first has to take a call, before tonight's performance can begin.

He stands in the corridor, and avoids eye contact with the arriving guests. He presses his phone against his ear, aware of how he must look; he nods, and he nods, and he nods, all the while listening to what his caller has to say. Okay, he finally says, his first word in. Thank you, he goes on to add; that would be nice.

The actor looks almost disinterested in the conversation. It wouldn't be a stretch to assume that he is merely waiting for the call to end. But eaves-droppers would detect a note of affection in his voice as he says, once again: Thank you. That's all I ask for . . . That's all I needed to hear. And finally, before he hangs up:

I love you guys too.

He sits on a chair, in the middle of the gallery at The Substation. There is hardly anything in the room aside from him and his chair, and a few other props, discreetly set aside. And there are his guests for the evening, of course: most of them stand, while some them sit, directly on the floor.

Tonight will be the ninety-ninth and final iteration of the performance. People have asked him what he will do after tonight, including the journalist who just spoke to him earlier, although Isaac has always maintained the same refrain: he has no idea. He will like to do nothing, actually.

What's the point of retiring if there are still things left to do? He is already doing all he can to focus on the now.

The performance is a dramatic re-enactment of *Cinema Paradiso*, 170 minutes long. Some nights the performance ends early, within 140 to 150 minutes; on one unique occasion it went on for nearly three hours, exhausting everyone in the room.

Isaac is the sole performer of this re-enactment, and also its director and dramaturg, sole stage and set manager. He is its sole lights and sound designer as well, with perhaps some assistance from the Substation intern. He has reduced the entirety of Giuseppe Tornatore's 1988 film into a dramatic monologue, employing different voices for different parts, as well as samples from the original film. He uses an old Walkman to provide music whenever necessary—one that he can still use perfectly well.

In the final act of the monologue he doesn't use a film reel, as one might expect, but a series of photographic slides instead: every night the images are used, and never to be used again, depicting shots of Singapore taken from the sixties to the nineties. These images have buildings and landscapes, faces and bodies; some of the faces belong to the everyday, some to the famous and well known, while others are exiled, nameless and forgotten, a diaspora of runaways from Singapore.

Isaac stands with his back before the projector, so that with every image that is flashed, onto the farthest wall of the gallery, there is an Isaac-shaped hole on every one of them, every projection, every image. He stands until the slides ends, plunging the gallery into a final darkness.

That is how every performance ends; that is when his guests leave.

Isaac never turns back to face them again, not even to say goodbye.

*　　*　　*

The first iteration of *PARADISE* took place on the 2nd of May, 2015.

Ninety-eight nights later, the date is the 8th of August, 2015, the time, 8pm: a manager from the Substation closes the glass doors of the gallery, and flashes a series of signs to the guests. Isaac then smiles, as though activated to life.

He looks at the guests in the gallery: his audience for the final evening. There are a handful of faces that he recognises in an instant, and some that only look vaguely familiar. But there is one face in the crowd that takes hold of him. It resonates, this face. It's a face that has returned to him, a face that hasn't aged a day—one that has caused his heart to skip.

The actor doesn't let this feeling pass. Instead he holds on to it; he presses his fingers deep into it. But however tight his clutch might be, the feeling doesn't burst. It never relents. He can do anything, with this feeling.

And so he begins.

28

Four months ago.

Daniel has to be prodded awake; his taxi driver has to reach towards his knee, and shake it, so that he might finally wake up. And he wakes with a start, blinking and sputtering, as though he had gone for too long a dive, and has just come up for air. He doesn't even know if the driver has realised his faux pas, taking a hold of his knee like that.

Hah, he says—I am here?

The taxi is presently stopped in front of a barrier gate; the uniformed men at the guardhouse are already looking at them, frowning, curious as to who they might be.

Bestari Heights, announces his driver. And the fee, from the checkpoint to Iskandar, is seventy-five Malaysian ringgit.

Daniel takes out his wallet. He counts the cash. Gràcies, he says, before he corrects himself: Terima kasih. Thank you.

All Daniel has is his duffel bag. He reaches inside and takes out his diary, which contains his notes, his schedule, his photos of Mateo; it also has a roughly drawn map of the estate and a set of directions, both of which he is using right now.

The road from the guardhouse stretches straight for a while, before branching off into multiple directions. Already, he has the sense that the place could be better laid out, and can't help but wonder what restrictions the developers had to contend with. There is a small field of grass to his left, which his map says to cut across; and while he walks he keeps note of the many unit numbers, plastered to the front of every home.

Daniel feels perturbed: half of the houses appear to be occupied, while the other half seem empty, barely furnished. But, more importantly—it's exactly how Jing described it in her book, a place with a barren spirit, though perhaps not so new anymore. He presses the doorbell once he reaches his destination, and sees the front door swing open. A face appears from across the driveway, and says:

Hey, Daniel.

He doesn't wave back. Hello, Jing, he replies. He takes several steps back when the gate swings open, its hinges squeaking as it moves, Daniel merely waiting for the gap to widen.

The woman looks good, Daniel thinks; she also looks like an exposed wire of a human being. There is a gauntness to her features, but an alertness too, her skin tightly stretched over her bone structure in a way that revealed not a frailty but a strength, one that she must have carried within her frame. He asks her how she's been anyway, and she tells him that she's okay. She's managing.

Managing? he says, a little amused. Like, you are on top of things, you mean?

Jing shrugs. I don't know about that, she says, though the days are liveable, yes. She asks him how he is doing as well, and Daniel decides to stick to the facts.

I left Isaac this morning, he says. I'm sure he told you.

Jing nods. He told me, she says, even though she must know that he didn't quite answer her question either. He then allows himself a smile, as he thinks about the few days he has spent with Isaac.

He seems fine, Daniel says. He looked quite cool, actually. He tells her about the rehearsal he observed the day before, for Isaac's upcoming show at The Substation: it was just the two of them, in the living room of the actor's penthouse suite, Daniel watching Isaac perform before a camera mounted on a tripod, using the same props he would use in a month's time.

I've never seen him act before, says Daniel. Not once throughout our friendship.

Daniel watches Jing nod again. He's sure she knows about their connection too, the one that has gone on without her and Mateo. He then notices the new look in her eyes, a look he has learnt to recognise by now, in the people he has already met all over the world; he waits for her to say it, to say she is sorry, for the loss in his life he's still learning to endure. But there's something else to her gaze too, and both of them know exactly why. Jing asks if Isaac had said anything helpful, anything illuminating about Mateo, and Daniel finds himself savouring it, the sound of his husband's name: it's as clear as a bell in the living room of her house, a sound with a near-physical quality and a thin, metallic edge. It's christening the moment, the time he and Jing are spending together right now. No, he tells her. Not really. Isaac told me to come find you, though.

A small smile creeps over the woman's face. Would you have come anyway, if he didn't tell you to do that? she asks, and Daniel finds his voice reduced to a bare whisper as he says: Oh, of course. Of course I would. You've always had a special place in his life, Jing.

Daniel casts his eyes around: there's barely anything inside the house, in the living room or in the kitchen. He looks up the main staircase.

Can I see him? asks Daniel. He is here, no?

He is, she says. He might be resting.

They walk up the stairs. The upper floor is just as bare as the one below, with a common area and three closed doors. Jing opens the one in the middle, the one nearest to the staircase, and hears her say: Hey, boy. Hey, babe. Uncle Danny's here.

There is a pause. Daniel lingers in the corridor, leaning against the nearest wall. His eyes are closed now.

Can you remember him? Uncle Matey's husband? he hears Jing say. He's here now, right outside . . . I'll go get him, all right?

Daniel quickly wipes his face. He makes sure to smile at least, when Jing reopens the door.

The boy is a pale mess. That's the conclusion he will arrive at, after a few minutes of staring. He's barely seventeen, Daniel thinks, as he says: Your parents told me about the accident; I remember your father telling me when it happened. He asks, half-heartedly, how Yong-he is feeling today.

The boy stares at him, without judgement. Yong-he has thick and furry brows, the same as his father's, and the same jaw as well. But the rest of him, his eyes and his lips, even the shape of his ears, and the texture of his hair—all Jing, he believes. It occurs to Daniel that the older this boy gets, the clearer this distinction will become.

I can walk, by the way. I can show you, the boy says.

Daniel balks at the sudden offer, but he is startled too by the boy's baritone, deep and rich. He and Yong-he turn to Jing, seated at the corner of the bed, wanting to know what she thinks of the idea.

Show him, she says. Show Uncle Danny.

The boy grits his teeth, as though eager, finally, to rise to the challenge. He lifts the blanket away, and slowly shifts his weight to the edge of the mattress. Daniel can't help but stare at Yong-he's legs, still covered in gauze and bandages; he can also see more of them around the right side of his torso, through the loose holes of his baggy singlet. Help me stand? says the boy, and Daniel quickly offers him his hands; the boy takes them, his weight a staggering, tottering, pivoting thing. But he is still strong, somehow, as he puts an arm against the wall, allowing him to prop his weight against a support that isn't Daniel's.

Watch, he says. The boy takes a step forward, followed by another; he takes a third, and a fourth, his breathing only slightly heavier. Still, a look of awe and horror sweeps over Daniel's face; it's all too much to bear, all too much to hide from the child. And yet Yong-he has the strength and the sensitivity to give Daniel a smile.

Hey, he says. This is good, you know.

Daniel nods, in spite of himself; he feels chided, even admonished, though he is sure that that was not the boy's intention. Daniel lifts the cuff of his trousers, revealing to him the ankle of his prosthetic.

It took me a whole month, he says. To stand on both feet. Daniel then watches, his hands ever ready to catch the boy, as Yong-he brings himself back to the mattress. He says that Jing told him, about what had happened to Daniel's leg.

Can I ask you something?

Daniel nods. Anything, he says.

The boy pauses. What does a bomb feel like? he asks, and Daniel can't help but feel taken aback by the question. But it's just a flash, he's soon to realise: the flash of a memory that's nearly three decades old by now. Daniel tells him it's like solid air.

Solid . . . ?

He nods again. My mother called it a hand of God.

Yong-he's eyes naturally drift towards his own hands, blotched with colour, but scab-free. Daniel asks if he remembers anything of the accident at all, the one that injured him like this. Yong-he now glances at his mother, as he says he does not. He's trying to, he says. And Daniel reaches out a hand, and places it on the boy's knee, as he tells him not to try too hard, causing a look of relief to cross over the boy's face. But Daniel nevertheless sees something more like guilt, as Yong-he begins to avert his gaze.

I still can't recall who he is, the boy says. But I'm sorry about what happened to Uncle Matey.

And that's it, Daniel thinks. This is all it takes. The horror and awe he felt earlier now mix into a quiver, as he remembers how much Mateo had loved him, and how much the boy, as a child, had loved him back. Daniel's eyes blink, rapidly, as the tears threaten to flow again; he finds himself standing up, all of a sudden, saying that he appreciates it. It's okay, he says. I'm okay, aha. I hope you are too, boy.

Jing later shows him to his bedroom: the third room in the house, the spare.

I've made the bed and got you a pillow, some sheets. It should be enough for the night, she says.

Daniel thanks her. He then asks her about Yong-he. His accident was in January, yes?

That's right.

So he's recovering, he says. He's recovering fast.

Jing nods. It's only been three months, she says. But things are looking good.

Daniel sits on the bed. But his memory?

No.

Still?

Jing merely smiles at the question; it nearly looks like a smirk, in exactly the way Daniel remembers it. I talk to him, she says. I tell him things, stories, anecdotes. Anything to help make him recall, to prompt something in his mind. But sometimes he looks at me like—like he knows, you know?

Know what?

She pauses. That I once did it for a living, she says. Tell stories.

Daniel wipes his eyes, his nose; he was tempted to bring his copy of the book with him, but thought against it in the end. At least you still have him, Jing. That is a blessing, he says. You must realise this, Jing.

She pauses again, her eyes fixed on his. He doesn't know what's going through her mind, till she says: I keep going over the details.

Of course, says Daniel. I'm sure.

She blinks. Oh, no, says Jing. You misunderstand . . . I meant, about Mateo. Sorry. I just keep going over what you told me, and I, I almost can't—I don't think I've accepted it, yet.

Daniel wipes his eyes once again. Aha, he says. Right. He doesn't know if he's fully accepted it, either. He had obtained Jing's new handphone number, her Malaysian one, from Isaac around two weeks prior to this visit; he then sent her several messages via WhatsApp about how Mateo had gone missing, messages about how he had got a call one morning, from a foreign-looking number, which turned out to be the Spanish Embassy in Seoul. It was like he had disappeared, they'd said, on board one of the ferries that serviced the Fukuoka-Busan route; the ferry had docked at the terminal, and the crew were clearing the vessel for the trip back to Japan when they found all of his bags, but not his body.

The news had stunned him. Air as hard as concrete; air like the back of God's hand, knuckle to the face. The authorities had done their own investigations and found them inconclusive, unable to verify with certainty if Mateo had even jumped. It truly was as if the man had just disappeared, they said.

Do you know what his last words to me were? says Daniel. Jing shakes her head. He says that Mateo had called him, about four days before he went on the ferry.

From Seoul?

He nods. Mateo was doing business, with some of the galleries there, says Daniel. He then called me, out of the blue, and told me to go to a bookstore, any bookstore in Barcelona . . . He told me to check the internet too, Amazon or eBay or any of the larger sites. He wanted me to find a book by a Korean poet.

Jing takes her phone out, and sits next to him. She asks if he has the poet's name.

Ki Hyongdo, says Daniel. He then spells it out for her, as Jing attempts to key it into the search bar of her mobile browser. He watches the results pop up on Jing's screen, even though he already knows there aren't that many of them. You know him? he asks, as Jing continues to scroll through her browser, and he can't help but feel crestfallen when Jing says no. He can't help but feel crushed again.

Mateo got introduced to this woman who once worked at a cinema, he says. The Pagoda Theatre, in Seoul. The place has many stories, apparently. But the most famous one involves the poet.

Jing looks up from the screen of her phone. She asks him what happened, to this poet from Seoul.

He died there, says Daniel. In 1989. He was twenty-eight at the time.

Jing grows quiet. She looks at her phone again, before putting it down. She asks Daniel how the poet had passed away, and Daniel says to her: That's the thing. No one really knows. They just found him in the cinema, dead. He probably had a stroke, or a heart attack.

Jing frowned. Mateo told you all this?

He shakes his head. Not the whole story. Hah. But I pieced it together, with a few calls.

Jing falls silent once more, with an increasingly pained look on her face. And then you didn't hear from Mateo . . . ?

Not for a few days, he says.

And then you got the call.

He nods. He then reaches into his bag, and takes out his diary; he shows her Mateo's old statements, the last of his financial transactions, made in Seoul and then in Tokyo. He tells Jing about how he had pieced it together, his journey to Kyoto, where he stayed at the Mitsui Garden Hotel in Shinmachi. Mateo then went to a pachinko parlour, on his last night in Japan: a place called King, Daniel says, though I have no idea why. Mateo was never the type to gamble.

The next morning was when he took a bullet train to Fukuoka, where he got on that ferry to South Korea. I know what he did, says Daniel, but I have no idea why, aha. I tried—I even tried to use a map of Kyoto, to trace his movements, to see if some sort of pattern would emerge . . . But I only got more confused, the hotel and the parlour being so far away from one another. Like I said, I don't know. I still have no idea, Jing, he says, shutting the diary, unable to show her his notes any longer.

Daniel closes his eyes, in another attempt to stem the weeping.

In your book, he says—people can come back. People can come back, after they're gone.

Jing nods. She nods as she places a hand on Daniel's back.

But your mother never came back, did she, he says, and Jing's shaking her head this time, as she tells him no.

Daniel stares at the ceiling. He doesn't sleep. It's always at the point of sleeping when he finds his mind drifting back to Mateo, always to Mateo, for his warmth, his strong aroma, even the sound of his teeth grinding. Daniel's body tosses and turns with the thought of what Mateo could do to him too, restless with want, for the wet of Mateo's tongue, the strong flick of it over his sphincter. He pines and starts to sweat, under the limp ministrations of his ceiling fan, and he tears his blanket off, overcome first by lust and then the longing, his utter longing for a home that no longer exists.

Daniel fumbles for his prosthesis, and attaches it in the dark. He steps out of his bedroom, wanting water from the kitchen downstairs. It's how he notices the door to Jing's bedroom, wide open.

He steps inside: empty bed. He then checks her toilet: no Jing either.

The room has a balcony that faces the street outside. It doesn't even have any curtains. Daniel is halfway towards the balcony when he hears it, a sharp, metallic creak.

The front gate swings open. He feels confused as he stares at Jing's escaping figure—but it's her, most definitely.

He heads down the stairs, reminding himself to be slow, and careful—he is in his mid-fifties, after all. And when he walks past the open gate, and sees her down the road, she's wearing nothing but her nightclothes and a pair of slippers. He can't help it, Daniel: he calls out her name.

Jing, he says. *Jing!*

She stops. Her arms fall to her side. He walks towards her, asks her what she is doing. She turns around, taking in deep breaths, her frame practically skeletal under the amber of the streetlight.

Still awake? she says, keeping her tone casual.

You and me both, he says. He then asks her again, what she's doing outside, when he finally catches up to her.

It's just something I do. Once in a while, Jing replies.

Daniel stares at her, still confused. What *are* you doing?

Jing's gaze doesn't waver. You read my book, she says. Didn't you?

He did, is what he wants to say. He knew exactly why she came here, from the moment he received her address from Isaac. And he wants to tell her about how he is being taken back by more than a decade, back to that scene with the four of them, talking within the study.

He can't be here still, he says. Milton. Is he?

Jing looks away. There are insects above her, swirling around the bulb of the streetlight beside her. I've been so lonely, is what she says to him in the end. And I don't know what to believe in anymore.

He'll pass Jing a photo, when he leaves the following morning: in it is her, and Mateo, and another Asian girl he doesn't recognise, smiling at what seems to be a flat party. He can only presume it's from their time in London, which might also mean that this other girl here, with the bangs and the mole under her eye: it's Tori Yamamoto.

Jing takes the photo with both hands. She stares at it, intensely, at their twenty-something-year-old selves. I can't—I can't remember when this was taken, she says. Not even where. Daniel watches her trace a finger over her friends' faces, before, finally, her own. I can't believe this, is all she says.

Out Daniel goes, with his duffel bag in tow. He makes his way out of Bestari Heights, following the same road and the same houses, and crossing the same, small field of grass. At the guardhouse he asks if any taxis come by here, and they say no, making crosses with their arms and hands; he will have to walk to the end of the road, where the edge of town is, they say.

He thanks them and he goes. He is confronted immediately by the longest road he has ever had to walk, compensated only by the sight of the angsana trees, so frightfully tall, making a grand canopy over both lanes. Daniel walks, and walks, until he reaches a short row of shophouses, and finds a pleasant-looking diner. When he steps inside he asks a member of the staff, a young girl, where he might grab a taxi if he wants to.

The girl seems to be around Yong-he's age, possibly older, but not by much. In spite of the smiley badge pinned to the front of her red tee, the girl looks absolutely disgusted by Daniel's shirt, and how drenched it is with sweat. She nevertheless points to the road outside, indicating to him the large building opposite the café, and the equally huge car park laid out before it.

The girl asks him where he is going.

Singapore, he says. I have a flight from Changi Airport.

She gives him a thumbs-up. There is a bus, she says. It can take you straight to the checkpoint. Is that good enough for you?

It is, he says, thank you. He turns back to her. Your English . . . Aha. What is your accent?

The girl stares at him, seemingly bored and entertained by his existence at the same time. The accent is "mid-Atlantic", she says. I go to an international high school.

Daniel smiles. Do you like school?

She shrugs. My parents would kill me if I dropped out.

But you work part time here?

She nods; the look she's giving him bears no sign of changing. My beloved summer vacation—I came here last year, and I'm back in town again, she says, gesturing towards the entire diner. She tells him that this is her grandparents' place, and that her Nenek's back in the kitchen. But it's weird, she adds. Daniel asks her weird how.

Weird town, she says. Weirder neighbours. The girl then cocks her head to the side, and asks him where he's from.

I'm from Spain, he says. I'm based in Barcelona.

The girl nods almost approvingly. Spain, she says, in a more wistful voice. I've never been to Spain. She then grabs a jug, and begins to fill up a glass with cold water. Do you like being an adult? she asks.

Ah, the young, and all of their damn questions; Daniel thinks of Yong-he again, the poor bedridden kid, and genuinely doesn't know what to say. I am not sure, aha, is how he replies, and the girl nods another time, as though she understands. She then asks him what he's doing here, in Johor Bahru, of all the places in the world. He tells her he's visiting a friend.

My name is Daniel, by the way.

The girl finally smiles at him. Welcome to JB, Daniel. It's not gonna miss you. She then lifts the glass of cold water to her lips, instead of passing it to him, like he thought she would. I'm Emi, she says, before jutting her chin towards the door of the diner. Looks like your bus is here.

Daniel boards the bus, and quickly buys a ticket from the driver. He catches Emi waving at him, still standing by the roadside, still holding on to that damn glass of water. He waves back at her, cheered nonetheless by her youth, her candour.

Emi is the first person he has spoken to who hasn't given him the look: the look Isaac had, and the look Jing had too, and even their son. He remembers the look his friends and family had given him, especially at the beginning, when he had to meet them, and talk to them, the sheer horror upon hearing that Mateo had essentially vanished. He was on a ferry when it happened, he kept saying. His bags were the only thing he left behind. They were married for ten years, going on eleven; Mateo was forty-five years old, and would be turning forty-six in May.

The bus gets moving. Daniel watches Emi walk away, back into her grandparents' diner; it doesn't register to him how similar she looks, to the girl in the photo he handed to Jing that morning. He fails to notice the same mole that Emi has on her cheek too.

Daniel puts one hand over a knee. Now that he is finally seated, he can feel the strain of the morning come to him, as a dull but familiar ache in his joint. Daniel holds his other hand over his mouth as he keeps his gaze outward, out onto Iskandar. He wants to commit the landscape to his memory, this scorching, shimmering, noon-lit scene, even as the air-conditioning is blasting from the vents, causing the sweat on his shirt to feel ice cold on his skin. The girl is right, says Daniel to himself: it's not gonna miss me, this town.

29

Jing begins to write a message. *Daniel just left,* she sends. And because it is only April, and the performance won't start for another month, she manages to get a reply in half an hour.

How was he? says Isaac's message. She types.

He is strong, her message says. *And devastated.* Jing then sends him a photo of the photo: of the three of them, as undergraduates, in a random flat in London.

You're the only one left, he says.

A new sadness rises within Jing, though she doesn't want to show it. *Of course I am,* she types. *No one can get rid of me. I'm a cockroach,* she says, with a humour she's proud to muster again.

Jing waits for Isaac's reply. And it comes, twelve minutes later.

I have a meeting, he says. *Talk to you later.* And then, later that night: *I hope Yong-he is well.*

June 2005.

Her book has been published, not necessarily to great acclaim, but to surprisingly good sales; it's nothing less than what she has predicted. Before the reporters can descend on her house, Jing has already packed her bags, and piled them all into her second-hand car.

There's nobody to say goodbye to, save her grandfather; Isaac has already taken the boy with him, to the newly purchased penthouse on Grange Road.

Her grandfather, predictably, is in the garden when it's time. In fact, he's watering the tabebuia tree.

Ah Pa, she says. You take care, okay.

He looks at her. He doesn't even say a word. He knows her marriage is over; he knows there's nothing more to say. He just nods.

Jing tries to imagine what her grandmother would say, if she were still alive. Why do you have to publish the book? she'd undeniably ask. Who tell you you have to send it to a publisher? And her imaginary answer to this would always give her pause; it would make her pause, literally, in the moment after fastening her seat belt behind the driver's wheel.

It's what he needs.

Who?

Isaac lah, who else.

Isaac? her Ah Ma would say. For what?

To be the protagonist, she'd say to her grandmother: the good guy in our story.

She relies on both her memory and a map for what comes next: from Tuas she crosses the strait and enters Johor Bahru, before she arrives at the township of Iskandar. Once she finds herself at the roundabout, she goes around it several times, until she eventually decides which is the right exit to take. When Jing is finally at Bestari Heights, she finds herself lost again, driving down all of its lanes, until she is finally convinced that maybe this, this house, the one on this corner—this is the one.

Jing turns off the engine of her car. She steps out of the vehicle, and slowly approaches the gate. Both the gate and the house are identical to everything else at Bestari Heights. And because Jing isn't tall enough to look over the gate, she peers instead, through the metal slats, doing her best to recall if she is right.

It seems like she is, she tells herself, though there does seem to be more furniture in the living room of the house.

Jing walks over to the intercom; this is also new, she notes. She presses the button for the doorbell, and it works, though no one seems to be responding to it. She tries the doorbell again.

Nothing.

Jing turns back to her car. All her shit is inside it: her clothes and toiletries, all her cash, her documents and the books that matter. She is aware that there is a version of events that can play out, one in which she is simply seated in her car, waiting for something, anything, to happen. She can turn the engine off and have the windows down, baking in the damn vehicle, for all she cares.

Jing drives the car out of Bestari Heights and checks herself into the nearest motel. When she returns to the house, sometime in the evening, she is glad, overjoyed even, to see that there is a light on downstairs. She presses the doorbell, again and again.

Nothing. No one comes out to see who it is. Nobody's interested in the fact that she's here.

She panics, is what happens next. It's the wrong house, is all she thinks. Jing walks down the road, and starts to look into all of the neighbouring units, occupied and unoccupied. Doubt sets in, uncertainty scrambling her plans: she doesn't know anything for sure anymore. Jing looks, and looks, until she is at the very end of the road, where she sees a sign pasted to the gate of the unit. It says the house is for sale; there is even a handphone number, attached to the notice—a direct number to the owner of the place.

When the owner picks up her call, Jing realises it's a supremely upset Teochew auntie, lamenting in a combination of dialect and Mandarin about all the issues the house has been riddled with. The air-con units, the kitchen sink, even the tap in the garden—all of it has a problem, did she know? Even some of the streetlights in the area don't turn on sometimes. She wants to sue the developer, is what the livid auntie says, except the developer appears to have run off somewhere. The damn bastard is uncontactable, and now, this auntie—she has no idea why Bestari Heights was even built in the first place. She doesn't know why she bought a house here at all.

All Jing does is listen. She listens, until she finally asks this auntie if she's willing to rent her the place.

Rent? says the auntie. You're not buying? Jing has yet to even reply in the affirmative when the auntie states her price.

You want or not? presses the auntie. She says she can always negotiate.

Jing closes her eyes; she needs a time out soon, from the painful back-and-forth between the English and Mandarin voices in her head. She also needs to squat, on the road, to fully accommodate all the mental sums she has to perform in her brain.

The book would continue to sell, whether she liked it or not; she has years and years of savings accumulated, what with Isaac having paid for practically everything in their marriage. She even has her mother's estate, the art that is still being sold and collected and loaned to institutions. Someone somewhere will always be paying for rights to her images, her words, her work. Even the insurance payout over her mother's disappearance is finally close to being settled. That and the fact that she can sell this car.

Jing tells the owner she can move in the next day. But why? asks the auntie. Why you want to move here? And Jing tells her that she just wants to, that's all. She doesn't know how to say "vendetta" in Mandarin either.

This is how the years pass by. Nobody, save for her landlord, knows where she is.

In the email account she no longer uses, messages pile up, year after year, informing her that her book remains well in circulation. It's a literary sensation, apparently. On the fifth anniversary of *The Horvallan*, her

Hotmail becomes bombarded with requests for interviews, creative writing workshops, appearances at festivals; even the occasional request related to her mother still comes to Jing, even after she has ceded control of Han Aw's estate to Isaac, with the idea that it would be Yong-he's to manage one day.

Her inbox floods until it finally jams. Every email to Jing gets an automatic sender's notification, stating that she's no longer able to receive any more emails. And then nothing, truly nothing, actually comes through to her anymore. Jing gets to relinquish this mode of contact, and enter her own season of solitude.

Jing still heads out, on some nights. But there is a routine she follows, so to speak. She checks every room, opens every door; she makes sure her house is clear, before anything else. And then she goes.

Not every house can be explored: the one closest to her has a chain on the gate; the one after that has a dog, chained to a pillar.

It is the third-nearest house that she manages to break into. It's the first house in Bestari Heights she gets to explore; both the gate and the front door are unlocked, miraculously.

She shines a light from her phone, casting it about the living room.

She already knows that this isn't it. All of it is in the wrong orientation: the stairs, the kitchen, even the garden outside. A mirror world.

Jing still lingers inside it for a while regardless.

There are nights when she returns to the original house—the one she had thought was his. Was theirs. Jing still presses the doorbell from time to time, whenever the lights are on. And then she runs over to the gate of the house opposite, just across the road; it is unoccupied, of course, though the gate does squeak like the rest.

She waits. She squats, and stares. She waits for somebody to come out, show up. Anything. But nobody ever does.

One night her eyes focus on something else. It's not the gate of the house she's staring at any longer, nor is it the windows, aglow from within. It's a plant she's staring at, a tree, its thick branches just poking over the wall that surrounds their yard.

In time it will continue to grow, taller and bigger. In time, she will recognise the plant for what it is.

Tabebuia.

She gets a call from Isaac in the first week of 2015. Her iPhone lights up, and buzzes, while a part of her already knows somehow: it's bad.

Yong-he was in a traffic accident, he says.

A groan escapes from Jing's throat. She is already on all fours, on the floor of her living room; she can't even recall her own accident now, the one with Isaac's and Milton's cars, without feeling like she might lose her balance.

Jing, says Isaac. Jing. Come on.

She forces the sick in her throat to subside; she exhales deeply, but quickly, determined to hold the panic at bay. Isaac, she finally says. Is he—

Alive, yes. But it's bad.

She asks him how bad, followed by: What happened?

He tells her: that he had slipped out the previous night; that their boy was next seen riding a motorcycle, down Ang Mo Kio Avenue One; that Isaac had always known he liked to slip out; that he didn't know, however, how Yong-he had a motorcycle to begin with.

But he's—Isaac. He's still sixteen.

Yes.

So he's underage.

Yes.

Jing's entire body is on the floor now. She curls up as she keeps a hand over her eyes. This is the cost, she says to herself; this is the price her family will keep paying.

And then?

He crossed a red light, says Isaac.

No.

And then a bus came for him.

Fuck. Fuck.

It's bad, says Isaac. But I think he'll be all right. Jing wants to discuss why their boy was even there in the first place, so clearly en route to their old home at Lorong Chuan, but she's afraid of asking the wrong questions at the wrong time. It's only later, after Isaac tells her about the incoming swarm of reporters and police officers, when he adds: You should come.

It's the month of March 2015, when Jing finds herself in her car, once again, over the causeway, once again. It's a rental she'll have to return in less than a week's time. And she has a fellow passenger too, seated on her left.

This is . . . Malaysia?

That's right, says Jing.

Indonesia, he then says: another country.

You're right again, says Jing.

The boy begins to list more countries to himself. Vietnam. Thailand. China. Russia. Mexico. Egypt. Australia. He then turns to her. Spain?

Jing falls quiet. Yong-he stares at her, and then falls quiet too. Soon they reach border control.

Johor Bahru, he suddenly says.

Yes.

Is-Is—Iskandar.

Yes.

Bestari . . . Heights.

Jing nods. Your new home.

Isaac, she texts him, sometime in May. *Yong-he wants to know why you're not here.*

Tell him I have to work, comes the reply.

So I can tell him about your play? she asks.

He doesn't reply for another hour. *Of course,* he says. He then sends her a photograph, of a simple but handsome brochure, advertising the details of his performance. *PARADISE*, it says. *2 May–8 Aug 2015, 8pm. The Substation (Gallery). Free Admission / Invite Only / Donations Encouraged.*

She types another message. *This is daily?*

Yes, I told you.

But—every night? Weekdays and weekends?

Yes, he says. *99 nights in total.*

Jing is astounded; he's actually doing this. *Will you be okay?* she asks.

I'll be fine, comes his reply. *I'll be alive.*

Jing texts him about his work at The Substation again, this time in early June. *Yong-he wants to see you in action.*

How is he doing? he asks.

Good, she says. *We tried walking down the stairs.*

How was that?

Jing wonders what to say. *He tried,* says her message. *And then he got tired. But he made it all the way down, and I cried.*

Isaac doesn't respond. But he will call her that night and ask: Why are you still there?

Jing doesn't even have to ask what he means by the question. She tells him she doesn't know.

Is it guilt? he asks.

Maybe, she says.

Is it love? he asks next. Do you still love him?

Jing keeps quiet. It pains her to hear how calm he sounds, the way he's asking her these questions. And it pains her, too, to hear her tell him: I'm not sure, Isaac. Let me figure out that part too.

Jing receives a video clip, on a night in early June. It is late, but she knows that her son is awake; he's playing a movie on his new iPad, a gift sent by courier from his father that afternoon. Jing enters his room and sits beside him, downloading the clip for them both.

This is Pa? Yong-he asks. That's him?

Jing nods. In a way, she says.

The clip begins to play: Isaac is seated on a chair, re-enacting a pivotal scene from *Cinema Paradiso*; he has on a brown cardigan over a white shirt, and a pair of beige chinos. His hair is neatly cut and gelled back, while his eyes are eager, entreating. The lighting causes his very figure to glow, while the gallery behind him recedes into the shadows.

Isaac plays a tape on his Walkman: it's Alfredo from the film, his dialogue in Italian. Isaac then speaks in English, in the gaps between Alfredo's sentences; it's as though he is directly translating Alfredo's story to Toto in real time.

He tells the story of how a king gave a feast, once upon a time, with his daughter in attendance. He speaks of a soldier standing guard, watching the most beautiful princess of the realm go by, falling in love the instant he lays his eyes upon the young woman. And while Isaac speaks of the soldier's hopeless love, and how he could only dream of being together with the king's daughter, Jing finds herself swept, in the midst of an unexpected swoon, back to the moment when they first met: to that first evening, in the kitchen of the ryokan, Isaac looking over his shoulder while Jing stood by the entryway. Isaac tells the story of the soldier meeting the princess one day, letting her know that he can no longer live without her love, and Jing can feel it again, an old swelling in her chest, her thin heart growing and beating with new blood.

"If you can wait, for a hundred days and a hundred nights under my balcony," said the princess to the soldier, "I promise to be yours at the very end."

In the clip, Isaac has both hands on his knees, telling the audience about how the soldier had waited for a day, two days, ten days, twenty; his eyes go red as he speaks of the princess, standing by the balustrade, watching the soldier stand for her sake, all for her heart at the end of a hundred days. By the ninetieth day, however, the soldier was all dry, all white, unable to stand: the actor's tears begin to stream as he describes how all the strength has left the soldier, in his fight against the wind, the rain, the snow, the beasts. He was not even capable of sleeping any longer, for even the act of sleeping required a certain strength too.

Isaac turns the volume down on his Walkman. The soldier remained like this till the ninety-ninth night, says Isaac, when he stood up and walked away. He knew it was a lie, believing the princess would be his the next day. And he would have perished, too, if he had stayed to see the princess break her promise to him in the end. But after ninety-nine nights, and only ninety-nine, the soldier could still live in that grand delusion: he could still imagine that she'd be there, waiting for him to reappear; he'd leave his spirit beneath her balcony, ever ready to receive the love he knew he'd never attain.

That dream alone was enough for them both, says Isaac, seconds before his clip to Jing ends.

Jing sends him a picture, the following week.

Look at him, she says. *Our boy lasted the whole way down.*

And then, the week after that—

Now he's outside.

It's sometime later, sometime around the start of July, when Isaac finally tells her about the car.

What car? she asks.

He sends her a picture. *Do you see it?*

She waits for the picture to fully download. It's the double glass doors of The Substation's gallery; it's possible to see Armenian Street through the doors, that section of kerb right outside the building. She zooms in on the picture, allowing it to fill the entire screen of her phone.

And then the worst thing happens, like a corrective against her hope. It's pitiful to think that she ever once entertained the idea that things would be okay once again. What felt like a ripening fruit became no more than a seed, her very heart seizing and then closing up once again with despair.

What is that? she types, as tears fill her eyes. *What's that outside?*

He replies a minute later.

I don't know, he says, *but it's gone now*—words that Jing can barely read on her phone.

30

There is no clear beginning to the story of Neo Yong-he. It is only a wide and ongoing now, an existence in the present tense, sharply edged with pain.

The month is June, nearly July, and the year, 2015. He is sixteen, turning seventeen, and he is managing, he thinks. His father is an actor, performing in what he believes to be the final show of his life. His mother is, well—his mother. She stands beside him, watching him with wary eyes.

Thirty minutes? she says. He nods.

That's good.

He does not take a step, and remains standing for a while, as they wait for the gate to swing close behind them. Every time he is confronted by the outside world, be it in real life or on the internet, he has to brace himself, find the centre within himself, as though the soaking in of information were a physical process too.

He catches his mother pocketing the remote in her pocket, and he thinks: Bermudas—another word for "shorts". While they wait he begins to recite other things too, like a mantra of the neighbourhood: A street, with lanes. A house, and a tree. Each of these things have many names too, and he finds himself wanting to know, out of the usual curiosity, what the name for the nearest tree is.

His mother is oblivious to his inner monologue; the gate finally closes, with a dull, anticlimactic clang. Shall we? she says, and he nods again. She asks him left, or right.

He looks: down left is the rest of their street, flanked by two long rows of houses. This scene, right here, has more in common with the suburb in *Edward Scissorhands* than any other Google Image search result of Malaysia.

Let's go right, he says.

They begin walking. As they walk, his mother holds onto his arm, in case anything happens. She asks if he needs his crutches, and he says he does not.

I'm asking just in case, she says.

I know, he says in return. Thanks, Ma.

They take a couple of minutes to round their first corner. Yong-he asks his mother if they will be going back to Singapore soon.

Why? asks Jing. You need a doctor?

Sure, says Yong-he, keeping his voice light. And to see Pa too.

His mother falls silent; it's just as well, Yong-he thinks. There is a half-mown field of grass on the other side of the road, in the middle of which stands a playground, abandoned and dirty looking. Yong-he can also identify the guardhouse, just beyond, next to the main gate of Bestari Heights.

The more he stares across the field, the more he notices the air, rippling, from the heat of the afternoon sun. And then, like a door opening—

There was a Caltex, he says.

What?

Across the road, he says. At our old house.

Mother and child look at one another. Neither of them has yet to take a further step. You're really remembering, she says, but he has to mentally push her comment aside. Next to the Caltex was a field of grass too, he says. In the middle was a—a path. (No: a footpath.) It led to—

A playground, says his mother. That's right. There's one here too.

They pause, calculating the distance between here and there. You sure you want to go? she asks. It's a bit far away. But Yong-he says he wants to, and his mother has to nod again. There is a sudden slack in the way she's holding him, however, which he interprets as an unwillingness to do what he says. The boy tugs on her arm anyway, ignoring the shaking in his legs. Please take me there, he says to his mother, even as his pain ripples like the air above the sun-baked grass.

They stand next to one another, their feet half-sunken in the loose grains of the sandpit. Streaks of dirt discolour the otherwise brightly painted playground, parts of which he readily names: rocking horse, monkey bars, slide. He asks his mother if they ever used the playground back home, and she looks at him, the two unclear about what the other is thinking about.

I never brought you there, she says. You were six or seven when you and Pa stopped living at Lorong Chuan.

Yong-he feels sad; he wants to know what kind of mother she is, even though he doesn't have another one to compare her to. Who did you bring? he asks his mother next, and she smiles at him, in a way both tired and sad.

Someone else, my dear.

Yong-he rests his gaze on her. In this new story of his, what he has found harder to name, and infinitely stranger too, is the way he feels about things, about people, about places he could only wish of being in. And because one's convalescence is always a matter of time, he has spent many hours on YouTube alone, listening to song after song, live and pre-recorded, with lyrics and without lyrics; he'd read the comments left behind by people too, expressing everything from doubt to adoration, some posting entire confessionals for others to read, reply, even rebut. Yong-he realised that there was an infinite number of ways to explain emotions, to elaborate upon them, anecdotally qualify them. But the naming of these feelings, the stating of them, always felt elusive to him, if not overly simplistic an exercise. As he continued to gaze at his mother, for instance, was it sorrow he felt, or was it pity? What could describe the way he looked at Bestari Heights, with the implicit knowledge, somehow, that this place was never their home? What's the emotion that comes with understanding that home is somewhere else, would always be somewhere else, for him and his mother both?

Your Pa and I have been thinking a bit. He says you might have gone there often, the playground, behind the Caltex. Just you, his mother says.

Yong-he asks if this was before the accident. Her mother nods, and asks if he wants to know why. He nods in return. His mother's grip on his arm trembles now.

It's because of a book I wrote, she says. We don't know how you got to read it, but you must have either gone to the library, or bought an old copy. She pauses, and sniffs. I didn't even think about what it'd do to you.

Yong-he stares down at his feet; he and his mother continue to stand in the sun, for a few more minutes. Home wasn't just somewhere across the sea, is the thought that passes through his mind: home was a place locked away, sealed in another time. It was the kind of place you couldn't reach towards alone.

It is in middle of the month—the second week of a hot, blistering July—when he sees her for the first time. The weather is so humid, the very air so irradiated with a steaming, thickening moisture, that he has to blink and focus on what he is seeing exactly, as he stands on the top of the slide. Yong-he can't help but gasp when the words girl, bicycle and fast, all flash past his mind before suddenly arriving at the one word— *beautiful*—which stays. The abstraction lingers, trembling, at the forefront of his mind.

She's beautiful, he thinks, before adding, rather lamely: Wow.

The girl catches him staring at her. She pedals the long, circular route around the playground, following the lanes of Bestari Heights, before braking, and alighting from her bicycle.

She cuts across the grass, briskly walking towards him with a quizzical look on her face; she takes off her backpack, the moment she reaches the edge of the sandpit, and lets it fall on the ground. From the bottom of the slide, she says:

I've seen you before.

He blinks. Really?

She doesn't nod or shake her head; she merely stares at him, scanning him as though he were an alien.

You have a very obvious red cap that you keep wearing.

He blinks; he reaches for the brim, brushing it with his fingers.

I do?

The girl squints. My grandfather also says you have difficulty walking. My grandmother thinks something bad must have happened to you.

Yong-he blushes now with embarrassment. The girl was just being kind, then, with the comment about his cap.

You live here? he asks.

The girl turns and points. Her house is in Bestari Heights, all right—but wherever she's pointing to seems far away from his mother's unit.

There are very few families here, the girl says. So my grandparents definitely notice when someone new arrives. It's like an event.

Yong-he can't help but smile. His smile grows even wider when the girl smiles back. She then comes closer to him, by taking a few steps up the slide. Yong-he braces himself, and doesn't dare to make a move, noticing the streaks of long hair that stick to her face.

You live with an older woman, don't you?

He nods. That's my mother.

Of course, she says. Your mom. He can almost see her file the information away, ready to report to her grandparents the moment she heads back home. Her eyes, so bright, make him think of sunflower seeds too.

Where is she now?

My Ma? says Yong-he. Back home.

So you walked here all by yourself?

He nods.

Was that hard?

He nods again.

But you're okay?

He runs his hand over a thigh. I'm okay now, he says.

The girl looks towards her bicycle, before turning her head back to him.

I can give you a ride home, if you want.

Yong-he smiles again. You know where my house is?

The girl shrugs. Sure, I do.

She steps off the slide. Yong-he scoots his way down, giving himself a gentle push with his arms. He notices how the girl can't help but look at his legs, at the purplish scars that still wrap around his calves. She then gives him a hand, and hoists him up, all the time saying to himself, yes, yes, hell yes, when he gets to show her how much progress he's made. He barely limps, now.

Yong-he sits on the saddle behind the girl. He nervously puts his arms around her waist. Yong-he waits for the girl to regain her bearings, to resettle into this new weight, this new centre of gravity between them.

Hey, he suddenly says. Your bag.

She looks. Her bag's still at the corner of the sandpit, and she doesn't seem to mind. I'll come back for it, she says, and even her breath smells sweet to him, like candy. And then she pedals away, without warning, saying:

I'm Emi, by the way.

He relaxes in time. It's his first time on a bicycle, but he's already loosening his hold around her waist, settling into a posture that doesn't feel new to him at all. He is overcome by a strange sense of ease, of familiarity; he wonders if this too is another sort of remembering, one that goes beyond the mere recollection of words.

I'm Yong-he, he says to Emi.

*   *   *

The boy sees Emi again the following day, and the day after that. During the weekend, sometime in the late evening, he hears her first—the sharp ring of her bell—and knows it is time to cut across his mother's room, straight towards the balcony. He sees her with her bicycle, just outside the gate of his house, and the girl sees him too, waving dramatically from the road.

What are you doing! he hears her shout.

He laughs. He blushes too, overcome by his own shyness, even as he can hear the neighbourhood ring with the echo of her voice. He points upwards, towards the full moon and says, I've just been looking at it. I'm a nerd, sorry. And when Emi looks up as well, he finds himself transfixed yet again, by the fine line of her profile. It starts from the sharp edge of her nose, and it runs, tenderly, down to the slender base of her throat.

Emi turns her attention back to him. She asks if he would like to hang out again, by the playground in the field, her voice still echoing across Bestari Heights without a care. He gestures at her to wait, and turns around, back into his bedroom.

His mother is already standing by the doorway, looking at him. She asks him who that is, the girl outside.

A neighbour, he says.

Is she nice? she asks.

He blushes again. She is.

His mother nods. She isn't smiling, but she isn't exactly upset either.

Please be careful, she says. You've only just started to walk.

I know, he says.

Remember your keys. There's only my copy and yours.

He says that he will.

Don't stay out too late, is her final wish to the boy, and he nods. He can't help but feel the weight of his mother's gaze, resting on the back of his neck, as he goes down the flight of stairs, one steady step at a time. His chest pounds and pounds, stretching tight and hard like the skin of a drum—but it is exactly this feeling, whatever it is, that reassures him somehow that he'll make it.

When he is finally outside, Yong-he gets on the back of Emi's bicycle, and asks if she might go a little faster tonight.

How fast? she asks.

He nearly laughs. As fast as you can.

They sit at the top of the slide. The moon, as full as ever, takes centre stage within a cloudless sky. Emi has a plastic bag, which she had earlier retrieved from the basket in front of her bicycle. She hands it over to him. He asks her what it is, and she says, Tempura. Yong-he asks if they speak Japanese back home, and she says that they do, of course, aside from a smattering of Bahasa Melayu.

There's a small community of expats here, she says. Every time the families meet is insane.

Yong-he reaches into the plastic bag: he lifts the lid of at the Tupperware container inside and discovers an assortment of fried food, such as crab sticks, prawns and mushrooms, all packed together over a sheet of parchment paper. Emi reaches into the plastic bag too and takes out a pair of chopsticks, offering it to him.

Is this all for me?

Emi nods. My grandmother told me to look out for you.

Yong-he looks at her. Words fail him again; he doesn't know what to say, how to convey the exact parameters of his gratitude; it's the first time he has felt care and concern from people who are not his parents.

They've never even met me, he says.

Emi shrugs. I'm sure you will. One day.

Yong-he picks up a crab stick with his chopsticks, and takes a crunchy, greasy bite. It's unlike anything he has ever tasted before. Emi watches every move of his.

It's good, isn't it?

He nods, eagerly. So good, he says. It's so good.

Emi smiles. It's a smile strong enough to make his brain stall. Does she know? he begins to wonder. How close her face is to his now? How he can smell her too, that combination of shampoo and sweat? It makes him want to die all over again, his desire for her blooming and unfurling at a rate so busy, so distracting, and so all over the place, that he is almost prevented from hearing what she says to him next.

There's something my grandparents are curious about. Is it okay if I ask?

He nods another time.

Emi's smile softens. We've seen your mom around, she says. But not your dad.

Yong-he blinks; he almost forgets to keep chewing. His face falls, somewhat.

Do you have a dad? she asks.

He nods. I do, he says. But he's busy.

Emi's voice remains kind. Where is he? she asks, a tad softer. It makes Yong-he want to hold her face in his hands, to press her cheek against his own. Instead he shrugs and says: Somewhere, another planet. Doing what he needs to do.

Half an hour later they see a car, coming in through the security gates. It's half past nine, according to her watch; Emi knows it's her grandparents, coming home after they've closed the diner.

Yong-he watches Emi go down the slide. He watches her cross the sand-pit and then the grass, towards the road. The car slows down to a crawl.

A window lowers; a light switches on, from inside the car. Yong-he can see an elderly man and woman, smiling at Emi. Jii-chan, she says, Nek. Okaeri.

Is that the one? asks Emi's grandmother.

Yong-he himself goes down the slide, and walks to the edge of the sand-pit. He gives a short wave when Emi points directly at him. Everyone smiles as the smell of exhaust fogs up the air.

Hello, says Yong-he. Thank—thank you for the tempura. Terima kasih.

Sama-sama, says Emi's grandmother. Come closer.

Yong-he does, slowly. The two adults are smiling at him. Emi's grandfather then says something in Japanese, causing Emi to turn to Yong-he. She asks if he'd like to come over, to their place, and Yong-he wonders out loud if it might be too late.

It won't be long, boy, says Emi's grandmother. Just for a while. My husband can drive you back too.

He can't help it. Okay, says Yong-he. Okay. Thank you.

Emi's grandparents, it turns out, live on the other end of his road, which still makes for quite a distance. And yet it is an odd comfort to find that the neighbouring houses are just as empty as the ones that surround his own.

O-cha? says Emi's grandfather. O-mizu?

Emi translates for him: Tea? Water?

Yong-he chooses tea.

The four of them step out of the car. The first thing Yong-he notices is their garden: it is replete with flowering bushes and large, extravagant ferns. A tree stands closest to the porch and the driveway, the green of its leaves as pale as the ash-like colour on its bark, its blossoms powdery white and soft. A flower falls from a branch just then, down onto the grass, spinning in quick circles.

A light comes on: it shines from the living room, and spills through the tall windowpanes, out onto the porch and the garden.

Yong-he steps inside. Emi tells him to wait, to stay in the living room while she accompanies her grandfather up the stairs. Yong-he nods, and doesn't move, taking in the wider details of their home: paraphernalia, souvenirs and photographs of all sizes, cluttering every available space and corner he could see. He has never known what it is like to be in the presence of so many things before, to be amidst so many objects of affection. And each object, surely, has a name of its own too; each object, a story, or at least a part of a story.

Now, he thinks: he might be a part of that story too.

Emi's grandmother emerges from the kitchen. She carries a tray with both hands, bearing coasters, a few glasses and a tumbler of iced tea. She goes up to him, and seems to reconsider something.

How about you and Emi sit in the garden? she asks. It's nicer there.

Yong-he holds the front door open for her as she steps out, leading him down the porch. He has never had an image for the word *grandmother*, and now he is glad to have one. Emi's grandmother places the tray down in the middle of a bench, while they sit on the opposite ends. The woman asks him if he is feeling okay, and he nods.

She pours him a cup of tea. I made this myself. Ceylon, with some dried fruits. How is it?

He tastes it. It's unlike anything he's ever had before. He asks her what it is again, and the woman raises her eyebrows at him.

You still haven't told me if it's good or not, she says.

Oh, says Yong-he. It's very good. He then asks how he might address her, and Emi's grandmother laughs.

Call me Nek, she says. Or Nenek. Actually, no, just Nek.

Okay, he says. It's very good, Nek. It's really nice and . . . sweet? But also—

Bitter.

He nods. Yes.

Nek continues to smile at him. I ask you something, yah?

Yong-he nods again.

Your house, she says. It looks very lonely.

Yong-he continues to smile at her, even though he cannot help but agree. It's just me and my Ma, he says. Nek then asks how his Ma is faring, and he tells her that she's good. She cares for me, very much. Nek then asks Yong-he what she does, aside from caring for him all day. He tells her that she's a writer, an author.

Have you read her books?

Yong-he shakes his head. She's written one book, he says. But it's not available online.

Nek appears confused. You don't have a physical copy?

Yong-he looks down into his glass of tea. I don't think Ma is very proud of the book, he says to Nek. I try to read what I can on the internet, but it's hard.

Why? asks Nek. Is it not well known?

He shakes his head. It's very well known.

Emi's grandmother stares at him for a while. Why can't you just talk to her about it? Nek asks. Like you and me, right now?

Yong-he shrugs. We just can't, he says. We don't. He says it might be easier for her to keep quiet about it, though Nek seems unconvinced. Is it easy for you, though? she asks, and Yong-he shrugs again. Is love meant to be easy? Yong-he says, without a single trace of irony in his voice, which causes Nek to laugh again.

Oh! she says, smacking Yong-he on the arm. Boy, what have you been watching? He sniggers along.

Sorry, he says. I watch too many movies.

Nek asks him what his favourite movie is. Yong-he blushes and adjusts his cap, before revealing his answer: *Edward Scissorhands*. He says he likes *When Harry Met Sally* too, and Nek laughs some more, clapping her hands.

Ah, alamak. Poor Emi. I need to warn her about you.

Yong-he drains the rest of his tea. Nek pours him a second glass. They then turn to the tree in front of them, just as they catch a glance of Emi too, walking back down the stairs.

Yong-he asks if the tree has a name. You mean, what kind? says Nek. Tabebuia.

The boy nods. It's very pretty, he says, and he can hear Nek murmuring out of appreciation. He can hear the door opening too, the sound of Emi putting on her slippers.

It blooms two times a year. Sometimes three, says Nek. But you can never predict when.

Never? says Yong-he.

Nek sighs. We tried. We've been trying to, she says. But the tree only blooms when it wants to, and when it happens, all of the ground is filled with flowers. So many flowers, I tell you.

Yong-he looks at the base of the tree: there are only a few blooms on the grass, wilting at various rates, which is to be expected for such a young tree. He then smells a familiar sweetness once Emi stands behind them on the bench, pouring herself a glass of the Ceylon tea.

I ask you something, says Nek to Yong-he. What do you want to be, when you grow up?

The boy makes a face. He says he hasn't thought so far yet. He doesn't even know how many jobs there are in the world. But Nek lets out a soft laugh, almost like a giggle, and tells him it's okay.

Just be what I tell my granddaughter too, she says, before turning back to Emi. What do I tell you?

She shrugs. Just be a good person? she says. No matter what happens?

Nek nods, satisfied, and leaves the two children alone with the tea. Emi takes her grandmother's place, the kids watching the old woman walk back into the house.

Yong-he asks Emi where her parents are. She tells him they're back home, in Yokohama. Yong-he then asks her about the jobs they have, and she says that her father sells beer, a really popular beer in Japan. Her mother, on the other hand, is a tennis coach, says Emi. She was the star of the varsity team where her father went to university. He then asks Emi what their home is like, and she paints him a picture, of a house on a hillside, overlooking the sea, and the boy has to do everything in his power to imagine what she's describing. The three of them live with her paternal grandmother, who cooks everything in the house, she says. Her paternal grandfather passed away unfortunately, way before she was even born.

But sometimes, Emi tells him, if I pay enough attention—I can catch my father and my grandmother trade a secret look, a look that always ends in a small smile. And that's when she knows, says Emi, that they're thinking of her grandfather, the one who passed away too soon. And the more she's able to catch them trade this look with one another, the more Emi can feel the full presence of her family, all members present, in spite of the loss; she can feel what it means to be connected to something, which is also why she loves spending her summers here too. And as Emi tells him all of this she's gazing back at the tabebuia tree, while Yong-he is overcome with the distinct feeling that here, right now: this is the moment a new chapter in his story might finally begin. And then Emi gasps, and turns to him, just as he's placing a hand over hers—just as they catch a bloom spinning, and falling, directly onto her shoulder.

31

Transcript of interview conducted by Marie Chandran-Lee, with Isaac Neo at The Substation (Gallery), 8 Aug 2015, 1830 hours.

MARIE CHANDRAN-LEE This is where I sit?

ISAAC NEO Yes. Right across from me.

CHANDRAN-LEE Oh, okay. *(laughs)* This . . . this is a great space.

NEO It is, isn't it? Do you notice how your voice travels . . . ?

CHANDRAN-LEE Oh, yes. Yes, I do. I was going to say that this space has many memories for me, actually. *(pause)* And yes, in response to what you just said: I was at last night's performance, and I did notice it, the acoustics in the room. *(pause)* Thank you for taking the time to speak with me today, by the way. Before we begin, though, can I just confirm—

NEO What?

CHANDRAN-LEE *(pause)* Is it true? That I'm the only interviewer you've agreed to see?

NEO Yes, Marie. That's right.

CHANDRAN-LEE Oh! Well, the pleasure is really—it's really all mine, then. *(laughs)* I can't help but feel today is an important day for you.

NEO It is, yes.

CHANDRAN-LEE How are you feeling?

NEO I'm good. I'm excited.

CHANDRAN-LEE And what are you excited for?

NEO Hmm, well. *(pause)* Today is my last day as an actor.

CHANDRAN-LEE It is, indeed. Let's cut to the chase, then. Very little is written about this performance of yours, though it does clearly state that this will be your swan song, so to speak. Were you always planning to retire this year?

NEO Not exactly. I was always planning to retire, at some point.

CHANDRAN-LEE I see. So why today, of all days, if I might ask?

NEO You mean, on the eve of National Day? *(laughs)* I, uh—I think I've given enough of my life here, to this country, to put it simply.

CHANDRAN-LEE Oh. Are you—are you planning to emigrate?

NEO *(laughs)* No, sorry. I see how that might have sounded. *(laughs)* But I am planning to leave, in a way. In some sense of the word. I think it's time.

CHANDRAN-LEE *(pause)* Again, sorry to belabour the question—but why is that, Isaac? I think our readers would like to know why you, Isaac Neo, have finally decided to retire from the spotlight. We know, for instance, that after the scandal of 2005, you left Mediacorp, only to pursue a full-time career in theatre. In that sense, you never really stopped acting; if anything, the Horvallan affair created an entirely different path for you as an actor over the past ten years. *(pause)* So why stop now? Or, more specifically—what's stopping you, right now?

NEO Hmm. It's been a long ten years, Marie. And I've been, uh—I've been very unhappy. I've been unhappy for quite some time.

CHANDRAN-LEE Can you tell me how so?

NEO Sure, Marie. The uh, the Horvallan affair, if that's what we're calling it—I can see why she had to publish it, actually. I can see the reasons. I think we both saw it as an opportunity, you know, to start a new life for ourselves. To start again, stop with the lies . . . It was important also for Jing and I to be alone, I think, to be truly alone, and uh—learn to live with that loneliness, in a way. But this year was different. Very different, for our family. *(pause)* I'm sure you remember my son's accident.

CHANDRAN-LEE Of course. *(pause; sound of paper)* Neo Yong- he, aged sixteen: riding a Suzuki SV 650 when he crashed into a bus on the 8th of Jan, 8.42pm, at the intersection between CTE and Ang Mo Kio Avenue One. It caused a massive three-hour jam that evening, and was in all of the newspapers the following day. *(sound of paper)* Were you changed, you think? By the accident?

NEO That's a good question. People usually ask how I feel, which, after a while . . . I found that question pretty stupid. *(pause)* I hate to admit this, but the accident made me realise that Jing and I have been pretty selfish, actually. Really—really fucking selfish.

CHANDRAN-LEE *(pause)* What do you mean?

NEO I mean, I think Jing and I, we—we were so wrapped up in our own shit that we uh, we just—we didn't think about how our lives would affect our son's.

CHANDRAN-LEE Again—what do you mean by that?

NEO He, well—and can this, uh—can this be off the record, Marie?

CHANDRAN-LEE Sure.

NEO *(pause)* I think my son got a copy of *The Horvallan*. Even though it's been years since it was reprinted, I'm sure it's still easy to find. And I believe, at some point, that my son thought he was the Horvallan.

CHANDRAN-LEE *(pause)* The character?

NEO Yeah.

CHANDRAN-LEE: Wait, he—what?

NEO *(pause)* Yeah. It's a theory, but . . . it kinda fits, actually. It explains the sudden recklessness in his behaviour, over the past few years, and the motorcycling too. I mean, you've read the book, yes?

CHANDRAN-LEE Of course. We all did.

NEO Heh. There's this bit in the final scene, where Milton tells Jing it's not about her, or him, or me. Remember?

CHANDRAN-LEE Yes, I do.

NEO Great. Well, I think anybody reading that portion would assume that Milton was reminding her, you know, that the story was just a story.

That it's about no one. But maybe my son read that bit, and thought it was an invitation instead, to wonder about who else in her life could be the one.

CHANDRAN-LEE *(pause)* But how? How could he come to the idea that he could be the Horvallan?

NEO I don't know.

CHANDRAN-LEE You never spoke with one another, about this theory?

NEO Uh, no, no. Like I said, Marie: it's just a working theory.

CHANDRAN-LEE *(pause)* And is he well? His injuries were pretty bad, if I remember correctly.

NEO Yes, they were. They were awful. But he's with his mother now, away from Singapore, which is good. He gets to recover in peace, away from . . . the eyes. And he gets to be with his mother, too.

CHANDRAN-LEE Are you willing to disclose where Jing is?

NEO I can, Marie. But I don't think I should.

CHANDRAN-LEE Sure, Isaac. But wherever she is now—she's been by herself, that whole time?

NEO Yes.

CHANDRAN-LEE Did she ever return to see you or your son? Have you ever sent your son to see her?

NEO No.

CHANDRAN-LEE But now that Yong-he is with Jing—he's well?

NEO Yes. Very well, actually. He's walking again, which is—which is amazing. It's better than anything the doctors said, actually. But his memory, uh—that's another thing, altogether. Who knows when he'll ever get anything back. *(pause)* He used to call me Daddy, you know.

CHANDRAN-LEE And?

NEO After he became a teen he started calling me Dad, in an effort to, I dunno—be more serious, I guess. Once, I think, he even called me by my name . . . But now, it's—I'm not sure. He calls Jing Ma now, and calls me Pa, and I don't know who taught him to do that. It could be Jing but, I guess—it's just strange how the mind works.

CHANDRAN-LEE *(pause)* On that note: shall we talk about this performance? The one you've titled *PARADISE*?

NEO (laughs) Sure, of course. Did you enjoy it, last night?

CHANDRAN-LEE Oh, yes. Yes. I thought it was affecting, troubling and deeply moving, of course. But I have to say: *PARADISE* is also a demanding piece of work.

NEO *(laughs)* You're right. It's very long.

CHANDRAN-LEE 170 minutes long. No intermission. Are you not exhausted?

NEO No. Not at all. Does that surprise you? *(laughs)* But yes, you're right—I have seen people go to the toilet, and never come back.

CHANDRAN-LEE But isn't that by design? *(sound of paper)* You state in the beginning that once you leave the gallery, it's not possible to reenter.

NEO Hah. I did do that, yes.

CHANDRAN-LEE *(pause)* And did you—did you always have The Substation in mind for *PARADISE*? This gallery, specifically, to perform the work?

NEO Yes, in a way. At this point I can't imagine the work taking place anywhere else.

CHANDRAN-LEE Did Alan have a say in the conception of the performance?

NEO Alan Oei? *(pause)* No, not much. But I do think it was an alignment in the universe when I heard about his plans—that he was creating a year-long series of programmes themed "Now and Nostalgia". It was an alignment that allowed me to situate the work here, in this building, for three months straight.

CHANDRAN-LEE And what inspired you, Isaac, to create this work?

NEO Aside from the film itself, you mean?

CHANDRAN-LEE *(laughs)* We can talk about the film if you want! It's a fabulous film.

NEO It is. *(laughs)* You know, the first time I saw it, I was at a point in my life, Marie, when I knew that a great change was going to happen. A massive change. My wife and I had a big secret, you see: I had mine, and she had hers. And when I told her about my secret, she—she completely accepted it. And she told me she'd still love me, and that it wouldn't change a thing between us at all. But what would break us, I think, was the fact that she found out that I had known about her secret too, long before she was even prepared to tell me about it. And that, I think, was the thing she couldn't accept. That was the thing that led to us separating. *(pause)* When I think back to the film, of course, I think back to the moment when I felt like anything could happen. Anything could truly happen, Marie. It was a moment when my life could have taken any number of turns, and the potentiality of my life—it was there. It was all there. I was, in essence, still in the very middle of a story. And I think now, as I'm approaching my retirement, effectively—I too feel like anything could happen. And it's a feeling I absolutely want to reclaim again, to feel again, down to my very bones. I want that in my life again.

CHANDRAN-LEE The ability to change?

NEO Yes, yes. That's absolutely right, Marie. That's exactly right.

CHANDRAN-LEE *(pause)* I suppose it's fitting, in a way, that the film itself is also about change.

NEO Yes. About progress, no? And all of the destruction that comes when we want to build something new.

CHANDRAN-LEE Yes. But it's also just a story, isn't it, Isaac.

NEO Pardon?

CHANDRAN-LEE The film, *Cinema Paradiso*. The book, The Horvallan. They're all just stories. But even then, these stories: they can still—

NEO Affect us. Change us. Become an . . . indelible part of us.

CHANDRAN-LEE *(pause)* Do you think happiness is possible, Isaac?

NEO What?

CHANDRAN-LEE Earlier, you told me: that you were unhappy. Unhappy, for a long time. *(pause)* We don't have to—

NEO No, no. I'm still thinking, Marie. *(pause)* You know, a friend of mine once said to me that something good can come from something equally tragic. That a beauty can always arise from the pain. Do you think that answers your question, Marie?

CHANDRAN-LEE Yes. Yes, I think it does. *(pause)* Can we talk about that final sequence?

NEO Sure. In the film? Or in the work?

CHANDRAN-LEE Why not both? I can still picture it in my mind, actually: you, standing against the farthest wall, while a series of images project over you. *(sound of paper)* Is it true? That every night is a different series of images?

NEO Yes, that's right.

CHANDRAN-LEE What informs your selection of these images?

NEO Hmm. Pure instinct? *(laughs)* Some nights have a theme, while on other nights they have something more like, uh, an organising principle, so to speak. But, broadly speaking—the images really function as a mosaic of history. They function as snaps of a life.

CHANDRAN-LEE Your life, you mean? Or do you mean this in a broader sense, like, life in Singapore?

NEO Hmm. Again, it depends. What did you see last night?

CHANDRAN-LEE *(sound of paper)* What I have here—

NEO Without looking at your notes, Marie.

CHANDRAN-LEE Oh. *(pause)* They were largely landscapes, shots of places. I remember recognising images of Bishan, Chinatown, even Serangoon Gardens. But there were also places that felt more European to me, am I right?

NEO That's right. *(pause)* Pardon me, Marie, but—can I show you something?

CHANDRAN-LEE Show me what, Isaac?

NEO *(sound of footsteps)* I was thinking of showing you the images I'd be projecting tonight. Would that be okay? We can treat it as a tech run.

CHANDRAN-LEE Oh. Oh my. Okay, sure.

NEO All right. Let me turn on the projector. *(pause; sound of a switch)* Here we go.

CHANDRAN-LEE Okay. *(pause)* Oh. *(pause; sound of footsteps)* Oh, wow. *(pause)* Is that—?

NEO Yeah.

CHANDRAN-LEE And that—?

NEO Yes.

CHANDRAN-LEE *(gasp)* That—that image. Han Aw. *(pause)* I knew it.

NEO What do you know?

CHANDRAN-LEE That you—you remember. You actually remember who I am.

NEO *(pause)* You and I were here, in this very gallery. You handed me a pamphlet. *(pause)* I asked you what your favourite artwork was, and you showed me.

CHANDRAN-LEE I did, yes. I told you about it, Han Aw's work: *A STORY.* *(pause)* I was just an intern then, a gallery-sitter. I was nineteen years old.

NEO And I was twenty-four. I was just a young man. *(pause)* You were important to me, you know?

CHANDRAN-LEE What? How so?

NEO *(pause; sound of footsteps)* It was just something you said, Marie. You gave me the conviction I needed, that night.

CHANDRAN-LEE Hah. Right. Still, I—I can't believe you know who I am! I can't believe you remember. *(pause)* So are you going to do what Han Aw did? Your mother-in-law? *(pause)* Are you going to walk out of here, once you're done with your story?

NEO Hmm. Yes, that's right. I think so.

CHANDRAN-LEE And then what, Isaac? Never to return?

NEO Yes, Marie. No looking back. *(pause)* Not while I'm heading into the now.

32

The boy had gone out of Bestari Heights, earlier today. Jing asks him where to, and he says:

The diner down the road. The one opposite Giant.

Jing has an idea of what this diner is: she would have come across it, multiple times, on her weekly trips to the hypermarket. She asks him why there, and the boy tells her it's where Emi works. For the holidays, he says.

Jing looks down at the packet of bee hoon before her, unable to tell if this is good or bad news. She asks Yong-he when the girl's holidays are coming to an end.

Mid-August, he says, as he takes a drink of water.

And then? Jing asks.

Yong-he pauses, as though debating how much he ought to tell her. She flies back home, he says. To her parents, in Japan.

Jing does her very best to not overtly react. She's not based here, she says, in as neutral a tone as possible, but her son sounds glum nevertheless. No, he says, she's not. She lives in Yokohama.

Jing allows herself a small sigh; it's painfully obvious, how her boy feels about this girl. She asks if he had walked the whole way, from here to the diner, and Yong-he looks at her, aghast. He tells her he didn't—Ma, he says, of course not—and so Jing asks how he'd made the journey then. He tells her he rode on Emi's bike, and it's a piece of information that slices right through her, like a pair of open scissors, the cut both clean and uneven. She feels like he's already being taken away from her. Need I remind you how you ended up like this? says Jing, as the two now look at one another, aware of what the other is thinking. And although the real question isn't who to blame, but who ought to be absolved from it, Yong-he's still the child here, while she's inevitably the adult. He's the one who gets to decide if he's feeling benevolent or not.

I sit behind her, she hears him say. And then we go to the diner together.

The clock in the living room chimes 6pm; they're sharing a packet of kai lan and a packet of stir-fried beef, aside from the bee hoon. Yong-he takes more of the noodles while he's bright red in the ears, burning with adoration for a girl she hasn't even met.

So she knows?

About?

About what happened to you. About how you got here, says Jing.

Her son nods. His scars, though fading, remain obvious to the naked eye. As much as I know, of course, he says.

Jing sighs again. They haven't talked about his memory lately, not since their excursion to the playground; they've hardly talked to one another, in fact, not since he became friends with the girl.

And she's, well—she's safe?

Ma, says Yong-he. What a weird word to use. He starts attacking his noodles. She's good to me, he says.

You stupid darling, Jing thinks. You stupid, idiotic, foolish babe. How many people will he meet in his lifetime? How many more people will he fall in love with? she wants to ask. How many more people will he allow to enter his heart, and to inhabit him, reside within him, in this intimate, inaccessible, unknowable kind of way?

Jing purses her lips together. But Yong-he is looking at her, patiently.

Ma, he says.

Yah?

The boy picks up a piece of beef with his chopsticks, and offers it to her. Pa should be free, right? Once his performance is over, he says.

She notices the slight way his hand trembles, even though his grip is mostly steady now. She lifts her plate up to receive it, and then savours the piece of beef in her mouth, even as she's realising that there's only a fortnight left to the show. Jing hasn't thought at all about what will happen to their family once *PARADISE* comes to an end; she hasn't thought at all about what will happen to her if Isaac chooses to take Yong-he back. So much is changing, she's starting to realise. So much is beginning to change, without her.

But then Emi drops by the following morning, and Jing can feel a piece of her, a piece she thought she had long lost, returning steadily to her body. She clicks opens their front gate and watches the girl take a tentative step into her house, pushing her bicycle in as she says, Hello, auntie.

Hello, says Jing. She has to blink, several times, at how much the girl looks like Tori. Are—are you Emi? she asks, her voice soft and unsteady. It's stunning to see the girl step away from the daylight into the shadow of her driveway, like a mirage taking on mass, solidifying into something real.

That's me, the girl says. I'm waiting for Yong-he.

Okay, says Jing, still staring. She has to force herself to look away, even though her very self feels full, feels immense the more she looks at the girl. I'm Jing, she later says. You can call me Auntie Jing, if that makes you more comfortable. The girl nods, and follows her in.

Jing brings Emi to the one couch they have, while pointing in the direction of the stairs. Yong-he will be down in a moment, Jing says, while the girl makes a quick but blatant examination of her still-bare house. Yong-he tells me you're here till the middle of the month, she says.

The girl nods again, before asking Jing a question in turn. Auntie Jing, she says—you were a writer, weren't you?

Jing licks her lips. The question comes as a laceration, though it's a smaller cut, something her sense of self can better withstand this time; she shouldn't feel so surprised by what her son must be sharing about his mother, especially when it's about a part of herself she had long chosen to relinquish. I'm not a writer, she says to Emi. Or rather, I should say—I don't write. Not anymore.

They then hear a noise, from upstairs: it's Yong-he, ready to head out for the day. And the noise jolts Jing into sudden action somehow—she doesn't even know why, but she's getting up from the couch, and walking towards the kitchen, where she last placed the photo that Daniel had given her a few months ago, slotted now between the pages of the biography she's currently reading.

I want to show you something, she says to Emi, from a time when I was younger. She holds the photo out to the girl, placing a finger next to Tori's face. I had a friend who looked just like you, she says. Exactly like you, Jing says again, as she can feel the long-lost pieces of her older self coming together, rearranging themselves into the semblance of a newer whole. But when she tears her gaze away from the photo to glance at Emi, she finds the girl looking back at her, too, as though she has something on her cheeks.

Auntie, she says. Are—are you okay?

Jing quickly blinks; she feels them then, the snot and the tears, and it makes her want to laugh, out of sheer embarrassment. I'm fine, she says, as she quickly wipes them away; she can see her son's shadow now, coming round from the top of the stairs. Ignore me, she says. I'm just a silly woman.

Jing waits till it's the early evening before she decides to give Isaac a call. Ever since he'd sent her that photo of the taxi, parked outside The Substation, he'd been sending her more messages, more frequently, telling her his theory about their son and her book, and what might have caused the accident to transpire. She hasn't replied to him, however, not for nearly a month at this point, leaving his messages and his photos to her on WhatsApp unread; she's still afraid of that photo of the taxi, as though it were something that Isaac had called ahead of time, ready to take off as soon as he is done with the show.

Isaac picks her call up after a couple of rings, and asks her immediately if something is wrong. But nothing is wrong, is what Jing wants to say; she's just standing outside her home, watching a strong wind descend upon Bestari Heights, causing a great rustling to come from the distant trees.

Yong-he made a new friend, she says.

He did?

A neighbour, apparently. But she won't be here for long, Jing says.

Isaac asks for the neighbour's name. Jing closes her eyes, while the wind is beginning to threaten to sweep her off her feet.

Her name's Emi.

Emi?

Yah, she says. Emi. Jing waits for the current gust to die down, before she adds: The girl looks exactly like Tori, Isaac.

Jing keeps her eyes closed, while Isaac remains quiet. Neither of them speak. The sound of the wind continues, shaking the leaves and the branches of faraway angsanas; she can feel her hair being whipped to the side, strands coming loose from the tight braid that falls down to her waist.

They go cycling together, apparently.

He clears his throat. Do they?

Yes, she says. She rides the bike. Yong-he sits behind her.

So it's romantic, says Isaac, to which Jing replies: Oh, definitely. Jing then picks at the dry skin on her lower lip, while the sun quickly sets over the neighbourhood; she can see all the light in the world, right on the brink of fading, as a line of dark clouds gather on the other end of the sky.

I think we can trust her, Isaac.

To look after him? he asks.

To make him better, too, she adds, before they pause again.

Look, says Isaac. It's past seven. I have to get ready now.

Jing says she understands. It's showtime.

Yah, he says. That's right. Can I call you back? he asks, after another short pause, and Jing says that he can. She's willing to talk now. And she can tell she's made him happy, from the new lilt in his voice.

Great, he says. I'm glad to hear that, Jing. But you have to pick up, he adds, after a quick beat. You have to pick up, he says again, when you see my name on your phone. And Jing's nodding, to herself, just as she's trying to stem a fresh wave of tears.

Okay, Isaac.

Okay, he says back. Thank you, Jing. Goodbye.

Jing hangs up. She tucks her phone into the pocket of her shorts. She looks up and down the street, as she witnesses one of the gates swing open, screeching across the air.

There is nobody else about, she thinks.

Nobody else but her.

She does her rounds, that evening.

She first walks into every room of her house, just to see what is inside. She knows that there will only be a broom, for instance, in the storeroom beside the kitchen. A mop and a plastic pail, kept in the toilet across the hall.

Beside the storeroom is the maid's room. In there will be the washing machine, nothing more. Perhaps there might be their clothes, dripping on the drying rack: the upper one with her clothes, the lower one with her son's.

There are no clothes drying tonight.

In the toilet beside the kitchen is a faucet, which has been leaking for two weeks. The shower head is leaking as well, even though neither of them has been using it.

Upstairs, in Yong-he's bedroom: sheets that will be changed, in time. And then it's her favourite stop on the tour, the unoccupied bedroom. Usually there's a lizard, greeting her with a light smacking of its tongue— but all she sees is Daniel instead, putting his duffel bag down beside the foot of the bed.

At least you still have your son, he'd told her that night. That is a blessing, he said. You must realise this, Jing.

Jing takes a deep breath, and walks over to the bed. She sits on the mattress, and imagines Daniel beside her again, the heavy weight of his body compared to hers.

She takes her phone out, and reopens her chat with the man, his last message to her dated four months ago.

They can always come back, is the message she sends to him. *You are never alone.*

Finally, she's back outside, with a poncho on this time. The wind's still about, having a wild go at it; she can feel the wind and the coming rain, running its hand through everything in its path.

Jing looks over her shoulder, staring at her unit. She then goes down the road, down to the very end, to a house she hasn't spied on for the past couple of months. It's masochism, as well as a dangerous nostalgia, that's driving her to do any of this; she's still able to recall the entire inventory of things the new owners have added to the house. There is a car now, for one, as well as a scooter, parked in the driveway; there's proper furniture in the living room, all mismatched but eclectic. No two chairs around the dining table can even be considered the same.

Once she heard the television, airing a show or a movie in Japanese.

Once, she smelt a fragrance: of batter being fried.

Once, she felt like she could bathe in the warm light, emanating from a place she thought she once knew.

And now it's breathtaking, the gentle but searing sight: of a tabebuia tree, standing in their garden, bearing the new season's crown of fresh and lustrous blooms.

———

She then starts—she hears a bell from somewhere, the sharp ring of it. The bell rings, and rings, and rings again—

Whooo! goes a voice, from down the street. Whooo! Whooo! Whoooo!

Jing makes a dash towards the opposite house; it's still unoccupied, thank heavens, and the gate is furthermore unlocked. It screeches all the same as she swings it open, and it screeches another time as she swings it shut, the very sound alone threatening to give her hives. She squats and stares through the slats, at the sight of a boy coming round a corner of the road, clumsily riding a bicycle.

Whooo! he says, as he makes the corner. Yes!

A girl runs behind him, running after the bicycle; Jing can hear the slap of the girl's sneakers against the tarmac, clapping and then echoing off the neighbouring houses. Her laugh is sweet, and high-pitched, as she says to the boy—Stop! Dude, you're crazy! She laughs again: You're gonna hurt yourself!

The boy laughs as well: another alien, unfamiliar sound. His is a laugh that doesn't echo, but one that she can absorb, into her very soul. I'm not gonna! he says. I'll be good, I will.

The two come to a stop before her. Jing's eyes widen as the gate of the warm house finally swings open. An older woman emerges from the front door.

Tadaima, she says.

Okaeri, Nek, says Emi.

Come in, hurry, says the older woman. Come in before the storm arrives. You take your time, Yong-he . . .

Her son laughs again. He laughs, unreservedly, to the point where she can't take any more of it. It makes her want to laugh too, as she wonders— Who has he become? When did he ever get so tall? Didn't she just see him a few hours ago, that very same afternoon? Jing continues to stare: all she wants is a confirmation, that this young man she's seeing—it's still her child, her son. It's still the one she's been taking care of all year long. But all she has instead is the sight of his back, followed by a mere outline of his frame—and then nothing at all, once the gate swings shut again—nothing but the memory of who he used to be.

Later that night, she enters her bedroom, failing to take off her poncho.

She unplugs her phone, now fully charged beside her bed. *Jing,* says a message. *I saw the taxi again.*

Jing puts her hands together; she gives herself a minute, and unlocks her phone. She has to call him, she knows, because she's shaking too damn much right now. Isaac picks up, in less than a ring, and she puts him on speaker.

Is it still there? she asks.

No, he replies.

She's shaking, shaking—as though the storm outside had followed into her room.

Did you see anyone?

He pauses. No.

Do you want to go? she asks, while lightning flashes through her window, and he says he doesn't know. He doesn't know if he even has a choice. But all he knows, he says to her, is that the taxi's no longer here. I don't think it'll come back, he says. He then asks if she's still there, and she says she is, she is. She's just scared. She asks if he's scared too, and she can hear his voice now, drawn down to a frightened whisper. I'm not, he says, as she stares at her phone—at the sight of his name on the screen. It's not fear that I'm feeling, right now.

And then the day comes: the 8th of August, 2015.

Jing pushes her cart across the floor of the Giant hypermarket, excessively large and exceedingly quiet. Grey light filters from the ceiling, down onto a presentation of wild colours: boxes and cans and bottles and containers, all in abundance and neatly arranged, in orderly, towering rows. Even getting sunflower oil can feel like an intimidating, unreal task. As Jing walks down the aisles, one after the next, she hears the sole sound of her cart, rattling across the hypermarket, aware that she might be the only one here.

Imagine: she might be the only person left in Iskandar, Johor Bahru, for all Jing knows. And here she is, nevertheless, shopping for groceries.

Jing is nearly done when she hears a sound: a beep from one of the cash registers. She sees the one cashier on duty, putting things into a plastic bag, the customer she's serving being none other than Emi.

The girl looks over her shoulder. She smiles, and waves. Auntie Jing, she says. I thought it might be you. And she'll wait for her, outside the hypermarket, both of them heading down the travellator towards the first floor, where there are little restaurants, IT stores and shops selling bubble tea. Jing asks Emi what she's got, and she reveals the contents of her bag: Yakult, chewing gum, a mango and batteries. The girl then glances at Jing's bags, and asks if she needs help carrying them.

Oh, I'm okay, Jing says. I do this very often. She then asks Emi if she has time to spare. I'm thinking of getting a small bite. Would you like to join me, Emi?

The girl adjusts the smiley badge on her T-shirt. Sure, she says. I'm not needed for another while.

The two of them find a table at a Chinese restaurant, with a dining area that extends outside the building. Jing can spot Emi's diner from here, the one her grandparents own, along the shophouses across the street. Its storefront is the only one that's painted sky blue.

You're working today?

The girl nods.

How are you finding it?

It's okay, she says. I can think of worse things to do. Emi smiles at Jing. My Jii-chan says I should run my own place one day.

Jing smiles back at the girl. Is Yong-he there, right now?

He didn't tell you? says Emi, as worry passes over the girl's face. And Jing can't help but smirk, with a small sense of déjà vu, as she hears Emi talk about how much her grandparents adore him.

It's okay, Jing says. It's all right, Emi. I'm really envious of you, in fact. Of the both of you, really. You guys make loving look so easy. Emi then gawks, at what Jing just said to her, and it causes her smirk to soften into a smile.

I'm gonna tell you something, Emi. And all you have to do is listen to me. Okay?

Emi nods. A waiter comes, bearing a glass of water for each of them, and Jing thanks the waiter before she speaks.

I wrote a book once, she says. And I have a copy of it, of the very first edition, locked away in a suitcase in my room. I'm thinking of handing it to Yong-he soon, she says, as her eyes flit over to Emi's, the girl gawking once again.

Why?

Jing shrugs. I feel like he needs to read it. It's a part of our history, she says. He'll have to read the book first, if he ever wants to return to Singapore. It's the only right thing to do, I think.

She pauses. She's now thinking of the possible consequences, all of the possible ways she could split her family apart again. You're probably wondering if it's still necessary, Jing says. I find myself asking that too, you know. I'm wondering if it's worth it. I'm wondering if we haven't caused enough damage to him already. I'm wondering if I won't regret re-inviting the possibility that I might lose him another time.

Jing shakes her head, and then she keeps her eyes closed, for just a few seconds. I probably will, she says. And I'll most likely regret it, Emi. But he needs to know, I think; he needs to know how we ended up like this. And he'll be hurt when he learns what his mother is like, I know. I know what it's like, to have a mother who hurts you, who only ever does things from her point of view. Which is why, Jing says, as she reopens her eyes, and looks at Emi—this is why I need you to be there for him, okay? Even if you're not here. Even if he's just a friend to you, at the end of the day. Even if you're all the way back in Japan. Even if that's where you think your real life is.

The two look at one another, across the table of this Chinese restaurant: she and this girl who's like a carbon copy of Tori. And even though Emi doesn't say a word, even though she might never even care about this life-altering fact, the girl does nod, eventually. The girl agrees to be there, for the person whose life Jing brought into being, and it's enough to cause her aged heart to ache.

I wish I was more worthy of love, she says to Emi. I wish that life wasn't so cruel, or that it isn't full of suffering. But that's just life, isn't it? That's just a perfectly ordinary part of life. What I really need is less fear, because fear, oh boy—that can be a very, very powerful thing, Emi. It can compel you to hide, to run away from the hurt, to do whatever it takes, so long as you feel safe again. But I'm realising, now, that love is the thing that can make you stay. Love is the thing that brings you back. Love will lead you all the way.

Jing then laughs; she's shaking her head, knowing that she's probably said too much to the girl. She takes her phone out anyway, to a screen lit up with notifications, with unopened messages from Isaac: messages she would never have received if she hadn't reached out to him, and assured him that she was here, and that they were still a part of one another's lives. Isn't that a kind of love too?

She shows Emi her phone. I wish I had this, when I was younger, she says. Obviously we did not have this, in the eighties or the nineties. Nothing close.

She puts her phone down on the table, before turning back to Emi. Take photos of him, will you? Videos too, she says. Every day with Yong-he is a miracle to me, except now he's choosing to spend them with you. All while you're still here, of course. I'll give you my number, too, so—so do send me what you can, will you? Can you also do that for me?

Emi blinks. For sure, she says. I can do that, Auntie Jing.

Jing continues to smile at her. I hope I didn't scare you.

The girl blushes. She takes her phone out from her pocket anyway. I have more videos than photos. Is that okay?

Jing nods, quickly; it's embarrassing how eager she is. I'll take anything you have, she says.

Emi scrolls through her phone: the thumbnails of her photos and videos blur across her screen, and it's enough to make Jing's heart feel like it might ache again, with fullness, to the point of bursting. The two then exchange numbers, in the restaurant, just as Jing's dessert finally arrives. It's a bowl of ice kachang.

Do you want some? Jing asks. Emi shakes her head. I have to head back to the diner, she says. But thank you.

Oh, no, says Jing. No, thank you, Emi. Thank you for listening to me, she adds. You should go.

Jing eventually steps out of the restaurant, ready for the long walk back home. Her hands are laden with the weight of her purchases. The apples and onions and potatoes, in particular, weigh awfully like sandbags. But it's what the curry requires, according to the internet.

Her eyes squint against the face of another setting sun; it'll still be another half an hour before it's the moon's turn to rise. She glances towards the sky, noting its special, particular hue, while there's whooping and cheering down the length of the road, coming from two figures ahead of her.

It's her son, riding a bicycle, over the bridge that's built across the gully. Emi stands behind him, taking a video on her phone, all while the boy wobbles and regains his composure, his sense of balance on her bike.

Come on! she hears Emi say. Keep going! You can do it!

All Jing can do now is stand, and watch. It's all she can ever do now, the standing, the watching; learning to let things go while holding on to them all the same. Here she is caught, between the beauty and the pain, and it's a pretty good place to be. And she doesn't even have the right, no right to be here, partaking in the joy of this place.

Her son is still going; he's laughing, the whole way. It's a blessing, is the thought that goes through her mind: to see him zip away and then turn back around, his eyes lighting up as he shouts down the road: Hey! Hey, Ma! Are you seeing this also, Ma? And it's a blessing too, she thinks, as Emi whips her head around, her face pulled apart by a smile she'd never seen Tori make in her life.

Jing walks up to Emi, and puts her bags down. She's taking her phone out too, overcome by a sense of duty, not to anyone else but her own heart, this time. I can't possibly leave everything to the girl, she's saying to herself; I'm gonna have to do some of my own work too. And as she's taking pictures of him, and videos of them, Jing's also able to see, with all the clarity the present moment has bestowed upon her, how life has managed to sustain itself all this while: from front to back, start to end; from one person to another, one loss to the next. She's being blown wide open to a cavalcade of feeling, running right through the fresh rupture in her heart; she can feel the edges of her long-broken self, threaded back together via the through-line of love.

33

But there's still Isaac to think about, at this point of the story.

His phone rings. Isaac stands in the corridor of The Substation, and avoids eye contact with the arriving guests. He makes a hurried goodbye to the journalist, with promises to see her again soon. Email me, he says to her—we'll resume our chat another time, Marie. He then presses his phone against his ear, and he nods, and he nods, listening intently to what his wife has to say. I'm sorry, she'll then say, at the end of her story—for everything, Isaac. I really am.

Isaac won't know how to respond to this. An okay is all he can manage for now, and he'll hear Jing's disbelief, at the lameness of his response. Well, she says, you're truly the best, and it forces him this time to hold back a laugh. Thank you, he says, as sincerely as he can, while he hears the sound of other people, in the background of Jing's call. It's his son, he realises: his son with another girl.

I'll send you photos, Jing says, as though reading his mind. You've never seen them together, have you? she adds. She then tells him about her plans, about how they'll drive straight to his place for a couple of nights: they'll pack their bags the moment Emi flies back to Japan. Isaac has to lower his voice, and hide his smile from the guests.

That would be nice, he says.

Both of them pause again. It's as though they're catching their breaths, stunned by the future that's awaiting them still. But Jing, as ever, continues to surprise him.

We'll understand, Isaac, is what she says next. Whatever you choose, whenever it's time to go—we'll always understand.

He's trembling. Thank you, he says. And he'll mean it when he adds that that was all he needed to hear. And although he hasn't seen her in a while, he's still able to picture her face, smirking at him from the other end of the line.

We love you, Isaac, she says to him. And he'll find himself telling her he loves them both too.

Later, that same evening: Isaac stares at the final image of his performance, and waits for the last guest to leave the gallery. It takes everyone a few minutes before he hears his signal, a light knock on the glass of the double doors.

He turns. It's the programmes manager again, tireless and capable, the invisible hand behind his show. I'm gonna lock up the office, says Selene through the glass. You lock the front doors as usual before you leave, okay? They agree to meet again, on the day after the holidays, so that Isaac might clear the gallery and hand over his keys to the building.

Is that it? he proceeds to wonder. Nobody else? From the darkness of the gallery he watches Selene take her leave, waving goodbye to her another time. He then looks around the gallery for a few additional minutes, just to be absolutely certain that he's truly alone. Whatever happened to the face that he was sure he'd just seen—amongst the others in the audience tonight?

He doesn't know. He makes one final scan of the gallery, before turning back to the projector; he reloads the night's images and replays them, one by one.

There's a shot of him at Chomp Chomp, and then another on Caldecott Hill. There's one of him at his wedding offering a cup of tea, to Ah Pa and

Ah Ma in the living room of their house. And then other shots of his life proceed to scroll by, of him and his wife and their only son: there's one of them at the hospital, on the day Yong-he was born; there's another at his preschool, on the day of a choir performance. There's one of them together, seated in the cabin of a plane, and another of them with Daniel, at the Gothic Quarter of Barcelona; there's also a shot of them with Mateo, by the marina at Isla Cristina. The sky's a soft pink above the mouth of the Carreras River, while the four of them squint against the flash of Daniel's camera.

And then there's that photo, of course, of him and his parents, together with his sister at the zoo. There's also a photo of him with a younger Sherry Wong, posing before a mirror in a hotel room in KL.

The second-to-last image is that photo of Han Aw, on the floor of the gallery with a marker in her hand. But the image that follows is a video clip of Jing, standing in the middle of a bamboo grove. The Handycam blurs and refocuses on the back of her white blouse, while he hears the sound of his own breathing over the unedited footage.

Ready, says Jing, her voice in the far distance. We're now recording, replies Isaac, his voice loud and up close. She then waits, and screams, before she falls silent once again; Jing then looks over her shoulder, with a relieved smile on her face, her eyes directly on the camera as she says: We're done.

He pops open the door to the closet, while the gallery is still dark. He finds his backpack, and stuffs his cardigan inside. He then puts in the Walkman he took from his father, causing him to be taken back, to the scene of his parents' bedroom, taking all the things he thought he deserved. But the memory has to continue, which means he's now on the floor of the room next door, sharing a final moment with the sister he left behind.

He's not a good person, he says to himself. It's impossible to him that anyone could think that.

This is a routine he's built over the past ninety-nine nights; it's as much a ritual to him as the acting, the performing, the clicking through of the photos. Isaac unplugs the projector as part of his final step, and is coiling up the cord when it happens, of course. The silver light pierces through the glass of the double doors, streaming in directly from Armenian Street.

It's inevitable, is what this is. And he feels it too, right on time, the flutter he had felt earlier in his chest. He brings himself over to the double doors of the gallery, and sees a taxi slow to a stop, just outside The Substation. And although the light it's emitting is stronger than ever, causing him to flinch, and to squint, and to hold a hand up before his eyes, he can still spy a passenger—in the backseat of the car! He then gasps, and backs away, and presses his back against the wall beside the doors, just as the door to the driver's seat pops open.

An eternity proceeds to pass; his heart hammers away in his chest. Is that her? he thinks. Is that her in the backseat, the same way he last found her—all those years ago? But all Isaac can see is the opposite wall, which means that all he can do now is listen through the doors. He hears the engine of the taxi, and the sound of the driver's door closing; he then hears the driver's footsteps, down the corridor, past the box-office booth. And then nothing, not for a while, till he hears the flush of a urinal and the sound of hands being washed. And in the bright swathe of the light that's now cutting into the gallery, the shadow of a figure starts to grow before his eyes, its shape looming larger and longer than anything he's ever seen— and he swears he's not afraid, of whatever that's going to happen. He has no fear, of whatever's coming next. He just doesn't know what will happen to everyone else, now that life, at long last, is restarting once more.

Ah, says a voice, like the first note of a song: The Bravest Boy in the Universe Is Finally Free to Go. And then Isaac can't help it, he's snapping his head back towards the street—the moment he hears the sound of the other car door opening.

ACKNOWLEDGEMENTS

I have many people to thank: my family, of course, for their tireless support and acceptance of my black sheep lifestyle. Wong Yiping and Magdalene Yeow, for being the two people I emailed a PDF of my manuscript at the age of twenty-eight; Pigar Mahdar, for being that person I needed to email with an updated PDF at the age of twenty-nine. Yuki Shirato, for his sensitivity read; Selene Yap, for being okay with appearing in the book; Cyril Wong, for letting me use that *Oneiros* section as an epigraph in Part III: PARADISE; the late Ho Poh Fun, for writing "Thoughtscapes Singapore", which I've partially used as an epigraph in Part II: HORVALLA, with kind permission from her family. Thanks also to Sharmini Aphrodite, Joses Ho and Tse Hao Guang, for reading the very first draft of the manuscript; to Jennifer Hamilton-Emery, for reading the second; to Yu-Mei Balasingamchow, Eve Hoon and Anna Power, for reading the third; and to Daryl Lim Wei Jie, for reading the fourth.

My heart also goes to the people who supported me in other ways while I worked on my novel. To Sophia Schoepfer and Micca Wright, for letting me crash at your flat in Stoke Newington that snowy December; to the Clarke Ruschimskys—Patricia, Bill and Ana—for being so kind and so generous (that drive out of Madrid! the barbecue and swim at your gorgeous home!) in June 2018, and for entertaining all my random questions about Spain, the Spanish language and summer vacations at Isla Cristina;

to Emma Betsy Welton and Marit, and to Johan Pehrson and Siri, for hosting me over the heartbreaking midsummer that year in Sweden. To Han Yujoo and all the other people who worked and hung out at Bad Bad Books / Oulipopress in Mangwon-ro, in January 2019—for the Japanese mah jong, endless amounts of coffee, and always driving me back to Yeonhui.

I would also like to thank my colleagues at Sing Lit Station—thank you Azira, Klarissa, Jon and Joshua for being such a supportive team whenever I fucked off to write; to the Seoul Foundation of Arts and Culture, for the month-long residency at Seoul Art Space Yeonhui; to the National Arts Council for the 2017 Creation Grant (it was really good money, and I wish I had asked for more). And many thanks to Epigram Books, of course: to my publisher Edmund Wee, for taking another chance on me; my editor Jason Erik Lundberg, without whom the story (so damn long!) wouldn't be what it is right now; my line editor Eldes Tran, who made me feel nothing but cradled across every single sentence in the manuscript; and to my cover designer Nikki Rosales, for the back-and-forth on WhatsApp, ever patient, ever kind. Thank you also to the judges of the 2021 Epigram Books Fiction Prize: Wahyuni Hadi, Monica Lim, Gareth Richards, Sim Wai Chew and Edmund Wee once again. Further thanks need to be made to the Gaudy Boy team—to Jee, to Kim, to Ally, and to Flora, to Jennifer, to Susan—for making this American edition in 2024 possible.

Finally, some notes. The sections of Kyu Sakamoto's song "Sukiyaki", found in Part I: RANDEN, were translated from the Japanese by yours truly. Alfredo's story in *Cinema Paradiso*, found in Part II: HORVALLA and Part III: PARADISE, was paraphrased from the film and whatever English subtitles I had access to at the time. Needless to say, The Substation depicted in Part III: PARADISE is an alternate version of The Substation we have in our reality.

ABOUT THE AUTHOR

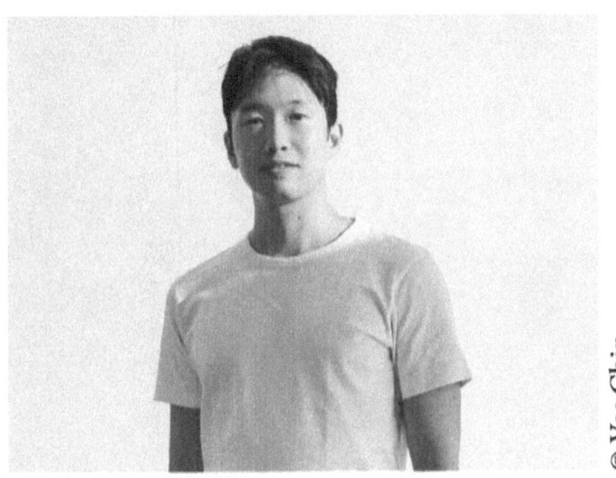

Daryl Qilin Yam (b. 1991) is a writer, editor and arts organiser from Singapore. He is the author of the novella *Shantih Shantih Shantih* (2021), shortlisted for the 2022 Singapore Literature Prize, and the novel *Lovelier, Lonelier* (2021), which was longlisted for the 2023 International Dublin Literary Award.

He co-founded the literary charity Sing Lit Station. His writing has appeared in periodicals and publications such as the *Berlin Quarterly, Mekong Review, Sewanee Review*, the *Straits Times* and the *Epigram Books Collection of Best New Singapore Short Stories* anthology series. His first novel, *Kappa Quartet* (2016), was selected by the *Business Times* as one of the best novels of the year, and described by *QLRS* as "[breaking] new ground in Singaporean writing . . . a shimmering and poignant novel, an immensely sympathetic and humane exploration of our existential condition."

ABOUT

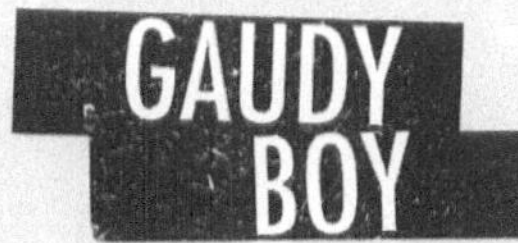

From the Latin *gaudium*, meaning "joy," Gaudy Boy publishes books that delight readers with the various powers of art. The name is taken from the poem "Gaudy Turnout," by Singaporean poet Arthur Yap, about his time abroad in Leeds, the United Kingdom. Similarly inspired by such diasporic wanderings and migrations, Gaudy Boy brings literary works by authors of Asian heritage to the attention of an American audience and beyond. Established in 2018 as the imprint of the New York City–based literary nonprofit Singapore Unbound, we publish poetry, fiction, and literary nonfiction.

Visit our website at www.singaporeunbound.org/gaudyboy.

Winners of the Gaudy Boy Poetry Book Prize

Waking Up to the Pattern Left By a Snail Overnight, by Jim Pascual Agustin

Time Regime, by Jhani Randhawa

Object Permanence, by Nica Bengzon

Play for Time, by Paula Mendoza

Autobiography of Horse, by Jenifer Sang Eun Park

The Experiment of the Tropics, by Lawrence Lacambra Ypil

Fiction and Nonfiction

Picking off new shoots will not stop the spring, edited by Ko Ko Thett and Brian Haman

The Infinite Library and Other Stories, by Victor Fernando R. Ocampo

The Sweetest Fruits, by Monique Truong

And the Walls Come Crumbling Down, by Tania De Rozario

The Foley Artist, by Ricco Villanueva Siasoco

Malay Sketches, by Alfian Sa'at

Bengal Hound, by Rahad Abir

From Gaudy Boy Translates

Amanat, edited by Zaure Batayeva and Shelley Fairweather-Vega

Ulirát, edited by Tilde Acuña, John Bengan, Daryll Delgado, Amado Anthony G. Mendoza III, and Kristine Ong Muslim

Other Series

New Singapore Poetries, edited by Marylyn Tan and Jee Leong Koh

Suspect: Volume 1, Year 1, edited by Jee Leong Koh